LOSS OF LIFE

MARK FARRINGTON

Legacy Book Press LLC

Camanche, Iowa

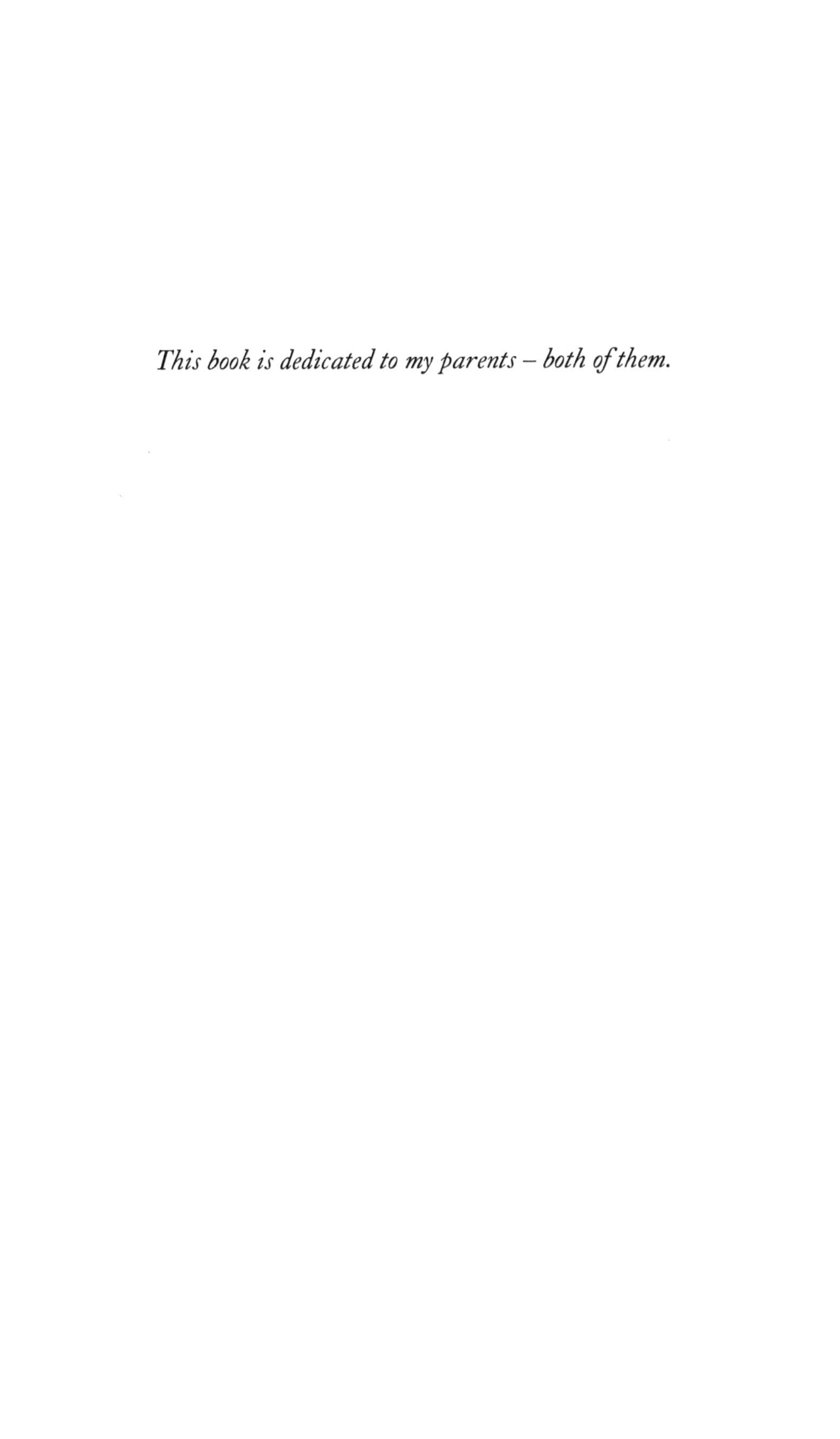

This book is dedicated to my parents – both of them.

Table of Contents

To be without stories means…to be without memories, which means something like being without a self.

Kay Young and Jeffrey L. Saver
The Neurology of Narrative

Forgiving presupposes remembering.

Paul Tillich

PART ONE

Chapter One

A voice summoned me back. "Hello, Mr. Winton. It's time to wake up now."

My eyelids wouldn't open. That stuck-together sensation was the only thing I felt. Not arms or legs or a body. Glued-together eyelids and a painful dryness in my throat. A croaking sound escaped. "Water."

"There you are. Welcome back."

I tried again. "Water."

"You can't have any." The voice faded, then returned. "Here. You can have a little ice."

Something cold and wet touched my tongue. Crystals of bliss, too soon gone. "More." Heard as if underwater. My eyes sprang open: I watched a dark brown hand approach, tasted more diamond drops.

"Go easy."

I struggled to focus. I was sitting in a chair facing a shadow-covered wall. A bright light from somewhere made me squint. Behind me, something beeped. A woman in green walked past, the keeper of precious ice, but I could not make my head move to follow her.

"You've been in an accident, Mr. Winton." A different voice, another green woman. "You're doing okay now. The doctors fixed you up."

Until that moment, I had been only a pinprick of consciousness. Now, suddenly, I became a body, and instantly, jolts of pain attacked: a knife-slash in my right knee, stiffness in my neck and shoulders, a squishiness in my abdomen, as if my stomach had been cut open and my guts put on display.

More noise, grunts sounding like they were coming from a cave, more electrified pain. A panic raced through me.

"There, there," said one of the green women. "Best not to move around."

"You just relax, Mr. Winton. We'll take care of you," promised green woman 2, although I could see neither of them now, sitting tense and rigid, already understanding that movement equaled pain.

They called me Mr. Winton. The name meant nothing to me. I didn't know where I was, what accident had put me there, what I'd been doing before. I didn't know what I'd been doing my whole life. I didn't know, as my eyelids closed, if they would ever open again.

. . .

I floated in a world of dreams, where unfamiliar people moved past as if I was no more than air they could pass through. At other times, when sharp light pierced my eyes, blue people appeared, touching me, prodding me, pricking me, while people in white stood nearby, speaking in voices like burbling brooks, and sometimes, green people wheeled me away, down shadowy corridors and into rooms that were always cold.

At night, the children came. There were two of them. I thought they were children because they were small, with tiny voices. They woke me with stabbing pain in my hand or arm. I felt the heat of a body pressed against my back, but in the darkness it was impossible to make out features. "I'm sorry," she whispered. "I have to change this."

"Ow," I spit when the needle forced its way in. The child apologized again. She seemed too young and tiny to inflict such pain.

After she left, I wondered if I had dreamt her.

The other child was better at her job. I barely noticed the needles sliding in and out. Sometimes I didn't even awaken, and knew she'd come only from the fresh tape holding the needle in a new location, a purple bruise showing where it had been before.

In rare, almost-lucid moments, I thought perhaps they weren't children. There might have been only one of them, better at finding veins on some days than others.

But I didn't question. I lay quiet and still, and did what I was told.

. . .

There was no moment of sudden awakening. I simply opened my eyes one morning to discover that everything — light, colors, objects — was sharper and more distinct, no longer viewed as if through a rain-spattered window. I saw the hard edges of a counter and a half-open door, a row of straight-backed chairs such as you might find in a cafeteria or schoolroom lined up along one wall, a larger armchair in an open space beyond the foot of my bed. Straight ahead I could see a window, through which the blue of the sky looked solid as a wall, and even the sunlight appeared to have substance. And I saw a woman putting linens into a cabinet.

She was young, in her twenties perhaps, tall and thin, with dark hair cut short. She was dressed in blue: blue top, blue slacks, white shoes. I thought she looked familiar, although I wasn't sure if I recognized her or just the color of her uniform. Blue was the color nurses wore, while technicians were green, and white coats, doctors. At least, that was the conclusion I'd reached, and whether or not it was accurate, it satisfied me.

I lay on my back, eyes open, although when the woman moved about the room, a brace around my neck prevented me from turning my head to follow her. I was always wary of the pain. Several times while sleeping, I'd move in ways that roused a pain that woke me, and left me fearful of closing my eyes.

"Hello!" she said, sounding excited. "How are you this morning?"

I wanted to tell her the world seemed clearer today, but words took effort, and threatened to distract me from my main priority, keeping docile all those parts of my body waiting to rebel. I felt surrounded by a pack of hungry wolves.

Consequently, I grunted something that came close to "Okay."

"You look better." She drew one of the chairs beside my bed. She had a cheery voice, not overdone or phony, and a bright face. She asked me to rate my pain today, on a scale of one to ten. I vaguely recalled being asked that before, but I couldn't remember what number I'd chosen.

Today, I had no easy answer – a good sign, I thought. "Right now, staying perfectly still, it's a zero," I told her, the words coming easier than I'd feared, though no louder than a whisper. "When I move, it's maybe an eight."

She grinned; those were probably more words than I'd spoken in total since I'd arrived. "Do you want to sit up?"

Dreading trying to push myself up, I started to say no, when I remembered that the bed could do the work for me. "Yes," I said, as she pressed the button that raised my head and shoulders. When she asked if I could sit forward so she could adjust my pillow, I gritted my teeth, squeezed my hands into fists, and leaned forward. Only after she finished did I release the breath I was holding.

"You're doing great," she said, and sat down again. "I'm Dana. I'll forgive you if you don't remember."

That word "remember" changed my mood. Although I'd mostly been content to give in to the limbo world of drug-assisted sleep, I'd had moments when I tried to seek clarity. Always, I came up empty. I was Mr. Winton. I'd been in an accident. I could remember nothing more.

Dana filled in a few blanks. I was in Fairfax Hospital, in Fairfax, Virginia. That surprised me. I didn't know where my home was but Virginia seemed an alien place. I'd been in an automobile accident that had been quite serious, but the doctors were pleased with how I was recovering. "I think the doctor may come in to see you later today," she said.

"I don't remember," I said, meaning the accident, although I could have meant anything.

"That's okay," she replied. "You just concentrate on getting better."

She stood. I didn't want her to leave. "The accident," I blurted. "Did I hurt anyone?"

She seemed touched by the question. "No," she said. "You were alone. You ran into a tree." She sighed. "You only hurt yourself."

The doctor did visit me, but not for another day. In the meantime, the most exciting thing I did was sit up in bed, swing my legs over the edge, and, with Dana's help, stand up. I was wobbly at first, and weak, but she moved a chair nearby so I could sit. That allowed her to change the bedclothes without having to work around my obstructing body.

I liked Dana. She was friendly but didn't chatter or batter me with questions. Our conversations, such as they were, centered around my creature comforts: Are you finished eating? Do you need the bathroom? On a scale of one to ten, how's your pain? I wanted to ask what she knew about me, but feared revealing how much I couldn't remember. Dana praised how well I was doing, but would her assessment change if she realized my brain had become a black hole? I struggled to remember something, trying to conjure some image of where I lived, people I knew, but searching my past was like walking through a house emptied of everything, the furniture and all signs of anyone having lived there before.

The doctor was short and stocky, with thick hands and unusual eyes. "Good afternoon, Mr. Winton. How are you doing today?"

I replied, "Better," the stock response that seemed to please Dana each morning when she asked the same question.

"I am Dr. Shinomoto. Do you remember me?"

I gave a gesture that might have meant, "Maybe."

He drew a chair close and sat. "You have had an accident, Mr. Winton." He spoke slowly, distinctly, as if words were lumps of clay he needed to mold before releasing. "It was very serious, but you are healing acceptably."

He examined those parts of me that had been the epicenters of my pain. A couple times his touch caused a hiss or a grunt to leak out of me, but mostly I remained still and quiet, not wanting to reveal anything that might cause him to change his assessment that I was "healing acceptably."

Finished with the examination, the doctor again took his seat. He seemed pleased by what he'd found, but I tensed when he asked, "Do you feel strong enough to answer a few questions?"

This is it, I thought, and sighed. "I'll try."

The doctor explained that in addition to the injuries to my body, there had been some trauma to my brain. So he already knew my condition. Of course I'd never really believed I could hide from these people what seemed to me a far more serious injury than a torn-up knee or a sliced-open abdomen. I was a body with a brain that seemed to function well enough with what was immediately in front of me, but which shut off completely when I turned around to look toward my past. I had not only lost my memories; I'd lost all sense of myself. I'd lost my life.

Did the doctor know all that?

He was still speaking. "Although there was trauma, the tests we have conducted suggest there has been no irreversible damage. At this time we have no reason to doubt you will recover completely."

That was encouraging, although I remained wary, as the doctor finally got around to his questions.

"Do you know where you are, Mr. Winton?"

"The hospital," I replied.

"Do you remember the accident that brought you here?"

"No, I'm afraid I don't."

The doctor smiled reassuringly. "That's quite all right. Do you know where this hospital is located?"

"Fairfax, Virginia," I said, my gaze avoiding Dana, standing at the foot of my bed writing notes on a clipboard.

The doctor paused, and I steeled myself for the tougher questions, some as basic as Where do you live? Where do you work? What is your first name? Instead, the doctor slipped off his glasses and stood. "You are doing well, Mr. Winton. Please continue to rest and recover."

A bubble of anger popped inside me. That was it for his questions? How much did he really know? What was he not telling me?

But I remained silent as he put his chair back with the others and headed for the door. There he turned back. "A colleague will be stopping by, perhaps tomorrow. Dr. Clark." He paused, as if debating whether to say more. Then he left.

• • •

What is it like to lose one's memory? I couldn't have described it this way then, but perhaps you've been in the middle of a conversation, and you reach for a word or name to complete your thought, only the word has vanished, you grab only air. "Sorry, I've lost the word I was thinking of," you might say. Now imagine it's not a word that's vanished, but everything you have learned, all knowledge you've accumulated over the course of your life, everything that assures you that yes, you have existed. All of that is gone.

There is no substance to your life. You are the shell of a crab left behind, the skin a snake has shed. You are a stick figure, without weight or substance, nothing to distinguish you from all the other stick figures even a child could draw.

And you fight to keep at bay the possibility that you might have to spend the rest of your life this way.

· · ·

I identified Dr. Clark by her white coat. She arrived lugging an overflowing bag and acting as if she was late, although I'd been given no indication of when to expect her. She introduced herself and asked how I was feeling. "Better," I said.

"Give me a moment to get settled, then we'll have a little chat, shall we?"

She brought a chair close to my bed and set her bag on the floor. She was about my age, with whitish blonde hair and a face that suggested she'd seen a lot that had left her both wise and a little tired. A sweet scent drifted toward me when she leaned close.

I ran a hand through my messy, too-long hair and over the scratchy beard I'd developed. So far, I hadn't shaved, or even asked to see a mirror, not sure I was ready to confront the stranger who might stare back at me.

She pulled the bag into her lap and dug out a notebook and a pen. "That's better," she said, settling into the chair, assuming a posture that seemed casual, in a businesslike way.

"Perhaps we can start with a few questions?"

I nodded, feeling my body tense.

"Can you tell me your first name, Mr. Winton?"

"Matthew."

"Do you have a middle name?"

"Arthur."

"How old are you, Mr. Winton?"

"Forty-one."

"Your birthdate?"

"May 14, 1956."

"Can you tell me today's date?"

"September." I added an apologetic laugh. "I'm not sure what day exactly. The days kind of blend together here."

"And the year?"

"1997."

She paused to write on her pad. I tried not to look smug or self-satisfied. The truth was, I'd cheated: earlier that morning, I'd found my name, age, and birthdate on a form Dana inadvertently left by my bed. Adding 41 to 1956 gave me the current year.

I felt guilty; I wanted to trust Dr. Clark. But doctors can't put a cast around your brain or give you a pill to help you remember. Dr. Shinomoto had discovered there'd been trauma to my brain, but I suspected he had no way of knowing how severely my brain had been affected. I doubted doctors would send home a patient who didn't even know where he lived. What they might do instead frightened me into concealing the truth.

But Dr. Clark's next question hadn't been answered on that form.

"Can you tell me where you live, Mr. Winton?"

It felt like I'd been holding onto ropes attached to flimsy walls that would collapse if I relaxed even a little. I prepared to let those ropes go.

Suddenly an address popped into my head. I blurted, "10 Division Street, Mansfield, Massachusetts 01230."

The pen in Dr. Clark's hand stopped moving. With her head down, I couldn't see her expression. Her writing was indecipherable, even if I hadn't been looking at it upside down.

She resumed writing, more energetically, then closed her pen and slipped the pad into her bag. Were the questions over? Had I passed? I wasn't sure about that address I'd given her, but overall, I'd have graded my performance B+.

"So how are you feeling?" she asked, assuming a more relaxed posture.

About to say, "Better," I recalled I'd already given that response. "Not too bad. There's less pain than before. I must be feeling better, because I'm getting tired of lying in bed all the time."

"We'll get you up and walking about soon."

"Everyone's treated me well."

"From what Dr. Shinomoto's told me, you're quite lucky."

I recalled him telling me that too. No doubt my injuries could have been worse, although I hadn't given much thought to what "worse" might mean.

"I imagine you're anxious to get back to work." She paused. "What is it that you do?"

She said it as casually as if we'd been chatting about the weather, but she had me and we both knew it. Bristling, I wanted to accuse her of cheating, even though I was the one who'd been snowballing her. Or trying to.

"The truth is, there are some things I've been having trouble remembering. Basic things like where I work. Stuff like that."

She retrieved her pad. "Tell me about those things."

I looked toward the two windows on the distant wall. Only sky was visible, thick and lumpy, like oatmeal.

"It's everything," I said, and let those metaphorical ropes go. "I don't know who I am. I don't know anything. Those things I got right – I didn't remember them. I read them on a piece of paper."

No longer writing, she studied me. I couldn't bring myself to look into her eyes, afraid of what I might see there: shock, pity, judgement.

Moisture dribbling off my chin made me realize I was crying. Dr. Clark handed me a box of tissues. She had to rise to reach them, and before sitting back down, she gave my shoulder a comforting squeeze.

When I regained control, she asked if I felt strong enough to continue. I nodded.

"I'm curious about that address you gave me. Division Street, Mansfield, Massachusetts?"

"I don't know where it came from. It just popped into my head."

"This hospital is in Virginia. Apparently, you've lived in this state the last nine years."

That shocked me. When I'd said Massachusetts, it had clearly felt like home. Virginia was the home of Robert E. Lee. The cradle of the Confederacy.

"Did you remember something?"

"Robert E. Lee."

"What do you know about Robert E. Lee?"

I explained that he was the general who led the Confederate army against the Union.

"You're familiar with the Civil War?"

"We studied it in school. In eighth grade history. Bruce Catton. We read a book by him."

"And where did this happen?"

"In Massachusetts," I said, and it hit me. "Mansfield, Massachusetts."

"Where, quite likely, you lived in a house at 10 Division Street."

So I did remember something. I had a functioning memory after all. Acknowledging that unlocked a flood of memories: a red house on a hill, a yard surrounded by woods, a dirt path leading to a pond with lily pads, croaking frogs, insects I called "darning needles." Walking beside a bald, slightly-built man. My grandfather.

Dr. Clark wrote it all down. "Tell me something else you remember."

I described a giant rock, whale rock we called it, at the top of a hill, the intersection of Division Street and Christian Hill Road, where I got the school bus; the high school where my father worked as janitor and took me to sometimes in the evening so I could play basketball while he cleaned the empty school. The house my family moved to when I was in fifth grade, closer to town.

Dr. Clark wrote everything down. I could tell from her energy that this discovery was important. And yet, all these memories came from my childhood. She said I'd lived in Virginia for nine years. I had no recollection of that. Or of anything beyond eighth grade.

Exhausted, I didn't protest when Dr. Clark suggested we stop. These days, I had no reserve; if I got tired, I couldn't push through.

"I'll come back tomorrow," she promised. Even though it was rude, I let my eyes close before she'd left the room.

• • •

The next day, a short, heavyset woman with a pleasant face came to my room. She introduced herself as Mrs. Gutierrez, the hospital's social worker. When asking how I was doing ("Not bad," I replied, wanting to move on from, "Better"), she called me Professor, then handed me a cluster of papers. "Dr. Clark wanted you to see this."

The two pages contained a long list, with my name at the top of page one, below the heading "Curriculum Vitae." Below my name was an address: #17 Old Winchester Road, Blue Meadow, Virginia. There was a phone number too, and some shorthand I didn't understand: mwinton1@unv.edu.

"It's like a resume for college professors," Mrs. Guiterrez interjected, noticing my puzzlement.

I was a college professor?

The next heading was "Education." It listed "MFA, Fiction Writing, University of Louisville, 1988." Then, "B.A., Carver College, 1977," and some phrases that meant nothing: "cum laude, Phi Beta Kappa." The heading "Teaching Experience" followed. I'd been at the University of Northern Virginia for the last nine years, first as an assistant professor, then an associate professor. Prior to that I taught English and Dramatics at a place called Warrentown Friends School in Pennsylvania. I'd published about a dozen writings, a mix of "short fiction" and "pedagogy"; I'd given readings, led workshops, been on panels at conferences. I belonged to an organization called AWP.

I indeed had a life: this paper proved it. I had an actual home, too, with an address I could give to any taxi driver who would take me there. I nodded at Mrs. Gutierrez, grinning wildly. I not only had a life, that life had a shape.

But my excitement waned as I realized I felt no connection to anything written on these pages. I may have done these things, but I could remember nothing. I couldn't picture Warrentown Friends

School, or the University of Northern Virginia, couldn't feel what it might be like to work there. This "curriculum vitae" might have my name at the top, but it felt as if it belonged to a stranger.

Another concern began to weigh on me. "My parents," I said. "Has someone notified them?"

I didn't like the shadow that crossed Mrs. Gutierrez's face. "Dr. Clark has that information," she said, in an apologetic tone. "She'll come by later to speak with you." Then she mentioned how in the days ahead, she would be helping me prepare to go home, and my excitement returned. I wasn't sure what "preparing to go home" would involve; it wasn't as if I'd suddenly gone blind and had to learn to negotiate a dark world. On the other hand, I thought, I was exactly that: a man gone blind.

• • •

"You've suffered a trauma, Mr. Winton," Dr. Clark explained. "Some memory loss is not uncommon in these circumstances. The mind needs to heal, just as does the body."

She had taken her familiar chair beside my bed. I was sitting up, feeling hopeful. If they were thinking about sending me home, my condition couldn't be too severe.

"Many patients can't remember the trauma they experienced," Dr. Clark continued. "There are rare cases of people who lose all memory, all the way back to birth. You have some memories – you can remember your childhood. That's a positive sign."

I suffered a concussion, she explained. But tests showed no permanent damage to the brain. No sign of disease, either; I didn't have Alzheimer's, or what she called "early onset dementia."
"There's much we don't know about the brain. But from what we can see so far, it's reasonable to believe that in time, your memory will return."

"In time?"

"I'm afraid that's the best we can say."

I tried to hold on to the positive. My brain wasn't damaged, it just needed time to heal. My memory would come back. In time. Probably.

"My parents," I asked her. "Have you been able to locate them? I'm sure my mother would come and help out."

Dr. Clark looked down at her lap. When she began, "I'm sorry," a tremor passed through me. I heard the rest as if in a tunnel. My mother passed away in 1984, thirteen years ago, from cancer. My father died from a heart attack, just this past summer.

My gaze locked onto the metal bar across the foot of my bed. It helped having something solid to hold onto, even if I couldn't physically reach it. I clutched it with my eyes, and it helped hold me up. It hurt to think that my mother had died and I wasn't there for her. But I would have been there. I just couldn't remember it, and that made it feel like she had died all over again.

"What can I do," I asked Dr. Clark, "to get my memory back?"

"You have those memories from your childhood. Explore them. See what else you can remember."

• • •

My body continued to heal. I still moved warily, as much from memory of pain as the actual sensation. One day I was allowed to get up and walk to the bathroom, Dana holding one arm as I dragged my IV pole along with the other.

I glimpsed a shaggy face in the mirror. My hair was wild, and my new beard had narrow streaks of red and white mixed in with the brown. I wasn't sure how to get a haircut, but I definitely needed a shave. Maybe after I rested, I thought, since just this little effort had tired me out.

Parts of my face seemed familiar to me – the small, slightly upturned nose, the narrow mouth. And yet, I didn't recognize this face. I couldn't remember ever peering into it before; studying it now, I didn't think, *Oh yes, it's Matthew Winton's face.*

I peered into my eyes. They were a light green, intense but cautious. As if aware they were being threatened. As if there was something vital they had to protect.

After lunch I convinced Dana to let me return to the bathroom to shave. I was able to take a shower, after a fashion, and having clean and combed hair made me feel almost like a regular human being. My long hair felt odd tickling the back of my neck.

Later, I asked Dana if she'd ever had a patient with amnesia. She said no, but mentioned someone named Agatha Christie. When I said I'd love to read about people like that, she replied, "Let me see what I can do."

The next day she brought me a book called, *Stranger than Fiction: True Stories of Amnesia*. Although it mentioned a few people who couldn't remember what they'd been doing five minutes before, most had conditions not unlike mine. Often, doctors could identify what caused the amnesia – for instance, the man who lost all memory after a fall in the bathtub – but there also was a woman who woke up one day and couldn't remember the last fifteen years of her life, didn't recognize her husband or ten-year-old son. The doctors never discovered what had happened to her, but – I underlined this part – "her memory returned slowly, most of it restored within eight weeks." There were cases where memories returned suddenly, such as the man who'd lost two decades of his life but recovered all his memories in an instant during an operation that was similar to another operation he'd had twenty years before.

There were also stories of people who faked amnesia to escape some trouble in their past. Others who showed up somewhere far from home with no recollection of who they were, gave themselves new names and went on to live full lives totally different from the one they'd lost. And while a few of the cases went back as far as World War I, most had happened recently, one as recent as 1988.

It was comforting to think that even people who never recovered their memories hadn't let amnesia mean the end of their life.

No one ended up in an insane asylum, which was one of those wild fears that swirled around me in the empty darkness of two a.m. The woman who'd recovered her memory in eight weeks gave me the most hope. I wondered if she'd done things to help her memory return. Perhaps I could do those things too.

"Explore the memories you have," Dr. Clark had said.

What did I remember? A pond, beside a narrow sandy road with a strip of dandelions and other weeds along the center, woods on either side. The water inky black, with a gray-white film along the top, the darkness reflecting upside-down trees. A turtle sunning itself on a half-submerged log. A croaking bullfrog, hiding in the reeds, dragon flies darting above the water's surface. The hot sun tempered by a breeze.

The pond was far enough into the woods that we could no longer hear cars, lawn mowers, or barking dogs. Only the birds and the breeze.

My grandfather and I used to walk there. I was six, maybe seven. My grandfather was a slight, serious man who lost all his hair and many of his teeth as a young man, due to an unspecified illness. He came to the U.S. from Germany at the age of 14, along with his mother and younger sister. At sixteen, he enlisted in the Army and fought in World War I, to prove he was no longer German. But he had a German personality: strict, organized, and demanding, at least toward his daughter, my mother. My grandparents lived with us on Division Street, and I could recall marveling at how my mother – who usually seemed to me the most powerful person in the world – always deferred to her father. He was sharp with her and his criticisms cowed her. With me he was gentle and instructive, with a wry sense of humor. I could not recall my grandfather ever being cross with me.

A half mile beyond the pond was the largest body of water I'd ever seen. Far off, beyond the opposite shore, a church tower rose into the sky.

The water was the town reservoir, the church one of the buildings in the small neighboring town of Housatonic. But at six, I
didn't know that. I knew the largest bodies of water on earth were
called oceans, and I knew France, where my grandfather had
fought a war, was across the ocean. So I stood in front of my class
at school and told everyone how I had looked across the ocean and
seen France.

My teacher told my mother I had a remarkable imagination.
But I wasn't making it up. I was speaking fact.

Chapter Two

I was waiting for my lunch when a visitor showed up. It was a special day: I was out of bed, ensconced in the big armchair, and I'd been allowed to order my lunch from a menu, rather than making do with whatever they chose to bring. I'd ordered roast chicken, rice, green beans, and what I looked forward to most: chocolate pudding.

My visitor was a policewoman. She looked young, perhaps in her twenties, with hair the color of straw pinned up in a bun. She was athletic looking, confident in the way she stood, weight evenly balanced. Her expression was friendly, but I tensed up at her presence. I'd seen security guards walk past my open doorway, but this was "real police" – a phrase I'd heard recently on a cop show on the TV in my room. She wore a navy blue uniform with a badge and a little walkie-talkie pinned at the shoulder, handcuffs, and a gun on her belt. She slowly twirled her hat held in both hands.

I tried to relax. Maybe I had a guilty conscience lurking somewhere in my fugitive memory. Once or twice, Dana had used the phrase "according to the police investigation," and those words set me on edge. What was there to investigate? Another problem with amnesia: you can't remember what you might have done.

"How are you today?" the officer asked, stopping a respectful distance from my chair.

"I'm waiting for my lunch," I said, a finality in my voice I hoped didn't offend her.

She introduced herself as Officer Sarah Madison. "I won't take up much of your time."

"You're investigating the accident," I said.

"We're just completing our report." She smiled. "There's always a report."

That smile seemed genuine, making me think I could trust her. But I'd learned from those cop shows that police used tricks to knock you off guard.

"It was just an accident, right?"

"That's what we've determined, yes."

I relaxed. Dana had already told me no one else was involved in the accident, no one had been hurt. Other than me, and my car.

"I'm afraid I can't be of much help," I told her. "I don't remember any of it."

"Yes," she said, with no surprise.

"You know about that? That I can't remember?"

"We spoke with your doctors."

"What did they tell you?"

She shrugged. "Just that. You're suffering from a memory lapse."

That was a new phrase. It had an attractive temporary sound.

"Well," she said, and placed her hat over her hair. "I won't take up more of your time. I was in the area and thought I'd stop by and see if you remembered anything."

I shook my head. "Sorry."

"You keep getting better."

Suddenly I didn't want her to go. "Wait!" burst out of me. It sounded desperate; I might as well have shouted, "Help!" It startled both of us.

"Could I ask you a couple questions?"

Nodding, she came back into the room, the hat coming off again.

"It's hard to get any information," I said, to restore some face. I considered admitting that she was my first visitor, but that would have sounded pathetic. "You were at the accident?"

"My partner and me. We answered the call."

"You found me?"

"The EMT's got there first. They got you out."

That sounded serious, and I recalled how both my doctors had said I was lucky. Until that moment, I hadn't considered what unlucky might have meant.

Thinking she might want to sit, I gestured toward the chairs along the wall, but she declined. "I don't want to cut into your lunch time," she said.

"I haven't had many visitors. I think my friends are waiting until I get better." I forced a laugh. "Not that I'll be able to recognize them when they do show up."

Officer Madison returned a polite smile, but I could tell from her shifting weight that she wanted to go.

A pressure was building behind my eyes. This had happened a few times lately, pressure that overwhelmed like an ocean wave. Usually it came late at night, and I always fought it, even when I was alone, not wanting to end up blubbering like a frightened baby. This wave was stronger than most, and I clenched my fists and turned my head away, coughed to cover what might have been a whimper.

Out of the corner of my eye, I glimpsed movement. "No," I said, holding out my arm, and Officer Madison halted a few feet away. "I'm all right." I forced myself to sit up, wincing when I moved in a way my body didn't like.

"I know it must be hard," she said, and I thought she might.

"I can handle it most of the time." I wiped the moisture from my eyes. "Once in a while it sneaks up on me."

Now I wanted her to leave, but didn't want to be rude. Fortunately, creaky wheels in the hall came to the rescue, announcing the appearance of the woman pushing the cart with my lunch.

Officer Madison moved out of the way as the woman set down

my tray.

On my birthday when I was a kid, I got to pick my birthday meal, which was usually roast chicken, mashed potatoes, corn, and chocolate cake. All preceded by me getting to lick out the pot with the icing. I knew this meal wouldn't measure up to those, but it smelled inviting. The chocolate pudding sat like the goal post at the end of a football field.

Officer Madison retreated to the doorway. "I'm glad you're doing better," she said, and on went her hat. It cast a shadow over her forehead and eyes. "Enjoy your lunch."

. . .

Another day, another visitor. A man this time, in a suit it looked like he'd slept in. Straddling the entrance as if it were the edge of an ocean, he gazed longingly down the hall, as if hoping to be rescued. Lying in bed, having just awoken from a nap, I had to clear my throat in order to call, "Hello."

My voice seemed to startle him. He visibly collected himself and marched in.

He was tall, and carried a beaten-up, bulging leather briefcase and a winter coat draped over one arm that had me seeking the window to make sure it was still the warm September day I remembered. He had thinning blond hair and pale skin, and there was something doughy about him. I was thinking he might be a salesman, when he said, "They've given you your own room," sounding both surprised and impressed.

I tried to indicate I shared his reaction. Thus far I'd avoided wondering why I'd been given this big room; it was too easy for paranoia to leak in.

He'd come as far as the foot of my bed. Still unsure if he was a lost salesman or someone who might actually know me, I gestured toward the chairs along the wall. "Would you like to put down your things?"

He laid his coat down carefully, then brought over a chair, still carrying his briefcase. He pretty much ignored me, settling in the chair, unclipping the flaps on the briefcase he'd hoisted onto his lap, and rooting around until he withdrew an oversized white envelope. "This is for you," he said, looking a little like a boy handing his mother a present he'd proudly picked out all by himself.

Inside was a giant greeting card. On the cover, a bunch of goofy looking cartoon people stood around an empty desk, all holding glasses of champagne. The caption read, "We're looking forward to celebrating your return." Despite the caption, the picture looked to me as if the person whose desk they'd gathered around had died.

Inside the card were twenty-five or thirty ink-penned signatures, the writing tiny and twisty, hard to decipher even if the names had been familiar. The messages were generic: "Get well soon," and "Miss you," most ending in exclamation marks.

My colleagues from the university, I decided. And this must be the professor chosen to deliver the message. It made sense: the disheveled suit, overstuffed briefcase, the way he'd paid me no mind as he got himself settled, as if preparing to teach his class; they all fit the image of a college professor that had formed in my mind.

"We all miss you very much," the man said. "We're hoping for a speedy return."

Those words sounded familiar, and scanning the inside of the card, I found that exact sentiment written near the center. "We all miss you very much. We're hoping for a speedy return. Signed, Franz."

So this was Franz.

"Thank you," I told him. "That was nice of you. Of everyone."

Mission accomplished, he sat back, looking pleased.

I thought I should show more enthusiasm. Here at last was a real visitor, a colleague, perhaps a friend. But what I wanted most was information.

"Has anyone from the hospital spoken with you?"

"They called Irma."

I didn't ask who Irma was. "What did they tell her?"

"You were in an automobile accident."

"Did they say anything else?"

He considered, then perked up. "Yes, I almost forgot." He sat up in a formal way. "I'm pleased to inform you that the university has granted your request for a full medical leave through the end of the fall semester. We all want you to rest and recover."

I tried to look surprised, although the social worker had given me the same news yesterday. "That's great," I said, then, "Did the hospital say anything about my...condition?"

"I don't believe they went into detail."

I didn't want to go into detail either, but I had to say something. He clearly didn't know, and tip-toeing around my "condition" required too much energy. "I've lost my memory."

He didn't react with the shock I expected. "You've had an accident. It's common not to recall the details."

"It's not just the accident. I don't remember anything at all, going back over twenty years."

Franz' eyebrows pinched. He tended to look away from me when he spoke, then stared into my eyes while listening. He studied me closely now, and then something clicked, and he flashed an awkward smile. "You don't know who I am."

"Sorry, I don't."

"And those people who signed the card?"

I shook my head. "Sorry."

He was silent as his brain recalculated. Then he leapt to his feet. "Franz Bergstrom," he announced, thrusting out his hand. "English Department Chair."

I took his hand, which felt a bit like a wet dishrag. "Matthew Winton." I grinned.

It took him a moment to get the joke. "Yes, of course," he said at last.

Another silence followed. His brain must have been working in overdrive. "Nothing?" he asked at last, in a timid voice.

"The doctors are convinced it's temporary."

"What have they told you?"

I went through the spiel: no permanent damage, no Alzheimer's or anything like that. "They're sure my memory will come back in time."

An exaggeration, but not a complete lie. Dr. Clark said I should proceed with that mind frame, assuming my memory would return.

Franz was rummaging in his briefcase again, collecting papers. "I brought you these." He waved a stack. "Start-of-the-semester memos, the schedule of faculty meetings, things like that. I don't imagine they'll mean much to you now."

"You never know," I replied. "Sometimes the smallest things can open up the floodgates." I didn't believe that, but Franz seemed pleased when I took the papers and laid them on the table beside my bed.

Another awkward silence followed. There were questions I could have asked, but I was wary. I had trouble imagining that Franz would have been a close friend. I was getting tired, and I didn't have the energy to hide it.

To his credit, Franz noticed. "I should let you rest." He put back his chair, picked up his coat.

"Thank you for coming. And thank everyone for the card."

"Take care of yourself. We all miss you," he said, but passed on repeating his wish for a speedy return.

• • •

A couple days later, a young women appeared in my doorway. Her enthusiastic "Hello" and the bouncy way she came right to my bed suggested she knew me, and was happy to see me.

"How are you doing today?" she asked.

"I'm still here," I said, and she grinned.

She looked vaguely familiar. She wasn't a nurse, instead dressed casually, in jeans and an unbuttoned white shirt over a blue top, and very white sneakers. I felt a flash of excitement: could she be someone I knew from before the accident, her familiarity now a leak in the dam holding back my memories? I wanted to blurt out a whole list of questions, but decided to be patient. *I'm a patient patient*, I thought.

Then I noticed how she was standing, feet apart, weight firmly planted. If she'd had a hat, she would have been twirling it in her hands.

"Officer Madison?"

"You remembered!"

I may have winced, because she looked embarrassed. "Sorry. Poor choice of words."

Her brownish-blonde hair was tied back in a ponytail, and she didn't look as bulky out of uniform. "You look different," I said.

"It's my day off."

"Which you chose to spend at the hospital, visiting poor schmucks like me?"

"Actually, my mother volunteers in the gift shop downstairs. I came by to pick her up. We're going to lunch."

"I don't suppose you'd consider taking me along? I've had my fill of this room."

She laughed. "I don't think they'd let me do that."

"No, I guess not." I tugged at my robe. "I'm not exactly dressed for it, either."

"You look good," she said. "Your face has a lot more color."

"There's more of it to see," I replied, having finally shaved that morning. Also, yesterday Dana had cut my hair. Not a professional job, but it made me feel less feral.

There were other improvements, too. I could get up on my own, use the bathroom whenever I wanted without having to call a nurse. I'd even taken a short walk down the hall yesterday. My lower back had started to bother me, lying in bed so much, but the cut on my forehead was improving, my knee had grown sturdier, and as long as I avoided sudden twisting movements, my stitched-together abdomen remained calm.

I'd been close to dozing off, but Officer Madison's appearance perked me up. It was Saturday, and Dana didn't work on weekends. The nurses taking her place always seemed in a hurry to get somewhere else.

"Do you have a few minutes?" I asked, glancing at the clock, although I had no idea what time she was supposed to meet her mother.

She said, "Sure," and drew over one of the chairs.

"Could you tell me more about the accident? We were talking about it the other day, but we got interrupted by my lunch."

"Which looked and smelled delicious."

"They told me I hit a tree."

Her expression turned serious. "Yes."

"It was late at night?"

"Around 2 a.m."

"And the area's remote?"

"It's pretty rural. Woods mostly. No houses nearby."

"You don't know what I was doing there? Where I might have been going?"

"We were hoping you would tell us that."

I shook my head. "When I woke up in the hospital, it felt like I was being born. Or maybe like that guy, who was that, he was in some story. He slept for twenty years."

"Rip Van Winkle?"

I considered, but the drawer in my brain containing that type of information wouldn't open. "Maybe. I don't know."

She looked at my card, smiled at the picture. "From my colleagues at work."

"That was nice of them."

"Yeah. I'll thank them, if I ever remember who they are."

That came out a little harsher than I'd intended, and was met with silence. I'd noticed that from time to time, anger snuck to the surface. I couldn't say what I was angry about, but Dr. Clark said the feeling was normal.

There was something else I felt, also normal, but poorly timed. I needed to use the bathroom.

With apologies, I explained the situation to Officer Madison.

Although I was able to get up by myself, it was a bit of a production, and if she wanted to leave first, that was fine.

"I still have a few minutes," she said. "Are you sure I can't help?"

I shook my head. "It's better if I do it myself."

She rose, backing away, even though I was getting out the other side of the bed. I inched to the edge, each move deliberate. I had to turn onto my side to get enough leverage to push myself into a sitting position, my feet now almost touching the floor. I clenched my fists, which I'd found helped with the pain, and slid forward enough for my bare feet to meet the cool tile floor.

This was where I could have used help; when Dana was there, she'd face me and hold out her arm for me to grasp, to propel me to my feet. I could have asked Officer Madison, but pride wouldn't let me. It was a mistake, as pulling myself up, I twisted the wrong way, and a lightning bolt of pain shot across my lower back. My knee buckled, and only by grabbing the bar at the end of the bed did I keep from falling. I couldn't stifle a groan.

I felt a presence behind me, a steadying hand on my arm. "I'm okay," I said, as the pain in my back receded and my knee settled into place. I thanked Officer Madison, who slowly backed away.

I was able to make it into the bathroom on my own. When I came out, I was surprised to find Officer Madison still there. She'd moved to the far end of the room and was gazing out the window. "Your mother's probably wondering where you are," I said.

"She's never ready on time anyway."

Since it was close to my lunchtime too, I headed for the armchair. With its fat sturdy arms, it was easier to get into and out of than the bed. But I sat down before remembering the blanket I always used to cover my legs. As I looked side to side, hoping it might be close enough for me to reach, Officer Madison plucked the folded blanket off a counter and brought it to me. "Do you need this?" she asked.

I almost made a joke about her becoming a nurse, if this policing didn't work out, but I held back, not wanting to offend her. I thought of another joke, about how over lunch she could tell her mother about her exciting morning helping an invalid get out of bed, but I held that back, too. I felt bad that she'd had to witness that, but maybe that was just my own pride, too.

"What's it like," she said, "having amnesia?"

She'd moved her chair closer. It was small compared to my armchair and I felt like I was sitting on a throne. It was an uncomfortable feeling.

After a few moments I said, "It's like you're in this big storage room, drawers and drawers everywhere, all labeled with the parts of your life. Only each time you open a drawer, you find there's nothing in it.

"Everything is new. You might think that would be exciting, but it means you have no references, no confidence that you can do something because you know you've done it before. I wasn't joking before, about being asleep for twenty years. It feels that way, like you haven't even been alive.

"And the worst thing are the people. Not you, not the people here, but the people who knew you before. Are they your friends? Maybe they're people you pissed off or hurt. Even when they tell you about yourself, how do you know that's really who you are?"

I hadn't meant to go on like that, but once started, it was hard to stop. Sarah had seemed interested, but I hated sounding pathetic.

And while I didn't want her to leave, I heard myself saying, "I keep waiting to hear over the loudspeaker, 'Officer Madison, call your mother. Stat!'"

She rose with a sigh. "You're right. I should go."

"Thank you for coming by."

At the doorway, she paused. "Maybe I'll stop by again some time, if that's okay? The station's not too far from here."

"My door is always open," I said, then winced, because what I should have said, plain and simple, was, "I'd like that very much."

. . .

As I became convinced the hospital really would allow me to go home, dread began to color my excitement. How did one respond when going to a place he's never been before, and knows nothing about? Never mind that this place was the home I'd been living in for years. It felt like a first time. Too much of my life, I thought, now felt like a first time.

There was an added problem to going home: I had to figure out how to get there. Blue Meadow was some thirty miles west of the hospital; Dana had shown me a map. "Don't you know anyone who could drive you?" she asked. I tried to soften the disgust in my expression; she was only trying to help. But during my whole time in the hospital, Franz Bergstrom had been my only legitimate visitor, and I was not going to ask him. He'd mentioned someone named Irma, but who was she, and why would she help if I asked?

There was also the issue of clothing. The clothes I'd been wearing had to be cut off at the accident scene. Other than that horrible gown, my entire wardrobe now consisted of a pair of shorts, a robe, and those thick socks with tread on the bottom that could double as shoes. Not exactly a "traveling outfit."

True to her word, Mrs. Gutierrez began preparing me to live on my own. She told me about a home health care service, where someone could visit me a couple times a week and take care of anything I couldn't do myself. She had me sign some papers that allowed me to withdraw money from my bank. She arranged visits from a physical therapist, who helped me get stronger and improve my balance. She sent in an occupational therapist, who explained how to do basic things: buy groceries, clothes, and household items; do laundry; pay bills; balance a checkbook. The occupational therapist also introduced me to cell phones and computers, which remained mysterious to me.

It appeared that when I did go home, it would have to be by taxi. I had never ridden in a taxi before, not that I could remember. There was a small hotel on Railroad Street in Mansfield, in between a row of bars, where women reeking of perfume sometimes stood out front, and taxis waited in the street. When I was a kid, I was forbidden to walk on that side of Railroad Street, although a few times I did, until one of the women – who looked young and colorful from a distance but messy and caked with makeup, up close – asked me if I could light her lipstick-stained cigarette, sending me racing away, heart pounding.

Angrily, I reminded myself I wasn't a twelve-year-old kid anymore, and most taxi drivers weren't like the ones parked outside the Mansfield Hotel.

I continued exploring my childhood memories, but the wall sealing off the last twenty-eight years of my life remained impenetrable. "I don't know what I'll do if it doesn't come back," I told Dr. Clark, who visited regularly. I was a teacher who had no clue how, or even what, to teach. "I don't think I have any other skills," I said.

She reassured me I was still in the process of healing. "Once you're back in the familiar places of your life, surrounded by familiar things, you may well find yourself remembering." She encouraged me to be patient and kind to myself. She also gave me the card of a therapist to see after I got home.

I always felt better after talking with Dr. Clark. But my confidence faded late at night when I couldn't sleep and the floor was so quiet and empty I felt like the only person left alive. September to January wasn't such a long time. The university might extend my leave an additional semester, but probably without pay. Still, I'd been astonished when Mrs. Gutierrez showed me how much money I had in my bank account. However I'd been living my life before, it hadn't required much money.

One day Mrs. Gutierrez brought me an envelope with a clear plastic bag inside. The bag contained what was in my wallet at the time of the accident: seven dollar bills, a driver's license, a social security card, another card she identified as a credit card, a couple of business cards bearing my name, and a coupon for two dollars off the next purchase at Giant Supermarket. There was also a key, likely to my home.

The social security card had brown stains that looked like gravy. At my puzzled expression, Mrs. Gutierrez said, "Blood." She was holding onto my insurance card, she added, but other items, such as my wallet, "weren't worth saving."

During my time in the hospital, I'd been careful to avoid the sight of my own blood. The first time I watched them drawing blood, I almost passed out from the image of the purplish-red liquid leaving my body. It didn't hurt, but the visual bothered me. After that, whenever the doctors or nurses took blood or changed a bandage, I closed my eyes or looked away.

Holding the stained card in my hand, I remembered a car placed outside my middle school during a week focused on safe driving. The car was crinkled up like an accordion, and while most of the students in my class marveled at the mangled metal, I couldn't stop staring at the brown stains spattered across the front seat, the dash, and even the steering wheel. These stains, I thought, were all that was left of the driver.

What was I doing at 2 a.m. on a Sunday, driving on a remote road miles from my house? Did I look away at the wrong moment? Fall asleep at the wheel? I remembered deciding as a kid that the driver of that crashed car must have been speeding or drinking. That was the lesson we future drivers were supposed to learn: that by driving safely and following the laws, we'd be spared from a similar consequence.

Unless – I thought suddenly, then pushed that thought away – avoiding a crash wasn't the driver's goal.

• • •

The appearance of the uniformed policewoman in my doorway made me realize I'd been hoping she would visit me again. "Hello!" I said, sitting up in my armchair, not hiding my wide grin.

She grinned too. "I heard you got some good news." At my puzzled look, she said, "I spoke to Dana."

"You know Dana?"

She laughed. "We were in high school together. A lot of people live in this area, but it's still like a bunch of small towns."

It was late on a Friday, dusk settling outside the window. Dana had already left, and I figured Officer Madison had just finished her shift, too. The "good news" was that I would soon be going home. Not right away; the doctors wanted to keep me over the weekend to make sure I didn't have any setbacks. If all went well, I'd be leaving on Monday or Tuesday.

"So how are you doing?" she asked. She'd taken her familiar stance, weight centered, hat in both hands.

I laughed. "Body's good, mind not so much."

"Nothing new on the memory front?"

"I'm beginning to think I need to learn a new trade."

When she gestured questioningly at the chairs along the wall, I said, "Sure," and she brought one over and sat down. I sensed there was something she wanted to say, and that made me wary. As far as I could tell, she was still "investigating" my accident.

"Dana mentioned you've been having something of a logistical challenge around getting home." Her gaze locked on mine. Her eyes were light blue, like a milky sky.

I didn't know how to respond. I was a little peeved Dana should share what seemed private information. "I'll manage," I said finally.

"I've been thinking maybe I could help you out."

She paused to study me again. It felt like I was some skittish animal, and she was approaching me cautiously, one slow step at a time. I shrugged and gave a flick of my hand, that she should go on.

"I go hiking sometimes, out where you live. I was planning on heading out there this weekend. If you wanted, I could stop at your house, pick up some of your clothes, whatever else you might need."

"You'd do that?"

"Like I said, I'll be out there anyway."

I broke away from her intense eye contact and gazed toward the window. Apparently Dana had shared that I didn't have any clothes to wear, too. Being fully dressed might make me feel more human. At least it would save some embarrassment. On the other hand, did I want a police officer walking into my home when I had no idea what she might find there? For all I knew, there could be a dead body in my living room, and I'd been fleeing that late Sunday night.

But my time in the hospital had taught me that sometimes you had to give up that desire to control and put yourself in the hands of others. It was hard for me; I seemed to have a lot of pride.

"If you don't mind doing that," I said, "it would be a big help."

"Great! And then when they finally let you go, I'll come by and give you a lift home."

"You can't do that."

"It'll be better than taking a taxi."

I studied her. There was a playful innocence in her expression but it could have been an act. "Why would you do this?"

"What? Offer to give a ride to a guy who needs a ride?"

"This is more than that."

"Is it? I like to help people. It's a big reason I became a cop."

Maybe she was right, it wasn't such a big deal. It was easy to imagine her going out of her way to help people, giving a drunk a ride home, helping an old person carry their bags. Helping a person in need. That's what I was, as much as it stung to admit it.

"When they release me, you'll probably be at work."

"Naw, they always keep people until late in the day. I'll tell Dana I'm coming by around four. She'll take care of everything."

"It sounds like you two have it all planned out."

"Just trying to be helpful."

I flashed a wry smile. "Can we take the cruiser?"

That brought a laugh. "I'd get in trouble for that."

"You have your own car?"

"I do. She runs like a dream."

"Better than my car, I'm sure." I'd intended it as a joke, but it landed with a thud. I had no idea what my car looked like after the crash, but Officer Madison had seen it, and she wasn't laughing.

"You're sure this won't be a bother for you?"

"I'm glad I can help."

And with that, the medicine ball lodged in my gut for the last few days suddenly deflated. I couldn't hold back a laugh. I was going home.

. . .

The weekend passed slowly. Freed of my IV, I could move around at will, but there's a limit to how many times a person can walk down a hall and back.

Worry scared away sleep for most of Sunday night. Why would I ever want to leave this place where everyone takes care of my every need? What made me think I could survive on my own? What if I went home and discovered I couldn't manage? The hospital wouldn't take me back.

"You're under no pressure," Dr. Clark assured me. "If anything feels like it's too much, you don't have to do it. Step back, relax, save that task for another day."

I wished I could take Dr. Clark home with me. Or at least call her up when I needed to hear a calming voice. I'd asked if I could continue seeing her, but she said she had a limited private practice. The therapist she'd recommended should be fine.

Lying in bed, I watched the darkness turn to soup and then a cleaner light. I was eating breakfast when Dana brought in a paper bag. Inside were a shirt and jeans, underwear, socks, sneakers. And a handwritten note: "Where you live is way cool!" Signed, Officer Sarah Madison.

Chapter Three

Apparently, the law required all patients to leave the hospital in a wheelchair, pushed by a young person still in high school, dressed in red and white stripes. That's how I got my first taste of the outdoors (in what seemed like twenty-some years), the bright setting sun, a humid breeze, the smell of cut grass and apples. And lots of cars.

They were lined up on the street at the end of the drive, three lanes going in each direction, jam-packed and inching along. "You can leave me here," I said over my shoulder. "It looks like my ride is going to be late."

She answered with a single breathy word I couldn't make out, but she didn't move. Maybe she'd been ordered, "Stay with your wheelchair until it's empty."

This was my first chance to look around. What I'd been thinking of as a hospital was more like a small city. I couldn't see the main hospital building, since I was sitting on the ground in front of it, but multiple buildings rose up around me, six or eight stories high, made mostly of brick. One was a parking garage, even though at the edge of the grounds I spotted an open blacktopped area also filled with cars.

I'd welled up a little getting ready to leave. Dr. Shinomoto came by for one final check, and Dr. Clark stopped in to say goodbye. Dana gave me a hug, and I thanked all of them, genuinely grateful for all they had done for me. I hadn't expected to feel sadness overwhelming the anxiety bubbling in my stomach.

Down the street, a single car broke free from the pack and headed up the drive. It was small and rounded and pink, I could make out, fighting the glare of the sun.

It had to circle a roundabout to pull up to the front entrance. The engine made a choking sound and the car seemed to tremble when it was turned off. A moment later, Officer Sarah Madison popped out. She wore her full police uniform, and I chuckled at the sight of her emerging from that little pink car.

"Can I get up now?" I asked over my shoulder, wriggling to the edge of the chair. Getting no response, I stood. I wanted to show the world I was above their wheelchair law, but rising too fast made me dizzy, and I stumbled a bit. "Whoa," said Officer Madison, but I righted myself before she could reach me, and assured her I was fine.

"Take your time," she said.

When she took my arm, I let her guide me to her car and help settle me in the seat. She reached across me to buckle a strap that ran from my right shoulder to my left hip. "This is a seat belt," Officer Madison instructed. "You may not remember this. You wear it whenever you're in a car."

I didn't like the way it confined me, but I wasn't about to argue.

The car swayed a bit when Officer Madison got in. A stick with a ball on the end rose up between our seats, and when her hand settled on it, I inched away.

She noticed my expression. "What?"

"I didn't picture you driving a pink car."

"She's not pink, she's salmon. And her name is Mrs. Dalloway."

I was going to quip, "Married, is she?" but decided not to poke fun at a car obviously dear to her heart.

She pulled away from the curb, and we both gazed down at the jammed-up road. "When I was in high school," she said, "that was a one-lane road in each direction."

"Do we have to go that way?"

"No way." Laughing, she made a sharp turn onto a narrow drive that circled behind the main hospital building. "What kind of cop would I be if I couldn't get around traffic?"

We followed a road running parallel to the superhighway but with none of the traffic, through neighborhoods with modest-sized houses and modest-sized yards, a couple schools, and lots of churches.

"So you grew up around here?" I asked, remembering she'd gone to high school with Dana.

"I'm one of the few. Most people who live here now came from somewhere else. They like to tell you that, how they're not from around here, and how great the place they left was."

"I promise I won't do that."

She grinned, getting the joke.

We stopped at a traffic light at the top of a hill. Below lay clusters of giant houses and some big shopping centers. "This is Centreville," Officer Madison said. "I live here – not in one of those McMansions."

The big houses all looked the same, except they were situated at different angles and the front doors were different colors, so the owners could find their own, I guess. Then a gasp escaped me: in the distance, humps of mountains rolled across the horizon.

"Do you remember something?"

I pointed ahead. "Are we going there?"

"That's the Shenandoahs. We're heading in that direction, but you don't live that far out. I'd say you're on the cusp of them."

Those mountains brought a sense of relief. I could picture the mountains where I grew up, a kind of protective wall. It made more sense that I would choose to live near mountains.

"I go hiking there sometimes," Officer Madison said. "It helps keep me sane."

The terrain began to change after that, fields with straw-colored grass baking in the sun, clusters of woods, and always in the distance, the blue and hazy Shenandoahs.

"This is Manassas," she said, although all I could see around us were woods and fields. "Stonewall Jackson, JEB Stuart? We're going through the battlefield."

"The Civil War," I said.

"That's the one. Some people around here act like they're still fighting it. And I don't mean re-enactments."

"Officer Madison?"

"You can call me Sarah. Even when I'm in uniform."

"Okay, Sarah." Her first name came easier than I'd expected. Officer Sarah Madison was a mouthful. "Thank you for doing this. For everything, really."

"I'm glad I could help."

"I should pay you something for your trouble."

She shook her head.

"But you came out here over the weekend, too. For my clothes."

"That was purely for pleasure. There are some great bike routes around here. I just stopped at your place on the way."

I was still a little anxious about her going to my house. In one of my crazier dreams, we arrived to find a bunch of police waiting in my house to arrest me.

"So I guess you didn't find any dead bodies in my pantry," I said.

She gave me a pinched-eyebrow look. "Just joking." I added, "That's another thing that happens when you lose your memory. You start imagining all sorts of crazy things you might have done."

She smiled. "You're clear. Anyway, you don't have a pantry."

But when I asked her to describe my home, she wouldn't. She wanted it to be a surprise.

We rode for a while in silence, and I had a chance to study her. She was attractive, in a wholesome way. I was struck again how her eyes, her whole face, seemed to promise, "You can trust me." Was that look genuine, or cultivated for her job?

Last night I'd come up with a bunch of questions to ask her, to be polite and to pass the time. I started by asking if she still had family in the area.

"My mother's still in the house I grew up in. That's in Falls Church – that's closer in toward the District." She paused, then explained, "Washington, D.C." She was in teaching mode, or maybe just being extra sensitive to me knowing nothing

She had three brothers, all older than her. The oldest was in the military, married with two children, stationed in Germany. Another was a high school teacher in Houston, Texas. The third, whose name was Bobby, was "out West somewhere" working on a ranch. "Bobby claims he's still trying to find himself, but to me, he's a guy who likes to work on ranches. What else is there to find?"

Her mother still lived in the house Sarah grew up in. "That's in Vienna. Vienna, Virginia, not Vienna, Austria. Or Vienna, Georgia, which I've been told is pronounced, Vy-eena. It's on the other side of Fairfax, not far from the hospital."

Her mother, she said, was convinced that one day all her children would decide to visit at the same time, spouses and grandchildren in tow, and they'd need a place to stay. "So she hangs onto that house, even though it's way too big for her now."

Her father passed away two years ago. I told her I was sorry. "It was hard on all of us," Sarah said, "especially my mother."

When I asked why she became a police officer, she thought a while before responding.

"It wasn't some big event. I know it was like that for some people on the force, something happened and they didn't like feeling helpless. With me, it's mostly what I told you before. I like helping people.

"In college I started out majoring in Sociology. I thought, what better way to help people than to study human behavior. But it didn't work out for me. The Sociology I studied treated people like statistics and guinea pigs. Maybe all Sociology isn't like that, but what I saw turned me off.

"In this job I get to help individual people in need. I don't walk a beat or anything, not in the suburbs, but I feel like I know the people I come in contact with. I can deal with them face to face."

"Some of them probably aren't very nice," I offered.

She made a snorting noise. "I admit at first I was naïve. Altruistic is a word more to my liking. I thought any situation could be handled with calm reasoning and a little compassion. Fortunately, I had a partner who set me straight."

"Was that the partner who was with you at my accident?"

"No, Sully – my first partner – he retired last year. He's off in Montana now, fly fishing his heart out. At least I hope he is. That's all he ever talked about doing when he retired.

"I'm still new at this. I did well at the academy, but I'm still learning the job. Things are better for women than they used to be, at least that's what all the men tell me."

"They treat you all right?"

She laughed. "It was rougher growing up with three brothers."

She grew quiet, and I was content to look out the window. I was getting tired, my eyelids wanting to close. I toyed with a fantasy: if only I could get home and go to sleep, I might wake up to find this had all been a dream.

Suddenly her arm shot out, pointing to a sign that said, "Entering Blue Meadow, established 1765." When I sat up, it became clear I'd been expecting my world would suddenly become familiar, now that I was home. But I looked out at a small town, as unfamiliar as every other place we'd passed through. There was a market; a hardware store; a church; and the post office, library and town hall all inside the same red brick building.

The car slowed even more. "Close your eyes," Sarah said.

I made a face.

"Come on. Humor me."

Sighing, I obeyed.

The car took a right turn, slowed to a crawl, then stopped. "Okay, you can look now."

We were in a parking lot, a huge empty swatch of asphalt, no other cars in sight. The building in front of us didn't look like a house, exactly; it was boxy, one story, brown with a tin roof. It didn't have a front door.

I looked to Sarah, who was grinning madly. And then something clicked. "Is this a train station?"

"Didn't I tell you? It's way cool."

"I live in a train station?"

"It's not a train station anymore. The trains stopped running through here about ten years ago. It's a residence now. Your residence. With lots of parking for your friends," she added. "Welcome home."

I was confused. I could remember a train station in Mansfield when I was growing up. Dusty wood floors, hard wooden benches along the walls. We kids used to put pennies on the tracks for the train to flatten.

But nobody lived in that train station.

"Be careful getting out."

I bristled. I wasn't an invalid. All the same, I was careful to steady myself once I'd climbed out of the car.

The parking lot was enormous. I guess they needed it when the trains were running. It was a wasted space now, with only me.

When Sarah headed around the side of the building, I followed. She walked up to the door but a concrete walkway in back distracted me. That would have been the platform where people waited for the train, I realized. A gulley ran between the platform and the wooded hill rising up behind it. At the bottom, a single set of tracks ran over sharp black rocks and dark brown ties stained, cracked, and rotted.

Sarah waited at the door. I reached into my jeans pocket for the key, but found it empty. Panic shot through me. Had I forgotten the key? Would Sarah have to drive all the way back just to get it? Then she held out her fist, opened it, and sheepishly, I plucked the key off her palm. "You do the honors," she said.

I paused to collect myself before I stepped into shadows and a slightly musty smell. I was in a narrow space, the kitchen, with sink, cabinets, and appliances along one wall and a table in the middle. Between the table and the opposite wall was barely enough space to squeeze by.

Ahead was a larger, darker area. I approached as if nearing the edge of a cliff. "Sorry," came from behind me, and the space ahead burst with light. "This used to be the waiting room," Sarah said.

It didn't look like a waiting room. The walls were a soft blue, the floor mostly covered by two rugs, the wood in between shiny and new. Clusters of furniture divided the open space into smaller areas: two upholstered chairs facing a TV in one part, a round table with a lamp and telephone in another. Something that looked like a combination radio and record player sat on a stand in another corner, while in back a couch had been turned to face the double sliding glass doors that looked out on the concrete platform and the hill beyond.

Then there were the books. One whole wall, from the front of the room to the back, lined with bookcases, eight or nine of them, each one seven or eight feet high. Each jammed full of books, so many books that on several shelves, books lying on their sides had been piled on rows of books standing up. Could I have read all these books? Not unless reading was all I'd been doing the last twenty-eight years.

"You doing okay?"

I'd forgotten Sarah. I didn't know what to say. "It's a lot to take in," I managed.

"I know. And there's more. Come look at this."

She led me to a door with a window looking into a small office that faced the front of the building. "This must have been the ticket office. These windows probably opened. Pay your money, get your ticket, ride the train." She said it in a sing-song way. She seemed more excited than I was. But then she could remember being here before.

To me, this was a stranger's home.

"Are you okay?" she asked.

"I'm just a little tired."

"You look pale."

"I just need a little rest."

She pointed to a shadowed hallway. "Your bedroom's down here."

My body felt weighted, my legs wobbly. Sarah stayed close behind me, the way Dana had followed me the first few times I'd tried to walk. "I just need to rest," I said, pushing the words out on a weak breath.

I halted at the bathroom door. "I should go in here first," I said, and fortunately, she didn't try to follow. I felt a little better after splashing cold water on my face, but I was like a flashlight with dying batteries, it was hard to tell how much light was left.

"I'm really sorry," I told Sarah. "I haven't built up any reserves yet."

She assured me she understood, I shouldn't worry.

"I really appreciate everything you've done for me." A weak laugh slipped out of me, that threatened to end up as tears. "I can't thank you enough."

We kept on like that, me thanking her, she saying she was glad she could help, until I knew I'd collapse if I didn't get off my feet. No longer even caring how rude I was being, I finally trudged off to my bedroom, and without even bothering to take in my surroundings, I flopped down onto the bed, closed my eyes, and let go of the world.

. . .

I dreamt I was in a play, waiting backstage to go on and deliver my lines. I didn't know what those lines were, or even what play I was in. I thought if only I could see those lines, I'd remember them, but none of the people around me had a script. I didn't recognize any of those people, nor did they seem concerned about my plight.

I woke up still mired in anxiety from the dream. I was sweating under my clothes and breathing rapidly. Expecting to see drab hospital colors and to hear beeping from the machines behind me, I lay still, letting my eyes absorb the blue walls, the glowing lamp on the dresser, the clothes poking out the open closet door.

Cautiously, I drew up my shirt and strained to look at my abdomen. A whitish line with a row of marks, almost like train tracks, ran straight across, just above my navel, scars from the way I'd been cut, then sutured. Bruises on my hands and arms from all the needles. A left leg that barked when it moved. It had not been a dream.

I played back the ride here, how fatigued I'd grown, how I'd walked away from Officer Sarah Madison. Would I ever see her again? Did I even thank her?

It felt like a weight was bearing down on me. I had to get up, but I didn't want to move. I reached for Dr. Clark's words: "Ask yourself, What do I feel up to doing now? If anything feels like too much, let it pass. You can always come back to it later."

What did I feel up to doing now? I'd like to take a shower. Eat something. Judging from the shadows, the sun had set, although it didn't feel late. I didn't think I'd slept that long. I'd brought home a packet full of instructions and helpful advice, but I didn't feel like doing homework now. The thought of never seeing Officer Madison again made me sad. There'd been a television in my "waiting room." Maybe I could park myself in front of that and take a pass on thinking and feeling.

Sarah had left the light on in the main room, and from somewhere came a cool breeze. Had she left the windows open?

I sensed a presence before I saw, curled up in a chair beneath a standing lamp, reading a book, Officer Sarah Madison.

"You're here!" blurted out of me.

She uncurled her body, closed the book around one finger to hold her place, and stood. "How are you feeling? Were you able to sleep?"

"I thought you'd be gone," I said, then quickly apologized. "I'm not awake yet."

"It's good you slept. You look better."

"What are you reading?"

"Alice in Wonderland." She held it up. "I never read it as a kid but I always wanted to. It's pretty strange."

"You can have it."

"I'm not going to take your book."

I gestured toward the rows and rows of them. "I doubt I'll miss it."

"Even so, I'm not going to take it. But I will borrow it. And you can be sure I'll return it in a reasonable amount of time. My aunt Fredericka has been a librarian for forty years. She instilled excellent library etiquette in my whole family."

"Do you call her Aunt Fred?"

"Not if I want to live."

I grinned. If she borrowed my book, then I'd see her again when she returned it.

She set the book down after marking her place with a scrap of paper. "I thought I'd stick around until you woke up. I know it's been a long day."

"What time is it?"

"Almost eight."

I laughed. "No wonder I'm hungry. In the hospital, they serve dinner at five o'clock sharp."

"I'm afraid you don't have much here," she said, and I followed her into the kitchen. "I took the liberty of throwing out a few things that had gone bad. That left some graham crackers, orange juice, a few frozen things in the freezer, but nothing to make a meal out of."

"Hard to get excited about graham crackers and orange juice for dinner."

"So," she said, "I walked over to that Mom-and-Pop grocery and picked up this." She opened the freezer door theatrically and slid out a flat box. "Do you like pizza?"

I hesitated. I knew what pizza was, mostly from television commercials. They hadn't served it at the hospital, and I couldn't remember eating it as a kid.

"Everybody likes pizza," Sarah announced. "It'll be a treat for you."

She set the pizza box down and fiddled with the stove. "Do you have –" she began, stopped herself, then said, "Sorry," and opened and closed several cabinet doors until she found a flat tray to put the pizza on. When the pizza was in the oven, she turned to face me. "I picked up a few other things, some bread so you can have toast in the morning, milk, and coffee, since I noticed you had a coffee maker.

"I've set a timer on the oven. When it goes off, just turn the oven off and your pizza will be ready."

"You have to stay," I said a little too desperately. My heart was racing. It was frustrating, because I felt thirteen again, anxious about talking with a girl I liked. "No matter how much I discover I like pizza," I said, calmer now, "there's no way I can eat that whole thing myself."

"It's also good cold." She smiled. "But I'll accept your offer."

While we waited for the pizza, she helped me organize my pills. There were two I needed to take twice a day, and another only when I felt pain. "You can make a chart and just check them off when you take them. They have weekly containers, too. You put the pills you need to take in a compartment for each day, a.m. and p.m. Then the empty container will remind you that you took them." I had an image of her explaining the same system to her mother, and hoped she didn't see me that way.

She also helped me sort my mail. The pile consisted mostly of bills, which she made me promise to pay in the morning. Mrs. Gutierrez had told me I had some kind of automatic payment for my rent, so I was okay there. Sarah warned there might be some late fees I'd have to pay, but assured me they wouldn't shut off any services without a warning.

There was nothing in the pile that resembled a card or personal letter, no envelope with human handwriting. If Sarah wondered about that, she hid it well.

The pizza was good, and I ate the two pieces Sarah put on my plate and then accepted a third. Sarah was content with two, so there was some left over. "You can have it for breakfast," she said.

When she went off to the bathroom, I decided to do something to impress her. The occupational therapist showed me how to make coffee, and I confidently filled the coffee maker with water, added coffee, and turned it on. Excited, I got out two cups.

When she returned, the gurgling caught her attention. I'd positioned myself to block her view. "Something smells good," she said, and grinning, I stepped away with fanfare.

"I thought you might like some coffee."

"Good beans," she said, which puzzled me, until she explained it's just an expression.

When the coffee maker turned silent, I announced, "Here we go," and slid out the carafe. But something didn't look right. Tiny black dots floated in the liquid, like little bugs. Peering over my shoulder, Sarah made a "Hmm" sound, then raised the lid. "Ah, I see. We seem to have forgotten the filter."

Her use of "we" didn't soften the fact that I alone had screwed up.

"It's no big deal. Easily fixed." I moved out of the way as she found a paper cone and poured coffee through it into another container. "Good as new," she announced, filling our two cups.

As we drank the coffee, Sarah remained in instructor mode, explaining how there was no Metro this far from the city, but busses ran everywhere, and the library had schedules. Clearly she was preparing for her departure. Like a mother giving final instructions to her child on the first day of school, I thought. "Don't lose your milk money, be sure to sharpen your pencils when you get to class."

"I don't know what I would have done without your help today," I told her.

She looked embarrassed. "I'm glad I could be there."

Not wanting to think I was a dullard who couldn't read the tea leaves, I told her, "You have to go."

"Five a.m. comes early."

"I'm really grateful."

"Maybe I could give you a call later in the week, see how you're doing?"

"Yes," I said quickly. "I'd like that."

"I don't know your phone number."

Neither did I. As I looked around, Sarah said, "It's probably written on your phone."

It was, and after I gave it to her, she wrote down her own. "This is my cell phone. If you call when I'm at work, I won't answer."

It was fully dark outside, only a faint glow of light rising up in the distance from the tiny center of town. Around the edge of my property came a steady, "chooking" noise.

"Cicadas," Sarah said. "They pop up every seven years." She laughed. "Literally."

"So they won't know who the president is, either."

"William Jefferson Clinton. There's a photo of him in every police station in the country."

"As long as it's not a wanted poster."

She laughed again. "Some people think it ought to be."

It didn't really matter, I thought, who the president was, or what cicadas did or didn't know. What mattered, I thought, was that Sarah seemed nearly as reluctant to go as I was to see her go.

Then something popped into my head. "I owe you money for the groceries."

She shrugged. "We can take care of it next time."

Those last two words made me smile.

"You take care of yourself," she said.

"I'll be okay."

"It'll come back. All of it."

A nod was all I could manage.

She stepped back, extending her arm, taking my hand and shaking it vigorously. Like we'd just made a business deal. Her grip strong and her grin showing lots of straight white teeth.

When our arms stilled, her hand still clasped mine. She gave it a gentle squeeze. "Be well," she said. When she let go, I felt the loss.

I watched her headlights lance across the parking lot, then the red slashes of tail lights as her car paused at the entrance, then finally pulled out onto the road.

Inside, the leftover pizza smell only made me feel more alone. Cleaning up, I noticed, lying on a chair in the waiting room, a scrap of paper sticking out to mark the place, *Alice in Wonderland.*

Chapter Four

On my first day home, I pretended to be Columbo, examining the home of a criminal to learn about the man through the details of his home. It only mildly disturbed me that I could remember a TV character from the 1960s, complete with rumpled suit and trench coat, better than I could recall every woman I might have loved in the past twenty-five years.

First, I made coffee, with a filter this time. Then I let my gaze roam. The furniture in the waiting room was basic, old and mismatched but in good shape. The whole area was clean, with very little dust, considering how long I'd been away. Each smaller area seemed purposefully arranged. I could discern no clear order in the arrangement of the books, but I might have found a logic, had I known anything about the books I was looking at.

Was this fellow, this Matthew Winton, a stickler for neatness? Perhaps he'd tidied up before leaving, not planning to return for a while. There'd been no overnight bag in my car, not even a thermos of coffee. Where was Matthew Winton heading?

The small office facing the front of the building – the ticket office, Sarah had called it – looked equally well kept. A desk pushed up to the window, looking out over the parking lot and a farmhouse across the road, contained only a lamp, a cup full of pens and pencils, and a dish with paper clips and a few coins. A manual typewriter sat on a small table to one side of the desk. Stacks of papers were piled up on shelves built into the wall, along with a dozen or so more books. There were a couple posters on the wall that meant nothing to me, no photographs on the desk. Everything, both in the office and out in the waiting room, seemed functional, without personality, and, I thought, lonely.

Had Matthew Winton been a recluse? That would explain the lack of visitors to the hospital, the absence of personal well-wishes.

I sat down at the desk. My desk. This Columbo thing wasn't working; he always solved the case in ninety minutes. I'd been at it longer and had nothing. Opening the top desk drawer, I felt relief at how messy it was: loose papers stuffed in, pens and more paper clips, an old checkbook register, a bottle of aspirin, a melted Baby Ruth candy bar, blank postcards, bill receipts, rubber bands, band aids, a box of staples, scotch tape, a pair of sun glasses, a set of keys, perhaps a spare set belonging to my old and now totaled car.

The post cards I might have bought at a museum. One showed the face of an old smiling bald man with a mustache and round-rimmed glasses, identified on the back as "Mohandas Gandhi (1869 – 1948), Indian leader," while another one with colorful designs, said "Matisse cutouts" on the back.

I also discovered a birthday card, a drawing of a cartoon cowboy falling headfirst over his horse, above the caption, "Another one bites the dust." Inside, written in ink "Oh well, forty's better than the alternative. With love, Jessie." Whoever Jessie was, they'd sent their birthday wishes "with love."

The papers on the built-in shelves were all from school. Things called a "Syllabus," which seemed to be outlines of courses I taught, with titles like "Fiction Techniques" and "Voice in Modern Fiction." What did I know about voice in modern fiction? Apparently, Professor Winton knew a lot, as many of the papers were student writings, along with what seemed to me intelligent comments made by the professor. Professor Winton knew his stuff. Amnesiac Winton knew next to nothing.

The top shelf contained books with titles like *Making Shapely Fiction*, *The Art of Fiction*, *Becoming a Writer*, and *Writing Fiction: A Guide to the Narrative Craft*. The only books I recalled reading as a kid were about some boy named Tom Swift, and the Bruce Catton book in eighth grade history class. Comic books and *Mad Magazine*. If I read these books on writing carefully, would they teach me how to teach my students?

I cautioned myself not to get discouraged. My memory would come back in time. Everyone said so. What choice did I have but to believe?

In a corner of one shelf sat a metal box, a little bigger than a loaf of bread. A musty smell seeped out when I opened it. The yellowed papers inside looked fragile, and I handled them with care.

The first paper I unfolded was my birth certificate. Matthew Arthur Winton entered the world at 8:02 a.m. on May 14, 1956. Parents Irene Margaret Winton and Edwin Joseph Winton. There was even a tiny footprint, no bigger than my thumbprint would be now.

At first, the document brought elation, and validation, too: I was who people said I was, I had lived forty-one years. But as I sat there, I began to feel even more separated from this person whose proof of birth I held in my hand. Not as if he was another person, as in my Columbo game. But as if he had died, and I was his ghost, combing back through his life.

When I was a kid, I used to pretend that I could make myself invisible. As long as I didn't make eye contact with another person, that person wouldn't see me – a handy trick, especially when ogling the voluptuous women on the cover of detective magazines at Marvin's Drugs. My go-to escape, probably, whenever doing something I knew my mother would disapprove of.

Now I felt invisible, without wanting to be.

I found other papers in the box, such as a notice that Charles A. Heller, my grandfather, had been elected secretary of the Long

Island chapter of the National Linotype Operators Union. Dated September 30, 1938.

There was also a playbill for something called *West Side Story*, nothing professional, just black ink on orange construction paper, a silhouette of city buildings and a fire escape on the front, and a cast list inside. None of the names were familiar, until I got near the bottom of the list, where the character of "Doc" was played by Matthew Winton. The play was performed at Bear Mountain Regional High School in Mansfield, Massachusetts, April 19-21, 1973. I would have been in eleventh grade.

In the bottom of the box were a handful of photographs. The one on top, its colors faded, showed four elderly people seated in a row of lawn chairs in front of a house. The two women were both heavyset, with white hair, while one man was muscular, with a crewcut, and the other – my grandfather – slight and bald. I identified my grandmother, remembered the other couple as my great aunt and uncle: my grandmother's brother, a truck driver with rough, powerful hands, and my aunt, who spoke with a Scottish brogue and jokingly said things like, "Yer bum's oot the windae," and "My heid's full o' mince," and was, as far as I could recall, the only one in my family ever to tickle me, which she did relentlessly.

Aunt Cathy. Uncle George. My grandmother, Maggie May. My grandfather, Charles.

Written on the back, in pencil, was "August 2, 1964." I'd have been eight. I always got excited when told my great aunt and uncle were visiting. As soon as they called to say they were leaving their home, I rushed outside to wait for them. It never quite registered that the home they were leaving was in New Jersey, and it would be hours before they arrived at our house.

In the next photograph, two women stood side by side in front of a flower garden. I recognized my mother immediately, pushing away a twinge of sadness. The other woman was my great uncle's daughter Lily. She was tall and thin, older than my mother by as much as ten years, elegant and comfortable in front of the camera, unlike my mother, who seemed to be shrinking away, embarrassed, even guilty. As if the camera might reveal something she wished to hide.

The next two photos were from my parents' wedding. The first formal: woman and man, bride and groom. My father a cheery-faced young man with dark curly hair, in a dark suit and tie, looking like a kid having the best Christmas ever. His puffed-out chest made him look both proud and timid at the same time. My mother, also dark haired and an inch or two taller, looked uncomfortable, as if uncertain she was in the right place. In the second photo, they stood beside a wedding cake, my father holding up a slice in his bare hand, pretending to be about to cram it into his new bride's mouth, while she looked like she wanted to be a sport but her heart wasn't in it.

These were my observations, anyway. I had very few memories of my father from my childhood. He always seemed to be working, and my mother seemed more relaxed when he wasn't around. I believed – although I wasn't sure why I thought this – that she regretted marrying him.

The final photo was a portrait of my mother, taken at some point before she got married. It looked professionally done, a black and white photograph splashed with color, and I recalled that she'd worked in a photographer's studio during the war, one of her jobs painting colors onto black and white photographs.

In the bathroom I held the photo beside my own face in the mirror. There was a clear resemblance in the small mouth and slightly upturned nose. Her brown eyes revealed a vulnerability I suspected she felt inside. I had my father's green eyes, but I could remember looking in the mirror at the hospital and seeing a person inside simultaneously trying to hide and desperate to break free. Did she feel the same?

Studying this photo brought memories. My mother had an irrational fear of snakes, so severe that in seventh-grade science class, she screamed and hurled her book across the room when she came upon a photo of one. Her father – so different from the man I knew as my grandfather – took her to the zoo and made her touch a boa constrictor, believing it would cure her. It didn't.

She loved baseball, but her father wouldn't play catch with her, wouldn't take her with him to see his beloved Brooklyn Dodgers. Baseball wasn't a game for girls, he said. After the war, she wanted to be an artist but got married instead.

I remembered my mother as unhappy. Unfulfilled. Her parents lived with us throughout my childhood, and I suspected her father criticized her parenting skills. I remembered being told how at four or five, I often ran away from my mother in stores, even down Main Street in Mansfield. I preferred believing I wasn't fleeing from her but rather running toward something exciting, wanting her to come along. But I had no idea what was in my mind or heart. Eventually, they put me in a harness when we went out in public.

Even with my grandfather's companionship, as a child I fixated on my mother. To me, she had near mystical powers. "Take your raincoat," she'd tell me as I left for school, despite the cloudless sky, and of course, I'd come home in a downpour. In Sunday School, we were told that Jesus watched over us, He could see us all the time, and I somehow passed on those Jesus powers to my mother. I took everything she said as literal truth.

I returned to my parents' wedding photos. My father I remembered as easy-going and eager to please, who too often said or did the wrong thing in her presence. Whenever she got angry or frustrated, she usually blamed him.

I see her in our house, the house we moved to later, after both my grandparents died. She glares at my father. "How can you be so stupid?" She doesn't want a reply, but my father offers one, and then he laughs his nervous laugh, which she hates. "Go ahead and laugh," she says. "You won't be laughing when you wake up some morning to find me gone."

What was my father's sin that time? He went to the store for her. She asked him to buy a head of lettuce. He came back with cabbage instead.

⋯

After a while I took a break and walked into town to pay bills. The town seemed barely a town, smaller even than the three-block-long Main Street of Mansfield, although it made sense that I'd be drawn here. A few people were walking about, and I toyed with a fantasy where someone rushed out of their building shouting, "Matthew, old friend. Where have you been?" But no friend appeared.

I visited the Route 66 Diner, situated at the end of the off ramp to its namesake highway. Ordering coffee, I made eye contact with the waitress, tall and big-boned, middle aged, with some gray dusting her reddish blonde hair. "This may sound weird," I began, "but could I ask you a question? Do I look familiar to you? Have you seen me in here before?"

It was embarrassing to sit there while she examined me. "You've maybe been in here before," she said finally, "but you're not a regular."

"I don't look familiar?"

She shook her head, vaguely apologetic, then walked off to tend to her next customer.

Next I visited the grocery. Without a plan, I browsed the aisles, picking out things I could remember liking: frozen waffles, ice cream, hot dogs, French fries, bologna, white bread. The perfect haul – for a twelve-year-old.

⋯

Later, with shadows draped across the parking lot, hedges, and street outside, I studied more closely the two hangings on my office wall. One was a framed art poster of a woman lying in a field gazing up at a house. Underneath it said, "Christina's World, National Gallery of Art." The second was a framed cover of a literary magazine, the front and back laid flat. Titled *October Mountain: An Anthology of Berkshire Writers*, the magazine was dated Fall, 1992.

On the back portion was a list of contributors: Herman Melville, Nathanial Hawthorne, W.E.B. DuBois, Edith Wharton, and nearly twenty other names, none of which meant anything, until near the bottom, I found "Matthew Winton."

Of course, I thought. Matthew Winton wasn't just a college professor, he was a writer. He'd written stories, perhaps about his own past. Maybe those stories could show me my life.

I found a copy of *October Mountain* among the books on teaching fiction. It was a slim paperback, an impressionistic sketch of a mountain on the front, black lines against a purple background. Flipping the book over, I again read through the contributors' names. Perhaps some of these people were friends of mine, we might have exchanged letters complimenting each other's stories. The title said we are all Berkshire writers; Mansfield was part of Berkshire County. Perhaps I'd sat down over beers with some of these people.

For the first time, I felt genuinely hopeful. Opening *October Mountain* and finding my name and the title of the story in the table of contents, excited and nervous both, I turned to that page and began to read.

· · ·

The Radio

"Into the arena comes the somber and menacing figure of Charles "Sonny" Liston, aptly named the most frightening man in the world."

People said the war changed your father but your mother disagreed. "It just gave him license," she said. You were six or seven when you heard her say this to her friend Angela, and you thought "license" meant driver's license and wondered, *Was he too young to drive but they let him because of the war?*

You know now that license meant permission, to do whatever the fuck he wanted, not give a shit about anyone or anything if he didn't feel like it. Like some innocent prisoner finally let out of jail, owed something he knew he'd never get back, so he took what he wanted as compensation, the rest be damned.

You used to listen to your mother tell of all the exciting things she dreamed of doing once her husband was gone. It was reasonable: eleven years her senior, he smoked and drank and abused his body, while she spent most of her time at home. Who thought she could die at thirty-seven? He smoked; she got cancer. Close to the end, you heard her whisper, "I never imagined it could be like this."

She whispered something else near the end, too. Her trembling, bone-thin fingers clutching to your shirt, she hissed out a single plea: "Look after him. He's a child."

You stand in his room now, "their room" you still call it in your head, and imagine you can still smell the trace of your mother's scent, a mix of perfume and baking, something you've thought of as the smell of home, but another smell overpowers the memory, the stink of sweat and grime and unwashed bedclothes, the smell of unchecked man. The room is divided in half now, your mother's side untouched except that her vanity's been cleared off, after the old man swept into drawers everything he couldn't use, sell or throw away. On the other side, the bed looks like he wrestled a grizzly in his sleep; cigarette butts spilling out of a multitude of ashtrays, dirty clothes strangling a chair.

Near the bed, which you refuse to sit on, sits the radio squeezed between the lamp and an overflowing ashtray on the bedside table. The size of a small loaf of bread, it's bone-colored, dented and dirty, with dust wedged into crevices and cigarette burns on top that remind you of spy movies where interrogators use glowing cigarettes for torture. The dial that turns the thing on and off is loose, despite being sated with glue, electrical tape hugs slits in the wire, and the bent prongs have to be continually reshaped before being plugged in. But the radio works: you listen to it sometimes in the afternoons, sliding the dial away from his swing music to find Sam Cooke, The Drifters, Marvin Gaye. The reception is best late at night, and you've already tested it to make sure it will bring in the station you'll need tomorrow.

Outside there's a ruckus; the old man is alien to quiet. You hurry out of his room, close the door behind you, your chest thumping. Outside the old man curses and jangles, searching for keys. Before he can begin pounding, you collect yourself, walk over and wrap your sweaty hand around the doorknob and jerk the door open. Hunched over, his dark eyes peer up without raising his head, guilty and predatory, a narrow smile slicing his lips. "Good," you say, already turning away. "I was about to start dinner."

"Now he has to make his fists do what his mouth has predicted."
"This boy who said he'd make the ugly bear look silly."

He never said he was proud you were his son. Now he seems to want a daughter, or a maid. You do the cleaning, the laundry, the shopping with bills he leaves on the table at the end of each week, whatever's left after booze and gambling and the spending money he keeps for himself. You've learned to cook a few things, sausages and mashed potatoes; you can heat up a can of peas. He pushes all the food together into one messy pile and you wince, remembering the distaste on your mother's lips, his prickly answer: "What? It all goes to the same place." And then, "This is how a man eats in war."

"Tomorrow night," you say, peering up at him to be sure he's listening. He won't look at you because he knows you want him to. "It starts at ten o'clock." You need to remind him, not because you fear he'll forget but because you can't believe he's giving in so easily. There might be a hint of invitation there, too.

He spears a whole sausage and bites off one end. His fingers have been broken more than once, and the gnarled middle finger sticks up as if it's saying, "Fuck you" and "Come here," both at the same time.

"They can kill each other for all I care. Two convicts fighting for the championship of the world."

"He's not a convict. Just Sonny, and he's done his time."

This time he waits until your eyes find his. "Sooner or later," he says, "they all end up in jail."

You let time pass. "You gonna be home?" you ask. "Tomorrow night?"

He shrugs, as if what he'll do tomorrow night is a question only God can answer. He doesn't often come home straight from work, but how late he's out depends on factors you don't want to know.

"I might move the radio into my room. Reception's better close to the window."

He glances over to where the television ought to be. It was never much of a television, tiny and full of dents, with a bent antenna topped by aluminum foil that brought in two snowy channels when the weather was clear, but it's broken now, needing a new picture tube, sitting in the back room of the repair shop at the end of Main Street, because you can't stretch the recent cash far enough to pay for the repair. Not that it would matter for tomorrow night. If it were on TV, the channel'd never reach here.

He shovels food into his mouth, a mountain green and white and sausage grey. "Knock yourself out."

"He's hurt him in the body with a right hand. Clay is hurt. He's got to keep moving, keep away."

You're almost sixteen and yearn to get away. But there are no good options. You could join the army, lie about your age, but you'd likely end up in the jungle fighting a war nobody calls a war. College is impossible: in school you keep quiet, stay out of people's way, do only what you must. You could just take off, keep your face to the setting sun, sleep beneath underpasses. But there's snow on the ground and temperatures thudding below zero. Winter is no time for flight.

The simple truth: even if you want to go, you can't.

• • •

There's a row of bars along Railroad Street, solid doors always closed, windows darkened, smells of beer and piss seeping up from the ground in front. His stomping grounds, and he goes there after dinner, returns late rubber-legged, wearing a snarling, goofy expression. You tell yourself to leave him be, but you can't stop from snagging an arm as he's about to greet the floor, tugging to keep him upright, half-dragging him over to flop down on the couch. He isn't a big man, not a brute, but sinewy and coiled like a snake, sober anyway. But even sober, he's clumsy. When he got frisky—play-slapping your face to get a rise, or when you were younger, planting his hand atop your head and shouting at you, "Swing, come on, punch your old man, swing like you mean it," and your arms flailed until they ached as his taut arm held you too far away to pummel more than air; even when he snatched your mother and wrestled her around the room in what he called a dance—something usually got smashed.

He struck you in anger only once. It was silly: you were five or six, wanted to watch cartoons on Sunday morning, rebelled against going with your mother to church. He never went, why should you? Sitting on the floor in front of the TV, you refused to put on your socks. "Please," your mother said, not for the first time. "We're going to be late." Your rebuttals joined with tears, sweet salty snot sliding down your upper lip. He walked in, wearing just his boxers, finally out of bed. "Please," she said again, but this time she turned to him. "Do something."

Maybe he sensed her frustration, heard the unspoken, "For once in your life…" Maybe he was just hungover and ornery. "Put on the damn socks," he said, and when you replied, "I don't want to," the next thing you saw was a blur shooting out of the sky, lifting you up, a noise somewhere then an explosion in the bones of your cheek, knocking you back into your mother's womb, the world all around you under water.

Splayed out on the couch, he slips back and forth between snoring and struggling to get up. During one of the latter attempts, you offer an arm and he grabs it, hoists himself. He totters, gains purchase, draws his arm free. Steadied, he stares into your eyes, his own eyes crinkling, not so much like he doesn't know you but as if you look different than you always looked before. You see it too, impossible you didn't notice before, how long has it been true: with both of you standing straight, he has to look up to find your eyes.

"Fuck," he says, a general appraisal. Turns toward his room. You can see the tension in his back and neck, knowing you're watching, he's trying real hard not to sway.

In the morning as he's leaving you remind him, "It starts at ten o'clock."

"I got my own plans," he shoots back. "Don't pay no mind to me."

"There's the bell and they're still fighting."

After dinner, you bring the radio into the kitchen, clean up while Sam Cooke sings "You Send Me." Later, fighting yawns, you consider a nap but fear you won't wake up. You catch yourself glancing at the apartment door, expecting what? Him to come barging in, spoil everything. The one thing he's really good at, spoiling everything.

A little after nine you carry the radio into your bedroom, nestled on two palms like a gift on a pillow to be handed, knees bowed, to a king. You've already cleared space near the window, curtain drawn back. You've searched the papers at Mahoney's Smoke Shop to find the stations that will carry it, and you test them now, settling on the one that holds the steadiest connection. Even so, anxiety nibbles at your gut because two men are not talking about the fight to come, and you fear you've got something wrong, or maybe the people broadcasting the fight decided it was too much trouble to transmit to such an insignificant town in the middle of nowhere that you have been born and raised in.

Mouth dried out, you walk to the kitchen for a glass of water. And hear outside that familiar thumping and cursing, joined to something unfamiliar: a second voice, high pitched and giggly.

The door swings open. She's loose-limbed, her cheeks looking like they've been rubbed with raspberry powder. His arm is around her shoulders; is she holding him up, or is he keeping her from escaping? Still giggling, until her head raises up and her eyes lock on you and go wide and her cherry lips straighten. "My kid," he says. "Don't mind him."

He looks at you like he's just delivered a punch line. But she comes forward, daintily offers a hand. "Pleased to meet you," she says. You can smell her perfume like a wall of heat on a summer day, and up close she looks older, you can see makeup caked on the side of her face. Her hand is cool and soft, truly an offering, not a demand, and you remember from somewhere your mother telling you once that a lady will let you know how she wants you to take her hand. This one, you think, wants you to touch her like you're a prince preparing to try on Cinderella's slipper.

"Come on," he says, slips off his coat, takes hers when she holds it out, something that looks like fur but couldn't have ever been alive. He does a little dance step leading her forward, suddenly transformed into Fred Astaire, while she trails, a little awkward in her heels, and you back deeper into the kitchen.

Pausing outside his bedroom, he peers in, turns back to you. "Hey," he says. "Go get the radio, bring it out here. We feel like dancing." He says it like the phrase has some secret meaning for him and the woman, who kicks back her head and grins. There's a spot of lipstick on one of her front teeth, and underneath the perspiration lining her upper lip, you notice the trace of a mustache.

"Come on, kid, get a move on. Can't stop these feet from dancing!" He hops and skips like a drunkard in some old pirate movie.

You don't fight him. You tell yourself it has to do with the woman, but maybe that's an excuse. Maybe, you think, your whole life is an excuse.

He fiddles with the dial, finds his Swing. Her dress billows out, ending at her knees, and when he twirls her you try not to notice the flash of red beneath. The old man nimble, lost inside a rhythm as you've never seen him before. She's grinning madly, a little shriek of surprise and joy popping out of her as he takes her hands, draws her close, then steps back and twirls her, lets her float away like a spinning top before drawing her back again like he's hooked a fish, their chests bumping playfully, and then the two of them close together, hunched over, high stepping as if through fire.

The music speeds up, building, and their movements speed up too, their arms and legs flinging off sweat and booze and all the aches of living. Their expressions show they're gone, flown off away from each other, from themselves, from you, their bodies like desperate immature birds trying through sheer determination to take flight and follow their parents into the skies. And then it ends, the silence itself a kind of thud, and he grabs her and together they flop down onto the couch, she gasping, his grin showing yellowed pointy teeth. She finds a handkerchief from somewhere and dabs it to her face in a coquettish way. "Oh, Lordy," she says, as the next song starts, a waltz, and you imagine the two of them moving slowly around the room, their bodies glued together, imagine this going on forever, and she moves as if she's imagined it too, but he pulls her back when she tries to get up, brings her to him for a kiss. Easily won over, she utters a low sound from deep in her throat; is that what they call purring? Arranges herself against him, knees drawn up, this lengthening kiss not the end of something but the beginning.

Then they are up, their bodies never parting, and moving toward his open bedroom door. Somewhere inside he releases her, steps back outside and waits for your eyes to find his. You know what he is saying: you will eat this, swallow it like all the rest, and we will never speak of it because if we do, you know that you will lose, a first-round KO. Then, just before the door swings shut, a grin, and a glance at the clock: exactly ten.

"He's clubbing viciously, primitively and savagely to try to beat down this young challenger."

You snatch the radio, race to your room, use a chair to blockade the door. Caution yourself: cool, not frantic, as you slide the dial around the circle. You fear, with your luck, that you'll find the station ten seconds after he's been knocked cold, ten seconds before your old man will burst in, crowing, "I guess Pretty Boy ain't so pretty anymore."

"Clay can't see properly he's blinking and he's got something in his eyes."
"Liston will be merciless."
"Liston is hurting him now because Clay isn't putting up much defense, saying, I can't see, I can't see."

You find the station, hear the buzzing beneath the crackle: thousands of ringside insects. The announcers still using their anticipation voice.

A bell. You straddle your chair, leaning forward, fists clenched in your lap, rocking like a jockey begging his horse toward the finish line. Eyes fixed on the radio that transforms from plastic loaf of bread to a bridge that lets you not walk over and be there but rather, draw it all back into your mind. You see it, buoyant as a dream.

"Clay is playing on him now. He's taunting him, making a fool of the champion. Liston has got a scowl on his face now. His lips are twisted."

Noise outside your room: clumsy thumping, a curse, that high pitched response, serious now, giggling stilled. You twist toward the door, your heart thumping too, think, that chair won't keep him out. Think: let him come. Imagine yourself rising to full height, looking down on him. When fighters meet before the fight, in the middle of the ring, they stare into each other's eyes, the loser the first to flinch. You've seen it on the newsreels. You speak out loud, softly, "Come on in."

A distant door slams, muted but still sharp. Silence beyond your door.

"He's punishing the champion heavily."

He never embraced you, never looked at you with pride. Never taught you, no catch in the backyard, no pretending as you watched him shave. Never told you, "This is how to be a man." You thought he was keeping it a secret, that you didn't deserve to know.

He play-boxed with you, his fist always opening before it reached your cheek. The slap stung no worse than the humiliation of a father who believed you could not take a punch.

"He's making the champion look like a sparring partner."

Your mother wanted to be a dancer. But her Prussian father said no, and she never fought back.

You wonder: was your old man jealous of the affection she gave you? You could have told him, "She would have been devoted to you, if you'd let her."

"Liston now looking completely at sea. He doesn't know what it's all about."

Outside your door, it's quiet, the apartment empty. Your father's bed looks like a war's taken place there. There's no trace of your mother's perfume, not even in your imagination. Their room is not theirs anymore.

"What's happened? Clay has won. Clay has won after six rounds. It's all over and Cassius Clay is the new champion."

You stand in the middle of silence, surrounded by roars.

Soon you'll be sixteen. Maybe you'll head out after all, just keep moving. Find a place, anyplace better than here. It's cold now, but winter always gives way to spring.

The new truth: if you choose to go, you can.

The static on the radio melds with the crackle of the crowd. The announcers babble, and then suddenly, a clear voice, loud and sure, crowing from the top of the world:

"I don't have a mark on my face. I must be the greatest. I shook up the world. I am the king of the world. I'm pretty and I shook up the world."

Chapter Five

I needed to go to the university. First, I had to figure out how.

When the Blue Meadow Public Library opened at 10 a.m., I was waiting at the door. I felt comfortable in libraries; when I was a kid, I used to wander among the stacks on Saturday afternoons, picking out books at random. I didn't remember what those books were, but I felt at home among them, even when the librarians tried to convince me I should be in the children's section instead.

Housed in a single room on the first floor of the town hall, this library was tiny. I probably had more books at home. But I wasn't there for books, and spotting a row of computers along the wall, I asked the librarian, "Could I use one?"

"Of course," she said and smiled. "You have your pick." She was a small woman, grandmotherly, with a sweater draped over her shoulders and glasses hanging on a strap around her neck. It struck me that all the librarians I could remember looked like her, and I wondered where young librarians went while waiting to get older.

I settled at a computer on the end but quickly realized I was going to need help. The occupational therapist had taught me about computers, but hers was always turned on, while this one was dark and silent. Finding no obvious buttons to push, I raised a hand, feeling like a school kid who can't understand the instructions for a test.

The librarian hurried over. Of course she did. It struck me that librarians were like nurses – the good ones, anyway. Always looking to help.

"I'm afraid I don't know how to turn it on," I said, adding a nervous laugh that made me cringe, thinking of my father.

"Here." One button pushed and the screen lit up. "There you are."

As she turned away, I called to her again. None of the icons on the screen looked familiar.

"Where are you trying to go?"

"The World Wide Web," I said, because I couldn't remember if the other name was Internet or Intranet. "I'm looking for the University of Northern Virginia."

"That's easy." A couple clicks this time, and the screen filled with shiny brick buildings and happy college students.

The University of Northern Virginia was a new school, barely twenty years old, formerly a satellite of the University of Virginia. I wasn't surprised that none of the buildings looked familiar, not even Dana Hall, location of the English Department. I clicked "Faculty" and up popped a photo of Franz Bergstrom. According to his bio, he had a Ph.D. from Yale in Medieval Literature. I'd imagined he was European, born in Denmark perhaps, but he was from Ohio.

The list of English faculty was long, and the Matthew Winton appearing near the end hardly resembled the one staring at him on the screen. The English Department's Matthew had hair to his shoulders and a thick, neatly trimmed beard. His serious expression made him look like a combination scholar and mountain man. The short bio said nothing new.

The page offering maps and directions listed half a dozen routes to campus, all of them requiring a car. The university appeared to be in the same general area as the hospital.

"What are you trying to find?" asked the librarian when I again looked for help.

I told her I needed to get to the university, and I'd found directions but didn't have a car.

She brought me a brochure. "This should have what you need."

The bus schedule she handed me likely did have the information I needed, but I didn't know how to read it. I didn't need to ask for help, the pathetic expression on my face was easy to decipher.

She began circling bus numbers and times. "You can get it right out front here." She handed me the marked-up brochure. "You can keep this."

Leaving, I thanked her multiple times, deciding that when I returned I should bring her a gift. A book?

According to the schedule, the next bus wouldn't come for an hour. At home I put a few things into my backpack. I thought about taking *October Mountain*, thinking I might reread "The Radio," but I was angry at that story. The man in that story wasn't anything like my father. My mother didn't die when I was a teenager. The story took place in 1964, when I would have been eight. I remembered Cassius Clay, who later changed his name, although I couldn't remember to what.

My anger mixed with disappointment. I'd hoped that story would help me find my past. But almost nothing in it connected to my real life. A few things in the beginning reminded me of my mother, but even if she had died young, my father would never have acted that way. I would never have considered running away from home. The story was a lie.

• • •

Reaching the university required taking two busses. The first went through Manassas and Centreville, where Sarah said she lived, though not in one of the "McMansions" that dominated the landscape. The second went down a several-block-long Main Street before turning to climb a long hill.

There was a moment, when the bus stopped at the outer edge of the campus, that I considered staying on and letting it take me back home. Dr. Clark had advised me that it was okay to pass on anything that caused anxiety. But she also pointed out that facing those anxieties was the fastest way to grow. And if I went home now, I'd just have to go through the whole trip again tomorrow.

All the people walking around backed up the Internet's claim that 20,000 people attended the university. Judging from the parking lots, most of them drove cars.

Many of the people getting off the bus looked like college students, but there were a few older adults, and one woman with two small children. Before leaving home, I'd grabbed a baseball cap which I pulled low over my eyes. As one among 20,000, it seemed unlikely I'd run into anyone I knew crossing campus, but I'd have to visit the main English Department, if only to get directions to my office.

Apparently I'd arrived while classes were in session, a fortuitous accident that allowed me to roam the empty hallways on my way to the fourth floor of Dana Hall. Even as I neared the English Department's entrance, nothing looked familiar, but I was getting used to that being the norm.

Suddenly a rumbling sound passed through the building; doors flew open and a stampede of noise burst out ahead of students spilling into the hallway. I ducked into a bathroom, a horde of students following, and I locked myself in one of the stalls, amid whoops and grunts and other bathroom noises. "I can't believe he gave me that," complained one student. "He's such a prick."

He must have been referring to a teacher. Did they talk about me that way too?

The noise diminished, until it sounded as if only one student remained. When the door opened and closed, I breathed a sigh of relief.

Taking off my cap and smoothing down my hair, I studied myself in the mirror. Most of the cuts on my face had healed, although there was still a scab on my forehead, and puffy gray bags beneath my eyes. I looked like I went a few rounds with Cassius Clay, I thought, and smiled. Although the story hadn't shown any glimpses of my past, I kind of liked it as a story. *Maybe I'm a half-way decent writer after all*, I thought. Or was.

I wondered if I was dressed too casually. What were professors supposed to look like? Franz Bergstrom had worn a three-piece suit when visiting the hospital. But I didn't recall seeing any suits hanging in my closet.

"Get on with it," I muttered, and used that frustration to propel myself through the double doors into the main English Department area. Inside, I expected everyone to turn toward me and stare, but no one seemed to notice me at all.

I stepped up to a desk manned by a young man who barely glanced up. "Hello, Professor," he said.

Before I could respond, I heard a gasp, and someone rushed toward me. A tall woman with red hair in a cloud of perfume angled herself between me and the desk. "That's all right," she told the young man. "I'll help Professor Winton."

"I was looking for my office," I said, and she nodded in a knowing way.

"Of course. Come with me." She led me down a carpeted hallway, past a closed door with a placard that said, "Dr. Franz Bergstrom, Chair," and into the next office, belonging to "Irma Brown, Office Supervisor."

The room had a homey feel, with comfortable chairs and pillows, wall hangings, a soft rug. Drawings done by children covered a bulletin board, "To Grandma," written in red across the top, while clusters of framed photographs covered her desk, young children and teenage children, young adults and middle-aged adults, and Irma.

"I'm sorry," she whispered, reaching behind me to close the door. "Dr. Bergstrom forgot to mention you'd be coming by today."

"He didn't know. I should have called ahead, I guess."

"No, no. I'm sure he would have liked to see you, that's all. To say hello."

An awkward moment followed, where we faced each other and she looked into my eyes and I thought she might burst into tears. Then she lurched forward and hugged me, quickly letting me go. She was older than me, maybe old enough to be my mother, and I wondered if she and I had a special bond. Perhaps she felt like a mother to everyone in the department.

She picked a ring of keys off her desk. "I'll show you to your office."

I followed her down a back hall, bare walls and a drab bone-colored linoleum floor, and lots of closed doors. Irma walked fast, looking over her shoulder regularly to make sure I was still there. At the hospital, Franz Bergstrom had said my doctors spoke with Irma. She must know my condition.

Passing an open door, I looked in at a woman sitting at a desk, speaking with a student. Noticing me, the woman looked like she was about to leap to her feet, her expression surprised and excited both, before turning her attention back to her student.

Irma waited at the next door, where the placard read, "Professor Matthew Winton, Creative Writing." A spot for "Office hours" was blank.

"I'll order you a new key," Irma said, unlocking the door. "Unless you still have your old one."

I shook my head. "That's okay," she said, gentle and understanding. I felt like an invalid again, but I appreciated her taking charge. I was doing that a lot lately, stepping back to let others take charge. Was I that way before the accident, too?

My office was nothing like Irma's. It was bigger, but half of it was empty and bare, as if a second tenant had moved out. My half had a desk and chair, a bulletin board with only a few scraps of paper pinned to it, and a metal bookcase. No carpet or colorful hangings, no photographs on the desk.

Irma gave me a card with her name and phone number on it. "Call me if you need anything." She added, "You don't need to dial the full number for campus calls, just a 3 and the last four digits." She took the card back and wrote something on the other side. "This is the number for the tech office. In case you need to reset your password."

"Can I ask you something?" Already with one foot out the door, she turned back. "The doctors spoke to you?"

"Yes. Dr. Clark. A nice woman."

"What did she tell you?"

"You've lost your memory. Temporarily."

"Who else knows?"

"Dr. Bergstrom. He came to visit you at the hospital," she added, as if I might not remember.

"Nobody else?"

"Dr. Bergstrom told everyone you'd been in an automobile accident. You were recovering but would be on medical leave through the end of the semester."

It was better that way, I thought. Being in a car accident was less freakish than walking around without a memory.

From the doorway, Irma gave me that look again, like her eyes were welling up with tears. I tensed in case she attempted another hug, but instead she said, "It's wonderful to see you," and hurried away.

A few moments later there was a knock at my door. Figuring Irma had forgotten something, I was surprised to find the woman from the office next to mine. "My God, you're here." She rushed forward and wrapped her arms around me, holding me tight like she'd done this before. She was half a foot shorter than me, and I had to bend forward when she laid her cheek against my chest. Her hair smelled of lilacs.

Finally she let go. "How are you? You look good. I'm so sorry I didn't come to visit you. You know how I am with hospitals. Franz said you'd be out all semester. How do you feel?" All of it said on one breath.

She clearly wasn't just any colleague, and I decided to be direct. "I've lost my memory."

I expected the usual reassurance that not remembering an accident is normal, but her brown eyes suggested she saw something deeper. "How bad?"

"My whole adult life." She grimaced. "I'm okay with things happening now, it's not like I'll forget you five minutes after you leave. And I can remember stuff from my childhood. But I don't recall the accident, or anything that happened before that for a whole mess of years."

When she laid a hand on my arm, I can't say it felt familiar, but I didn't tense up. "I'm Jessie," she said, and grinned. "You and I, we're the creative writing program at this fine up-and-coming university."

I thought, birthday card Jessie. With love Jessie.

"Fuck!" she cried. "I'm late for class." She grabbed my arm, as if I was the one about to flee. "Can you stay? Please? I'll be back in an hour. Have you eaten? I'll pick up lunch for both of us. The Chinese place." She paused, recalibrated. "There's a Chinese place on campus. You like the Kung Pao chicken. I'll get you some, bring it after class."

I nodded. "I'll be here."

"It's so good to see you!" she cried, but she was already racing out the door. "I'll be back."

I dropped into my chair, suddenly exhausted. Had I really thought I could sneak into my office without encountering anyone? You should be pleased, I told myself. Jessie knows you, she should have lots to tell. And I wanted to know it all. Just maybe not so soon.

• • •

Jessie and I were hired at the same time, nine years ago, because the university wanted to enhance its creative writing program. She was the poet and I the fiction writer. We became friends quickly, and given how expensive it was to live in this area, we decided to share a house.

She told me all that amid the sweet and pungent aroma of Chinese food spread out across my desk. "This is what you always get," she'd said, setting down the container of Kung Pao chicken.

"So you say," I countered, and she laughed.

"That's right. I could say you always ate brussels sprouts for lunch and you wouldn't know if I was lying."

She dexterously handled chopsticks while eating her noodles. I fumbled with mine until she handed me a plastic fork.

"I guess I've forgotten how to use these," I said.

"You never could."

She was more relaxed, having finished her class. She'd apologized again for not visiting me in the hospital. "It was a shitty thing to do," she confessed, but I shrugged it off. "You really don't remember anything?"

"I remember my childhood, up to the age of thirteen or so. After that, nothing."

"You don't remember anything about your accident?"

"I hit a tree. So they tell me."

"It must be strange. Memories are how you know you've been alive. For people like us anyway, when you don't have kids."

She studied the signs of the accident still on my face. When her stare grew longer than necessary, I said, "What?"

"I was just remembering that line from *Man of La Mancha.* Whether the pitcher hits the stone, or the stone hits the pitcher, it's going to be bad for the pitcher."

"And I'm the pitcher."

She grinned sympathetically. "It looks that way."

While she'd been teaching, I'd managed to conquer my computer, helped by three phone conversations with IT. I'd discovered files under "Documents," but nearly all of them seemed to relate to my classes, and the rest seemed irrelevant. I also discovered 1,081 email messages in my Inbox, 279 of them marked "Unread." Going through them proved even more tedious than the documents: along with department and university notices I didn't care about were a shockingly high number of emails sent to me by mistake. They began "Dear Mick," or "Dear Makaya," and announced how excited I would be to learn of the upcoming conference on molecular engineering.

To clear my head, I'd wandered to the window and watched stragglers hurrying off to class. I liked that perspective, four flights up; I could see the world but it couldn't see me. There are creatures that live this way, I thought. They're called birds. "You remember birds, right?" I muttered. "The little feathery creatures with wings?"

It all seemed crazy, and passing a hand over my face, I wished I could snap my fingers and magically be back home. Or back in the hospital, not having to think or do anything for myself.

Next I investigated the bookcase. More student papers. How could students write so much? How could I read it? On the top shelf were a few thin books. One proved to be another collection of short stories, including one by Matthew Winton. The book was called *Blurred Boundaries: Stories of Fact or Fiction*, and purported to explore the uncertain line between true stories and those made up.

There was another book, slim with a black cover and a black-and-white photograph on the front of bare trees at the edge of a lake, rising up as their reflections dove straight down into the water. The book was called *Wilderness, Poems by Jessie Freer*. On the back was a photo of a younger Jessie, wearing glasses that made her look both studious and sexy, her brown hair shoulder length instead of cut short as it was now.

I read a few poems. They were spare, powerful, sensual. Filled with sharp, concrete images: a jagged mountain peak, a hand pump, a woodsman swinging an axe. Landscapes both rich and barren. At the same time, there was an intimacy to the poems, as if through these concrete images outside herself, Jessie was revealing the deepest parts of herself that most people would never share.

Handwriting on the title page caught my eye. Jessie had crossed out her printed name and written her signature. Below it, she'd added, "To my dear Matt, for helping me learn to believe in myself, and to believe in love." Dated April 30, six years ago.

As she continued to describe our friendship and how we built the creative writing program, my patience wore down, and I said, "So we've been friends all these years?"

Her expression changed, as if she'd pulled down a curtain. "Let's have some tea." She stood. "I have some in my office. I'll bring us both back a cup."

While she was gone, I cleaned off my desk. She returned carrying two mugs, steam floating out of them. Mine had milk. "That's how you take it," she said.

"We hit it off from the start," she began. "We became really good friends. I'd say we were like brother and sister, but I'm an only child, and so are you. Then something changed, I'm still not sure what it was, and suddenly the relationship changed. It surprised us both. We both had this thing about physical contact, we put up all these walls. One night, the walls came down."

She paused. Her eyes, dark brown and big, had a depth it would be easy to fall into. I thought of her poems. She looked like someone who knew what it was like to be hurt. Deeply.

"How long were we together?"

"About three years. I always thought – please don't be offended, I loved you dearly, I still do – I always felt we were two lonely people who came together at a time when we both needed someone to be close to. You know, let down our guard, be ourselves. We're both such private people, but you can't live that way all the time."

"I found your book," I said.

"That was a long time ago."

"Six years."

She laughed. "Which is how long I've been working on the next one."

"I read what you wrote, too. In the beginning of the book."

"It was true."

She didn't have to add, "It's not true anymore."

• • •

Later, I asked if she'd read my "boxing story."

"It's a beautiful story. That last line always makes me smile. 'I'm pretty and I shook up the world.'"

"I was trying – I thought maybe I could learn about my past, reading a story I'd written. I know fiction isn't true, but that story is a total lie."

"It has emotional truth," she said. "I can feel you in it. The longing, the frustration. It's like, you trace a story through a series of crossroads, and at each one, you have to find yourself." She chuckled. "At least, that's what I once heard Professor Winton say, when I visited his class."

I was content letting the topic drop. I wasn't ready to let Jessie see how little I remembered about writing and teaching.

After a while, she had to get ready for her next class. With many more questions I wanted to ask, we agreed to meet on a day when she wasn't teaching, when I would take her to lunch.

As she was about to leave, I said, "I hope I wasn't too much of a jerk, when we were together."

"You were never a jerk. You were sweet, considerate – most of the time. We both needed our privacy, but we understood that about each other. We had a few blowouts, but that's because we're so alike. We never want to admit that something bothers us, so we swallow it and let it fester. But it always comes out eventually."

She laughed. "I remember one time you got really mad about something, and when we finally worked out why, it came back to some night three months before, when we went to a movie I wanted to see because you never told me there was a different movie you wanted to see.

"But I did shit like that too. It was ingrained in both of us. If something bothers you, keep it to yourself."

I thought of how, whenever I walked into a room my mother was in, I always looked first to gauge her mood, so I could decide how I had to be.

Before she left, we hugged again. I still couldn't remember her, but holding her, and being held by her, brought a feeling I had known before, if rarely: that I was protected, and loved.

•••

I filled my backpack with books to take home, including Jessie's poems and the *Blurred Boundaries* book with my story. I put on my cap and followed the back route Jessie had shown me to avoid the main English Department.

The campus had looked quiet from the fourth floor, but descending, a sudden rush and rumble made the stairs shake, and I barely escaped the stampeding students bursting through the doors.

Having come out a different door than I'd entered, I needed a moment to orient myself. Suddenly I heard, "Matthew!" called out somewhere behind me. A woman's voice, not Jessie's, a plea edged with demand. I kept walking, even when the shout was repeated, telling myself there must be dozens of Matthews on the campus. But the next call froze me: "Professor Winton!"

I tugged my cap lower before turning. A young woman raced up to me, tall and blonde and out of breath. A student, certainly. Her expression mixed anger and worry, and she must have been cold, since gray clouds now blocked the sun, a cold wind sliced between the buildings, and she wore no coat.

"Where were you? I tried to call. Where did you go?" All said at the same angry and desperately fearful pitch. Entitled, too. It was hard for me to imagine a student accosting a professor like this.

She moved closer as students streamed past. Her cheeks had turned red from the cold, and regularly she had to reach up to finger away hair blown across her face. I tried to think of something benign to say to extricate myself, but she looked so insistent, I decided to simply tell the truth.

"I've been in an accident. I was in the hospital."

"So it's true! But you're all right now?"

"I'm okay," I said. Then, because that felt dangerous to admit, I added, "I'm still recovering."

"Mrs. Freer said you wouldn't be coming back. I thought you'd run away. I pictured you on the French Riviera. I knew you hadn't died. They would have told us if you'd died."

I couldn't help but smile. She was probably a creative writing student, with that imagination. "I'll be back next semester," I promised.

All the other students had dispersed, but she remained stubbornly close. Remembering how Irma had lurched forward to hug me, I tensed in case she did the same.

"I have to go," I said at last. "I have to catch the bus."

"I could drive you. I just have to borrow a car." She looked around, as if expecting someone to pop up and offer a key.

"I'll be fine. The bus is fine." I stepped away from her. "It was nice to see you." She looked unhappy but accepting. "I'm doing okay. I'll be back next semester."

I walked away, hunched over as if walking into a blizzard. Her final shout, fainter than before, proved she wasn't following. But it unnerved me all the same.

"I miss you!"

Chapter Six

At home, a red light flashed on my phone. It took me a few moments to figure out it was a message, and how to play it.

"Hi. It's Sarah Madison. I'm sorry I missed you.

"I just called to see how you were doing. Also, I forgot my book. Your book. The one you said I could borrow.

"I hope you're well and settling in."

I, too, was sorry I'd missed her, and wished there'd been more to her message. As much as I wanted to be left alone, hearing her voice excited me. I didn't really know Sarah, and I for sure didn't know myself. She'd been generous to me, but maybe she was that way with everyone in need. Dana had been kind and friendly toward me too, but probably forgot about me as soon as I left the hospital.

At least Sarah hadn't forgotten me, and I felt a rush thinking about calling her back. Anxiety, too. Should I call back right away? If I waited too long she might think I didn't want to talk to her. I didn't want to disrupt her dinner. Also I had no plan for what to say. It was frustrating. As a kid, I'd hated talking on the phone, unless it was with guys to arrange the next basketball game. At thirteen, talking to girls was agony.

"You're not thirteen," I hissed, but decided to wait another hour before calling her back.

At seven p.m. exactly, I dialed her number. I'd made a list of things to say, but got immediately flustered when she answered with, "Matthew! Hello!"

"How did you know it was me?"

A chuckle. "I have caller ID. I put your number in my phone so your name shows up when you call."

"I'm doing okay," I said, glancing at my notes.

"That's good to hear."

"I went to the university."

"That's impressive." She said it like she meant it, and my chest puffed up.

"I took the bus. Two busses, actually."

"You were able to figure out the schedule?" She laughed. "They always baffle me."

I didn't tell her the librarian helped.

After a pause, she said, "Listen. I have to do some shopping on Saturday, and I wondered if you might want to come along. There's a big mall on the other side of Fairfax. They have just about everything you could want. If you're looking to pick up some things–"

"Yes!" Almost shouted.

"Great. I'll swing by on Saturday morning and pick you up."

"I could meet you there. There must be a bus."

She said it would easier to pick me up. "I like being out there. It's peaceful."

I wasn't about to argue. Saturday now seemed like Christmas to me.

When we finally hung up, I replayed the conversation in my head. I could remember liking one girl in sixth grade. Her name was Suzanne Martin, and I sometimes followed her home from school – at a distance, of course, which was apparently the way boys at that age showed girls they liked them. We gave each other secret valentines, and at the sixth grade dance, where I spent most of the time on the boys' side, gazing across the gym at the few bold or bored girls dancing with each other, we ended up together for the last dance, a waltz, where I got to try out the steps my mother had taught me that afternoon. Suzanne was a better dancer than me, and I recalled my hand holding hers grew clammy, and once my other hand slipped too low on her back and she whispered, "Don't." But I couldn't remember what happened to Suzanne after that. Perhaps her family moved to a different town.

While pacing around my waiting room, wondering how I would be able to make it until Saturday, I remembered the books I'd brought back from the college. The premise of *Blurred Boundaries* was that because some fiction was borrowed from real life, and some nonfiction read like fiction, it was often hard to tell one from the other. The book presented stories without identifying them as fiction or nonfiction and asked the reader to guess. Hence the subtitle, "Fiction or Fact?"

I settled in the chair I'd found Sarah reading in the other night, opened to my story, and began to read.

MY FATHER'S COURT

There was a time the boy stood beside his father. Eight years old, ankle-deep in fresh-fallen snow, on the wide concrete step outside the back door of the high school gymnasium. A few straggling snowflakes flitter from an oatmeal sky. The boy's father takes off one glove, pins it in his armpit, and searches the brass key ring attached to his belt, isolating each key and holding it up to the diffused light of the street lamp behind them, because the light above the back door isn't working. "Have to fix that, too," the boy's father says about the bulb. "I'll catch hell from the coach if they have to tromp through here in the dark."

A laugh pops out of him in a cloud of cold air. The same laugh, nervous and childlike, that irritates the boy's mother so. *You won't think it's so funny,* he hears her say, *when you wake up some morning and find me gone.*

Recently, the boy has realized he and his father share the same curly dark hair and green eyes. They both like Abbott and Costello, who the boy's mother calls, *Idiots. A pair of clowns.*

"I don't think this is it," the boy's father says about one key, then forces it anyway. "I already tried this one, I think," he says about another. But this one turns, making the lock click free. "Eureka, Watson!" he cries. When he jerks open the door, the warm air pouring out stings the boy's tight cold cheeks. Even his eyebrows feel stiff.

"At least the furnace is working tonight," his father says. The boy follows him upstairs, imagining the horror of an ice-cold gym. "Here we are." The door closes, trapping them in the immense dark.

Lights pop on, a row of them, then another, and the formless dark gives way to a high ceiling and walls, and a floor of pure magic. To the boy it's as gloriously breathtaking as a baseball diamond; more so, because it is a floor and it's been painted – black lines around the edge and more in front of each basket, and in the center a big blue circle with a white "S" in the middle. Superman, the boy thinks, although he knows it stands for Stanton, the high school's name.

"We don't want to cross that line." His father points to the black border, and the boy steps back as if at the edge of a lake during spring thaw. "Not with our boots on, we don't." He laughs. "It's the law."

He unlocks a door in the corner that opens to a closet large as a garage. Inside are rolled-up mats, a folded trampoline. He drops the paper bag he's been carrying onto a card table in front, next to a rack of basketballs, and sits on a folding chair to yank off his boots. The boy tugs his off, too, and when his father picks them up they leave a little puddle of melted snow on the concrete floor.

"You have to wear sneakers to be allowed on the court," his father explains as they put theirs on. Their boots are lined up on top of the newspaper, the large boots and the small boots matching the way the boy and his father would look if they, too, stood side by side.

"Socks would be okay. They used to have sock hops. That's a dance. The kids took off their shoes and danced around the floor in their socks."

He grabs a long-handled dust mop. "You want to shoot baskets?" The boy shakes his head. His father removes his shirt, leaving him in a white tee bunched up in back, where the blue band of his boxer shorts sticks out above the waist of his pants.

As he pushes the dust mop, the floor that already shines, glows even brighter in his wake. There are wide empty lanes on either side of the court, then a single row of bleachers, eight feet high, against each wall. The boy is wondering how people will climb up there when his father puts a key into a hole in the cement-block wall, then grabs the bottom slat and begins to walk backwards, toward the court. The bleachers follow, opening like an accordion, one row and then another, and another above that.

When people start arriving, the boy finds a place on the stage behind one basket, where his father has lined up two rows of chairs. He sits on the end, next to the big red curtain that smells of mildew and dust. His father calls him over to meet the coach. "This is my son, Jay," his father says. "Jay, this is Coach Morelli."

The coach is taller than the boy's father, and muscular, with a weathered face beneath crewcut white hair. His huge, calloused hand swallows the boy's.

"Pleased to meet you, Jay." He has a deep voice and a face that seems unable to smile even when he wants to. The boy cannot bring himself to speak.

"I guess we've had enough snow to carry us through the whole winter," the boy's father says.

Suddenly the floor begins to tremble. There's a sound like stampeding horses, and the doors to the locker room burst open and a dozen enormous bodies pour forth, all dressed in blue and white.

All the players seem like giants. The boy has heard of professional players standing seven feet tall, but on television they all look small.

During warm-ups the boy moves to the balcony above the far basket. He likes the perspective of looking down over everything. Beyond where the players shoot lay-ups stands his father, arms folded, chatting to anyone who passes by.

The buzzer sounds in the gym, now bloated with heat and noise, and the boy races downstairs, hoping to make it back to the stage before the game begins. Halfway there, he hears the announcer say, "Will everyone please rise for our national anthem." The crowd rises in a single whoosh, and the boy freezes, backing into the people crowding around him, and placing his hand over his heart as a scratching sound fills the air, then the anthem explodes from the loudspeakers.

The moment it ends the boy races for the stage. People clap and stamp their feet. Passing the corner where his father has been standing, the boy spots him in the storage closet, bending over an old record player. He looks up and laughs. "Just call me Harry Phillip Sousa."

The game is close throughout the first half. Stanton's best player is Nate Williamson, the only black player on either team, a guard who darts around swiping the ball and racing away like a speedy little kid taunting bullies. The boy favors Tommy Bishop, a muscular forward who always seems to get the rebound. Big for his age and chubby, the boy can easily pretend to be Tommy, who has short dark hair neatly trimmed and a stoic expression whether he's just scored a basket or been called for a foul he didn't commit.

At halftime, his father buys the boy an ice cream sandwich that melts fast in the heat, coating his hands with chocolate and sticky cream. "You'd better go to the men's room and wash up," his father advises, leading him along the narrow trail between the court's black line and the first row of bleachers, saying hello to a half-dozen people along the way. A line stretches out through the propped-open bathroom door. Although relieved when his father leaves him, the boy feels lost in the forest of men.

When he comes out his father is pushing the big dust mop up and down the floor again. He decides to watch the second half from the balcony. Above and behind the basket, he has a clear view of Tommy Bishop muscling rebounds. The game is tense, the other team leading by three points as the fourth quarter begins. The movement and colors and noise and heat all merge together, and leaning over the balcony rail, the boy becomes Tommy Bishop grabbing a rebound, tapping it against the backboard so softly it drops through the hoop, bringing his team within one point with thirty seconds to play. The crowd leaps to its feet, then settles into rhythmic clapping as the other team calls time out.

When play resumes the other team plays keep-away to run out the clock, forcing Nate Williamson to foul their best shooter, a guard.

The lights on the scoreboard above where the boy's father stands read :09. The score is 54-53. The guard has one-and-one, getting the second shot only if he makes the first. Making both will put his team up by three, and there is no three-point shot.

A rumbling rises from every corner of the gym, crescendoing as the guard walks to the free throw line. "Miss it!" the boy screams.

The ball hits the rim, bounces once, and falls off into the sure hands of Tommy Bishop. He whips a pass to Nate Williamson, who slices between two opposing players racing down the court, stops at his favorite spot at the top of the key and goes straight into the air. The boy is perfectly positioned to watch the orange ball rise out of those two black hands, pause at its highest point as if it is a balloon about to float away, then drop through the hoop as the buzzer sounds and the crowd erupts.

The boy jumps up and down. On the court, players and fans mob Nate Williamson.

Later, after the gym has emptied, the boy's father removes his shirt again, lifts the bottom of the lowest bleacher and pushes until that row folds into the one above it, then both into the one above that, until all the bleachers again look like a single bench against the wall, eight feet high. Dust and trash coat the floor the bleachers covered.

Exhausted, the boy sits on the floor by the stage, wishing the players downstairs would finish dressing and leave so his father could take him home.

His father picks up something off the floor. "What do you know?" he says. "A quarter." He holds out his hand. "Here, you have it."

The quarter seems large compared to the nickels and dimes the boy is used to. "Sometimes I make out pretty good going through here," his father says, gesturing toward the trash. "The change falls out of people's pockets. One time I found a five-dollar bill."

This wakes the boy up. "I have to put the bleachers up on the other side," his father says. "If you want to look around here while I'm doing that, you can keep whatever you find." His words transform the trash heap into a treasure trove the boy searches methodically, unearthing another quarter, two dimes, and seven pennies.

"Now try the other side," his father instructs. "That side's where the visiting team's fans sit, so usually there are more adults." He laughs. "Adults have more money to lose than kids."

The dollar bill the boy finds folded up beneath a cup proves his father's words true. The boy will be a father himself, his own father gone, before he considers that his father might have planted it.

That night, he clutches the money in his sweaty palm, dreaming of baseball cards, midget race cars, Pez. Overcome by fatigue once again, he pushes the money carefully into his pants pocket and sits in the chair his father has taken down off the stage. "It won't be long now," his father says.

When the door opens, the boy jerks out of the sleep he's been tumbling into. Not five feet away, his shiny dark hair slicked back, a gym bag slung over one shoulder, stands Tommy Bishop. He wears a blue and white letterman's jacket with a football on the front, and snow boots nearly to his knees.

Nate Williamson follows him, wearing a gray rain coat that doesn't look warm enough for the winter, gray dress pants, and shiny black shoes.

"Drained that sucker, stopped on a dime." Nate's voice has a lilt like poetry.

The boy's father, scraping some gum stuck to the floor beneath the bleachers, calls, "Hey, boys."

"Hey, Skinner," Nate replies. The boy does not know what the nickname means, but it does not sound complimentary.

"Good game tonight, boys."

Tommy Bishop grabs a ball off the rack and flips it to Nate. "Show us the touch."

As Nate drops his bag and bounces the ball, the boy's father calls good-naturedly, "No shoes on the court, boys."

Nate ignores him. "You get under the basket," he tells Tommy. "Snatch that rebound and feed me the out-let pass."

"Come on, boys." His father has risen to his feet. "We don't want to damage the floor."

When Tommy tries to flip the ball off the rim, it goes through the hoop instead. "You got to miss, man. You got to miss so I can make my shot."

"Come on, boys," the boy's father says again

Tommy shoots and misses, but the ball skirts from his grasp and dribbles toward the boy's feet. He bends down and picks it up.

This next the boy will remember all his life. Tommy has taken several steps in his direction. Hands extended, he nods for the ball. Beneath his still-damp hair, there's a squareness to his jaw and the promise of something sim-ple and honest in his brown eyes. In the distance beyond Tommy's shoulder stands the boy's father. His baggy pants sag beneath the bulge of his belly. Pale bony shoulders, weak red face. The stick of the mop he holds rises taller than he is.

The boy will be unable to recall the emotion in his fa-ther's face. Understanding? Gentle forgiveness? His father was that kind of man. Or did he feel it like a knife the boy's hands pushed forward, instead of the ball that curled into the air, pausing at its highest point as if it were a bal-loon about to float away, before settling into the hands of Tommy Bishop, who spins and whips a pass to the already running Nate Williamson?

Nate catches the ball like a wide receiver, dribbles once to gain his balance, and rises into the air. The ball soars from his hand, clanks the rim, and drops harmlessly to one side.

"Shit," Nate hisses. Landing, his heel gashes a long black streak in the floor.

"That's all right," Tommy consoles. "You hit that shot when it counted."

"You got that right."

Nate grabs his bag. They button up their coats in preparation for the cold. "Take it easy, Skinner," Nate calls. "Little Skinner, too."

Cold air rushes in when they open the door. The boy's father laughs. "They're pretty excited about the game." He walks to the top of the key to inspect the damage done by Nate's shoes.

The boy waits in silence, thoughts turned to his mother sitting glumly in front of the television at home, while his father on hands and knees scrubs those marks with steel wool.

· · ·

This was more like it. My father used to be a janitor at Mansfield High School, and sometimes he'd come home after dinner and bring me back to play basketball in the gym while he cleaned the empty school. At least once, he took me to a game. I could picture the bright colors, the big white "M" in the middle of the deep blue circle at midcourt, the blue numbers on white jerseys. Feel the stickiness of the ice cream sandwich I ate while waiting in the line of men outside the bathroom at halftime. After the gym emptied, tee-shirt half untucked, my father pushed the wide broom up and down the floor.

The story was fact. A slice of my past.

Nor did my confidence waiver when I turned to the "Contributor's Notes" and read where the author said, "My story is fiction. When I was a child, my father worked as janitor at the local high school. He sometimes took me to basketball games like the one depicted in this story. But the events of the story are fictional."

No Nate Williamson, no Tommy Bishop. No last second, game-winning shot. And, probably, no moment where the boy had to choose between those two heroes and his father.

But the details were true. And the important characters. The father in the story was exactly as I remembered my real father. The mother was my mother.

More of the "emotional truth" Jessie had spoken of? To me, the mother seemed the most important person in the story, even though she never appeared. Throughout, the boy worried that his father wouldn't be up to the job he was tasked with. I felt that about my real father all throughout my childhood.

The story, I concluded, was mostly factual. And while it didn't fill a blank spot in my past, it showed me I could trust what I did remember, and encouraged me to keep looking for more.

Not only that, but reading it got me one hour closer to Saturday.

Chapter Seven

I had Sarah to thank for introducing me to the monstrosity known as the shopping mall. It was a hideous place, cold and noisy, a gigantic fish bowl without the water. All the noise swarmed around three open stories.

Since we got off to a late start, she led me to the food court first. Here a variety of noises and smells blended into something indeterminate but constant. People leaned over the rails on the floors above, peering down as if at the zoo. A dull light dropped through the milky panels of the roof.

Spotting a Chinese place, I ordered Kung Pao chicken. At least I wouldn't be risking something unknown. Sarah got Mexican and we sat at a table we had to wipe clean before setting down our trays. The Kung Pao chicken tasted like the cook had bleached out the flavor before serving, and Sarah wasn't thrilled with her choice, either.

"Sometimes you eat just to eat," she said. "To put something in your stomach."

I did feel better after eating.

So far, I hadn't felt anxious in her presence. It wasn't like a date, I told myself, just two friends going shopping.

While we ate, I told her about my trip to the college. My stories about Irma made her laugh. I didn't mention Jessie, or the student who cornered me as I was leaving.

"Nothing seemed familiar?" Sarah asked.

"Not really. Although my office was pretty much like I expected."

"Which was?"

"Drab. Barren. Like somebody just moved in and hadn't had a chance to decorate."

She grinned. "And how long have you been in that office?"

"Nine years."

As we were cleaning up, she asked if I needed clothes.

"I don't know. How much clothes do people normally have?"

"A lot more than you do."

That's right, she'd seen my wardrobe. If it could even be called that.

"Maybe I should take a look."

The problem wasn't finding clothes, but clothes I was willing to wear. I didn't like bright colors or crazy designs, I didn't like plaid or checks. "Maybe I'm okay on the clothes front," I said at last.

Sarah refused to give up. Getting me dressed better seemed one of her goals for the day. "Let's try one more place," she said, and took me to a store called "Midwestern Outfitters." I noticed the difference right away: these were clothes like the clothes I already owned. Sturdy material, plain solid colors, a basic design. When I slid a shirt off the rack and held it in front of me, Sarah, showing an amused grimace, pointed to a mirror, where I discovered the shirt I held was a twin to the one I was wearing.

"I knew I liked it for a reason," I said.

She gave me a look that said, "You're hopeless," but she didn't protest when I bought two shirts similar to ones I already owned, along with another pair of jeans, some socks and underwear.

"Sorry my clothes aren't flashier," I said as we walked back through the noisy hallway.

"That's okay. You dress like a Midwesterner."

Her tone didn't make it sound like a compliment. "What does that mean?"

"Your clothes are functional. Comfortable. You wear them to cover yourself."

What else are clothes for, I was about to ask, but I knew the answer: to make others see you a certain way. I could have accused Sarah of the same thing; out of uniform, she dressed comfortably. She didn't even wear makeup, which I liked, considering how many of the women I'd seen at college looked like they were headed to the prom. But I kept that to myself.

· · ·

Sarah informed me I had good manners. I opened doors for her without making a show of it, I walked beside her, not ahead or behind, and I listened when she spoke. "Some guys don't do that," she said, then corrected herself. "No need to be sexist. Some *people* don't do that, male or female. They're talking but not listening. They're too busy planning out their next amusing comment."

After she described those things, I tried to notice them in my behavior. But it was hard being natural and self-conscious, too.

· · ·

"Did you want to look at computers?" she asked. "You can probably get a laptop for a decent price."

I hadn't been thinking I needed one, having one at school. But my fingers had struggled to press down hard enough on the old manual typewriter at home, and I didn't want to go to campus every time I needed a computer. I wasn't sure what a "decent price" might be, but I remained astounded at how much money my bank account held. My only question (kept to myself) was, *What's a laptop?*

"It might be worth a look," I said.

To find computers, we had to go to a computer store. Of course, I thought, every store seems to sell only one thing these days.

When I was a kid, we did most of our shopping at Adams and Zayres, Adams being a grocery and Zayres selling everything else.

In the computer store, Sarah took the lead, and I was glad to follow. I couldn't believe all the huge colorful screens that looked more like televisions. "I really do feel like that Rip Van Winkle guy," I whispered to Sarah.

"I don't think he was real," she replied.

I had to be careful not to knock into anything with my big bag of clothes. "You're interested in laptops, right?" Sarah asked, pointing to a long table with rows of smaller machines that opened like clam shells. It dawned on me that they were called laptops because you could hold them in your lap. Ah, well. At least I hadn't shown Sarah my ignorance.

"Try one. See how it feels."

I wasn't sure what she meant. Each machine was chained to the table, so I couldn't pick it up. When she gestured toward the keyboard, I touched a few keys, and laughed at how the keys responded to even the lightest touch. "I like it," I said.

"Is there one you like better than the others?"

She stepped back to let me work my way down the row. Each computer had its own price, and I was a little shocked at how much these little things cost. A salesman appeared by my side and I tensed, but Sarah stepped in, saying, "We're only looking right now. We'll let you know if we need help," and the salesman wandered away.

Sarah ran through all the features I might or might not want: creating fancy designs (no), charts and graphs (no). "Watching movies?"

"Watching movies? Where?"

"On your computer."

"You mean like on TV?"

"Pretty much," she said.

I ended up picking out one in the middle: middle-sized, middle-priced. "You're doing all right for yourself today," Sarah said as we left the computer store.

"I want a phone like yours."

She nodded, grinning in approval. "You know where we have to go for that, don't you?"

"To the phone store?"

"To the phone store."

"There were no malls where I grew up," I told Sarah as we walked. I told her about Adams and Zayres. "On special occasions, before Christmas, or to get school clothes, we'd go to Pittsfield. That was a big city, we thought, and they had a department store that seemed huge, although it probably had only three or four floors. I remember there was an elevator. And they had one of those hot air blowers in the bathroom. I loved those things."

In the phone store I discovered that before I could buy a phone, I had to purchase a phone plan. Once again, I let Sarah do the negotiating.

"Leaping into the twentieth century," she said as we left the phone store. She seemed to find that amusing, though I didn't know why.

• • •

Leaving the mall loaded down with packages, I realized Sarah hadn't bought anything for herself. "Didn't you need some things too?" I asked, and she shrugged.

"Nothing essential. I can come back here any time."

I wasn't sure what to make of that. Instead of two friends going shopping, this felt more like charity. Not that I had a right to complain; Sarah's backseat was filled with things I'd have never bought on my own, or been able to carry home on a bus.

• • •

"Can I ask you about the accident?"

"Sure," she said, although I noticed her jaw tighten.

I'd been thinking about it a lot since I'd been home. It was just as big a blank as everything else since my early teens, but it was something I'd done recently, and I thought there might be clues. Why was I on that road so late on a Sunday night? With nothing in my car to suggest I was taking a trip. It made no sense.

We'd just passed through Centreville. "I don't think it's far from here, right?"

"It's a little north, but yeah, not too far."

I took a breath. "Could we ride over there? Seeing it might trigger something."

"There's not much to see."

"We don't have to, then," I said, but she turned at the next light and headed north.

Quickly, we left the suburbs behind. Sarah had once told me there were no woods in Fairfax, only the illusion of woods, but we were in dense woods now, treetops overhead almost touching, creating a strip of sky to mirror the strip of narrow road we drove on.

We didn't speak. Sarah had an advantage, she could keep her eyes on the road. She clearly thought this was a bad idea, and I was probably taking advantage of her good nature. But didn't she want me to remember?

I stiffened when the car slowed. Ahead the road veered to the left, a dirt road slicing off to the right. A chunk of land like a spear point in between, a giant oak tree at its center.

Sarah put on her turn signal, though there were no other cars in sight. She pulled onto the dirt road, pebbles pinging against the underside as the car came to a stop. When I got out, she stayed behind the wheel.

Most of the brush that must have been crushed had grown back, although I could make out some deep cuts in the rich black earth. The sun had sunk behind the trees, coating everything in shadow. Up and down the road, nothing looked familiar. The tree was a real giant, fat and healthy looking, except for the gash in the bark, about waist high. I reached out but couldn't bring myself to touch it. I'd been thinking of this tree as if it were lifeless as a rock, but it was a living thing I'd wounded with my car.

From a distance I studied the tree and the road. I stared until I could close my eyes and see the scene in the darkness behind my eyelids. No matter how hard I tried, I could not insert a moving car into the picture. I could not look out from the inside of that car.

There were no skid marks in the road. Sarah had mentioned this when she visited the hospital. What did that mean? I coached myself: reason it out. I could have fallen asleep. The way the road veered, the path I'd been on would have taken me into the tree. I must have hit it with great impact; perhaps I'd awoken at the last moment and stepped on the gas thinking it was the brake?

Perhaps a deer leapt out of the woods at the last moment and I swerved to avoid it? Sarah hadn't thought I was going at excessive speeds, but on a road like this, fifty or sixty would be dangerous.

Or maybe something went wrong with the car, jamming the steering or the wheels.

There was one other logical choice that I pushed away.

"Anything?" Sarah asked when I returned to the car. I shook my head, and she swung the car around and headed back.

We rode a while in silence. A voice in my head kept saying I should let it go, but I couldn't. "You and your partner," I began, "you're sure it was an accident."

"That's what we concluded, yes."

Maybe that should have satisfied me, but she added, "We didn't have enough evidence to conclude anything else."

"You thought about other possibilities?"

"We tried to work out how it might have happened."

I told her about my ideas, falling asleep or a springing deer, and she said either was possible. They hadn't found any malfunction in the car, "but it was wrecked pretty bad."

"There weren't any skid marks."

"No," she said.

"Did you wonder," I began, "if maybe it wasn't an accident?"

"My partner did."

That made me pause. I guess some part of me had been expecting, or hoping, she'd say, "No, we were pretty certain it didn't happen that way."

I wished I could erase this conversation, rewind everything back to when we left the mall. But I'd gone too far to stop now.

"He thought I'd hit the tree on purpose."

She kept her gaze on the road, her voice a monotone. "He thought it was possible."

Possible. That was better than "likely."

"You didn't agree?" I asked.

"We talked it over. There wasn't enough evidence. And you couldn't remember."

"No," I said, and we settled back into silence.

. . .

When we got home, Sarah showed me how to charge my phone. "It'll take a while," she said. I asked if she was hungry, showing her the brochure I'd got for the pizza place she'd said was so good, but she was in business mode. "First, let's set up your computer."

"Set up?" I'd assumed I could just plug it in and turn it on. Or call the tech guy at the university.

She gave me a look designed for a cute kid who'd just said something adorable.

After she finished with my computer, she went back to my phone. "What do you want for a password?" she asked.

"I need a password to use a phone?"

"To keep people from breaking into your phone," she explained, ignoring my irritation. "Something that's easy to remember."

She frowned, but didn't argue, when I offered "1, 2, 3, 4." I couldn't imagine anyone wanting to break into my phone. Not to mention that if they did break in, there'd be nothing to find.

She handed me the phone. It opened kind of like a clam shell. Inside, on a white screen under the heading "Contacts," was the name, "Sarah."

"Touch my name," she said.

I did, and magically, her phone rang.

"Now your phone has my number and I have yours in mine." She giggled. "If we were thirteen, that might mean we're going steady."

My expression must have betrayed something, because her face turned pink. "Sorry," she said. "Bad joke."

"What can I do to thank you?"

She looked hungrily toward the pizza shop brochure. "Feed me."

. . .

While we waited for the pizza, Sarah asked if she could read the story I'd told her I'd found, about the boy and his father and the basketball game. I told her, "Sure," in a casual way, but after she sat down to read it, I wandered to the back door and stared out into the darkness, feeling my stomach churn. My anxiety wasn't rational; she wasn't going to say, "You're a horrible writer and I've been wasting my time hanging around with you." It was more like that time in the hospital when I nearly fell on my face trying to get out of bed, and she was there to watch it all.

When she approached me, I was surprised to see that her eyes were red. Had she been crying?

"It's beautiful."

"I'm sorry," I said.

"No." She held up the book. "This is nothing to be sorry for."

Outside, a car door slammed.

"Pizza!" we both shouted at the same time.

. . .

"I never questioned if my parents loved each other," Sarah told me as we ate. "They were always pretty amorous around each other. It was embarrassing sometimes. One time I came home from college a day early and caught them going at it on the kitchen table. They were nearly sixty, for God's sake."

We were sitting across from each other at the kitchen table, stuffed from eating too much of the delicious pizza. I was still basking in the glow of Sarah liking my story. "I have trouble imagining my parents having sex even the one time that produced me," I told her.

"I feel sad for that boy." She gestured toward the book with my story. "He's been put in the middle between his mother and father, forced to choose. I feel sad for the father, too. He's trying so hard, he wants so badly to be loved. And the mother, why is she so unhappy?"

How could I answer that? I just shrugged.

"So this is fiction? I read the note in the back."

"I'm pretty sure most of it's true. I remember the gym, going to basketball games. My father sweeping the floor. I remember how he'd take off his shirt, he'd have this white undershirt on, and his underwear would be bunched up in back. It was embarrassing. I didn't want him to look that way. My heroes were Superman, Clutch Cargo."

"Clutch Cargo?"

I laughed. "He was a cartoon character. I don't remember much about him. But I'm sure he was really good at his job."

. . .

"I should be getting back," Sarah said, and rose. "Like Yogi said, it gets late early these days."

"Yogi Bear?"

"Yogi Berra," she corrected. "He was the real one."

I gave her *Alice in Wonderland,* along with the money she'd spent on groceries the other night, and walked her to her car. We ended up with her leaning back against it, me facing her, fists dug into my pants pockets.

"Thank you for today," I said.

"It takes two to party."

"With all the stuff I got, I shouldn't have to go shopping again for two or three years."

She laughed, while I stood there like a fool. I was thirteen again, with no clue how to say goodnight to a girl I liked.

She seemed to understand. "Let's try this." She reached out, took my hand in both of hers. "I really enjoyed spending the day with you. I hope we can see each other again. Would you like that?"

The playfulness in her eyes showed she was teasing. Even so, my face grew hot. I nodded.

"Good. Then I'll give you a call. Or you can call me. You've got my number."

"Yes," I croaked.

"But don't forget, I go to bed early."

"Yes."

"Good." I thought she was going to let my hand go and turn away, but instead she gripped me tighter and tugged me forward. With a giggle, she planted a quick kiss on my tight, closed lips, then spun around and opened her door. "Have a good night," she called in an amused and alluring way before she disappeared inside the car.

She might have glanced at me once or twice before she left, but in the darkness, I couldn't tell.

Chapter Eight

I needed a car. The bus system was cumbersome, and I refused to impose on Sarah. I had two appointments coming up, a follow-up with Dr. Shinomoto, and one with Dr. Bernard, the therapist Dr. Clark recommended. Both were in offices near the hospital.

The insurance company would be sending me a check for the value of my old car. But I didn't want to buy a car right away. Instead, as I searched for rental cars, a company called Wrecked Rentals caught my eye: "Good used cars, cheap. Rent by the day, week, or month." All I needed was a driver's license, proof of insurance, and a valid credit card. They'd even deliver the car to my door. I liked the irony of me driving a car from "Wrecked Rentals," even though it could end up being a car held together by duct tape.

I spent the morning cleaning. When the phone rang I got excited, thinking of Sarah, but it was a Home Health Care service asking if I wanted to arrange for a nurse to visit. I declined, and surprisingly, they didn't argue. I felt buoyed; I was taking back control of my life.

My wrecked rental turned out to be a 1991 Chevy Nova, no duct tape in sight. As I'd hoped, the same muscle memory that allowed me to remember the keys on a typewriter kicked in when I climbed behind the wheel. My hands settled natural-ly at two and ten o'clock, my foot moved smoothly between brake and gas. But driving proved more complicated than typ-ing. Backing up, I barely avoided scraping a post, and once, I came to a stop but forgot to put the car in park. Fortunately, I had my giant empty parking lot to practice in, and nobody to criticize me.

Eventually I felt ready to tackle the road. I headed west, where the traffic was lighter, and kept well under the speed limit, pulling to the side whenever a car came up behind me so it could pass. My body was tense, my hands gripping tight. Fortunately, traffic was light. The road curled between the mountains, water drip-ping down the rock walls rising up on either side. It was cool in the rocks' shadows, but beads of sweat pooled across my hairline. I had to consciously tell myself to breathe.

Then the land around me opened up, fields of tall grass seem-ing to stretch all the way to the distant mountains. The blue sky seemed enormous, the road ahead flat, straight, and empty. I felt tension in my leg, realized I was pressing hard on the gas. The car was going 60. It bucked, then took off like a wild horse set loose. I rolled down my window and laughed at the breeze smacking the side of my face. The needle on the dashboard now near 70. It was almost like flying.

At seventy-five, the car protested. I held on tight and leaned forward to put more weight on the gas. I felt powerful and free. I was vaguely aware of the great force I had to exert to maintain control of the shaking steering wheel, but mostly I leaned into the surprise and delight of giving myself up to speed. It was like being carried on an ocean wave, or in the midst of a tornado. As a kid, I'd always loved wind.

Then I saw the tree. A lone oak tree far ahead, reaching into the sky at the side of the road. My eyes struggled to hold their focus on the road. The tree seemed to have some kind of power, drawing me toward it.

There were no thoughts in my head. It was as if my conscious self had checked out, turned off, flown away. My body reacted on its own, independent of my will. It began calculating the angle I would have to take to head straight for that tree.

Ahead, a streak like lightening: the sun sparking off an approaching car. I jerked my foot off the gas. The car trembled even more slowing down than it had speeding up. Holding tight, I fixed my eyes on the lane in front of me as the car whizzed past in a blur.

Spotting a dirt drive, I pulled in, the tires kicking up pebbles. The car finally stilled, although it felt rather as if the car was still moving and it was the world itself that stopped. I rubbed the sweat from my eyes with the back of my hand. I was sitting in a small, empty, unpaved parking lot, in front of what looked like a one-room schoolhouse but was, the sign read, the Agape Church of God in Christ.

What had just happened? The allure of speed, yes, but something more. I hadn't made a decision, hadn't clutched to a plan, determined to see it through. Instead, I'd checked out. As if I'd given up my body to some force outside of me, allowing it to do with me as it wished.

Was this what had happened that Sunday night? There must have been some conscious thought involved; at some point, I must have decided I might do this. As much as I'd wondered why, I'd also been unable to understand how: how could I purposefully drive straight at a tree? Now I knew that answer. I just had to exile the part of me that thinks and feels, that tries to do what's right.

. . .

Dr. Shinomoto was pleased with my progress. He focused on the injuries to my body, and said I continued to "heal acceptably." When he asked about my memory, I mentioned typing and driving as, "Some kind of muscle memory," and he nodded but didn't comment. He was pleased I had an appointment with Dr. Bernard.

I drove there and back without incident, and stopped at a large supermarket in Manassas. Back at home, the local cable company came to set up my Internet. I was beginning to feel more comfortable at home, although it still felt as if I were squatting in another person's house. I told myself I should look through some of the books on my shelves, or read some papers from the courses I'd taught, but I couldn't work up the energy.

I took a long walk up the hill behind the train station, into the woods. At one point I got lost, but eventually I found my way home. I was used to getting lost in woods; when I was a kid, I got it in my head that North was always the direction I was facing, East always to my right, West to my left, South behind. I don't know where that idea came from; I'd hardly considered myself the center of the universe. But it often led to me returning home – to a silent angry mother and a dinner table stripped of everything except my empty plate – hours late.

At least now no one waited and wondered if something had happened to me. The more I recalled from my childhood, the more it seemed I must have been a terror to my mother. I remembered once when a friend named Arthur came to play at my house. We must have been six or seven. We were outside and got into a fight over something I'm sure was trivial, and Arthur announced he was going home. "Okay," I said, and as he trudged off, I went back to my game. I don't know whether ten minutes or an hour passed before my mother stuck her head out the door and asked, "Where's Arthur?"

"He went home," I casually replied. He lived ten miles away.

There was the time my mother discovered a nest of snakes beneath the front steps of our house. My father and grandfather tore apart the steps and killed all the snakes, while my mother remained locked in her bedroom, trembling. I got out my kid's plastic shovel to help my father and grandfather, and although they mainly just let me watch, as they were cleaning up I scooped a severed snake head onto my shovel and ran inside to give my mother indisputable proof that all the snakes were dead. I don't remember her reaction, but as I was told after my accident, it's common not to remember traumatic moments.

The morning of my appointment with Dr. Bernard, I woke up with anxiety bubbling inside. I almost called to cancel. It wasn't just that Dr. Bernard wasn't Dr. Clark. There were things I didn't want to talk about, my experience in the car chief among them.

On the way, I developed a game plan. If I had to mention Sarah, I'd refer to her as "one of the police officers who helped me." Jessie was simply "a colleague at work." I'd somehow remembered how to drive and did so without incident. Nothing else had come back to me.

On the other hand, if Dr. Bernard suggested something like hypnosis as a way to recapture my memories, I'd probably jump at the chance.

The waiting room was small, decorated in shades of blue to instill a sense of calm, with paintings depicting pastoral scenes. The receptionist gave me a clipboard full of mostly basic questions, and the more complicated ones I simply answered with, "I had an accident and lost my memory." That was really all the doctor needed to know. No need to write a book about it.

After returning the clipboard, I closed my eyes, expecting a long wait. But a moment later a door opened and a man who had to be Dr. Bernard emerged. He was tall and very thin, with thick gray hair and a neatly trimmed gray beard. He wore a three-piece suit and a handkerchief of the same color as his tie poking out his jacket pocket.

I was disappointed. The thirteen-year-old part of me had been hoping Dr. Bernard would magically transform into Dr. Clark. Or at least her twin brother.

His movements were exact and refined as he shook my hand and led me into an office full of deep reds and browns, and dark, heavy furniture: a large, probably antique desk, a leather couch and chair, a bookcase crammed with old, fat books. It wasn't cluttered but there was very little space to move around. It smelled different, too, after the artificial freshness of the waiting room, and for a moment I was transported back to the old library in Mansfield where I sometimes spent Saturday afternoons wandering the stacks. The image vanished as Dr. Bernard told me to take a seat. Offered the couch or a chair, I took the chair.

The room was full of shadows, with a muted light coming from two lamps in the corners, and one bright curved lamp aimed directly at the papers scattered across Dr. Bernard's desk. Multiple diplomas filled one wall, along with a framed photograph of a green doorway on the second floor of a gray building, with no stairway to get to it.

Eventually, Dr. Bernard swiveled his desk chair to face me and rolled closer. He looked up from the white pad in his lap. "So, Mr. Winton, what brings you here today?"

"Dr. Clark suggested it might be helpful for me to talk with you."

I thought that would give me an advantage, but he didn't seem to know who Dr. Clark was. "And why did Dr. Clark suggest that?"

"I was in an accident." I forced myself to meet his gaze. His eyes were the color of dishwater, but sharp. He studied me the way a zookeeper might a new exhibit. I wondered if he'd read what I wrote on the form.

"A car accident," I explained. "I'm better now, physically, but I seem to have lost my memory." An embarrassed laugh popped out.

Dr. Bernard jotted something on his pad, using what looked like an expensive pen. His hands were large, the fingers very long and delicate, tufts of dark hair above the knuckles. "When did this accident occur?"

"The end of August."

"And did you suffer a blow to the head in this accident?"

"I suffered blows all over," I said, then laughed to cover what seemed to me a surly tone. A deep breath helped calm me, as I explained that Dr. Shinomoto's tests had concluded there was no permanent damage to my brain.

"Do you have a family, Mr. Winton?"

The question threw me off track. "What? No."

"Your parents?"

"Both dead."

"Never been married? No children?"

I almost said, *Not that I know of.* Instead, I shook my head.

"What do you do for a living, Mr. Winton?"

"I teach at Northern Virginia University."

That seemed to interest him. "My daughter graduated from there. It's an up-and-coming school."

I nodded. As if I knew.

"What do you teach?"

"Writing."

"Really!" Even more interested now, he uncrossed his legs and sat up, as if having totally revised his view of this patient.

"What do you write? Articles?"

"Fiction, mostly." At least I had evidence of that.

"I've long dreamed of writing a novel. I know the story inside and out. But so far I've confined myself to professional articles. What is it they say? 'Write what you know.'"

I nodded, returning Dr. Bernard's smile.

"Are you teaching now?"

"I'm on medical leave. They expect me back in January."

"And how does that make you feel?"

My hands kneaded each other in my lap. They were hot, damp, and slippery. The words were right there waiting behind the door in my mind; I only had to open it. *I'm scared. I don't know what to do. I don't remember the books I've read, the lessons I've taught. I don't remember how to teach. I don't know anything. And then the other day, while driving...*

"I'm anxious," I said. "As anyone would be."

"Have you had headaches, since you got home from the hospital?"

I shook my head. He was reclining again, one long leg crossed over the other knee. I would have liked to see what he was writing, but he held the pad up so that only the back was visible.

"Are you eating regularly? Getting fresh air, exercise? Going to the bathroom regularly? How are you sleeping?"

"I'm good with all those things."

"Mood swings?"

"I'm pretty calm most of the time. I get frustrated now and then, but even when I'm anxious, I tend to keep it inside."

"Yes," he said, as if this were a test and I'd answered correctly. "Do you dream?"

"I'm sorry?"

"Do you have many dreams, when you sleep?"

"A few, I guess."

"How about the people in your dreams. Do you recognize them?"

I sat up. The question intrigued me. "My parents," I said, trying to recall. "There are other people but I don't think I know who they are. Sometimes one starts out as a stranger but later morphs into my mother."

"Have you done much writing since the accident?"

He seemed to like these sudden shifts in topics. "Not really," I said without thinking, then wondered if that would lower his estimation of me. Is a writer who doesn't write still a writer?

He looked up. "Why haven't you? Been writing."

The answer seemed obvious to me: I didn't know how. "I don't know," I said.

"Why don't you try?"

When the doctor leaned forward, I got a look at his pad: as expected, the writing was illegible. "You said you had memories from your childhood," the doctor continued. "Why not write some of them down? The more open you are to the memories you can access, the more opportunity you give yourself to recall other memories as well."

I wanted to argue, but Dr. Clark had said something similar, too. I felt a flicker of hope. If I really was a writer, could I write my way back into my memory? But I heard myself say, "I was wondering if maybe hypnosis might help."

The doctor shook his head. "I'm afraid that's not in the cards. Hypnosis is dicey, for one thing, and when it does work, it's usually focused on one incident. You've got too many years of incidents you're looking to recover."

"But you think it might work with my writing?"

He grinned. "Write what you know."

· · ·

Back home and exhausted, I was about to take a nap when the phone rang. I hurried into the waiting room and picked up the receiver, but heard only a dial tone. Then it rang again. Not the phone I was holding, but the mobile phone I'd left on the kitchen table.

In the little window when I flipped it open, I saw, "Sarah."

"Sarah," I said, grinning.

"It works! You saw my name?"

"I did."

She laughed. "So how are you?"

"I rented a car."

The silence was so sudden and complete, I'd have sworn there was cold air coming out of the phone.

"Do you have to pick it up?"

"They delivered it the other day. I just drove to Fairfax and back. I had an appointment with my doctor."

"Is everything okay?"

"Everything's fine. It was just a follow-up."

I didn't mention the therapist. Technically, that didn't mean I'd lied.

"I was very careful," I said, meaning with the car. "At first I practiced. It was great having this huge empty parking lot. It all came back. Not that I remembered driving, but I seemed to know what to do. I'm taking it slowly. I'm not ready for – what's that big race?"

"The Indy 500?"

"Yeah. I'll have to work up to that one."

Sarah laughed, but without much enthusiasm. "I'm practicing safe driving," I said, which was something I'd heard on a TV ad recently. No way was I going to tell Sarah about my first driving experience.

"So you got a car," she said. "Any other new developments?"

"I've been practicing my culinary skills."

"Have you now?"

"I have. And I've been thinking, after all you've done for me, I should do something nice for you."

"You don't have to do anything."

"I'd like to. I want to. So I was wondering if maybe this weekend, if you're free, I could cook you a nice dinner. It won't be anything fancy, but I know how to roast a mean chicken."

"Does the chicken have to be mean for you to roast it?"

It was a relief to hear her joking. "Mean or kind, I'll roast them all."

"You make it sound so romantic."

"Does that mean you'll come?"

"I can't do Saturday. But Sunday's good."

"That sounds right. A Sunday chicken dinner."

"It'll be good to see you," she said, and sounded like she meant it. "But you don't have to do anything special for me."

"I want to."

"You don't owe me anything."

We kept at it, until finally she relented. "I'd be nuts to turn down a free meal."

"So you'll come?"

"Of course," she said, as if she'd been planning to accept all along. "I need to take my mother to church in the morning, but I should be able to get there by one."

"Great!"

In the pause that followed, I heard her suppress a yawn. "You're tired," I said.

"Don't take it personally. It's been a long week."

"I'll let you go. But Sunday's okay, right? We're on for Sunday?"

"We're on for Sunday."

After we hung up, I didn't know what to do with all that energy. At the same time, part of me kept glancing at the phone, waiting for her to call back to say she'd changed her mind.

• • •

I started pacing. I was in an in-between place, too tired to take a long walk, too charged up to nap. Thinking about Sarah coming on Sunday was beginning to make me anxious, so instead I focused on Dr. Bernard's advice: write what you know. An image had been following me of late, me as a boy sitting on the hardwood floor in the hallway of our house, beside a closed bathroom door. I knew that image, could feel the hardness of the floor beneath my butt.

So far I hadn't done much with my computer beyond playing Solitaire. I turned it on, settled in front, raised my hands above the keyboard, emptied my mind, and began to type.

• • •

"How can you be so stupid? You just don't care."

You watch your father's expression, sheepish, embarrassed, like a little kid who tried and failed to do a good deed he should never have been expected to accomplish in the first place. You think, *Please don't laugh*, that way he has of nervous laughter when he doesn't want her to be angry but doesn't realize how that laugh, even from anxiety, makes her madder.

Your mother's veins stand out in her neck, her hands clenched into fists. You don't agree with her assessment: your father isn't stupid, he just doesn't stop to think is all. He's not careless, he cares too much, but that doesn't make him careful. If anything, it works the opposite way.

Your father is a small man, wiry, with a thin neck and shoulders and a bit of a paunch. He's got curly dark hair and green eyes, same as you, and you can't change the eyes but you've tried everything to straighten your hair, exorcise those curls. It doesn't matter, because even when your hair sits flat on your head, you look in the mirror and see your father's eyes.

Your mother has turned away, still talking, more general now, lamenting. "I can't have anything. Honest to God. What did I do to deserve this?" Picking up and putting down the cabbage, which was supposed to be a head of lettuce. That's what she sent him to the store to buy, lettuce for the roast beef sandwich she planned to enjoy after he went to work.

"How can you be so stupid?" she repeats, shaking the cabbage like a severed head in her palm.

"The boy, I asked the boy," your father replies, with earnestness. "The kid who works in the grocery. He knew me from school, back when I used to be the janitor. His name is Preston."

"He played a trick on you," she sends back. "A joke. Here comes old Easy Eddie, the perfect mark. I'm surprised he didn't ask you for money in order to point you in the right direction. The wrong direction," she corrects.

You cringe; the truth is, you can imagine your father paying a guy who works in the grocery for directions.

"He told me that was lettuce," your father says, but your mother doesn't want an argument, she wants to vent her troubles, and you know the best thing your father can do is stand there, arms sagging at his sides, and take it silently. Like you. But he won't.

"Honestly," she says, and looks like she's going to toss the cabbage into the trash, then opens the fridge and drops it in. "I can't have anything!"

And then he does it, that laugh, like a kid's snicker in the back of a classroom, even though he doesn't mean it that way, it's nerves pure and simple, a desperate hope to convince her it's a simple mistake, easily corrected. "I'll go back," he says.

She makes a disbelieving sound.

"I'll go back now."

"Save it," she answers. "Don't bother. It's too late now." She glares at him. "Don't you understand?" she demands, as if only an idiot wouldn't, yet you know he doesn't. He's not like you, he doesn't focus so intently on her, watch for every sign, every nuance. He doesn't make reading her the most important job of his life.

"It'll only take a few minutes," he says.

"Stop it!" Her scream is so much more hopeless than before. "I can't have anything," she says again, pacing about the kitchen like she must do something important but can't remember what. "You'll see. You'll get yours. You'll wake up some morning and find me gone." Her eyes leave him to find you, hook you and reel you in. "Both of you."

Your father is putting on his jacket, holding the car keys in his hand.

"You'll be the death of me." She stops and stares. "Is that what you want? Keep it up. You'll put me in an early grave."

She halts, then her eyes drop to the floor and for a moment, it's as if she's forgotten where she is, who she is, just for an instant, and then she turns and runs toward the bathroom, one hand pressed to her mouth, like she's going to throw up, you thought the first time this happened but you've learned all these moves too well by now. She's holding in her tears, she refuses to share them, locking them in her head that might explode if she doesn't corral it, until the bathroom door slams shut and you hear the lock turn. A few moments of silence follow, and then the wailing begins.

Your father looks at you, that hopeless look, that laugh; if he had the words he might say, "Don't think too much of this, don't take it to heart," but of course you do. You have always believed everything your mother says, taken every word as literal truth. From the first time she threatened to leave, you have been waiting for the morning you'll wake up to find her gone.

Your father steps up to the closed bathroom door. "Irene," he says. The wailing takes no note of his voice; it's as if he's never spoken.

"It's all right. Come out now."

Her crying makes you think of the one time you heard cows being slaughtered.

"Irene," your father tries again, leaning ridiculously close to the slit between the door and the frame. "I'm going back to the grocery. I'll get the lettuce. It won't take long." He pauses; does he really expect a reply? That the door will open and she'll emerge full of love and gratitude?

"I'm going now. I'll be right back."

He looks at you but doesn't speak, one more little laugh, like a smoker's cough. You turn away as the door shuts behind you.

You are ten, you are twelve, you are older than that; the only difference is that later, you no longer wrote letters of apology you left on her pillow, inventing errors you made that caused her such pain, vowing to never make them again. As you got older, you no longer stayed sitting on the hallway floor until she came out, hung around until she said something trivial enough to let you know it was over and she was your mother again. Instead, you went upstairs as soon as she came out and played your music, loud, and sang along, your voice making up in volume what it lacked in quality. *A winter's day. In a deep and dark December.*

Chapter Nine

When she arrived on Sunday, Sarah looked like a different person. She wore a knit dress of burnt reds with bits of gray and blue mixed in, stockings, and dressy shoes. Her loose hair sat on her shoulders, bouncing when she walked, forcing her to tuck it behind her ears, from which hung jangly earrings. She wore lipstick, and makeup that brought a rosiness to her cheeks.

She looked older, serious in a different way than in her uniform, like someone who fit right into a world I'd never belonged to, and never would.

At the same time, I felt a stirring of sexual desire.

"You didn't have to dress for dinner," I joked.

"I didn't." Said in a huffy, irritated way, as she yanked her familiar backpack from the back seat of her car. "These are coming off as soon as I get inside." Flashing a sly grin, she added, "Don't worry, I've got replacements."

She walked right past me. "I'm going to commandeer your bathroom."

While she was in there, I changed shirts, putting on a long one I could leave untucked, to hide what had become a stubborn erection.

Sarah re-appeared wearing jeans and a white shirt, unbuttoned, over a tight, stretchy sky-blue top, and sneakers. Hair in the familiar ponytail, earrings gone, face scrubbed clean. "That's better," she said. "I feel like myself again."

When she came toward me, I braced for a quick kiss, but she veered at the last minute and peered out the window. "That's the rental?"

"My 'wrecked rental,' to be exact. That's the name of the company."

She went "Hmmf," as if she didn't appreciate the humor.

"It runs good. I've been careful." Except once, I didn't add.

One thing she hadn't removed was her familiar flowery scent. Noticing that, I tried not to imagine her changing her clothes in the bathroom.

"You like your new computer?"

She clearly wanted me to say yes. Fortunately, I didn't have to lie. "I do."

"Sorry I was late. I had to bring my mother home after church, and I didn't want to take the time to change. Hence the Sunday-go-to-meetin' clothes."

I wondered absently if I'd committed a sin, lusting for Sarah in her church clothes. "You looked nice," I told her.

"I clean up good sometimes," she said, in a bad hillbilly accent that splashed cold water on my desire.

Then I noticed she wasn't wearing a bra. Her shirt had opened, and her nipples poked out against the stretchy blue fabric. I looked away, trailed her into the kitchen, where she got a glass of water. When she faced me again, my eyes were like a stubborn dog that caught a scent he won't let go.

"So what time's dinner?"

Panic flared. I hadn't started anything. "I was thinking we'd eat later, but I can start it now if you want."

"No, later's fine." I'd settled in next to her, both of us leaning against the counter, until she straightened and began wandering, a bit aimlessly, around the kitchen table.

"What I really need is fresh air. Exercise." She looked at me and grinned. "I need to frolic."

"And where does one go," I asked, "to frolic?"

"I know a place, if you're game."

"Where is it?"

"You'll see when we get there."

Before leaving, I stopped in the bathroom. Her dress hung on a hanger, bra and pantyhose draped over a towel rack behind. I splashed cold water on my face, remembering how as a kid – ten years old? Twelve? – I used to lust at the pictures of women's underwear in the Montgomery Ward catalogue. A few mornings ago, I'd awoken with a painful erection and had pleasured myself, the first time I could remember. I'd imagined a woman who was probably Sarah, although I didn't focus much on her face. It was over quickly, and was generally unsatisfying, and afterwards, I felt guilty. Now I wondered if I was afraid of sex, or of letting Sarah see I had sexual urges. I still remembered that sixth-grade dance when my hand had slid too low on Suzanne Martin's back. "Don't," she'd hissed, and I'd felt shameful and exposed. "You're not in sixth grade anymore," I muttered, "even if your notions about sex are stuck there."

I didn't want to jeopardize my friendship with Sarah. I was more than ten years older than her, and I was hardly what anyone would consider a "catch." It was hard enough believing someone like Sarah would want to spend time with me, let alone become intimate. I told my reflection in the mirror, "Don't fuck this up."

Outside, when she said, "I'll drive," I didn't object.

We stopped at the grocery and picked up bread and cheese, grapes, and bottled water. It was a sunny day, warm as summer, and we rolled down the windows as we headed west toward the mountains. Even with her hair captured in a ponytail, a few wisps of Sarah's hair flew across her face in the breeze, while my hair flew and flipped all over the place, and we had to shout to be heard. Eventually, we closed the windows.

She asked about my trip to the college. "You didn't say much on the phone."

"Most people didn't pay me any mind. It was no big deal, I guess."

"What was it like being there?"

"Kind of like when I first came home. There I was, standing in some stranger's office, trying to figure out what that person was like from what I saw there."

"And what did you conclude?"

"That Matthew Winton needs an interior decorator."

She grinned, turning to make eye contact. I loved how, when I said something clever, she appreciated not just what I'd said, but that it was me who'd said it. She made me feel clever.

"I think we need some music!" Sarah cried as the windows came down again, the breeze racing through. The music coming on was hard, angry, loud, and energetic. "Start me up!" she shrieked along with the singer. "Start me up, I'll never stop." Grinning madly, she looked at me as if she wanted me to sing along too. I don't think I would have dared, even if I'd known the lyrics.

When the song ended, the announcer mentioned The Rolling Stones, which rang a bell. A different song started playing in my head.

> *She would never say where she came from*
> *Yesterday don't matter if it's gone*

The song continued in my head, all the way to the refrain.

"Sarah?" I asked. "Do you know a song called 'Ruby Tuesday'?"

"That's an old one."

"It's a real song?"

"Of course. Do you remember it?"

"I do."

Her excitement said she was thinking like me: if I could remember a song from my adult years, that might constitute a memory. But after considering, she frowned. "That's old though. They probably made it thirty years ago."

When I would have been eleven.

"I did read something once about music and amnesia," she said, "about how some people can remember songs even when they've forgotten everything else. Have you listened to other music since you've been home?"

It stunned me that I hadn't. A section of my waiting room was set up just for that purpose.

"You should do a test. Find some recent music, see if you can remember the lyrics." She grinned. "Although I will say, if you're going to remember only one song, you could do a lot worse than the Rolling Stones."

· · ·

Her surprise turned out to be a place called Big Sky Farm, a state park with a farmhouse nestled at the foot of a mountain, vast meadows spreading out in front. When I quipped about frolicking in the grass, she said, "No way, Mister," and pointed to the top of the mountain. "We're heading up there."

She said it in a mock-serious way, admitting we didn't have to go all the way, and we could take our time, but my pride made me answer, "I can make it," despite a dubious look from Sarah, her gaze going straight for my not-quite-fully-recovered left knee.

"We'll take it easy," she repeated, and her face lit up. "It's way cool up there."

The climb wasn't as strenuous as I'd feared, and Sarah helped by carrying our stuff. The summer-like weather brought out lots of people, and nearing the top, we struggled searching for a secluded spot. We finally climbed onto a huge, rounded rock, where the view was spectacular, a checkerboard of fields and farmland spreading out almost to the horizon, melting into a misty white in the distance, where it was hard to tell if the ragged shapes between earth and sky were clouds or more mountains.

It was the sky that gave the park its name, this sky that was crystal blue and enormous.

"It's even more incredible at night," Sarah said. "Northern Virginia's not great for seeing stars, but the view here can be incredible."

She spread out a blanket and the food. "We came up here once at night, me and some friends, it was after senior prom. The park closes at dusk but it's easy to sneak in. We didn't have any flashlights, maybe one person had a cigarette lighter, but we climbed all the way to the top. I can't believe we didn't all break our legs."

I smiled. She'd slipped off her outer shirt, and I struggled to corral my gaze, looking from her eyes to the view below. I sat carefully, hiding my renewed erection.

"So you were pretty wild growing up," I said.

She snorted. "Hardly. I had my moments. I got detention once senior year. The whole school was shocked. Here I was, the top student in my class, Miss Goody Two Shoes, who always followed the rules, doing something that got me detention."

"What did you do?"

"I skipped class to sneak out to the woods with my boyfriend."

Lucky guy, I thought, but I feigned a shocked look. "You? In the woods with a boy?"

Shouts nearby halted her reply. A trio of boys, perhaps ten years old, came galloping along the path at the base of the rock we sat on. They smacked sticks against the rock, then hurled them like spears over the cliff below. Sarah and I exchanged a raised-eyebrows look and remained silent until they tromped away.

I turned back to her. "So when we were rudely interrupted, I believe you were telling me about skipping class to go neck in the woods with your boyfriend."

"We weren't necking. We probably held hands, maybe we kissed a little, but that's all. Trust me, I was a very good girl." She laughed. "Most of the time."

"I want to hear about the other times."

"I can't reveal stuff like that on a first date."

"I thought the mall was our first date."

She shook her head. "That was shopping. You can't go shopping on a first date. A first date has to be fun."

"This is fun," I said, gazing across the patchwork of distant fields. We both stood, facing each other. I was nervous, but my body seemed to know what it wanted to do. At least one part of it did. Then my hands reached to her shoulders, my arms opening as she inched forward. Just relax, I told myself. You've done this before, even if you can't remember it. Let your body show the way.

Our faces came close, heads angled, and our lips came together. We kissed hard, lips pushing against teeth, and then her tongue pushed into my mouth and I opened to accept it, groaning a little and pressing my hips against her, feeling my firmness, and her desire. My tongue entered her mouth, our lips pressing so hard I tasted something salty that might have been blood. But mostly I wasn't thinking, just feeling, letting my body respond. It felt unbearable and I wanted to keep feeling it forever.

Unfortunately, "forever" lasted only seconds, as loud, close-by shrieks announced the return of the three boys. This time they stopped right at the base of our rock and began hurling stones over the cliff, making explosion noises, as if each stone was a grenade. Wordlessly, Sarah and I arranged our clothing, gathered our things, and started back down, careful to follow a path far away from where the boys were bombing.

. . .

We went down the mountain like two strangers who just happened to choose the same path. Back in her car, I said, "It's an incredible place," just to end the silence.

"I'm glad you liked it," she replied. Then she rolled down her window and turned on the radio.

When the pressure got too heavy, I said, "Maybe we should talk." I had to shout it twice before she turned off the radio, then a third time at almost-normal volume.

"You mean about what a pain kids can be?"

"You'd think a climb like that would have sapped their energy."

We were still shouting, until finally she rolled up the window.

"I really like you," I said.

She glanced at me, but she was paying the lightly-traveled road more attention than it deserved. "I like you too."

"You've done so much for me."

"Don't go there." A sharpness to her tone. Then she laughed. "It's good those kids came back. We were on our way to embarrassing ourselves big time. Or maybe getting arrested."

I tried to come up with a clever retort, but couldn't ignore the serious things we needed to discuss. Like how I might have been ten years older than her, but emotionally – sexually – my brain seemed stuck at thirteen. Like how on that rock, she seemed as willing as me, but how did I know I could trust that I was reading her correctly?

"I don't want to screw this up," I said.

She didn't reply, but I was glad I'd said it.

The surroundings grew familiar. We passed the Agape Church of God in Christ, passed through the shadows from the rock walls. The last stretch of road I'd walked on many times.

She parked next to my wrecked rental but made no move to get out of the car. I tensed, wondering if she was going to say it would be better for both of us if she just went home. Instead she took my hand, her thumb reaching around to caress the back of it. "I really like you too," she said. "What happened back there felt right, in the moment. Maybe we can just go along that way, play it by ear, not overthink things, respond to things in the moment."

"Overthinking is the one thing I do well."

She gave me a mock slap on the arm. "It's not the only thing. From what I hear, you also make a mean chicken."

I wanted to hug her, but the gearshift was in the way.

Inside, she asked if she could take a shower. "I feel kind of grungy," she said.

I told her sure, I should probably take one myself.

"You go first," she said, and when I objected, she pointed out that if I showered first, I could start the dinner sooner. Laughing, she assumed a pleading, pathetic pose. "You like this? It's my 'lean and hungry look.'"

. . .

In the shower, an image flashed: a shadow on the other side of the curtain, a sexy voice feigning innocence. *Might there be room for two?* The feeling strong enough I inched back the curtain to make sure no one was there.

Was it a memory? If a fantasy, it might have been based on something real. A scene from a movie perhaps. Or from my prior life.

I got out of the shower, toweled dry. I was erect again, and if Sarah had walked into the bathroom at that moment, I might have jumped her and torn off her clothes. If that would be okay with her. If she would want me to. How could I know? What did it even mean to "play things by ear"? What if one person's ear wanted something the other person's ear didn't? A thought popped into my head: when it came to sex, a wrong move could hurt someone severely. I didn't know where that idea came from but it felt like one of those truths burned into you. Had something bad happened in the past? Was my mind stuck at thirteen because that's where it wanted to be?

I found Sarah sitting on the Adirondack chair out back. "Bathroom's free," I told her.

As she slipped past me, I reached for her, but she brushed me away. "Save your fondling for that chicken," she said.

It was odd hearing my own shower running from another room. I tried not to imagine Sarah inside.

She came out again wearing her casual clothes, although her wet hair was loose. Her skin had a rosy sheen, and her scent was oddly familiar, until I realized she must have used my soap.

I'd told her that I'd written something the other day, and while the chicken was roasting, she asked if she could read it. I brought it up on my computer and left her in my office to read it. I'd been anxious when she read my story about the boy and his father at the basketball game, but this was worse. This was true, not fiction, and I could remember writing it.

"It's so sad," she said when she finally emerged; she'd taken a long time to read such a short piece. Not knowing how to reply, I told her I was sorry, then went to check on the chicken.

She took a seat at the kitchen table. "When I was growing up," she said, "I never doubted my parents loved me. My brothers, that was a bit more complicated, but my parents, even when they got angry with each other, or angry at me or my brothers, we always knew they loved us. That we'd always be a family.

"When my father passed, it was hard. It still is, especially on my mother. But we were all adults by then, we'd grown up with our parents there to comfort and support us. I never knew what it was like to grow up without all that. To grow up in fear.

"When I first met you, I thought, here's a person who has known a lot of sorrow. Now I think I understand at least a small part of why."

She played with a thread between her fingers as she talked, and fortunately, she only looked up at me a handful of times, but even so, I couldn't hold her gaze. I felt I'd made a mistake showing what I wrote. There was enough sorrow in the world; why write something that makes more people sad? Then I thought, it's me, who I am. Who I've been. Maybe it wasn't what she wanted.

I forced a laugh. "One thing you can say about my stories: they're great for killing the mood."

"They're beautiful," she said.

I wanted to believe she meant it, but I could only add another laugh, self-deprecating. "If you like being sad."

"My brother Brian likes to say that anger and sadness are two sides of the same coin. They're both reactions to being hurt.

They just take different directions. The angry person turns out-ward, blaming others, while the sad person turns inward, blam-ing themselves."

"Your brother Brian sounds like a smart guy."

She grinned. "Sometimes. Other times he's an asshole. But that's how brothers are."

Her saying "asshole" surprised me, even though she no doubt heard worse language in her job. But it helped to lighten the mood.

She asked if she could help and I said, no, it would be ready soon. She got up and wandered out back. Alone, I found myself thinking about my mother, how difficult I must have made her life growing up, even as I believed I only wanted to make her happy. I remembered how when she finally came out from crying in the bathroom, my mother acted as if nothing had happened, as if all the tears and threats and wailing could disappear if only we ig-nored them. I slunk off to my room, where I really did write her a letter apologizing for everything I'd done wrong, promising never to do those things again – even though I didn't know what those things might have been. Later, I snuck down and left my letter on her pillow, but she never acknowledged that, either.

There was more; there was always more. How I never under-stood what my father was thinking. How I resented him, con-vinced he was far from the man she wanted to spend her life with. I blamed him for my mother's unhappiness. Even as she, when angry at me, would hiss, "You're just like your father." When she said to him in frustration, "You'll put me in an early grave," I felt her accusing me, too.

I was glad I had the chicken to focus on, when Sarah returned. Dinner went well, with her complimenting me, and appearing to enjoy her food. I told her about my birthday dinner as a kid. "Ex-cept I forgot the chocolate cake," I said.

"It's not your birthday," she replied.

She helped me clean up, then I made coffee and we retreated to the platform in back. I had to bring out a kitchen chair because there was only one Adirondack. The sun had dipped below the hill in back, coating us in shadow, the sky slowly being drained of blue.

Feeling like I'd eaten too much, I got up and wandered along the platform. I didn't realize Sarah had followed until I turned back. She was very close and I dared to reach out, my hands settling on her hips. It felt natural and I left them there. Then she laid her arms out over my shoulders, straight out as if we were about to break into some crazy old-time dance. I peered left then right in an exaggerated way.

"What are you doing?"

"Looking for noisy kids."

"They won't save you now."

We came together tentatively at first, almost innocently, like two sixth graders trying to decide where it was okay to place our hands. In her eyes I saw a depth and a seriousness, a sadness, too, that unnerved me, but I met her gaze and hoped she could see as deeply into me. Our hips bumped, my erection brushing against her, and she giggled. I almost said, "What?" but instead I kissed her, my tongue entering her mouth first, and she groaned and pressed tightly into me, as if asking why it took us so long to reach this moment.

We did that crazy dance making our way from out back to the bedroom, some part of us always locked together, shedding clothes along the way. It was easy just to act and react, just to feel, because what I felt most was Sarah wanting this, wanting me.

Naked in my bed, I kissed her neck, her breasts, gently took a nipple between my teeth, making her gasp. I didn't have a plan, I let my body take over. My hand along one thigh, sliding into the slickness and bristly hair between her legs, and she gasped again, her whole body tensing, and I loved being able to make her feel that way.

Our bodies shifted, and suddenly something warm and solid snaked around my penis. My body jerked back, as if it really was a snake. Her hand fled.

"Sorry," I gasped. Even in the settling darkness I could see concern in her face. "You surprised me, that's all."

But the power that had been surging through me had vanished as completely as if someone pulled a plug from its socket. My penis shriveled up.

"I can help," she said, and began to lower her head, but I caught her and drew her back. "What can I do?"

I didn't know what to tell her. I only knew that I was suddenly terrified of her hand, even more so of her mouth, touching me there. My body had jackknifed of its own accord, to protect that part of me. "It's not you," I said. "I don't know what's wrong."

"Maybe we can just lie here?"

I sighed. She'd been just as aroused as I was. "I could do something for you," I said.

"Let's just lie here," she replied, and nestled in my arms.

Chapter Ten

"This is going to sound strange," I told Jessie, as we sat in the campus's fancy restaurant, too expensive for students. Only a handful of tables were occupied, and we sat in a corner by ourselves, but our waitress kept coming over, bringing menus, filling our water glasses, asking if we were ready to order, then lurking nearby when we said we were not. I couldn't tell if we were her only table, during this mid-afternoon lull, or if she just wanted to speed us up so she could take a break. Jessie and I had exhausted all the less delicate subjects, and it was time to get to the point.

Sarah left late last night. She'd said all the right things: it happens to everyone from time to time, it's no big deal, I was tired, still taking medication. She loved just lying in my arms. And with a sly grin: we'll have to keep trying. But she, in her encouraging words, and me in my silence, stayed away from the real questions: why had my desire suddenly fled when she touched me, why had her offer to "help out" filled me with fear. What if it's not something that happens "sometimes," but always?

When she got out of bed and turned on the light to track down her scattered clothes, my desire rose. I covered myself with a blanket, not willing to get on that rollercoaster again.

In the morning, waking with a pulsing erection, I finished my-self off quickly and brutally. The equipment seemed to be work-ing all right. I couldn't tell if this was good news or bad. If the problem wasn't physical, it had to be in my brain.

Eventually, Jessie and I decided ordering might get the waitress to leave us alone. Remembering a childhood fondness for bacon, I ordered a BLT, while Jessie got a salad. The waitress looked disap-pointed, perhaps anticipating a meager tip, but finally disappeared.

Jessie looked brighter today, more relaxed. She'd greeted me warmly, but without the enthusiastic affection of the other day. Probably this was how we'd come to be with each other in the years since we stopped being a couple.

"So what's this big secret question you wanted to ask?" Mis-chief in her brown eyes.

"I just wanted to ask you," I looked around, leaned close, low-ered my voice, "about sex."

She made a face like she'd eaten something unpleasant. "You don't mean how to do it."

"Oh, no. Nothing like that. No."

She looked relieved.

"I'm wondering about – us. When we were together, I mean. As a couple. We probably had sex, right?"

A laugh popped out of her, followed by an apology. "Yes. We had sex."

"And it was okay?"

"Are you asking if you were a good lover?"

I shook my head. "It's more basic than that. I'm asking if I was able to . . . perform. If I ever had trouble in that department."

A toothy grin lit up her face. "Have you met someone? I mean, it's none of my business, but have you?"

I returned a scowl meant to say that yes, it was none of her business.

The waitress arrived with our food. We ate in silence, me fin-ishing my sandwich quickly and then having to wait while she poked through her enormous salad.

I called the waitress back and ordered coffee. When she brought it, Jessie asked for a container so she could take home the remaining two-thirds of her salad. We waited while the waitress cleared our dishes, brought the container, then went back for the coffee and the bill.

"The change is for you," I told her, remembering what my grandfather used to say when he treated the family to dinner. The change amounted to a decent tip, and finally, the waitress looked satisfied.

I struggled for words to get back on track. "Why don't we go to my office?" Jessie asked. On the way, I told her about my visit to the therapist. "I was hoping maybe he'd put me under hypnosis and I'd remember everything. But he didn't think that was a good idea."

"We used to talk about that a lot," Jessie said. "You seeing somebody." She laughed. "I've been seeing my therapist for twenty years. I still drive home twice a month for our sessions. But you always resisted. You'd say, 'writing is my therapy,' which it is, of course. But it can also be helpful to get a professional opinion."

I didn't tell her I wasn't impressed with the therapist. Although after last night, I'd been pondering a second appointment.

Jessie's office was divided into a workspace and a place to relax in, her desk with its computer and filing cabinet on one side, and two easy chairs, a rug, and a small, fancy bookcase on the other. Several lamps allowed her to avoid the harsh overhead light, while the wall held framed posters from the National Gallery of Art: Berthe Morisot, Mary Cassat, Frieda Kahlo. There was also a framed photograph of a street painter standing in front of a café in Paris, the café duplicated in miniature on the street painter's canvas.

Jessie ushered me toward the easy chairs, but when I hesitated she said, "Uh oh."

"What?"

"Your shoulders. You've got them raised to the bottom of your ears. That only happens when there's something you don't want to do."

"I'm that obvious?"

"To me you are."

"Maybe we can sit at your desk?"

"That's fine." She took her desk chair while I settled in the straight-backed one facing her. Grinning, she rubbed her hands together as if about to dig into a huge meal after not eating for days. "So. Let's talk about sex."

She said it loud, and I looked back at the door to make sure it was closed.

"Sorry," she said, "but this is kind of fun. It's not every day a guy asks me to grade his sexual performance."

"I'm not looking for a grade."

"I know. I'm sorry. I'm just having fun with you."

"All right," I admitted. "I met someone. It's still new, I don't know where it will lead. But last night we – well, we got going, I was feeling great, and then suddenly, I lost it. Like somebody pulled the plug."

"And you're worried this might be permanent?"

"God, I hope not."

"Maybe you should talk to your doctor. See if it's related to your accident."

I considered telling her everything worked fine this morning, when I was alone, but it was too embarrassing to admit. "When we were together, did I have that problem?"

"Not any more than most guys." She quickly added, "Not that I have much experience with other guys. But I'm pretty sure most guys have that problem from time to time, a lot more often than they admit. Did it happen when we were together? A few times, probably. When you were tired, or stressed, or had too much to drink. To be honest, I never thought much about it. It bothered you a lot more than it bothered me.

"Lots of guys inflate the value of their dick. They think it's all a woman wants. And maybe some women do. But most women want to be with a whole person. You can buy a pretty realistic dick, if that's all you want, and believe me, it's a hell of a lot less complicated that way." Now she was blushing, and she looked away when our gazes met.

She laid a hand on my arm. "You were a wonderful lover. You were attentive, you wanted to please me as much as please yourself. Maybe more.

"And you understood that when two people made love, it wasn't just something going on between genitalia."

Her words comforted me. Maybe I'd done at least one thing right in my life. But that didn't explain what happened last night.

"Was there anything I did that you didn't like? When we had sex, I mean."

"Not at all. You were adventurous, but also considerate. Sometimes you were so considerate it was frustrating. 'Is that okay?' you'd ask, when all I wanted was for you to go ahead and do it."

"What about me? Were there things I didn't like you doing to me?"

She thought a moment, then laughed. "Blow jobs. If you'll pardon my French."

"I didn't like it when you did that?"

"You wouldn't let me do it. I kind of forgot about that, but it was something that seemed odd. For most guys, a blow job is like Christmas morning. Frankly, I never much cared for giving them myself, so I can't say your preference bothered me.

"Now that I think of it, you didn't really like me touching you there at all. That got frustrating, when you were having problems but you wouldn't let me help. You loved being touched everywhere else. Just not there."

That's when everything had changed, when Sarah touched me there. But why? As Jessie said, something like that should have brought me great pleasure.

There was one more delicate question I wanted to ask. I began tentatively. "When we were together, did we ever talk about past relationships? People we'd been with before?"

She laughed gently. "That's something we chose not to inflict on each other."

"Did you ever sense — that I – "

She looked puzzled. Understandably so.

"I'm just wondering if we, when we, you know, for the first time – "

"You're wondering if you were a virgin?"

The word didn't sound right, but that did seem to be what I was asking.

She laughed, then apologized. "I doubt we ever talked about it directly, but I think I can say with confidence that no, you were not a virgin."

That made sense. I would have been thirty-two when we met.

Jessie was moving papers around on her desk, stacking books. She had only one class today but it was coming up. "You have to go," I said, and she nodded apologetically. I thanked her for taking the time to talk with me.

She grinned. "It beats 'Defining distinctions in student behavior in accordance with the precepts of the Ethics Committee.' That was the conversation I got trapped in this morning, when you rescued me."

• • •

After Jessie left, I checked my email. Only 32 unread messages this time, none from anyone I recognized other than Jessie forwarding department memos, including one that said registration for spring classes would start in four weeks. If I would tell her which two courses I wanted to teach, she said, she'd put them into the system.

I wondered if I should ask to take another semester off. They probably wouldn't pay me, but I could afford it. There was no guarantee that my memory would return by the end of spring, but at least I'd have more time. In the end, I asked Jessie to put me down for the same two courses I taught last spring – at least I had extensive notes for them – and figured I could always back out later.

I hadn't told her that I'd forgotten how to teach. We'd talked about my friends and family when we moved off the subject of sex. She'd never met my father, but she'd spoken with him often on the phone, and she thought he was a good and kind man. A friend of mine named Aaron came to visit while Jessie and I were still together. Aaron and I had gone to high school together, she told me, and I'd worked for him for a couple years in between college and grad school, though she didn't recall in what sort of job. She liked Aaron and described how the two of us stayed up half the night talking about everything from good movies to our eleventh grade history teacher. Aaron had several black belts in karate and a dark sense of humor; at the time of his visit, she recalled, he was reading a book called *The First Circle* and getting great amusement out of Solzhenitsyn's depiction of the toadies in Stalin's government. Unfortunately, for all she'd remembered, Jessie could not recall Aaron's last name.

She also recalled Aaron mentioning someone named Daniel, who she figured was also a friend. Something had happened to Daniel, but Aaron hadn't wanted to talk about it much, at least not to her. His last name, too, she didn't remember.

I typed "Aaron" into the search box on my email, but all that came up was an Aaron Rienza, clearly a student, and Jonas Aaron, whose email praised a certain brand of siding and was addressed to "Maurice."

"Daniel" produced the opposite problem: 27 emails to or from people named Daniel. But no one who might have been a friend.

I remembered seeing a soda machine in the hall but I didn't have any change. As I was searching my desk drawers for coins, I came upon a small plastic thing, about the size and shape of my thumb. I had no idea what it was, but it looked interesting, so I dropped it into my shirt pocket.

The phone rang. Instinctively I looked to my desk, but the sound came from inside my backpack. I tracked it down and smiled at the name on the front.

"Sarah."

"What are you doing?" Her voice energetic and playful.

"Are you at work?"

"I've been sitting at a desk all day doing paperwork, and I need-ed a break, so I came outside. It's just me and a half-dozen smok-ers loitering outside the station."

"Watch out you don't get a ticket," I said. "For loitering."

"Naw, I'm okay. I have connections."

Our initial playfulness dissipated, leaving an awkward silence. "You doing okay?" Sarah asked after a while.

"I'm at the college. I found the name of a friend from home, someone I grew up with. I thought maybe I'd have an email from him but I couldn't find any."

"Tell me his name."

"I only know his first name. It's Aaron. I don't know his last name."

"That could be a problem."

"Besides, isn't there a rule against using police things for per-sonal stuff?"

"That's not exactly how they phrase it in the rulebook, but yeah, basically, that's true."

Another silence. I decided I didn't like phones. While she was talking, I was able to imagine her, but in the silence it felt like she disappeared.

And without being able to see her face, I couldn't tell if she wanted to talk about last night, or had decided we should ignore it.

"So it turns out that I'm going to be free this weekend, Saturday and Sunday both," she said. "Any chance you'd like a visitor?"

The thought sent a jolt through me, fear and excitement both. I tried to cover it in the usual way, grasping for something clever. "And who might this visitor be?"

"I can think of someone."

"It shouldn't be just anyone. I live in a train station. Any visitor would need to appreciate the historical significance, not to men-tion the way-coolness, of such a structure."

She laughed at my borrowed phrase. "I think this visitor could be very appreciative."

We could have gone on like that, but something stirring down below made me nervous. "Then I will confidently say that yes, I would be pleased and flattered to have this visitor come see me this weekend."

She released a sigh like she'd just finished an uphill climb. "You really know how to make a girl work for her chicken."

"I have to cook for you too?"

"Actually, I was thinking I might make lasagna. My mother's recipe. You'll like it."

"I can bring some movies too. We can watch them on your laptop." She chuckled. "You've got twenty-eight years' worth of movies to catch up on."

I told her that sounded like fun, although the fear was coming back.

"All the smokers have finished their butts and gone back inside," she said. "I guess I ought to join them."

"I'll see you Saturday morning?"

"I could drive out on Friday night, but I'd probably just fall asleep when I arrived."

"I don't mind. Whatever you think is best."

We went back and forth a little more, seeking a gentle way to say goodbye. In the end I repeated that I'd see her on Saturday, and she said, "It'll be fun." Then we hung up. Or rather, she hung up, as I still wasn't quite sure how to end a call on my new phone.

Leaving, I noticed Jessie had returned from her class. About to rush in, I halted when I noticed she was with a student. I tried to signal, "Never mind," but she popped up and hurried into the hall.

"What's up?"

"I just wanted to ask you about this thing I found." I dug the plastic thing out of my pocket. "Do you know what this is?"

"USB stick."

"Okay," I said, letting her see my befuddlement.

"It's a storage drive. It holds files, stuff you want to backup or copy from your main computer."

"So whatever is here is also somewhere else?"

"Not necessarily. You could also use it instead of a hard drive. Save it here if you don't want it on your main computer."

"It has files on it?"

"It might. You'll have to take a look." She explained how to do it. "A menu should pop up, and you just follow the prompts."

Not wanting to go back to my office, I dropped the USB drive back into my shirt pocket. I hadn't been driving long, but I'd learned to avoid the roads during rush hour, which could start as early as three-thirty. I hurried to my car and made it home before traffic got too heavy.

I arrived to find a strange car parked in front of my house.

· · ·

It was an expensive one, a white Audi. No one inside.

"Finally! I've found you!"

The voice, desperate and relieved, came from behind some bushes, and belonged to the young woman who'd approached me the first time I returned to campus. As she ran toward me, I held up my hands to keep her from flinging herself into my arms.

"I thought you were dead. Mother said you had an accident and then you didn't come and you didn't come and Mrs. Freer announced she'd be taking over your class and I thought, My God he's in hospital somewhere dying and I don't even know where to look and no one will tell me one fucking thing." All said in one breath, anger rising at the end. "Not even Mother," she finished, looking like she was about to collapse from the effort.

"Then I saw you that day. You were so strange but I thought, he's alive! I know it was awkward but you hurt me." She looked at me, her blue eyes frail and forlorn. "You hurt me. You really did."

I told her I was sorry; what else could I say?

"But you're alive and we're here." She took another step toward me and I backed away again. She gave me an irritated, pleading look. "Please." She came forward again, getting close enough that I had to twist away.

"I'm not – recovered yet, not fully. I'm still feeling the effects."

"You almost died."

I couldn't tell if that was information she'd learned, perhaps from the mysterious Mother, or if it was a fiction she'd created. At least it seemed to dissuade her from embracing me. That gave me a chance to ponder what possible relationship I might have with this girl – for girl is how I saw her, on her way to becoming an attractive, even beautiful perhaps, woman but not there yet, with an awkwardness to her, a looseness in her limbs that made me think of a colt still getting used to its own legs. She was clearly a former student, but was she more, and if so, in what ways? And how much of what she intimated might be true?

Her body had curled in on itself; she looked a little mousey, her eyes downcast, as if she'd been chastised. "Listen," I said. "I think we need to talk. Maybe we should go inside."

That seemed to perk her up, and inside, she slipped off her coat, revealing a colorful sweater, hand-knitted perhaps, and very tight white jeans. Even her shoulder-length blonde hair seemed to bounce back to life, and it struck me how her physical appearance seemed to change according to her mood.

"I've missed you so." When she moved in close, it was harder to avoid her in the cramped kitchen, and finally I gave in, my arms going limp at my sides as she embraced me, turning her cheek to rest on my shoulder.

She drew back with a gasp. "Are you in pain?" She held her hands up between us, as if she was the one needing to fend me off.

"Come sit down." I led her to the kitchen table, taking the chair on the other side. "Do you want some coffee? I can make some. It'll only take a minute."

She didn't answer my question but I got up and made the coffee anyway. It was a relief having something mundane to focus on.

She sat in silence, not bothering to look over her shoulder at what I was doing behind her. When the coffee was ready, I set her cup in front of her. "I have milk if you want some. I'm not sure about sugar, but I'll look if you want me to."

"You don't remember!" she shouted, her voice quaking.

"I'm sorry?"

She glared at me. Anger made the gray bags under her eyes more noticeable, and her nose more prominent. It was slightly off center, suggesting it might have been broken once. "My coffee," she said, more composed now. "You don't even remember how I take it."

"Did you want sugar?"

"Black! No milk, no sugar! Black!" Then she crumbled, anger giving way to tears. "Why are you doing this to me?"

She glanced at the chair where she'd draped her coat, and for a moment I thought she was going to go charging off. A part of me would have liked nothing better. But whatever was going on with her – whatever might have gone on between us – needed to be faced.

I apologized again. "I've been ill," I said. "I need to explain."

I poured milk into my own coffee, then walked around the table to sit across from her. I didn't want to tell her the truth but sensed that she'd see through any fiction I made up. "I'll tell you everything, but I'm hoping we can keep this confidential, just between you and me. I'd rather it didn't get out."

She nodded, but I had no way of knowing if I could trust her. Sighing, I went on. "I was in an accident. It was quite severe. I was in the hospital."

"But you're all right now?"

"Physically, I'm doing well. The doctors think so. But there's something else." I paused, as if hoping some act of God would stop this now. When God demurred, I said, "I have amnesia."

"So it's true!"

That threw me. "You knew?"

"I overheard Mother talking with Dr. Bergstrom. He mentioned memory loss, and I thought they were talking about you but I wasn't sure. I was dying to ask Mother but we have all these rules you know. Can't discuss private matters, especially about the faculty."

She'd come alive again. I studied her. Her emotions, theatrical as they were, seemed genuine. She wasn't putting on airs so much as acting the way I suspected she'd lived her whole life, as the center of attention, the person in the room confident she was more important than everyone else, confident they knew it too. All likely covering a deep insecurity that she masked by allowing people to conclude she was simply spoiled.

"I have to ask you a question," I said. "Who is 'Mother'?"

She glared at me, incredulous, then she giggled. "You really do have amnesia. 'Mother' – as you used to know – is Dr. Felicia Sorenson, Dean of the School of Arts and Sciences."

"You're the daughter of the dean?"

She giggled again. "You don't know my name either, do you."

I shook my head, adding, "I can't help it. It's nothing personal."

"Ha!" popped out of her, though I couldn't read how to take it. "My name is Lisette. Pronounced as if the 's' is a 'z.' Lisette Sorenson. And you, dear sir, are madly in love with me."

I tried not to show how that chilled me. She wasn't paying close attention to me anyway, enjoying her own power.

"All right," she amended. "Maybe not madly in love. Not yet. But you'll come round in time."

Another giggle. "You really do have amnesia? I could tell you anything and you wouldn't know if I'd made it up."

"That would be cruel," I said.

"And you weren't cruel to me? Disappearing, not telling me where you were? Not even letting me know you were alive?"

I wanted to scream, I had amnesia! But I checked my anger. I needed to tread carefully with this daughter of the dean.

I got up for more coffee. "Black," I said while pouring hers, but she gave me a dirty look.

"It would help me," I said once I'd resumed my seat, "if you could tell me –" about our relationship came to mind, but I pushed that phrasing aside – "how we know each other."

"Ah," she said. "You want the truth?"

"Please."

She looked around. "Do you have anything to eat? I'm starving."

I found some cookies in the cabinet. "Oreos," she said. "The best." Taking one, she pulled apart the two halves, licked off the cream, then set both cookies down on a napkin. "Okay," she said, as if having finished a nourishing meal.

She was a freshman who started early by taking a summer class, Fiction Techniques, instructor, Matthew Winton. According to her, I'd loved her writing, even promising it would be publishable if she worked hard enough. We'd conferenced several times, and I'd promised to help her, so she signed up for my class this fall. "You're the best teacher in the whole college," she gushed. "You're passionate, patient, knowledgeable, and cute." She giggled. "When you get so intense, I want to jump all over you."

Her eyes flashed that suggestive grin that promised she was older than she looked. I ignored it.

"I just realized. You don't remember my writing." She didn't wait for a response. "You really liked it."

"I'm sure it was very good."

"You really don't know who I am?" Her eyes glistened a bit – with tears?

"The doctors believe my memory will come back in time. I've only just recovered from my physical injuries."

She lurched to her feet and circled the table. Still seated, I braced myself but didn't resist as she embraced me from behind. I could feel moisture on the back of my neck. She smelled of cigarette smoke, and I pictured her sitting in her car – her mother's car, most likely – chain smoking like her favorite writers, waiting for me to return.

"You must let me help you."

"There's nothing you can do. Not right now."

"I could speak to Mother."

"The university has been really good about this. It's just something I have to do myself."

I patted her hands, clasped across my chest, then waited until she let go before I stood.

"Will you let me know when you remember?"

"I will."

She slipped on her coat, and I followed her outside. I thought she might try to hug me again but she went right to her car. Her parting words surprised me: "Be kind to yourself." Watching her drive away, I wondered if maybe she knew me better than I thought.

• • •

Exhausted, I flopped on my bed, but I couldn't sleep. Eventually I dragged myself out of bed and forced myself to eat dinner. I was thinking how Lisette Sorenson reminded me of someone I'd known before. She had blonde hair like Sarah's, but longer and paler, as was her skin. Whereas Sarah's eyes were more of a grayish blue, Lisette's were blue as a clear winter sky, and lacked depth. But it wasn't Sarah she reminded me of, but someone else, who remained as blank as the rest of my recent past.

I decided to take a shower. Unbuttoning my shirt, I discovered the "USB stick" I'd brought back from campus in my pocket. Jessie had said there might be files there. Maybe something from Aaron? An address perhaps?

I turned on my computer and slid it in. A single folder appeared on the screen.

It was called, "New Book." Inside were several text files: "Beginning," "Junior_Year," "Beginning_Part 2," "A_New_Family," and "First_of_Many." Each one had a date from July or August of this year. I moved the cursor over the first file and double-clicked.

Chapter Eleven

Folder: New_Book
File Name: Beginning
Date Modified: 3 August 1997

You hated him at first. Jonathan Pirelli. Pompous and arrogant, with his slicked-back hair and his blue blazer, ascot knotted round his neck. A big phony, that's what your mother said. Big fish in a little pond. He exulted in committing your mother's most grievous sin: he sought attention. Sure, he'd acted on Broadway, but he'd only ever spoken one line: as a tutor gathering up his charges: "And how are all my little ducklings today?"

He knew your father, because he'd taught for years at the old Mansfield High, where your father worked as janitor, before they built the new regional school. He knew you too, from times your father brought you with him to school when you were younger. He was the most popular teacher in school, so you were surprised one day midway through your ninth-grade year, when he approached you standing by your locker, asked how your father was doing, and suggested you take his famous course, Acting and Directing.

You told him your father was good, thanked him, and said you'd keep his course in mind. You didn't sign up for it then, but changed your mind in the middle of tenth grade, not because of him but because you were in love with Suzanne Martin and heard she would be in the class.

The first day of class, he had everyone sit in the first three rows of the auditorium while he occupied a throne on stage. "In this class," he said, "we're going to read plays," and he gave everyone a script. "Later on, we'll act some."

Juniors and seniors mostly filled the class, his ducklings who had taken it before and re-enrolled every term. They sat in the front row, called him Mr. P, talked and joked with him. You cared only that Suzanne Martin was sitting in the row in front of you, silky black hair and perfume flowing over the back of the seat.

In tenth grade, you despised people who broke the rules and got away with it. When those people were teachers, they got worshipped by students you hated to admit you admired. Even when they weren't building sets for the next play, Mr. P's students got passes exempting them from study hall. They hung around the theater sleeping or listening to music; now and then a couple snuck behind the black curtains in the back corner of the stage and made out, or smoked dope up in the light booth or along the catwalk.

He was heavyset, not obese but shaped like a football standing on end. He was not athletic, although he could be surprisingly light on his feet, like a dancer or a cat. You played sports, but the most impressive athlete in Mr. P's class was Daniel Obanyan, six-foot four and two hundred twenty pounds, a Native American richness to his skin and hardness to his face and his muscles, straight black hair falling to his shoulders. Daniel O could have been all-state in three sports, if only he'd tried out for a team instead of spending all his time acting and playing guitar and writing poems (and smoking dope and making out).

You secretly wished you could be Daniel O, who was Mr. P's prized student. He sat in the exact center of the front row and got called up on stage the second week to act out a father-son scene with Mr. P in a drama written by Arthur Miller. "Even when you're sitting back resting your tushy in these comfy padded seats," Mr. P instructed, "that's the way you should be reading lines."

At the end of the year the class put on a play: *A Thousand Clowns*. The half dozen acting roles all went to long-time ducklings, while you and the rest of the class painted sets or stood off in the wings feeding lines in rehearsal whenever the actors stumbled. Still, you got your first pass exempting you from study hall – so that you really could work on sets – and in the class final exam, which involved pairs of students performing a short scene, Mr. P paired you with Suzanne Martin for a gender-neutral rendition of *Waiting for Godot*.

Junior year, you enrolled again. In Spring everyone's attention turned toward the big musical, *West Side Story*. You hoped for a significant part; you sang pretty well to the records you played in your room late at night, but in the end Mr. P cast you as Doc, one of the non-singing adults who came on stage only a couple times. Mr. P caught you looking downcast and put his arm around you. He put his arm around everyone, but this was the first time he'd taken you under his wing; he was – as one of the more clever students had once termed him – "the head duck." "You were in the running for Bernardo," he said, "but you look so mature, so much older than everyone else. I needed you to be an adult."

Believing every word he said, you perked up. As Bernardo he chose Daniel O.

The night of the cast party, your mother allowed you to drive the family car. Suzanne rode with you. You occasionally gave her rides to rehearsals, and a few times you stopped at Friendly's afterwards for coffee and French fries and intense conversation, but you didn't dare make any romantic overtures because she didn't seem interested and you were afraid of losing the friendship you had. Like all the other girls in the cast, she had moon eyes for Bernardo.

• • •

Folder: New_Book
File Name: Senior_ year, Part 1
Date Modified: 8 August 1997

Senior year you take his class again. Daniel and the other ducklings have graduated, and you get to sit in the front row. He's also advisor for the yearbook, and the English Department faculty have elected you the editor.

One day, passing in the hall, you try to look pleasant but your heart isn't in it. "What?" he says.

You shrug. "Nothing."

"It doesn't look like nothing. Come," he says, and turns around and walks back in the direction from which he's come. Outside the front office, he stops. You stop. "What's your next class?"

"English. Mrs. Eisenberg."

"I'll take care of it. Stay." He holds out a hand as for a dog in training, and enters the front office. The faces of the two secretaries immediately light up, and soon they are laughing, watching him as if he is the star on stage. Which he is.

He's back a few moments later. "Let's go," he says, and you follow him to the exit.

A light rain is falling and you wish you'd brought a jacket. The school sits in a valley facing the mountain for which it was named. When he turns away from the student parking lot toward the faculty cars, you have to scramble to keep at his heels. You spot his car, famous among his ducklings: a red Alfa Romeo.

This is the first time you've been in his car. It looks cramped but you both slide in easily. You note the leather seats, the stick shift; you don't know how to drive one of those. It sounds like an explosion starting, and the car trembles, but soon everything settles down. You feel suddenly cold, and noticing, he turns on the heat.

You want to ask what he told the secretaries, how he got you out of class, but you fear he'll think you're questioning his powers.

He zips around the other cars and soon, on the highway, he's doing seventy. Surreptitiously you brace yourself against the door. He seems to be enjoying himself, as if he drives this way all the time. He's left the windshield wipers on intermittent, so the world blurs, then one pass of the wipers and all is clear again. You catch yourself awaiting each new pass.

He pulls into Friendly's, leaves the car running. "How do you take your coffee?"

"Milk," you manage, and he's gone, returning with two coffee cups he hands you to hold. Then you're off again, taking the back route through town, passing only a few blocks from the house where you and your parents live, turning onto a dirt road that ends with him parking in an isolated spot a few feet from the deserted shore of Otis Lake.

"Warm enough now?" he asks, and you say "Sure" without thinking. He turns off the car and you hand him his coffee. It tastes good going down. You usually don't drink coffee in the morning, you're in too much of a rush to get to school, and you can buy soda in the machines but not coffee. Coffee is an adult drink, and in the eyes of those who run the school, students are not adults. Everyone believes this except Mr. P.

"So out with it," he says.

"What?"

"You've been mooning around as if somebody ran over your dog."

You can't help but laugh. But he won't let you off the hook. "So?"

"It's stupid," you say.

"I've heard stupid before. I'm familiar with the term."

"I don't know. I'm so tired of this town, this school. Of high school. I can't wait to get away."

"Who is she?"

He's smiling, his eyes tender but amused.

You consider arguing: why does it have to be a girl? "Suzanne Martin," you say.

"Still? I threw you two together so many times last year, by now you should be attached at the crotch."

"She has a boyfriend."

"I see."

"He's not in school. He dropped out. He's twenty. He works at the racetrack." When he doesn't respond, you continue. It feels like all your breath is galloping off with your words. "She says she might quit school herself, go off and live with him. I guess he makes the circuit of race tracks in the Northeast. I don't think he's important though. Some kind of exercise rider, maybe."

"So are you genuinely concerned for her welfare? Or just pissed off because you never got to fuck her?"

You flinch, glare at him.

"You do want to fuck her," he says. "Don't you?"

"It's not like that," you argue.

"You mean if she came up to you right now and asked you to go off with her somewhere so you could fuck, you'd say no?"

You give him your most disgusted look; you're offended by such language, such bluntness, such a crass idea. Inside, you believe yourself a coward, but on the outside, you strive to appear a gentleman. The rain spreads a film across the windshield, as if everything outside is out of focus, and only those things inside the car – the shiny dashboard, the brown knob on the gearshift, the wedding ring on the hand that's close to you, now that he's shifted toward you – are real.

You want to assure him you'd absolutely say no. As if there'd ever be a chance of something like that happening. But in a corner of your mind you're thinking, What if she convinced you she wanted to?

"To be honest, I don't know what I'd do. I've never been in that situation before."

"You're a virgin."

The term doesn't sound right; it makes you think of religion.

"Never fucked anyone," he explains when you don't respond.

Frowning, you shake your head.

"Ever get a blow job?"

You're certain your face is reddening. You squirm, wishing you'd never run into him in the hallway.

"I get it. Nice boys don't get blowjobs. Or is it, nice girls don't give them?"

You try an end run. "Why do they call it that anyway? It makes it sound like the girl is blowing out a candle."

"Ever seen a guy get a blowjob?"

You try to make your sigh sound like he's asked if you've ever watched someone slit their throat.

"Not even in a movie?"

You want to say, I don't watch those kind of movies. "No."

"Ever had a girl take out your dick and hold it in her hand?"

"I don't see why we have to get into my whole sexual history."

"Doesn't seem like much of a history to me."

You know he likes to shock. Wants to push you outside your comfort zone, force you to look at things you'd rather close your eyes to. You've seen him do it over and over with actors on stage. He presents it as philosophy: an actor's job to inhabit what makes other people flee.

It feels like he's been moving closer. He seems too big for his seat, for this small car. The door handle digs into your side; as he's sprawled, you've inched away.

"You do jerk off, right?"

You really don't want to respond. The truth is you jerk off a lot, so much that at times you've thought yourself abnormal. But you can't tell him that. What if he decides you're a freak? What if he tells the other ducklings, "Stay away from that guy"?

"I thought we were talking about Suzanne," you say.

"I don't think this is about Suzanne at all."

He takes a sip of coffee, opens the window, pours out what's left. You drink some of yours and hold onto it, even though the coffee is cold.

"Look," he says, turning toward you. "You're a talented kid. Not so much as an actor, you're okay on stage, but you're an amazing writer. I wish I could write as well as you. You can really go places with that talent."

All your frustration and discomfort flies away with those words. Does he mean it? He's often said what separates him from other teachers – from adults in general – is, he doesn't bullshit.

"But you're too timid. You're repressed. Too much a mama's boy. Too much a goddamned New Englander."

You're back to feeling stung, and for a moment you want to tell him you were born in New York City. But what good would that do? You only lived there the first six months of your life. Besides, the way he's described you is what you secretly fear is true.

"You want to be a nice guy. Your father's a nice guy, he really is. But that's all he is. You can be more."

He sits up. You recognize this voice: lecture mode. His passionate breath forms a cloud on the windshield. "Look at Hemingway, at Fitzgerald. They went out and took what they wanted, they embraced life. All life – the good, the bad, the ugly and the beautiful. The pure and the gross.

"You want life to be nice. Life isn't nice. It's this slobbering, bloody beast. You can climb onto its back and let it take you for a wild ride beyond your imaginings, or you can curl up and hide and hope it passes by without noticing you."

"I want to do something great," you hear yourself say. "I want to be special."

"Then you need to open your arms to life. All life. You can't sit back and cringe when somebody asks if you like taking your dick in your hand and jerking off. Or worse, glare at the person asking, as if you're a saint and they're demented. As if shit doesn't pour out of you the same way it pours out of every asshole that ever lived."

It's an acting challenge to convince him you mean what he wants you to say. "You're right," you tell him. "I want to be open to life. I don't know how."

"For a start, stop trying to ignore the parts of life that aren't pretty. Stop asking yourself, *What will my mother think of this?* before you decide what *you* think of it. That's your biggest problem: you try to pretend you're the son you think she'll approve of. Everything else, you despise. Stop running from life because you've decided she would not approve."

You want to defend your mother, but you stay quiet. This assessment, too, you have secretly believed is true. When you can, you try to be perfect for her. And when you can't, you pretend you're invisible.

What's more astounding is how well he seems to know your mother. You can recall the two of them meeting only once, last spring, to say hello before one of the performances of *West Side Story.*

Something shifts in Mr. P's manner, and you understand it's time to go. His hand taps your thigh. "You'll get there," he says, "if you want to." He grins, his eyes full of promise. "I'll help."

"I do," you vow.

• • •

Folder: New_Book
File Name: Senior_Year_Part_2
Date Modified: 11 August 1997

"Has anyone ever talked with you about sex before?"

You're sitting in his car, same spot, except a blanket of ice and snow carpets the surface of the lake. He keeps his car running, the heat on, no lights inside or out except for the vague misty light from a nearly full moon.

You've been having these conversations regularly of late. He rarely takes you out of school, but he's made you assistant director of the Spring musical, and he picks you up sometimes to drive you to evening rehearsal. After everyone has gone home, he'll get coffee and drive you here, for conversation.

You are no longer surprised, or squeamish, when the subject turns to sex. It always does.

"Not my parents," you tell him. "My mother couldn't talk about that, of course, and my father – well, you know my father."

"None of your friends?"

"Not really. I always thought they knew stuff I didn't – I didn't want them to see how inexperienced I was."

"What about movies? Books?"

You laugh. *"Portnoy's Complaint.* I actually believed I was the only person in the world who masturbated, until I read that book. Then I figured, me and Philip Roth were the only two."

Even in the darkness you can make out his smile.

"I'm serious," you tell him. "That's a true story."

He reaches over and scruffs the back of your neck. You've even gotten used to this playful touching, mostly. At least you believe you've successfully hidden the urge to flinch when you spot his hand approaching.

"It's time for your lessons to begin."

· · ·

Over the next weeks, he teaches you. The lake is a favorite spot for these lessons, but any empty parking lot will do, and a few times, with the two of you the last to leave a late-night rehearsal, you'll get into his car and he'll drive from one corner of the school parking lot to the other, settling in on the far side overlooking the athletic fields, too remote for any cars on the highway to spot you.

He explains a woman's anatomy first. How a woman's nipples can get erect, hard as an eraser, how you can nibble them lightly between your teeth. The parts of the female genitalia, what each one is named. Where to touch, rub, gently pinch. What you can do with your tongue.

You are seventeen but you feel like seven.

You tell him everything, how at twelve you felt a pulsing intensity between your legs one early morning, and half asleep, brought your hand down low, no conscious thought, and out shot something hot and wet. You thought it must be blood, that you were dying, until terrified you drew back the blanket and discovered a substance you'd never seen before. You thought you'd pissed yourself but this was different, more like the phlegm you hacked up from a cold. It felt like a spider's web when you rubbed your fingers through it. Meanwhile, your penis, which had seemed so full of force, now hung limp.

"You honestly had no idea what happened?"

You shrug. "Where would I learn about that? I had only myself, a vivid imagination and very few facts." You laugh. "That's a dangerous combination."

These lessons don't cover anatomy only; he teaches philosophy too. How sex is the most intimate way two people have to express their love for each other. How there's also fucking, which is simply having a good time. How all life has to be sought out and embraced; if you're going to be a writer, you have to be able to understand the mind of a rapist or a serial killer just as deeply as the mind of a hero or a saint.

"That doesn't mean you go out and rape or kill someone," he explains. "It means you accept that you could — that you have it in you to understand someone who does those things, because in different circumstances, in a different world, you could have done them, too."

Experience is all. It's the pathway to everything you dream of accomplishing. A writer writes from experience. Every moment of living is an opportunity to gather more experience. Your mother is afraid of experience. She wants you to be afraid, too.

"Sometimes I think I might be gay," you say.

"Do you find yourself sexually attracted to men?"

You don't, have never imagined yourself that way, even accidentally. All your fantasies involve women. "I don't know," you tell him, and laugh. "I play football and all, but most of those guys, I don't even like them. They feel like some other species to me."

"That's because you're sensitive. Most guys aren't allowed to be sensitive. Or they're afraid to be." He turns to you. "Just because you're sensitive doesn't mean you're gay."

This next pops out of its own accord: "I'm scared of women."

"That's because of your mother."

You've had this discussion before: your mother is too powerful, too controlling; she's held you back, needs to keep you close, fears letting you develop into your own person because then you'll leave her behind.

You've argued she wants the best for you. That she's afraid because she has so little joy in her life outside of you. She goes to all your games, your plays, serves you giant steaks for dinner when you come home late from practice, sitting with you at the table while your father is off somewhere working. She hasn't had a fair life, you argue. She was in love with a British officer during the war but he died. She wanted to be a painter but her father wouldn't allow it. She never thought she'd end up married to a man like your father.

These are arguments you never win.

"We were talking about fucking," he says. "How you don't like to say the word."

"I say 'fucking' all the time," you reply.

"As an adjective. Not a verb."

You almost say, What's the difference? But you hold back, because he'll tell you.

"Let me hear you say, 'I'd really like to fuck Suzanne Martin.'"

You look at him and laugh, as if he might be joking, although you know he's not. You decide to say it, to shut him up, but you can't push the words out. "It sounds vulgar," you tell him. "It's an insult to her."

"So Suzanne Martin doesn't fuck? Not with that twenty-year-old cowboy of hers?"

For a moment you picture it, her at least, in a stable; the guy remains a blur.

"You can't tell me you wouldn't like to give her a roll in the hay."

You blush, fearing he's seen into your fantasy.

"You'd love to fuck her brains out. Admit it."

"I would," you say, softly, as if the words might boomerang and strike you.

"Would what?"

"I'd love to fuck Suzanne Martin!" you shout, on a burst of energy and frustration.

He grins. "There. Feel better?"

You won't tell him, but you do.

• • •

Folder: New_ Book
File Name: A_New_Family?
Date Modified: 17 August 1997

That winter, living at home with your mother has been tense. All the little sins bug her: how loud you play your music; how you finish dinner quickly and rush off to your room; how you stay out too late on Saturday night. The big sins are worse: you've been receiving information from colleges in California, New Mexico, Hawaii. When the fat envelopes come she lays them on the kitchen counter so you have to pass her to pick them up. And the worse sin of all: you don't disguise that you'd rather be out with him than home with her.

There's still half a year to go. You don't know how you'll make it.

You are certain you've outgrown your life. This insignificant, stifling town; this insignificant, stifling school; this insignificant, stifling family. Everything conspires to keep you from the great things you know you could accomplish.

And for the first time you can remember, you voice in front of your mother some of the curses you've always smothered until you were locked away alone. You still can't hurl them at her face but shout as you stomp upstairs to your room while she stands in the kitchen smoking, her back to you. Then one Sunday night you say you're going out for a drive, and she replies, "No." You only want to get some air, drive around a while, maybe see if Suzanne Martin wants to meet at Friendly's, but it's late, there's an inch of new snow on the ground, and you fumble explaining why going out now is so important.

"You can't have the car," she says. "For one night, you can stay home."

It's her car, and you understand there've been times she's let you use it when she wanted it for herself. But this feels bigger than cars. This connects to all the years she's smothered you, all the fear you've inherited from her, to Hemingway and Fitzgerald, sexual repression, her desperation over losing control of you.

You walk to the back door, pull on your coat, grab the car keys off the hook. "I'm going," you say.

"You're not."

"You can't stop me."

You've always slid around each other, turning direct hits into glancing blows, but now she comes straight for you as you stand at the back door, reaches to snag the keys, and when you pull them away, her eyes lock onto yours, and suddenly you see yourselves not for how close you are but how far apart you will become. You don't move against her open palm rising toward you, you don't believe it, even after it leaves your cheek stinging. She gasps, perhaps not believing it herself, or perhaps because her hand stings as much as your face.

"Keep your fucking keys," you hiss, hurling them down. They skitter across the linoleum.

You're not sure how you make it outside, if she speaks or moves or remains statue still. A slip on the ice and the cold biting your ears break the spell, announcing you've forgotten a hat, worn shoes not suited for winter walking. But there's no going back, and you start moving, following some unspoken force within, imagining where the path you are on will lead, not believing you'll really get there.

Now you're crunching along the hard-packed snow on a back country road, the shapes around you merely different shades of dark, and above, a sky brilliant with stars. You've come the first couple miles on adrenaline, figure you shouldn't have more than a mile left to go. You're grateful for the winter coat, the scarf and mittens, but you wish you had something to cover your head. Your ears are so cold they burn, and your cheeks are stiff. The cold is beginning to drill into your feet now, too.

You pass a farmhouse, lights inside, smoke curling from the chimney. Imagine being invited to sit by the fire. That's all you need, a few minutes to warm by the fire. But that's fantasy, and you gaze to the other side, over snow-covered pastureland rolling back to woods.

You're walking to Mr. P's house. You will ask him to adopt you. You've heard he did this before, he and his wife brought a troubled teenage boy to live with them for a year. Under their influence, the boy changed from juvenile delinquent to police cadet.

His wife seems to like you. "Jonathan speaks very highly of you," she told you once.

Ahead, at last, you see his house. A large white house, not opulent, set back from the road. A light in the front room, another upstairs. You scrounge in your pocket, pull out a paper towel, take off your gloves, blow your nose. Blow warm breath into your palms and place them over your tingling ears.

You gaze up at the crescent moon. Think how crazy this is; it's probably ten o'clock by now on a Sunday night. All your anger at your mother has dissipated, or frozen up, and you think, *I should just go home*, but you can't bear the miles you'll have to walk just to keep this venture private. You could hitchhike but it's been a half hour since the last car passed.

You slip a little on the driveway, with its inch of new snow. Nearing, you can make out furniture in the living room, a bookcase in the back, no people. You think, What if they're off somewhere making love?

"Fucking," you mutter, a thin smile breaking your cold-tightened lips.

A figure moves past the window: his wife. You find her attractive, though plainer than you'd have guessed his wife would be. She's also an English teacher, at a rival high school. You've met her a few times, and once or twice, brought her into your fantasies.

You wonder what they do at night. Read a lot, listen to music. You doubt they watch much TV, PBS maybe. They might take turns making dinner, help each other cleaning up. Pause often to kiss or touch, speak to each other in loving tones. He told you once they have no children because they enjoy their life too much to let a child disrupt it. But he was talking about babies. If you lived here, you wouldn't be disruptive.

You clear your throat, approach the porch. The snow on your soles catches in the rubber mat on the top step, and you pause to kick your shoes clean. You hear a muted buzz when you press the doorbell. There's an inner wooden door and an outer glass one that will have to open outward. You back out of its way.

The porch light comes on. The inner door opens, a quizzical look on her face, perhaps worry too. She's wearing loose faded jeans and a bulky sweater. You've never seen her dressed casually, and this shocks you more than it should, the idea that maybe there's life being lived here you haven't imagined.

"Oh," she says, recognizing you, and pushes the glass door open a few inches. "Are you all right?" Her gaze searches beyond you, for a car no doubt. "Has something happened?"

"I'm okay," you assure her. "It's just – is Mr. P –" You can't bring yourself to call him "Jonathan," even though he's told you to.

"Come in," she says, and the welcome rush of heat mixes with the smell of her sweet perfume as you slip past her. You stay on the inside mat. Even though you kicked the snow off your shoes, they're wet, and the rich tan carpet looks brand new.

"Do you want some coffee or hot chocolate?" she asks. "You must be cold."

You shake your head. "I'm okay."

You can tell she feels awkward, and you hate yourself for causing this. "Jonathan's upstairs," she says. "I'll get him."

When she goes upstairs, you look around. There is a television off in a corner, but the chairs are arranged so that people sitting in them can look at each other, not like in your house where all the chairs directly face the set. There's a piano in back you can imagine him playing.

A shawl is draped across the chair you suspect Mrs. P has been sitting in. On a low table in front of her sits a stack of papers. Of course, Mrs. P is a more conventional English teacher than her husband; she grades papers. You cringe at having disturbed her. Does she need to finish grading before she can go to bed?

You hear muffled talking upstairs, then he comes down alone. He's also wearing a knitted sweater, but one badly stretched out of shape, with a hole near the elbow. He manages an amused smile when he looks at you, then he holds up a hand when you start to speak, puts on his coat, and opens the front door. "Let's go," he says, ushering you out.

You go down the steps while he stays on the top one, buttoning his coat. "Where's your car?" he asks. You shrug. "How'd you get here?"

You shrug again.

"What? Out for a midnight stroll, just thought you'd drop by to say hello?" You search for tension in his laugh but if it's there, he's hidden it well.

"I couldn't take it anymore," you say.

He's searching his pockets, not finding what he's after. "Stay here," he says, goes inside, returns holding car keys. "We'll take the Accord."

For the first time you notice the car sitting in front of the closed garage door. This must be his wife's car. He unlocks the doors, gets in and starts it, but as you join him he hops out again and begins brushing off the snow.

He's turned the heat full blast but only cold air's pouring out so far, biting like little needles when you get too close. You unzip your coat, stick your hands into the warmth of your armpits.

"I'm sorry," you say when he climbs back inside, but he doesn't answer, concentrating on backing out of the driveway. A tantalizing warmth slips out the heating vents.

He heads toward town, still not speaking, and you stay silent too, waiting for his cue. You don't wear a watch and there's no clock in the car, but it can't be midnight yet because Friendly's is still open. He gets the usual two coffees but instead of heading for your regular spot at the lake, he simply drives to the far end of the parking lot and puts the car in park.

"Talk to me," he says.

"We had a fight. My mother and me." Fearing that doesn't sound important enough, you add, "I can't take it anymore." And then, "She hit me."

Greeted by a chuckle. "You're a hell of a lot bigger than she is. I doubt she could hurt you much."

"She's never done that before."

"Were you acting like an asshole?"

"I just wanted to go out for a drive. You know? There's no peace and quiet, she's got that damn TV on all the time, I just wanted to go out and clear my head."

"It's late," he says. "It's Sunday night. It's cold as shit."

"I know. I'm sorry, I shouldn't have bothered you. And your wife," you add.

"I still can't believe you walked all the fucking way to my house." There's enough light to see his expression, more impressed than angry. "It must be ten degrees out there."

"I was hoping –" But you can't say what you want to. "I can't take it anymore."

When he doesn't reply, you say, "She's jealous. Of my friends, of how I'm going to get to leave home and go to college. She's jealous of you."

You look at him as you say this last, hoping it will stir something you haven't seen so far. "I can't live there anymore," you add.

He says, his voice calm, almost disinterested. "What are you going to do about it?"

"I don't know. Maybe I'll run away from home." A laugh, to make sure he knows you're joking.

"What you're going to do is figure out a way to deal with it. To make peace. You're impatient, I get that, but you're not going to fuck up your life just because you and your mother had a fight." He pauses, lets his voice settle. "Besides, if you really did run away now, your mother would be right there running alongside you."

You don't understand what he means. Perhaps sensing that, he explains, "You've got her so deeply ingrained in your head, it doesn't matter if she's there physically or not. You still think like her, you see the world like her, you judge yourself and other people the way you think she would judge them."

"But I'm not that way anymore. The stuff we've talked about –"

"Is like a few drops of fresh water tossed into an ocean. There's still way too much salt."

You sigh, drink your coffee, try to ease the tightness in your chest. The words are right there in your head, banging to get out: *What if I came to live with you? Only for a short time?* But you can't say them.

He taps your thigh. "Drink up," he says. "I'll take you home."

• • •

Folder: New_Book
File Name: First_of_Many
Date Modified: 23 August 1997

His hand settling on your thigh, warm, strong, mean-ing business. You struggle not to let him notice how you flinch, but he senses it anyway. "It's affection," he says. "That's all. Two people who care about each other, show-ing their affection."

You nod, want to say, I can't help it, but can't.

"It's not sex," he says, with an impish laugh. Then his hand slides between your legs and clamps down. You sit up and shrink, both at the same time. "That's sex," he says. "It's no big deal. Sex is fun, sex is play. Sex is affection tak-en to its natural endpoint."

You feel nothing beneath his hand; that part of you has died. No one but yourself has ever touched you there. At first his hand is like a blanket thrown over the area, but then it turns to individual fingers and you wriggle about, wondering if there's a way you can prove him wrong when he says you've made little progress, when your body proves him right.

You've recently turned 18. You've been hoping for a celebration, maybe he'd take you to a bar in New York State, where you can drink legally now. Instead, you end up in his car again, parked off a dirt road in the middle of the woods.

His head draws close enough that you feel the stubble of his whiskers on your cheek. "It's perfectly natural," he says. "Every animal on the planet has sex."

Your mind flies off, trying to think of an exception. An amoeba? You've read or heard somewhere that an earth-worm can have sex with itself. You try to imagine a mouse climbing on the back of another mouse, like rutting horses, but it all seems crazy. Why does it have to be so powerful? Why should it feel so intense, so encompassing – so good – when you use your own hand, and so opposite when the hand is his?

Now his hand slides along the inside of your thigh. Not long ago you went on a date, no girl you'd ever fall in love with, but before taking her home, you parked along a dirt road in the woods just like this and kissed; she let you feel her breasts (through her bra of course) and her hand rubbed this same spot on your thigh. It brought a lightning charge of pleasure. Now, the same touch from him makes you feel empty and forlorn.

You can understand his philosophy in the abstract. This means nothing. But why then does it feel like it means everything? You let your lips open when his mouth presses against yours, his fat snake tongue forcing its way inside. You manage to bring your arms up to embrace him. There's no passion in you, but you love him and you cherish all that he has done for you. You're convinced you've done nothing for him, ever, until now.

Chapter Twelve

I was stunned. It felt like I'd just been handed a piece of my life – a piece I did not want.

I stared at the words glowing on the screen in front of me. I needed to be calm and rational. I was a fiction writer; this could all be made up. Except it mentioned Suzanne Martin, the girl I'd had a crush on in sixth grade. Why would I make up a fictional character and then give her a real person's name? Could Daniel O. be the Daniel Jessie had said Aaron talked about? I'd found that playbill for *West Side Story* with me in the cast playing Doc. And reading about Mr. P., I was certain I had known him.

Most damning of all, it felt real.

Finding it hard to breathe, I went to the platform out back and gulped in air. It was a gray, lifeless day, the air thick and heavy, uncomfortably warm, with no breeze. It felt like a dreary rain was coming, but the sky was pale and still, with none of the angry, gray-bellied clouds that swirled around the sky before a real storm. I brushed a cobweb from the Adirondack chair and sat.

Some of it being true didn't mean all of it was true. Like that basketball story, the boy and his father were real but that particular game never happened. Since I'd been in a play that he directed,

I'd certainly known this Mr. P. But the details of the relationship – especially that last part – could have been made up.

Why I'd want to make up something like that eluded me. On the other hand, if it really happened, why would I ever put it into words that other people could read? A teenage boy being kissed by his male teacher wasn't exactly something you shouted to the world.

I shivered thinking about it, suddenly cold despite the heat-and-moisture-saturated air. This was what I'd been writing at the end of the summer. The date for the last entry was two days before my accident.

I felt drained but needed to move. I climbed down onto the railroad tracks and followed the curving trail around the bottom of the hill and into thick woods. When I was a kid I used to walk the railroad tracks past Green River where my grandfather took me to fish, and where later I rode to on my bicycle. The tracks ran parallel to the river, then they veered off into pasture and corn-fields, seeming to go on forever, and I imagined I was on my own, free and unencumbered, walking across the country.

These tracks remained locked in dense woods. Some of the rotted ties crumbled when I stepped on them, and the sharp rocks dug into the soles of my feet. I'd hoped that walking would help me feel stronger, but the opposite was happening. When I paused, I could feel the bristles on Mr. P.'s face pricking the delicate skin around my mouth, the fat snake of a tongue burrowing inside. I thought about the times with Sarah when I'd felt as if I was thirteen again, a timid and confused adolescent. Whatever had happened between me and Mr. P., I must have been seventeen or so at the time. But I felt suddenly younger than that, younger than thirteen even. When I pictured the two of us sitting in his car, he reaching toward me, I saw myself as a small, helpless child.

That child came to life and now hid inside me, convinced someone or something was tracking him, and could pounce at any time.

It wasn't rational, it wasn't fair. I wasn't a small child, I was a fully grown man. And yet, I felt terrified.

I turned around and headed home, alert to everything around me all the way.

• • •

That night I called Sarah. "I'm coming down with something," I told her, in the scratchy, burdened voice I'd perfected as a child pleading for a day off from school. "It's probably the flu."

It was the first true lie I'd told her, and it stung.

She made a sympathetic sound. "Are you in bed?"

"I just got out of bed to call you. I'll go back when I'm done."

"Drink plenty of liquids. When I come on Saturday, I'll make soup."

"I was thinking maybe you shouldn't come."

Her silence made it feel as if I'd slapped her. Quickly I explained, "I don't want you to catch what I've got."

"How do you feel? Do you have a sore throat?"

"A little." As a child I usually went for a stomachache, which could get better quickly, so I might not have to stay in bed all day. "A headache too. I feel achy all over."

"Do you have a temperature."

"I don't know."

A gentle laugh. "I bet you don't have a thermometer."

"Right now I only want to go back to bed."

"You should. Sleep is the best thing for you. Take some aspirin. Do you have aspirin?"

I said I did, fearing that if I said no, she'd drive out here to deliver it.

"Usually you can take two every four hours. Check the label on the bottle."

Instinct told me not to push a decision on the weekend, but I knew I'd feel better if it was settled. "What do we do about Saturday?"

"I've had my flu shot so you don't need to worry about giving it to me. It sounds like you might need someone to look after you."

176

"Being around me won't be very entertaining."

"You mean you won't be performing your famous song and dance routine?"

I guess I deserved her sarcasm. I should have known that "entertaining" wouldn't go over well.

"You go to bed, get some rest. It's only Thursday, we've got some time to decide. Tomorrow I'll call when I get home from work and we'll see how you feel. Does that sound okay?"

I told her yes. What else could I say?

After hanging up, I began to feel some of the symptoms I'd described to Sarah. Headache. Sore throat. Achiness all over. Can your mind create the flu?

I took some aspirin, laid around in front of the television for a while, then went to bed early, wrapping myself in blankets. I slept fitfully, plagued by a series of dreams. In one, a small boy raced across a series of flat mesas. They looked like a row of giant molars, a deep crevasse between each one. The boy was very small, mouse-sized, and the mesas enormous, each the size of a football field. The boy was colored yellow, the mesa's green, the crevasses black, wide and foreboding. If these mesas were teeth, the crevasses would be giant cavities. The boy appeared to be skipping. Perhaps he was happy. He had no idea of the danger he was in.

The dream changed. Another boy, the same age as the boy on the mesas, sat on a park bench in a clearing in the woods. His brother, ten or more years older, sat beside him. A figure appeared, a man's body with the head of a goat. The goat-headed man tapped the boy's brother on the shoulder and gestured toward the woods. The boy's brother rose and followed the goat-headed man into the woods. The goat-headed man acted as if he hadn't noticed the boy sitting beside his brother. Being left alone frightened the boy and he trailed his brother and the goat-headed man at a distance.

In the woods they came upon a village full of children singing and dancing. They were all very happy. They were small, almost the boy's size, but they behaved like adults. Their dance was very sexual. The boy's brother joined in.

Suddenly the boy was back on the bench, sitting by himself. The goat-headed man appeared and told the boy he didn't belong there. The boy wasn't sure if he meant the park bench or the village of old children dancing in the woods, but he was afraid to ask a question. He didn't like the goat-headed man but with his brother gone, there was no one else he could trust. The path they took to reach the village was now grown over with brush. The boy was confused: did he really have a brother? There was only the goat-headed man now.

I awoke to darkness, tangled in blankets and drenched in sweat. I felt like a shell, empty inside, even before I remembered why.

It was a little after two a.m. I did not sleep again. When the light of dawn spread throughout the room, I dragged myself out of bed and into the shower. The hot water was soothing, but afterwards, my body felt heavy and sore, my whole head clogged up as from a cold. The sunlight burned my eyes.

I resisted going back to bed. I didn't want to lie there wide awake, but I also feared a sleep haunted by more dreams. I made coffee and went into my office. The screen was dark, and I reached out a finger tentatively, as if reaching into fire, and tapped a key. The screen lit up, filled with words. My words, that I wished I'd never found, never written.

It was hard not blaming the USB stick. Sarah had warned me about computer viruses, and it felt as if this writing was a virus that had corrupted my whole life. It was hard to be rational when the feelings were so intense. I felt like a helpless child. I felt like a criminal. I felt like some kind of monster that, once seen for what I was, would scare away Sarah and anyone else who might ever have cared for me.

These feelings weren't rational. But they were real, and I didn't know how to shake them.

• • •

Our Friday night phone call went mostly as I'd expected, and feared. Sarah insisted on coming, and I had no energy to argue. It was hard to muster the effort to care.

In rare lucid moments, I tried to break down what was happening. In high school, a teenage boy had a relationship with a male teacher. The teacher kissed him, and touched him sexually. Judging by the reaction of the boy, it had been traumatic.

This boy had almost certainly been me, and at some level, I had never gotten over it. Perhaps I pushed it into some compartment with a metaphorical lock on the door. Perhaps I used Mr. P's language to pretend it was no big deal. Even if that last file was the end of everything, if nothing more took place between us, simply reading my own words had knocked me back to being a weak and frightened child.

Harder to pin down were the other feelings, that I was some sort of criminal, or a monster. The fact that it was a relationship between two males likely mattered, although I hadn't detected any negative feelings in me toward homosexuals or homosexuality. My feelings likely connected somehow back to my mother, as almost everything about me seemed to do. There were intimations in the writing that I'd let Mr. P. down, failed to be or do what I knew would please him. All these things probably contributed to my sense of myself as a miserable failure.

Was I such a miserable failure that I'd concluded, one late Sunday night, that I no longer deserved to live?

On Friday night I took a sleeping pill, hoping to smother all dreams. When I felt a weight pressing on the mattress and a hand laid flat upon my forehead, I thought I was back in the hospital. It felt like the middle of the night, although a gray and gloomy light filled the room.

"I don't think you have a fever," Sarah said, and for a moment, I confused her with Dale, not sure which was the nurse and which the police. "Slide this under your tongue," she said, and later, after taking it out, announced, "Ninety-nine."

"How did you get in?" I croaked.

"I'm a police officer. We have our ways." She laughed. "No, I'm kidding. You really need to remember to lock those sliding glass doors at night." A little guiltily, she added, "I knocked, but you didn't answer. I figured you'd be sleeping and didn't want to wake you. So I did a little investigating."

"Nancy Drew," came out of me.

"I was always partial to the Hardy Boys."

Just that brief exchange exhausted me, my eyes longing to close. Sarah noticed. "You rest. I brought some things to read. Later I'll make chicken soup." She grinned. "I brought some movies we can watch, too. When you feel up to it."

My mind was fuzzy. I recalled feeling dread about Sarah being here but I couldn't remember why. Then it came back to me. That story. Had I left it on my computer, left the computer on? What if Sarah went to watch a movie and stumbled upon that writing instead?

I yanked back the blankets and sat up, my feet reaching the floor just as the room began to spin. My head and shoulders felt too heavy to hold up, and with nothing to grab onto, I fell back, managing to curl into a fetal position and pull the blankets up to my chin. I couldn't believe I'd made myself sick just by pretending, but at least it would help convince Sarah I hadn't lied. But right then, all I wanted was sleep.

• • •

"You're up!"

Sarah sat at the kitchen table reading a magazine. I knew I was feeling better when a joke popped into my head about the magazine being something like *Guns and Ammo Quarterly*, and my more prudent side chose to stay quiet.

"How do you feel? Better?"

"Like I'm tired of lying in bed." Said with the frustration and fatigue of a person who'd been sick for days.

"You look better. Your face has more color."

I took a chair across from her at the table. "I really don't want to give you this," I said.

She put aside what turned out to be a women's magazine and got me a cup of coffee.

My first sip perked me up a little. Like chipping off the first layer of ice on a winter morning.

"What time did you get here?"

"You don't remember?"

"Time's a little blurry these days."

"Around eleven."

I remembered her weight on the mattress, the warm hand on my forehead. Something about a door I forgot to lock.

There was food laid out on the counter behind her. A big pot on the stove, a pile of chicken on a plate, a bowl of cooked white rice, a chopping board with diced carrots and celery. The bowls and chopping board didn't look familiar, and I didn't have a pot that big. Had she brought her whole kitchen?

Her backpack sat by the door, alongside a larger bag, an overnight bag, I realized, and it hit me that she would be staying the night with me. I forced myself to stand. "I need to take a shower," I announced.

When she came around the table, I stood with arms at my sides and accepted her gentle hug. "Do me a favor." She peered into my eyes. "Don't lock the door."

"I'm not an invalid."

"Humor me. Please?"

Her saintly patience felt grating. I never really understood her interest in me in the first place. Her first visit to the hospital was part of her job, but after that? One time she'd said she'd come by to pick up her mother who volunteered in the gift shop, but how did I even know if that was true? And volunteering to drive to my house and pick up my clothes, then drive me home when the hospital released me? She'd admitted she and her partner had questioned if what had happened was really an accident. They likely dismissed that theory for lack of evidence. Wasn't that how they phrased it on all the cop shows on TV? Lack of evidence, which didn't mean lack of guilt.

In the shower my mind started racing. What if Sarah and her partner really did believe my crash wasn't accidental, and they'd cooked up some scheme for Sarah to get close to me, pretending to be my friend so she could keep an eye on me? But why bother? I wasn't some bank robber who'd hidden away the loot. Why should it even matter to Sarah or her partner why my car had crashed – or if it might crash again?

Perhaps it wasn't a scheme, and Sarah was only looking out for me in case I really was suicidal. She seemed to disapprove when I told her I'd rented a car. She really did have a good heart, she liked to help people in need. Her interest in me was probably that: altruistic.

I fought those thoughts, even as they seemed more and more plausible. It wasn't as if she made me check in with her every day, like a parole officer. She knew I'd seen a shrink but didn't ask what we'd talked about. And the other day, when we'd torn off each other's clothes, wasn't altruism.

"Chill," I told myself. Just get through the weekend any way you can. You have a ready-made excuse: you really aren't feeling like yourself.

· · ·

The soup was excellent, and the aroma filled the house. Sarah even brought a loaf of Italian bread that went along nicely.

"Ideally," she said, "the broth should sit in the fridge overnight, but I didn't want to wait."

I told her it was perfect as it was.

I attempted to help her clean up, but she told me to go sit down and rest somewhere, and I plopped onto the couch and gazed at the backyard. Later, even though I heard her come up behind me, I jerked when she touched me, but soon relaxed into her firm and soothing hands massaging my shoulders.

I couldn't stifle a moan. "I'm guessing you didn't learn this at the police academy."

"A girl's got her secrets."

She leaned around and kissed me on the cheek. I turned so our lips could find each other but I could sense she wanted more than that, and I twisted free. "Sorry," I told her, "but I'm just not up for it." I didn't mean it in a sexual way but it could have applied.

"It's okay." She came round and sat on the couch, not too close. "Do you want to go back to bed for a while? I wouldn't mind a nap myself." Perhaps anticipating my response, she quickly added, "We could just lie together, sleep a bit. No need to do anything more."

"I don't know. It feels like all I've been doing lately is lying in bed."

We were silent a while, both staring out. A bright red cardinal alit on the platform and sat there, its head darting about.

"I brought movies. Do you want to watch a movie?'"

What I really wanted was to sit there dumbly, staring blankly at that cardinal and the chipmunk that ran out of and then back into a pile of leaves. "I'm sorry I'm so boring," I told Sarah without looking at her, then agreed we should watch a movie.

That perked her up, and she popped to her feet and disappeared, returning with a laptop I didn't recognize. "I brought mine," she said, setting it on the coffee table in front of us. "It's got a bigger screen and higher resolution."

She fiddled a bit, searching out an outlet to plug it in, collecting a handful of books to place under it to raise it up. When I offered to help she told me she had everything under control. With everything set up to her satisfaction, she disappeared again and returned holding two boxes about the size of hardcover books. "Two movies," she announced. "Courtesy of your friendly neighborhood Blockbuster Video."

She'd brought a drama and a comedy. *Casablanca*, she announced, "the great Humphrey Bogart and the even greater Ingrid Bergman," and "the funniest movie of all time, *Young Frankenstein*.

"What'll it be first? Tears of laughter or tears of sadness?"

I pointed to the hand holding the comedy.

"Excellent choice. *Young Frankenstein* it is. Get your popcorn, make your final trip to the bathroom, because once the movie starts, you won't want to step away." She announced it all like a carnival barker, then bowed and grinned at my applause. "Actually, I better take my own advice." She hurried off to the bathroom.

I did the same, and came out to find her bundled under a blanket, which she held up like a tent for me to slide under too. She wriggled, our hips and shoulders bumping. "Sorry I don't have popcorn," she said.

. . .

She was right: *Young Frankenstein* was silly, funny, clever, brilliant. The kind of movie that makes you forget about everything and just give in to laughing. Sarah had clearly seen it several times, as her laughter anticipated the best jokes, and occasionally she tapped me on the arm and warned me to "Get ready," or "Watch this." But in general she wasn't someone who liked to talk through movies, which I found a relief. We didn't cuddle, exactly, but our bodies remained touching, and that felt all right to me.

When it finished, she asked if I was hungry, but I was still full from the soup. "Do you want some coffee?"

I didn't, but told her I'd drink a cup if she made some. When she went off to the kitchen, I drew away the blanket and welcomed the cooler air. The clock said ten past five but my sense of time had been skewered by getting up so late. I thought how we had six or seven more hours to kill before we could go to bed. We had a second movie, but then what? And what about tomorrow? I felt guilty thinking that way, but I wished she hadn't come. I couldn't summon the energy to be entertaining.

We agreed to watch *Casablanca* next. Wanting something sweet with her coffee, Sarah came back with half a bag of Oreos. She ate her cookie like an adult, but in my mind I saw Lisette Sorenson pulling hers apart, and I twitched in discomfort, as if fearing Sarah would pick up Lisette's scent on the bag. That reminded me of the writing on my laptop, how I'd forgotten to check to make sure the computer was turned off, the writing erased, the USB stick hidden away. "Hold on," I told Sarah as she was about to start the movie. "I have to do something first."

The computer was off, the USB stick nowhere in sight. It took me a moment to remember that I'd put it into an envelope which I'd sealed and buried in the bottom of the metal box containing my birth certificate and other papers and photographs. It was still there. The box had an opening for a key to lock it, but I didn't have that key. I put it back on the shelf and piled papers on top of it.

I turned on the computer, worried that I was taking too long. If Sarah asked what I was doing, I'd tell her something vague like "I just remembered I had to take care of something." No folders came up, but a list appeared under "Home," with the names of each of the files containing writing. Had it automatically transferred everything? But when I clicked on the names of the files, I got a message saying these files could not be located.

"Take these away from me," Sarah said when I returned, handing over the bag of Oreos. "I can't be trusted." She headed toward the bathroom. "I'll be there in a minute," she called over her shoulder. "I just need to brush my teeth."

• • •

Casablanca was a good movie, and I could understand why it was popular, but I never connected to it. It clearly put Sarah in a romantic mood, and by the end, she was practically sitting on my lap. I felt a sexual spark when her hand rubbed my thigh, but I didn't respond, and her hand got no more adventurous than that.

"I'm sorry I'm so boring," I told her.

She was putting away her computer, putting back the books. "You're sick. You're entitled to be boring when you're sick."

Darkness had settled outside, and the air coming in through the screen was cold. I closed the sliding glass doors and drew the curtain across them, then returned to the couch. Sarah was still putting things away. When she sat beside me, we stared at the curtain as if still watching cardinals and chipmunks outside.

"I'm going to Massachusetts."

My words surprised me almost as much as they did Sarah. I'd thought, idly, that eventually I ought to visit my hometown, but my tone made it sound like I planned to leave in the morning.

We both stared off at nothing. "When?" she said at last.

"Soon," I said. "Maybe this week. Depends on how I feel."

More silence. I felt the cushions move as she shifted toward me. "Any chance you could hold off a few weeks?"

Our gazes met. "I have some vacation time coming, but I'd have to put in for it, and it would probably take a couple weeks to get approved. If you can wait, we could go up together, split the driving, have an adventure." She made a sweet, cajoling face, like a kid trying to convince her parents that ice cream won't spoil her dinner.

I couldn't understand what was happening. A few days ago, I'd been convinced I was falling in love with this woman, and now all I wanted to do was get away from her.

"I feel like I've been spinning my wheels," I said. "I mean, October's almost over." It wasn't, but she didn't correct me. "So many of my memories are connected to Massachusetts. They stop when I was twelve or thirteen, but I lived there into my twenties. There's so much more to remember. There's my friend Aaron, too. I went to school with him, he'll remember some things. Not to mention just being there, seeing familiar places, all that might trigger my memory."

"I'm not saying don't go. Of course you should go. But if you could hold off a little bit, we could go together."

"I have to do this alone." There was a finality in my voice that probably sounded cruel. Maybe I meant it to be. All the same, I tried to walk it back, just a little.

"I'd love to go up there sometime with you on vacation. But this doesn't feel like the time for that. This is not a vacation for me. This is me trying to get my life back."

"I know," she said, and I could tell she was hurt.

I sat up, took her hand. "I really like you. But I'm a mess right now. Two-thirds of my life is one big fucking blank. I'd say I don't feel like myself, except I have no clue what 'myself' is supposed to feel like. How can I be of any use to another person when I can't even find myself?"

Her head was down, her eyes watching my hand caress the back of hers. "I'm just concerned that it's such a long drive for you to make alone."

Anger flashed inside me, and I struggled to tamp it down. Did she think I was an invalid, that I couldn't drive a car? Or were we back to the accident again, that maybe I'd start looking for a new tree in Massachusetts?

I wasn't thinking straight. I wanted to tell her that: "I'm not thinking straight right now." But I feared she'd use it as a reason I should delay my trip. Ever since I'd announced I was going, the trip felt more and more a certainty, like something I'd planned out and scheduled weeks ago.

As my emotions settled, exhaustion returned. "I feel like crap," I said.

"Why don't you go to bed?"

It was barely nine-thirty. "Did something happen?" I could feel her watching me. "You seem different."

"I got sick," I said, louder than intended. "It's impossible enough dealing with this shit when you're healthy."

"I know," she said, but of course she didn't know. I didn't even know, although I could identify what had triggered it.

"I'm worn out," I said.

"Go on, go to bed. You need your sleep."

"Are you coming?"

"In a little while."

We both stood. I didn't know if I should kiss her or hug her or just exaggerate my tiredness and trudge off to bed. In the end, we opted for a brief hug. She rubbed my back before sending me off.

I wasn't shocked when later, she came in and sat on my bed. "Listen," she said. "I'm going to go home."

Only half awake, I said, "Stay."

"I will if you want me to, but I feel like I'm in the way. You need your rest" – she flashed a grin – "and I can tell you're not someone who likes to be babied."

"I'm sorry I'm so boring."

She made a dismissive sound and gave a flick of her wrist. "Get some rest, and maybe give me a call tomorrow. If you feel better and want to do something, I could come back out. Or if you just want someone to hang out with, I could bring more movies. But if you want to be alone, that's okay, I understand."

I laid my hand over hers on the mattress. I felt like a shit for the way I'd treated her, the crazy thoughts going through my head. I thought if the circumstances had been different, she'd have been a wonderful person to fall in love with.

All the same, I didn't call her on Sunday. Instead, I readied for my trip.

End Part One

PART TWO

Chapter Thirteen

According to my research, Mansfield, incorporated in 1721, was a town of four thousand, located in the southwestern corner of the state, close to both the Connecticut and New York State borders. The Housatonic River flowed through the south part of town, parallel to Main Street, and throughout the nineteenth and much of the twentieth centuries, three large paper mills had defined the town, but in the last decade, two of those mills had closed, and the third downsized considerably. The town now embraced tourism as its main source of employment and income, taking advantage of an emphasis on the arts that ran all through Berkshire County, especially in the summer.

The trip, though not easy, had been without incident. I'd determined to stay below the speed limit and hug the right lane, a strategy that worked for a little while. But the interstates had as many as four lanes each way, and cars entering and exiting clogged the right lane, so I traveled in the second lane, passed in the third, and kept a wary eye on cars coming up on me in the outer lane, sometimes at a hundred miles an hour.

Being careful got harder when four lanes suddenly reduced to two, or cars began passing me on both sides at the same time.

Even the slightest distraction, when traveling at high speed, sent my car leaking into another's lane, or pinned me in a row of cars going faster than felt safe. These slips invariably elicited a blaring horn blast from the cars around me, especially in New Jersey.

About half-way, I pulled into a rest stop, exhausted. I locked the doors and settled back, closing my eyes. At first it felt as if the car was still moving, but the next thing I knew, I was pushing myself up with a dry mouth and a stiff neck, not sure where I was, when it was, or how I got here in the first place. When it all came back to me, I went into the building, washed my face with cold water, and bought a coffee and a cinnamon bun whose smell proved better than its taste.

Back on the highway, I tried to perk up. Surprisingly, my wrecked rental had a CD player, and I'd brought with me a stack of CD's. In the early part of the trip, I listened mostly to classical music, as it helped relax me, but wanting more energy now, I turned to Bruce Springsteen and the Rolling Stones.

Yesterday, I'd tried Sarah's "music test," going through my stack of CD's to find one that had been recorded after 1970, when I would have been fourteen. I found one by someone named Rickie Lee Jones. On the case, it said, "copyright 1979." I liked the music, although at first it was hard to decipher the lyrics, but then she got to a refrain I recognized: "You've found the last chance Tex-a-co." Not just the words but the melody and rhythm, the drawing out of syllables, the fluctuation in her voice.

In the silence that followed the song's end, I heard another phrase: "Chuck E's in lo-huh-huhve." Sang in Rickie Lee Jones' voice, but playing not on the CD but inside my own head. A moment later, the next song began: "Chuck E's in Love."

Excited, I found another CD: Bruce Springsteen's *Born in the USA*. The jacket said 1984. When the title song began, a picture popped into my mind: a cabin, with a fireplace, and a red carpet. Music blasting: "Dancing in the Dark."

This may have been only a snapshot, but it felt like the bare bones of a memory.

When I finally left the Taconic Parkway for the narrow country road near Hillsdale, New York, I turned off the music and couldn't help but smile when I passed over the state line into Massachusetts. It struck me that I'd started responding to the subtleties of the road, slowing down before I reached a curve, anticipating the speed limit dropping as I approached a village. As a kid I'd likely been in cars that drove along this road, but child passengers wouldn't notice fluctuations in the speed limit. Something in me remembered driving here.

Excitement sparked as I neared the top of a hill. I wasn't sure why; I'd just passed a sign saying Mansfield was still three miles away. But at the crest of the hill, I gazed down at a river curling through fields and pastureland. There were buildings in the distance, but the river seemed cradled in its own natural world. I knew that river: Ice River, we called it, because the water was so cold. My grandfather used to take me there to fish and swim.

I pulled off and parked. The sun hung low behind me. Wispy clouds lined the horizon, the blue slowly draining from the sky. Below me the river was wide but shallow, the rocks shining even in the lengthening shadows. Farther on, I knew, was a pool at the base of a big rock, eight feet deep, where nine-year-old Matthew Winton's preferred dive was the cannonball. I could see myself in midair, body tucked, preparing for the impact.

Beyond the swimming hole, the river slid into dark and mysterious woods. An image popped into my mind, me navigating that portion of the river, climbing over fallen trees, wading through water waist-deep. Imagining myself as Jungle Jim, the character played by the actor who was also Tarzan.

How old was I then? My grandfather wouldn't have let me wander off alone down that potentially dangerous part of the river. Both my grandparents died within a week of each other when I was twelve. I must have come here alone, sometime after.

The approach to town took me first past the fairgrounds. Every September, the schools let out early on one Friday afternoon so that kids could spend the afternoon going on rides or trying to knock things off shelves or hook them with wooden rings, games everyone swore were fixed but paid money to play, nonetheless. Farmers exhibited animals and crops in barns, while the center-piece was the grandstand, where a thousand or more people gathered to watch the daily slate of thoroughbred races. The walkway under the grandstand was always dark, smelling of beer, urine, and popcorn, and littered with torn tickets bet on losing horses. In that walkway, where I was told never to go but often did, the grandstand trembled beneath the roaring crowd, and even with no view, it was easy to tell where on the oval track the horses were by the intensity of the noise.

This year's fair should have taken place a few weeks ago, but out-of-control weeds and waist-high grasses surrounded the buildings, marked by peeling paint and broken boards. In the open area, pieces left over from the frames of rides sat like ancient ruins, metal arms reaching into the sky, supporting only air. The paint on the giant billboard was so faded I could barely make out "Mansfield Fair," followed by "September," with dates faded out entirely.

It was disappointing to think that the fair may have closed for good. It had meant so much to all of us kids, the highlight of our first month back in school. Even though I must have witnessed this disrepair in recent trips back home, it felt as if it had gone from a place thriving with crowds and noise and exotic aromas, directly to this neglected ghost town, in the blink of an eye.

Modest old houses lined the next blocks. The houses got bigger and farther apart as I entered the main part of town, while on the other side of the street, a high stone wall surrounded "Mansfield Castle," what we kids called it, despite its sign proclaiming, "Mansfield Country Club. Members Only."

Then I was stopped at the town's one traffic light. To my left rose the red-brick town hall, next to the movie house, where my father would give me a few dollars so I could see a movie on Sunday afternoons. The building had once held stage plays and operas, and I liked sitting up in one of the rounded boxes along the side, where the view was limited but offered a shelf to hold popcorn and soda. Out of habit, I glanced at the marquee to see what movie was playing, only to read, in bold blue letters, "Thank you for 77 great years!" The movie house had closed.

I noticed other changes along Main Street: what used to be an A&P was now a car dealership; a former bank was now a restaurant called "The Vault." Gerard's Smoke Shop, where I used to buy candy on the way home from school, had disappeared, giving way to a store that sold pottery.

The second of the three-block-long Main Street was marked by Railroad Street, a horseshoe-shaped side street filled with bars and a seedy hotel, a street my mother often warned me to steer clear of, which only made me more determined to check it out. The bars all had heavy, solid doors and blacked-out windows, and the entrances smelled like the underbelly of the fair's grandstand, minus the popcorn. A woman or two, usually big-breasted and drenched in perfume, might be waiting in front of the hotel, and occasionally one might speak to me as I passed. I never spoke back, though I was more partial to those who called me "Young man" than one who named me "Little boy."

Railroad Street looked unchanged, still seedy as ever; also unchanged was the library on the next block, and the row of churches: Congregational, Episcopal, Methodist, and the largest of all, the white stone Catholic Church. At the end of that block – the end of Main Street – sat Marvin's Drugs.

Then Main Street curved, passing over the Housatonic River. I pulled off before I got there and gazed back at the town in my rear-view mirror. What I saw, what I'd just passed through, was the town of my childhood. There were memories here, but so far they went only as far as my early teens, whereas I'd lived here through college, then come back to live for a few years later on. Those were the years I needed to remember.

First, I needed a place to stay. The sun dropped relentlessly toward the tops of the mountains ringing this valley, and my back and shoulders ached from the tension of the drive.

The mile or two heading north, away from town, was crowded with houses and small businesses, pizza joints and liquor stores, a few car dealerships, and three different cemeteries. My parents must be buried in one of those cemeteries. My grandparents, too. It shocked me that I hadn't thought about this before, that I would find them here.

The road flattened out, the jagged top of Big Bear Mountain rising in the distance. Soon, I knew, the road would start climbing, continue past the high school, and on into the town of Old Bridge.

Suddenly I spotted a red brick building with a red and white sign: Friendly's.

I pulled off the road. At first, I focused my attention on the red-brick building, but then my gaze drifted to one single spot in the far corner of the parking lot. The spot was empty, and then suddenly it wasn't: a little red Alfa Romeo appeared, a big round man walking toward it with a coffee cup in each hand.

Anxiety rose inside me; I fought the urge to flee. Why had I come here anyway? If my memory planned to come back, it would do so of its own accord. Where I was, or how actively I tried to remember, most likely wouldn't matter.

I looked again at that parking space: empty. I released a breath I hadn't realized I was holding, relaxed my hands that had squeezed into fists. When anticipating this trip, I'd been excited about finding Aaron, and seeing familiar places. I hadn't let my mind dwell much on Mr. P. He would likely be in his sixties now, assuming he was real. Would I recognize him? Would he remember me? The writing on my laptop felt unfinished to me. How much more might there be?

I drove on. There were ghosts in this town. If I were going to stay, I would have to face them.

At the foot of the mountain, a motel sat next to a pond nestled in the woods. The units were all individual cabins, spaced well apart, and I pulled in beneath the vacancy sign and up to the office.

The bell on the door brought a young man, tall and very thin, from a back room. "What part of Virginia is Blue Meadow in?" he asked after I'd filled out the card. "My wife's from Chesapeake, that's down near Virginia Beach."

"It's pretty down there," I said, wanting to be polite, since I had no answer when he asked how long I planned to stay.

"It's pretty quiet now," he told me. "I don't expect we'll get busy until Thanksgiving, probably."

I hadn't seen any cars parked in front of the other units, and when I asked if I could have the end cabin, closest to the woods, he handed me the key. The room was clean and cozy enough, with a queen-sized bed, a chest of drawers, a table that could double as a desk, and a TV. A pleasant surprise was the small refrigerator beneath the sink in the otherwise tiny bathroom.

Each cabin had two plastic Adirondack chairs out front, and I settled into one, laying my jacket over my legs to counter the rapidly chilling air. I wanted to enjoy the chattering of the birds overhead, the occasional splash of a fish or frog in the now-shadow-covered pond, but my body still felt like it was moving, I was tired and hungry, and for the first time since forever, I craved alcohol.

With a groan I pulled myself up and drove back toward town, to the liquor store where I picked up a pre-packaged sandwich and a bag of Fritos, which I recalled liking as a kid. When it came to choosing alcohol, I let myself wander. My roaming kept returning me to shelves filled with Scotch, where a bottle called Dewars seemed brighter than the rest. Maybe it was all fatigue and imagination, but having no better way to decide, I added the bottle of Dewars to my basket and headed for the checkout.

Back at my cabin, following my impulse, I filled a glass half full, dropped in some ice, topped it off with water. My first taste was jarring: the Scotch, not yet cooled by the ice, burned when I swallowed. Worse was the taste of iodine that lingered on my tongue. Did I like this? Perhaps my "intuition" had played a trick on me?

The taste improved as the ice took effect. By the time I emptied the glass, it tasted like an entirely different drink, smooth and clean. I poured more and brought my food outside, where the settling darkness made the pond inky black, and trees that had lost their leaves stood like sentries, their bare limbs veins against the darkening sky. In the distance, a truck grinding its way up the mountain provided the only unnatural sound.

I had not spoken with Sarah since that night she'd left and gone home. I'd been telling myself I'd call when I arrived, but now that I was here, I grabbed at another excuse: I was tired, and a little drunk.

It was colder here than in Virginia, and I figured tomorrow I should buy a heavier coat. I had no other specific plans, but the more Scotch I drank, the more that seemed okay. And the Fritos, I thought, weren't bad at all.

Chapter Fourteen

I awoke to bright sunlight pouring past the curtains I forgot to close last night. Beside the clock, which said 7:13, sat a Scotch bottle with a shocking amount missing. I took a shower and dressed, then went outside and dried the dew off the Adirondack chair. The air was fresher and cleaner here than in Virginia, the sky and sun brighter, the colors more striking. In the distance, a woodpecker hammered away at a tree, while above me a crow seemed to take umbrage with me parking myself below his favorite branch.

I didn't have a specific plan for the day, but I knew I needed coffee. But thoughts of venturing out beyond the oasis of my little cottage made me anxious. I could feel a nebulous presence lurking out there, waiting for me. Realistically, the odds of running into one particular person in a town of four thousand weren't high. But my feelings weren't based in reality.

On my way out, I stopped in the motel office. The proprietor seemed pleased when I said I'd stay a week, maybe longer. I seemed to be his only customer.

I wasn't ready to tackle Friendly's, not even the take-out window, but I remembered passing a bagel shop in town. Along Main Street, I walked with my head down, my baseball cap tugged low over my eyes. The bagel shop had only a handful of customers, most of them high school age. I ordered a bagel and large coffee and took them back to my car.

On the way, I passed a store window displaying cowboy hats, boots, and leather vests. "Western Dreams" was the store's name. A sudden voice in my head made me halt: "They even have a store that sells cowboy clothes." My father's voice, spoken over the phone, expressing his befuddlement at the changes in this now tourist-focused town of Mansfield.

An image flashed: me talking on the phone, standing beside a table in a modest dining room, someone – Jessie? – sitting nearby. Was this a memory?

It was what I'd been hoping for: find someplace familiar from my past, sprinkle a little of that magic dust they used in TV crime shows to make invisible things visible, and watch my past re-appear.

A cluster of kids, middle-school age, crossed Main Street and headed down a hill, on their way to school. I started the car and followed them. At the bottom of the hill sat a large, square building attached to another larger building, L-shaped, three stories high, made of brick. A sign said, "Bear Mountain Regional Junior High School." This would have been the high school where my father worked as janitor, when he took me to basketball games. It became a junior high when Mansfield and Old Bridge merged their school districts; the new high school sat a few miles north of my motel, halfway between the two towns. That school opened when I was in ninth grade, and my class was the first to go through all four years there.

Sitting in my car across the street, I heard the echo of a basketball bouncing in an empty gym, listened to the eerie noises – a sliding desk, a creaking door – as I walked through the dark empty school looking for my father. Even though these were moments from my still-familiar childhood, I knew what I had to do: visit these places, and let the ghosts speak.

• • •

I bought a road map of Mansfield and surrounding areas. Even so, it was tricky finding the house I'd lived in when my parents and grandparents moved here from New York, when I was a baby. The house was only five miles outside of town but I must have driven twenty before I realized I'd missed a crucial intersection. At the top of a hill where Christian Hill Road crossed Division Street, I recognized the place where I used to wait for the school bus. Turning left, I paused at the top of a hill so steep I would have had to walk my bicycle up it, which I did over and over in order to feel the exhilaration of gliding back down.

Three-quarters of the way down the hill sat the house I spent the first ten years of my life in. Perched on a rise, surrounded by half an acre of cleared land running back to dense forest, it was a shockingly small house, compared to my memory. When I was a child, the house sat alone amid fields and forests; had I climbed onto the roof and looked around, I wouldn't have seen another house. Now, six other houses extended in a row up and down the hill, four on one side and two on the other.

At the bottom was an entrance into the woods, blocked off by a wrought-iron gate perhaps ten feet high, between two crumbling stone walls. On the other side lay the narrow sandy, weed-speckled road that my grandfather and I must have walked on, past the pond and up to the reservoir, where with enough imagination, I saw China.

The years had made the stone wall less stable, but I had no trouble climbing over it. The road had less sand than I remembered, just a light yellowish dusting covering hard-packed dirt. Most of the weeds were dried up, and the leaves had begun to turn colors on the oak trees mixed in with pines and white birch. In the distance a bullfrog croaked, and in my mind a seven-year-old boy raced ahead to the pond, to show his grandfather how well he had learned to skip stones.

The pond was as I remembered, except a few gray-bellied clouds had moved to block the sun, and in my mind this pond lived forever on a sunny summer day. A shorter walk than I remembered brought me to a tall fence and a warning: "No Trespassing. Property of the United States Government." The fence was electrified, and it stopped my progress too far away for me to see the reservoir, or any tall buildings on the other side. I was sure that years ago, my grandfather and I had been able to walk right up to the edge of this "ocean."

Before leaving, I walked up Division Street for one more look at my old house. Memories flooded my senses: me rolling in a pile of just-raked leaves, hiding behind trees or rocks having shootouts with imaginary bad guys, exploring the woods as if I were Daniel Boone. I knew my parents and grandparents were there, too, but I didn't try to summon them. I was having too much fun outside by myself, in my own private world, a world come alive through my imaginings.

. . .

When I was in fifth grade, my grandmother had a stroke that paralyzed her left side and affected her mind. Sometimes in the evenings, she'd start thinking she was a young girl and needed to go home. She called me "Charles," which was my grandfather's name, and she thought my mother was her mother. She had no idea who my grandfather was, and a couple times she woke in the middle of the night screaming because a strange man was sleeping in her bed.

Two years later, my grandmother died. A week after that, my grandfather followed, after falling in the bathtub. I could remember my grandmother lying in her bed, shortly before she died, the doctor standing over her. But I didn't recall her funeral, or anything of my grandfather's death.

By then we'd moved into a new house on Prospect Street, halfway up the hill behind town, close enough that I could walk to school. I had little memory of that house, but parked in front of it now, I saw that it was a modest house nestled amid larger homes, and I vaguely recalled that my parents had squabbles with my neighbors, doctors and lawyers mostly, who didn't appreciate a school janitor moving in to live among them. At least that's how my mother described it.

This house was only a couple blocks from Otis Lake, a small lake nestled in the woods. My friends and I used to swim there, although the lone beach was small and roped off by the lifeguard to ensure the smaller kids didn't venture out too far. Sometimes, we would sleep out in one of my friend's yards and go roaming in the middle of the night, strip off our clothes and swim from one side of the lake to the other. I wasn't a great swimmer and I hated when the seaweed tickled my belly like some teasing sea monster, but I always joined in whatever everyone else attempted.

I drove up to that lake, approaching on the back side, the public beach far away. Thick woods came right up to the bank on the far side, while a dirt road ran along the opposite side. I could remember riding my bicycle along that road, hiking across the very center of the lake in the thick snow and ice of winter.

Then a different image pushed out the others: me sitting in a car, small and cramped, backed into a narrow opening in these woods, settled between high mounds of snow. The car is running, hot air rising around my feet. A hand moves away from the steering wheel, settles on my thigh.

I took a breath, pushed it out. Ran a hand through my hair, my shoulders creeping up around my ears. Ghosts, I thought, that show up uninvited. Get used to them, I coached myself. That's why you're here.

• • •

Bear Mountain Regional High School was a square, one-story building that sat atop a flat-topped hill several hundred yards back from the main road. There were three tiers of parking, each identified by who was invited to park there: guests, faculty, or students. I arrived after four p.m., when only a handful of cars remained in the faculty lot. Both the football and boys' soccer teams were practicing on the athletic fields behind the school, while the girls' soccer team seemed to be playing a game, before a couple dozen spectators, on the field in front.

Three yellow busses were lined up along the side of the building. Students always used that side entrance, but as a guest, I walked around to the front, entering in the middle of the main hall. A trophy case just inside the door contained photographs and news clippings along with half a dozen trophies. I was pretty sure I'd played football and lacrosse, but I doubted I'd stood out enough to have my name or photo posted there.

The hall was empty and quiet. This is where my memory ended, but I was pleasantly surprised at how much of the school's layout I remembered. To my left was the principal's office, while to my right, beyond the closed double doors that blocked my vision, I knew the hallway continued in a horseshoe shape, with wings branching off for each of the major departments: Social Studies, Science, Math, Foreign Languages, English. On the other side, in the hall parallel to the one I stood on, were the more specialized areas, Business, Shop, Home Ec, Special Needs. In the middle were the three large spaces: the gym, the library, and the theater.

It was the theater whose red metal door I faced. I kept my distance, my back and shoulders tense.

Suddenly the door rattled, and I backed up as it opened. A woman emerged, younger than me, carrying a half-dozen books in one arm. She gave me a friendly smile before disappearing down the hall that led to the classrooms. Definitely a teacher, I thought; too old to be a student. Perhaps she'd had a meeting with Mr. P, or whatever his real name was. In my mind I could see the stage, the rows and rows of maroon colored seats and carpeting. Then another image appeared: myself in a corner of the stage, made up to look like an old man, my hair dusted white: "Doc."

That image stunned me. That play took place my junior year. I would have been almost seventeen.

Steeling myself, I opened the theater door. Darkness greeted me, and silence. No footsteps in the back, no rustling sounds, no light left on. If he'd been here, Mr. P was gone.

I exhaled. I couldn't tell if I was relieved not to have found him, or disappointed. I took some consolation in the strength I'd summoned to seek him out. When I opened that door, there had been no sign of the frightened little boy I had felt like before.

I headed to the main office. Through the glass wall, I could see lights on, but no one inside. Four chairs and a coffee table filled the waiting area inside, while behind a chest-high counter in the middle of the room were three desks, shelves filled with books, and a dark hallway leading to back offices. Two of the desktops were neatly arranged, the occupants likely gone for the day, but on the third a lamp was lit and a sweater draped over the back of the chair.

"Oh," popped out of the darkness, as a woman appeared, her arms filled with manilla folders she hastily dropped onto her desk. "I'm sorry," she said. "I didn't realize anyone had come in."

She was middle-aged, with peach colored hair and glasses hanging on a strap around her neck. "Can I help you?"

I explained I was a former student who hadn't been back in many years.

"I'm afraid school's out for the day. Most people have gone home. Except for the athletes –" she flashed an impish smile, "and those in detention."

I laughed. "I'm sure I fit into both groups during my time here."

She asked when I'd graduated, and seemed impressed with my answer. "You must have been the first class in the new building."

"I was in ninth grade when it opened."

"That's what I mean. The first class to go through all four years here. Although I guess you didn't start until a year later."

Puzzled, I asked what she meant.

"They had delays finishing the building, from what I recall. I've only been working here a few years but I've lived around here forever. The two towns had to use their old high school buildings until this one opened."

"When was that?"

"The fall of 1971. You would have been in tenth grade when you finally got into this building."

It took me a moment to realize what this meant. I'd been assuming my memory had stopped at thirteen. But I would have been fifteen in tenth grade. My knowledge of this building couldn't have come before then. It was only a year or two difference, but it felt like a big deal.

The woman looked anxious to start on those manilla folders, but I had more questions. "I was wondering about a teacher," I began. "I can't recall his name exactly. He was an English teacher but he directed plays."

After considering, she shook her head. "Ms. Lawrence directs the school plays. She's been here longer than I have, but I don't think she's much older than thirty. Maybe thirty-five."

The woman who'd come out of the auditorium, probably. "This was a man who taught when I was here."

She sighed. "Maureen might know." She gestured toward one of the empty desks. "But she's gone home for the day."

"Those books back there –" I pointed to the shelves behind her. "They wouldn't be –"

"Brilliant!" she cried before I could get out the word "yearbooks." She hurried to them. "What year did you say you graduated?" I told her again, and she ran her finger over a row of books and slid one free. With a triumphant grin, she laid it on the counter. "1974."

The cover looked unusual, a maroon stripe across the middle, in between strips of burlap. A circular silver seal embedded in one corner, and in the other, the name of the school and year. An interesting design.

"Can I look at this?"

She gestured toward the row of chairs. "I can't let you take it out of the office, but I'm here until five."

Thirty-five minutes. I settled in the chair farthest from the door. When the woman sat down at her desk, she disappeared from view.

Excited and wary both, I opened the book. Three names were listed as editors. Two I didn't recognize; the third was Matthew Winton. Below that was Art Director, Cheryl Alsop. She must have designed the cover. And below her name, the faculty advisor: Jonathan Piretti.

I found the faculty listings for the English Department: Jonathan Piretti, Director of Dramatics. Mr. P.

I paused, trying to steady my breathing. He wasn't here sitting next to me. It was only a book.

The yearbook's opening page contained a poem about the school, ironic in tone, the speaker a graduating senior who complains about the school in numerous ways before reluctantly admitting he'll miss it when he's gone. At the bottom, the author's initials, "M.W."

The first line was familiar: "Goodbye, Bear Mountain Regional High School of Mansfield, Massachusetts (I never could fit your whole name on one line.)" I'd written this poem. I remembered it.

Flipping to the senior photos, I went right to the W's. The Matthew Winton I found there was barely recognizable. He had long scraggly sideburns, and hair that looked like it couldn't decide whether to be straight or curly. The face was tense, repressed, super-serious, desperate to convince the world he was someone he feared he wasn't. I felt disconnected from this person in the photograph, who seemed disconnected from himself. Like most of the graduates, he gazed off toward some vaguely-imagined perfect future.

Underneath were a list of accomplishments: National Honor Society, honor roll every quarter, NCTE Outstanding Achievement Award, Yearbook Editor, Literary Magazine Editor, Football, Lacrosse, and three plays, *A Thousand Clowns*, *West Side Story*, and *The Fantasticks*.

I jumped to the section on the Spring play. I was hoping to find information on *West Side Story*, but that would have been my junior year. For *The Fantasticks*, I was listed as "assistant director." The director was Jonathan Piretti.

I turned the page and there we were: the two of us side by side, arms around each other and legs kicking like we were in some kind of chorus line. Both of us laughing, my head turned toward Mr. P, a look of pride and privilege on my face.

The caption read, "Mr. P and one of his prized ducklings in a lighter moment during rehearsals for *The Fantasticks*. (Were he and Matthew teaching the actors the can can?)"

He looked exactly as my writing had described him. A big man, not obese but heavy, with a rounded body, shaped like a football standing on end. A body that liked to be indulged. Dark hair neatly slicked back, an angular face with a beak of a nose and hardly any chin. He wore a dark shirt, the shirt collar open, an ascot tied round his neck. He looked amused but in control; his "lighter moment" appearing both spontaneous and rehearsed, no difference between actor and man.

I wore bell-bottom jeans, a shirt with an extra button undone at the neck, and what looked like cowboy boots. The photo presented a cool teacher who treated his students – selected ones, anyway – as special, and one student who had attained that lofty perch.

Mr. P looked about forty-five in the photograph. He must be retired now. Would he have gray hair? Would he have lost weight? How would he get by without his "ducklings"?

I must have made a noise, because the woman's head appeared over the counter. "Are you finished?"

I told her no, then asked a question. "Mr. Piretti is the teacher I was thinking of. He used to direct the plays. I guess he doesn't do that anymore, but do you know if he still teaches? Maybe he hasn't fully retired?"

She pulled another book from the shelf, the last in the row. "Last year," she said. "Ah, here we are," and she laid down the book, opened to photographs of the English faculty. Mr. P wasn't there.

I thanked her, promised to be done soon, and returned to my seat. The student photos were arranged alphabetically by last name, so I had to search through them to find someone named Aaron. With so little time, I forced myself not to linger on faces that seemed vaguely familiar, until I came to one that stopped me cold. A young woman with blonde hair, unsmiling, looking older, more mature than her classmates, attractive but plain looking, really, with a hardness to her features that probably would have intimidated most boys her age. Nothing striking about her except her name: Suzanne Martin.

An image popped: sitting across from her in a booth at Friendly's, late at night, drinking coffee and sharing a bowl of French fries. I stared again at the picture. She didn't photograph well; she was much prettier in person.

According to my writing, I'd been in love with her. Mr. P had pushed us together. But she had a boyfriend, someone older, no longer in high school.

I forced myself to move on. I finally found Aaron Segoyen, the only Aaron in the class. He had long dark hair to his shoulders, the beginning of a beard, and piercing eyes. He looked comfortable being who he was, not caring what others thought.

I would have liked to go back and linger over other photographs; there were memories here just waiting to reveal themselves. But the woman who had been so helpful stood at the counter, looking anxiously at the clock. I gave her back the book and thanked her. Leaving, I went out the side door, the exit only students used.

Chapter Fifteen

Aaron's house was small and long, a one-story building nestled in a grove of trees, across the street from a rocky, fast-flowing river. The house sat close to another, a big white farmhouse, which was unusual, as most of the houses in this neighborhood had large lawns.

Returning from the high school, I went to speak to the motel proprietor. The office was empty but the jingling bells on the front door coaxed him from a back room. In that room I could see a toddler standing up in a playpen. "Your child," I said, and his wide grin showed a mouthful of teeth.

"Shelly Anne. Our pride and joy."

Earlier, I'd phoned Jessie, to tell her where I was and ask if she remembered any more about Aaron. "I think he worked at a country inn," she told me. "Something about security."

I asked the proprietor if he knew of any country inns in the area, and he laughed.

"We've got country inns all over the place. You could spend a month and not stay in the same inn twice. Course, you'd end up going home broke."

Perhaps noticing my disappointment, he quickly added, "The most famous is the White Horse Inn. That's His Honor's place.

The Judge," he added, as if that would explain everything. "It's right on Main Street in Old Bridge. It pretty much is Old Bridge, at least the Main Street. You drive up there, you can't miss it."

"You wouldn't know how to find somebody's address when all you have is their name, would you?"

His eyebrows narrowed. "Somebody local?" I nodded, and he took a fat book off a shelf and plopped it on the counter. "This is a couple years old, but it'll work if the person hasn't moved lately."

The book made me feel like a fool: the local telephone directory.

I waited until dusk, figuring Aaron would be home from work. It was dark when I arrived, but there were no lights on, no car in the driveway, and I wasn't surprised when my knock brought no response.

As I was considering my next step, a car pulled into the half-circle in front of the farmhouse. A woman got out, a bag of groceries in one arm. Noticing me, she called out, "He's gone to work."

I stepped into the light, and her demeanor changed. "Oh, hi," she called, her tone suggesting surprise and delight. After setting down her groceries, she came toward me and gave me a gentle hug. "It's great to see you. Aaron will be thrilled."

Wanting to avoid a long story, I simply asked, "So he's at work?"

"He started a new schedule this summer. He got them to agree to four nights a week, but each night he works twelve hours." She glanced at her watch. "You just missed him."

"He's still at the inn?"

She rolled her eyes. "Until the day he dies."

I didn't ask which inn. The motel proprietor had been right, the White Horse Inn was impossible to miss. Driving by it, I'd felt something. Not a memory, just a feeling that this was the right place.

"Are you going to be here long?" the woman asked. She was tall and thin, perhaps a few years older than me. Before I could respond she said, "I'm sorry about your father. Aaron told me."

Nodding, I thanked her.

"Stop in and see him. You know how he loves company." Her laugh held a bit of sarcasm. "Him and that dog."

"I don't want to keep you," I told her. Clearly she and I had known each other, but I didn't sense we'd been close. "It was nice to see you."

She gave me another hug, then we both turned back to our cars.

• • •

The White Horse Inn filled one full block of Old Bridge's two-block long Main Street. An enormous building, five stories high, it was built in the late 1700s, according to the plaque in front of the building. The verandah running the length of the front was filled with people, despite an evening chill in the air. Everyone was well dressed, the men in suits, the women in colorful dresses. Even the children mimicked them in their little suits and dresses. Decorated in the orange and brown of autumn, with lots of pumpkins laid about, all under bright lights, the verandah looked like a stage ready for the play to begin. Strains of soft piano music drifted out from inside, while staff in red vests hustled to meet their guests' needs.

Apart from the verandah, Main Street was quiet. The block next to the Inn contained a Mom & Pop grocery, a cluster of specialty shops, and the public library, while on the other side of the street, a drugstore and an auto repair shop were flanked by huge homes with large lawns shaded by giant old trees. Old Bridge was the home to a number of wealthy families, I recalled, some of them famous artists, writers, and movie stars. Growing up, I'd been both attracted to and cowed by Old Bridge, the polar opposite of blue-collar Mansfield.

Just standing on the sidewalk in front of this inn triggered images: me walking along loose gravel in a parking lot, forcing heavy tired legs to trudge up endless stairs in the middle of the night. The smell of colored flakes in a bowl, something called potpourri.

The people on the verandah had begun to file inside, for dinner, probably. A red-vested employee closed the front doors, while another brought an Afghan to a white-haired woman sitting in a corner, unwilling to give up the fresh air. The lights in front grew stronger as the darkness settled in.

I wandered around to the parking lot in back, where loose pebbles slid underfoot, just as I'd envisioned a few moments ago. Passing behind what must have been the kitchen, I heard dishes clattering, people shouting over the hum of a giant fan. In my mind I saw rainbow-speckled liquid sloshing beneath an inch-high black rubber mat on the concrete floor in a room hot as a sauna.

Hearing footsteps approaching, I turned just in time to see a huge black dog charging toward me. I braced for the dog to leap.

"Ziggy!"

The dog halted instantly, letting out what sounded like an apologetic whine, and padded up to me, where he dropped something at my feet: a stick, chewed and gnarled and soaked with the dog's blubbering saliva.

"He's all right," came a deep voice out of the darkness. "He's big, but he's still got a puppy brain. He always wants to play."

The dog, a brown-and-black German Shepherd, lay flat on his belly, eyes fixed on the stick as if it were a small animal playing possum, and he was ready for the moment it came back to life. Behind him, a man stepped into the light.

"Aaron."

He grinned. "I thought it might be you." His hug was warm and strong and welcoming. "How you doing, Matty?"

"Just passing through," I lied. "I thought I'd stop in and say hello."

Aaron clapped me on the shoulder. "I'm glad you did."

He resembled his high school photo, although the jet black hair that had rested on his shoulders was cut short now, and speckled with gray. His brown eyes held the same intensity, and an impish invitation to view the world as he saw it.

He wore what looked like a policeman's uniform, except without the trimmings: no badge or epaulets or truncheon, no pistol, as Sarah had worn when she first visited me in the hospital. He carried what looked like a fat round clock in a leather casing hanging on a strap around his neck.

He was surprisingly small, only about five foot seven, and slim; wiry, his posture confident, balanced, and strong. A thought popped into my head and I decided to take the risk. "Are you still doing karate?"

"*Uechi-ryu,*" he said and laughed. "Yeah, it's the main reason I can keep working here without going insane."

"You didn't do that in high school. The *Uechi-ryu,*" I explained at his puzzled look, probably mispronouncing it. "You didn't start doing that until after high school."

He shrugged. "I've been practicing seventeen years now."

When he would have been in his twenties. Yet I had known that about him. In my mind I saw him standing in the center of an empty space on a wooden floor, the room bright, empty of furniture: a dojo was the word that came to me. A small group of people lined up along the far wall; an old man, white haired and tiny, really, but sinewy strong, taking a board and drawing it back, like a baseball batter preparing for the pitch, while Aaron stands tall, unflinching even when the batter swings, the board smashing across his stomach. It snaps in two, the broken piece flying across the room. A test, I recalled, for one of his many colored belts.

The image vanished, but I was buoyed. My memory was a skittish animal wanting to come home.

We'd walked a short distance when Ziggy raced up to me once again and dropped his stick at my feet.

"Ignore him," Aaron said.

Ziggy snatched up the stick and dropped it at Aaron's feet. When Aaron picked it up, Ziggy sat back on his haunches, poised to shoot off like a rocket – which he did, the moment Aaron hurled the stick into the darkness.

He was back in no time, dropping the stick at Aaron's feet again. "That's enough," Aaron said, and turned to me. "He'll do this all night if I let him."

When we continued walking, Ziggy picked up the stick and carried it, trotting along at Aaron's side.

"I don't think I had Ziggy the last time you were here. Damn, that was a long time ago, I still had Bear then. Bear was a big tough son of a bitch. Not like this guy." He gestured affectionately, but with a bit of attitude, at Ziggy. "This one's a big baby."

He suggested we get out of the cold. "I just finished a round, so we've got some time."

I followed him inside and up a flight of stairs with only security lights cutting the darkness. Entering an empty conference room, Aaron flipped on a few lights, slung off the clock and set it on a table, then dropped into a chair. "So how you doing?" he asked.

Such a simple question, but how to answer? "I guess I'm hanging in there."

"I was sorry to hear about your dad."

That's right, I thought. It was just this past summer. I must have come back for the funeral, but not seen Aaron.

"You know I lost my dad. About the same time as your mother, I know how hard it is." A bitter laugh popped out of him. "Now, my mother's a different story. That old battleax will outlive me."

Another detail remembered: Aaron's mother, a high school English teacher in another district, was an alcoholic. As was Aaron, before he started studying karate. *Uechi-ryu.*

"So I have to tell you something."

Whatever Aaron heard in my voice made him sit up, turning serious.

"I was in a car accident. Near the end of the summer. It was pretty bad I guess. I totaled my car, ended up in the hospital. I'm pretty much over my injuries."

"I'm glad you're okay."

"I am…There's something else. When I woke up after the accident, I'd pretty much lost my memory."

I flashed him a helpless, apologetic look. My words sounded crazy to me, as if I was stuck in a soap opera. I explained how mainly, I could remember only the first twelve or thirteen years of my life.

"I thought something seemed a little strange," he said.

"You mean stranger than normal strange?"

"You knew who I was."

"Kind of. I recognized you." I told him about going to the high school, looking through the yearbook. "You haven't changed that much. Except the hair's shorter."

He ran his hair over his head. He barely had enough hair to ruffle. "You know, Daniel and I were the first students in the history of the school district to get suspended for refusing to cut our hair."

I perked up at Daniel's name. Jessie had said Aaron mentioned someone named Daniel the time he came to visit. I hadn't found Daniel in the yearbook, but I recalled the Daniel in my writing.

"Yeah." Aaron chuckled. "Tenth grade. Daniel was a year ahead of us, but this was the year they opened the new school building, brought in the new principal. Miss Dunleavy was her name, I think, with the emphasis on the 'Miss,' because no man in his right mind would marry her.

"Anyway, it's the first day of school, maybe an hour in, and I get called to the principal's office. Daniel's already there waiting for me, and Miss Dunleavy takes us into her office and sits us down and explains that we have to cut our hair. School policy, she says. Boys can't have hair that falls below the ear.

"We both knew this was bullshit. I mean, no offense, but everybody knows Mansfield has always been full of reactionary tight-asses; in Old Bridge, let's just say we're more relaxed. But Miss Dunleavy, she's from Mansfield, and she asks us, 'Will you cut your hair?'

"I look at Daniel, I swear we could read each other's minds sometimes, and we both say in unison, 'We would prefer not to.' See, we'd read 'Bartleby the Scrivener' over the summer, and that kind of became our battle cry. 'We would prefer not to.'"

He was having fun telling this story. I nodded for him to go on, even though I didn't remember any of it.

"Of course Miss Dunleavy doesn't get it. I'm sure she never read Melville. Probably she never read anything, except *How to Be an Asshole Principal.* She thought we were saying we preferred not to cut our hair, but of course we would, school policy and all. So the next day, she's surprised to see us. She's especially freaked out by Daniel, who liked to keep his hair tied back but today has it hanging loose, practically down to his ass. She tells us again we have to cut our hair, and we say we would prefer not to. Understandably, this pisses her off, and she tells us if we don't cut our hair by tomorrow, we'll be suspended. So the next day, we get suspended."

He and Daniel enjoyed their vacation, he said, but it ended too soon. "We had some heavy hitters on our side. My father was a lieutenant colonel in the Army, and Daniel's dad was chief of police for Christ's sake. But what clinched it was, His Honor stepped in."

In deference to my amnesia, he explained that "His Honor" was Charles O'Malley, owner of the White Horse Inn, as well as several other establishments in the area, and a one-time high court judge. "One phone call and amazingly, the school had a new policy on the length of a guy's hair."

I waited, letting him relish the memory, before asking, "You and Daniel were good friends?"

Aaron's mood shifted. "We grew up together. He was like a big brother to me." He paused. "You knew him too. You guys were in that play together."

"West Side Story?" I ventured.

"Yeah. I could never figure out why Daniel agreed to that. He never volunteered for anything – except maybe to roll the next joint."

I thought back to the Daniel in my writing. It had to be the same guy.

"You guys weren't close," Aaron said, "but Daniel used to say how much he admired you."

That brought my eyes open wide. "He admired me?"

"He really did. He used to say how you always seemed to have it all together, like you had a plan for everything."

"I don't remember that," I said. "And I don't think it's because I lost my memory."

"I kind of thought that about you too," he told me. "When you did something, it always felt like you'd thought everything through beforehand, and arrived at the best course of action. Whereas the rest of us were just stumbling our way through the same old purple haze."

We both laughed, but his image of me was dismaying. I didn't need a memory to know I wasn't the confident, together teenager Aaron described. Most likely that was an image I sought to convey, and apparently, did a pretty good job of it.

Aaron got up, said he needed to do a round. "You up for a walk?"

"Sure."

As we were going down the stairs, I asked what Daniel was up to now.

Aaron took his time responding. We emerged into the chilled night air and he reached down and gently scratched Ziggy's neck. When he finally looked up, I could read in his eyes, not a warning exactly, but an acceptance that there were things in life that could drive a hole in your heart. "He's dead," Aaron said. "The motherfucker blew his brains out."

. . .

In silence we walked down to the Inn's kitchen, which was crowded, wet, and hot as a sauna. Just as I'd seen earlier in my mind, black rubber mats covered the floor, with rainbow-streaked liquid sloshing underneath. Big overhead fans rumbled, swirling the heat and sweet aromas, while the cooks, waitresses, and dishwashers moved around each other, orderly chaos in the cramped space.

I waited inside the doorway as Aaron crossed the room. Suddenly, I wasn't simply viewing this scene but participating in it: I was the one walking across those mats, squeezing past the kitchen workers, maneuvering into a tight corner, where I had to contort my body to reach the metal key I had to insert into the clock. I remembered that "a round" meant walking from the basement to the attic, stopping at each one of these key stations, metal boxes the size of a loaf of bread with a key hanging on a chain. The clock Aaron carried had an opening for the key, which would mark on a piece of paper inside the clock the exact time Aaron had been at this station. Supposedly the system had been set up for insurance purposes, but Aaron figured it was mainly to make sure the security guard didn't sneak off to some empty room for a two-hour nap in the middle of the night. Of course, His Honor – "the clever bastard," Aaron had called him – had placed those keys in the most hard-to-reach places.

• • •

I'd worn the uniform, felt the weight of the clock around my neck, blocked the pain as I raised and set down my hot, tired feet. I had worked here. I remembered it.

I followed Aaron through the basement, which was dank and cobwebby, the noise of the ceiling fans replaced by the rumble of a giant boiler. Water dripped in corners and the air smelled dingy. After Aaron hit the key station, we climbed up to a crowded lobby, where a silver-haired woman in an emerald green dress and lots of glittering jewelry played an elegant piano. I smelled the sweet, musky scent that earlier had drifted through my mind: potpourri.

As Aaron went for the key at the back of the crowded dining room, I slunk into a corner, too aware of my faded jeans and old jacket in this crowded room of well-dressed patrons. At least I'd stuffed my baseball cap into my jacket pocket. I kept an eye on Aaron, ready to announce, "I'm with him," if anyone asked why I was there.

But nobody seemed to notice me, and the three of us – Aaron and I, with Ziggy leading the way – went tromping up the stairs to the first floor of rooms. Unlike the bright and noisy dining room and lobby, everything was quiet here, the sconces on the wall dimmed, and it seemed like the middle of the night, despite the occasional bursts of noise rising up from downstairs, even through the heavy door Aaron had been careful to quietly close behind us.

"Any of this coming back to you?" Aaron asked, and laughed. "Stimulating though it is, I'm sure."

"I worked here," I said. "I did this job."

"You did. Three years you were here. You saved my ass that first winter, when Caroline and I were going through that shit.

"The divorce," he explained. "Caroline and I were together five, six years. We were splitting up, and on top of that, my old man was dying. And then I had to fucking fire Damian – he was my other guard, a real piece of work. I was working twelve hour shifts seven days a week, until you came on board. You saved my ass."

I asked if he could tell me more about that time.

I'd been teaching at a private Quaker school outside Philadelphia, he explained. He didn't know why I'd quit that job, but I'd suddenly moved back into my parents' house. Seventeen or eighteen years ago. I stopped by to visit with Aaron one night when he was working, and after reciting his recent troubles, he jokingly asked if I wanted a job. "I never dreamt you'd say yes," Aaron told me. "A shit job like this, it's okay for slobs like me, but you had a college degree. Tops in your class, or almost. I read about you. Phi Beta Kappa."

I remembered that phrase from my CV, although I still wasn't sure what it meant. I seriously doubted I was smarter than Aaron.

"How long did you say I worked here?" I asked as Aaron stretched to reach the key station chained between a radiator and a fire hydrant.

"Almost three years. I was able to get you a place after a while, a cabin on one of His Honor's properties, so you didn't have to live with your parents."

Even though we're just dancing in the dark. Heard as I stood on a red carpet in front of a fireplace in the main room of a modest cabin.

"Do you know why I left?"

"You were getting antsy. Not that I blame you. I've been here twenty years now, and I've been antsy for every one of them. You had options. You published a couple stories but you wanted to do more, and you started looking at graduate schools. Then your mother got sick. No offense, but once you told me her diagnosis, I knew you wouldn't be staying here much longer."

I avoided eye contact. I didn't want to talk about my mother.

"Did I ever tell you why I quit teaching at that Quaker school?"

He shook his head. "You never brought it up, and I never pushed. I figured if you wanted to talk about it you would, in your own time."

"I never said why I came back?"

"I just figured you needed a break from people. There are people around here but mostly they leave you alone. If they need you, they'll find you, but otherwise, you might as well be invisible. For a while anyway, I think you wanted that."

I tried not to feel discouraged. Don't worry about what you don't know, focus on what you do, Dr. Clark had said. I'd learned a lot being here with Aaron, and not just from what he'd told me. I'd seen myself existing in a past moment from my adult life.

The last key station was the worst. It required going into the attic and climbing up a rickety wooden ladder. The eaves made it impossible to stand up straight, and the floor consisted of beams a few feet apart, with nothing but insulation and plasterboard in between, so a slip could land you, if you were lucky, in the bed of the room below. The key station was attached low enough to a beam that Aaron had to drop to his knees to bring key and clock together, while I remained on the ladder, watching, and Ziggy waited at the bottom, peering up at the spot where he knew Aaron would reappear.

"Fucking Judge," Aaron muttered as we left the attic. There

was admiration in his voice when he called him "one deviously brilliant son of a bitch."

• • •

Outside, everything was quiet and still. The cold air felt refreshing, after the heat and potpourri inside.

Ziggy had reclaimed the stick he'd stashed somewhere earlier, and Aaron tossed it into the bushes at the edge of the parking lot. As he played with the dog, he filled me in on more stories from high school, including a party our AP History class threw specifically for me, because we'd been given six weeks to write a collaborative paper on what our ideal school would look like, had goofed off for five and a half of those weeks, and I'd ended up writing the whole paper myself in the last few days. It got an A.

When I asked if he remembered Suzanne Martin, he said he knew who she was but they'd never been close. I started when he added, "I think Daniel had the hots for her at one point."

"Daniel?"

"It was during that play. Daniel was Bernardo, and she was his girlfriend in the play. I think a little something developed, but it didn't last. She had a real boyfriend, I think."

We took another round, Ziggy again waiting at the bottom of the ladder as Aaron climbed up to the attic. Back outside, we sat at a picnic table at the edge of the parking lot. We hadn't spoken much going through the inn. "Can I ask you about Daniel?" I said after a while.

Ziggy dropped his ever-present stick at Aaron's feet, but Aaron turned away. "That's enough," he said. "No more." He was speaking to the dog but might have felt that about my question too. But he nodded, took a moment to collect himself, and began to speak.

After Daniel graduated, he went off to Emerson College in Boston. Aaron followed him a year later, and they shared an apartment. By then, Daniel had dropped out of college, and they spent most of their time, Aaron admitted, smoking dope, drinking, and carousing. "Daniel had some money from a rich aunt or something, and we picked up odd jobs when things got tight. But all we really cared about was dope and booze and women."

Aaron also dropped out of college at the end of his freshman year, and he and Daniel stayed in Boston. Aaron got a job working construction, and later, he started training dogs for the Boston Police Department. "I liked doing that," he said, "and for some reason, I was good at it. But it was hard holding that job with me and Daniel getting drunk and high every night. And for the Police Department, for Christ's sake.

"I met this guy, a true master, and started taking classes in *Ue-chi-ryu*. I quit drinking, and cut my hair. About a year later, I was back here visiting my folks, I ran into His Honor and he offered me this job. The dog training wasn't full-time, and I'd had enough of construction, so I decided to try it.

"Of course I had to move back here. Daniel took it hard, we stayed friends, but maybe he never forgave me. Although a year or two later, he moved back here too.

"He'd come by once in a while, hang out for a couple hours. The last time I saw him he said he was doing well. He wasn't drinking, and there was a woman he liked. I thought maybe he'd turned things around. God knows it happened for me.

"But that just made it harder, what he did."

Aaron had been working that night. Daniel must have driven down Main Street, right past the Inn, around two a.m. He continued a few miles out of town, to a field where lots of parties took place when we were in high school. The cast party for *West Side Story* had been in that field.

He drove his old Pontiac over the tall, dried grass and clumps of dirt and rock, until he reached the middle, where he swung a U-turn and shut off the engine. Nobody knew if there was significance in the placement of his car. He had a fifth of vodka and apparently drank it all. Then, sometime around 4 a.m., he stuck the barrel of a pistol into his mouth and pulled the trigger.

"Nobody could understand why he did it. He was such a private person anyway, and maybe I give myself too much credit, but I always thought if he wasn't going to talk to me about something, he wasn't going to talk to anyone." He paused. "He didn't talk to me."

Aaron gazed at the sky. The stars had shifted and grown brighter, and I remembered how at night, every hour brought change: the sky, the stars, the air, even the way you think and feel, was different at 1 a.m. than at 2 a.m., different again at 3 and 4.

I pulled my coat tighter. "Maybe it wasn't one thing that set him off," Aaron said. "Maybe it was the accumulation of everything. Living in his own skin was hard for him. He was convinced he was a horrible person. Maybe he just got tired of looking at his own face in the mirror."

It was hard to imagine Daniel – the Daniel I'd written about, that I was beginning to remember – believing he was a horrible person. In high school, if I'd been able to trade places with anyone, it would have been with Daniel.

The pain in Aaron's eyes was clear. "He was a motherfucker," he said, staring off into the darkness. "All the hearts he broke when he was alive. Then he turns around and breaks them all again."

"I'm sorry I wasn't around then," I said.

He waved off the apology. "You'd just got your job at the university. You were kicking ass.

"I came to D.C. to see you not long after that. You and Jessie was her name, right? I liked her a lot. Anyway, I probably wasn't very good company."

I admired Aaron for his strength and discipline and intelligence; for his integrity. I recalled him once saying that the proof of your integrity lies in what you do when you know that no one's watching. I admired him for what he'd overcome, too. I could also remember him telling me once – probably on one of those nights years ago when we'd strolled the Inn's parking lot together – how when he was as young as six or seven, his drunken mother used to scream that he would always be a worthless piece of shit. At that age, how could you not believe you were what your mother claimed you to be?

Aaron, Daniel, and I. We all believed ourselves to be horrible people. Aaron had overcome the burden of that; Daniel had not. I felt somewhere in between, still capable of choosing either direction.

• • •

A delivery truck pulled up in front of the inn, the driver tossing out stacks of newspapers. Regardless of the still-dark sky or the position of hands on the clock, I knew we were now at the true separation point between day and night. For me and Aaron, it was still yesterday, while this truck driver was living in tomorrow.

I didn't want to leave. There was still so much for us to talk about. I'd come here especially wanting to ask about Mr. P, but the time never seemed right, and now it was too late. Our bodies and minds were drained.

Aaron understood when I mentioned heading out. "I'm off on Monday," he said. "If you're still here, why don't you come over to the house. I'll make pizza and we'll shoot the shit."

I said I'd come, adding that I was impressed Aaron made his own pizza.

"It's the only way I know for sure what's in it – and what's not."

Before I left, we hugged. It felt like something I had never experienced before: the strength and assurance coming from him, the acceptance and even love for who I was, for being his friend. I tried to give that back to him, could only hope that I was able.

Chapter Sixteen

The sky was already brightening in the East, preparing to usher in the morning, when I got back to the motel. I lay in bed, my body achy but my mind racing. I'd loved spending time with Aaron, I'd learned a lot, and some honest-to-goodness memories had slipped through a crack in the dam holding back my past. I didn't expect the floodgates would suddenly open, but I'd seen and felt myself in places I'd stood fifteen years ago. I'd remembered.

As I lay restlessly in bed, I couldn't escape from Mr. P. I'd wanted to ask Aaron about him, perhaps summon the courage to tell Aaron everything. Aaron would have listened.

Now, strings of words floated like dissonant music. Eventually I got out of bed, squinting against the just-risen sun, and turned on my laptop. Holding my hands over the keyboard, I let go of all restraint.

...

Summoned, you trudge down the hall to the one pay telephone in an alcove next to the bathroom. Nine p.m. on a Thursday, your second month of college, and you've been debating whether to go to bed early, or try to bum something to drink, which likely would require spending time with guys you don't like, hanging out in Felder's room, from which laughter rafts out on a river of Led Zeppelin.

"Are you dressed?"

You know the voice but it leaves your mind befuddled.

"Get dressed. I'll pick you up in fifteen minutes."

You struggle to process. Mr. P is three hundred miles away, and he'll be there in fifteen minutes? Does he have magical powers beyond even what you've imagined?

...

You ended up going to his alma mater, a small, almost-Ivy-League private college in Maine, even though you didn't think you could get in, and your mother said they couldn't afford it unless you got major scholarships. Mr. P said, "Don't worry. I'll take care of it." You were accepted, and received $2,500 in scholarships from local organizations – one-half your tuition for freshman year – plus another $2,000 in work study from the college that promised to renew itself every year.

You've been in a relationship with Mr. P ever since that first night he kissed you. When warm summer nights brought too many people to where you used to park at the lake, he took you to a friend's house under construction, high up a mountain, looking down on the valley, no other houses nearby. He spread a blanket across the patchy grass, offering you a beer, lighting a joint, assuring you, "No one will bother us here."

For a while you talked, you baring your soul and he lecturing, instructing, praising, and encouraging, until he decided there'd been enough talking and leaned over and kissed you, hard enough that the bristles of his beard rubbed raw the tender flesh around your mouth. His hands began to roam, found their mark, then divided, one hand continuing to work while the other sought out your hand and directed it to him.

You were astonished that he was already so hard. You'd touched yourself enough you should have been an expert, but you didn't know what to do with his penis instead of your own. Or rather, you couldn't make your body obey; couldn't get up, turn round, approach him, explore him the way you would a female, learn what he liked, embrace the power you could hold over him, the power to grant pleasure.

Nor would your body allow itself to grant him that power over you. Your penis remained limp; parts of your body that had tingled when touched by your summer girl-friend – your thighs, your face, your neck – remained dead to all sensation.

Eventually, he turned away and finished himself off, while you fought tears at your miserable failure.

Those evenings happened throughout the summer. "I've missed you," he'd say after a week or two had gone by, now that you were a graduate and no longer saw him every day in class. His teachings now included how to thrive in college, people and places from his years there, and methods to seduce a girl so she'd finally have sex with you.

Each time, you told yourself, *Tonight we'll only talk.* Even so, you never protested when he moved you beyond. You thought of the sexual time as payback for all he'd done for you.

You thought you were taking his teachings to heart. And yet, to the fears you'd long had about having sex with women, your time with Mr. P added others: the fear that a perceptive woman would be able to tell, from looking at you or the way you moved or some other mysterious tell, what you and Mr. P had been doing; the fear that when the moment finally came for you to enter a woman, your penis would go as limp as it did for Mr. P.

Back in your room, you trade your sweatshirt for a button-down, make an effort to tame your hair, which has grown shaggy of late. You've been experimenting with a beard, just a few weeks now, and you ought to shave but there's no time. You grab your coat and head outside.

It's a cold night, the sky dense with stars. You've noticed that this northern sky holds more stars than the one at home. Or perhaps they merely shine brighter here.

When you hear the familiar sound, the buzzing of the Alfa Romeo, you realize that a part of you never believed he would come, that the phone call was imagined, or a prank. Your body tenses, but you're wearing a silly grin as you walk to the open window on the driver's side. "Get in," he barks.

He looks the same, the clothes, the hair, the expression, judgmental and amused. When you shut the door, turning off the interior light, he pats your face, draws back. "It's a bad look on you," he says. "Teenage mountain man."

You say, by way of apology but a pushback too, "I didn't have time to shave."

"Have you eaten?"

"Five o'clock," you say, because in college, that's when dinner is served.

"I haven't eaten," he says. "I'm famished," and quickly you've left the lights of the campus behind to speed down back country roads, the only light from the stars overhead and the spears shooting out from the front of his car.

He pulls into a restaurant near the Turnpike. "The Silent Woman," says the sign, beside a life-size cardboard woman dressed in Puritan clothes, with no head.

You had dinner here six weeks ago, when your mother

drove you to school. You're wondering if you should mention this when your face is grabbed, pincers on either side of your chin, and turned so his lips can descend upon you. "Definitely," he says when he's done with you. "If all the stores in this hick town didn't close at sunset, I'd take you to buy a razor right now."

You trail him into the restaurant, insides roiling out of fear that someone in the parking lot might have seen him kiss you, out of shame because your beard now feels like a mistake for all to see, like a stain on the front of your shirt or a broken zipper on your fly. There's also this: the irrational fear that someone in the restaurant will recognize you from before with your mother, and that somehow she will find out. But when Mr. P takes center stage, no one pays attention to you.

"You want a drink?" he asks when you are settled.

"I'm not old enough."

He looks puzzled. "Isn't it legal at eighteen?"

"Nineteen in Maine."

He grins. "Tonight, you're nineteen."

When the waiter comes you don't know what to order. Usually when he picks you up, Mr. P brings beer. You've also drunk Southern Comfort and Boone's Farm apple wine. Your mother let you drink rum cokes at New Year's, but you don't know if that's a real drink.

Mr. P says something that sounds like "Doors, rocks," and you say, "I'll have the same." The waiter writes it down without flinching and walks away.

He's here because of a retirement celebration for Irving Resnick, the director of the college Theater Department. Professor Resnick is one of a half-dozen people Mr. P told you to look up when you got to school, and to mention his name, although you haven't done that yet. "I thought it would be a nice surprise," says Mr. P. "Take you out for a decent meal, see how you're doing here at school."

"It's good," you say, hoping that answers both how you're doing and what you think of the surprise.

The waiter brings your drinks. "Here's to you," says Mr. P, raising his glass. "To the beginning of a great career."

You touch your glass to his and drink. It burns going down, but worse is the iodine taste assaulting your tongue. Can alcohol spoil?

"Easy," says Mr. P, wearing the same amused smile he's had on since you got into his car, as if he's being entertained by a cute baby or a frisky dog.

"Tell me about life at college," he demands, and when you don't reply fast enough, he asks, "Still a virgin?"

You force a laugh. "I'm working on it."

At home, he made you describe all the things you did with your summer girlfriend, things you tried that he taught you. When you gently took her nipple between your teeth and pressed down, she gasped and wriggled, and you thought that would be it for the night, forever, that she'd scream, "Stop," and never want to see you again, but she recovered quickly, baring her other breast and deftly moving you over, to spread the wealth, so to speak.

She let you slide your finger along the groove between her legs, outside, not inside, her underwear, but even so, you were amazed at how smooth and slick was the path your finger took. That was as far as you ever got with her, rounding third and heading home, you described it to yourself later, but the outfielder's throw beat you and the catcher tagged you out before you could score.

You didn't describe it that way for Mr. P, who didn't care about baseball. "She's saving herself," you explained.

"She's protecting herself," he replied. "She's afraid to lose control."

Now, sitting in The Silent Woman, he says, "Believe it

or not, there are actually females right here on this campus who love a good fuck. They're the ones you need to be on the lookout for."

Later, after your second dinner of the day, you end up back at his motel. "Take your clothes off," he says, drawing back the blankets on the bed. This is new; in his car or on the blanket beside the house-under-construction, you made do with unbuckled pants. You wish he'd turn off the light, but he's enjoying the spectacle. Enjoying your humiliation? Sure, you could flee the room, hitchhike back to campus – or, another Matthew Winton could – but you have given yourself to this man, your mind anyway, even as your body refuses to agree.

In the end, it is not so different, really. A point comes when you separate from yourself, one Matthew flying off to sit on a perch high above, looking down at the other Matthew being manipulated by Mr. P. When he takes you in his mouth, your body's determined inertia defeats his determined energy. He directs not just your hand but your head, positions you to take him, although thankfully, he jerks away from you before groaning, spurting all over the sheets. Vaguely, you are aware of other things he could have done to you, and you are relieved the night is over. Still, you feel once again the weight of having failed his test.

Dressing, he says, "This is our secret. We'll keep it till the day we die." When you don't respond, he says, "You know that, right? How important that is?"

He's said this before. Months ago, with you lying beside him beneath a mid-summer sky, he asked, "What do you tell your mother we do when we go out like this?"

In his voice, for the first time ever, you noticed uncertainty.

"I say we talk – about school stuff, acting, writing, the future. She doesn't ask much. I don't think she wants to know."

"You know you can't tell her about the things we do."

"Of course not," you reply. The idea seems ridiculous, that you would ever tell anyone. You're stung he felt the need to say it. You understand what you're both risking.

In his motel room bed, four miles from your college campus, a reminder seems even more unnecessary. You're convinced he got you into college, secured those scholarships. Who'd risk losing that?

Besides, a part of you believes him when he swears there's nothing wrong with what you do. You know you're not gay, though there would be nothing wrong if you were; other than sex, you've felt you have more in common with gay men than straight ones. It's other people, repressed, unenlightened, vindictive people who want to slay everyone who's different, everyone they fear – those are the ones who would destroy us, he says. Destroy him first, and you later.

You are loyal to your secret, loyal to Mr. P most of all. He has sacrificed much to help you realize your dreams. He's teaching you, and sex with him is the test to prove how much you've learned. Even when you continually fail, he doesn't condemn you. He won't give up on you.

. . .

A grainy darkness filled the room when I awoke. I didn't remember finishing what I'd been writing, getting up and crawling into bed, but I'd slept the day away, and when I touched the keyboard on my laptop, rows of words appeared. I didn't have to read them to remember what they said.

I knew what I had to do. Acceptance brought a tightness to my chest, and a quickening in my veins, and I channeled Dr. Clark's voice: Not today. Tomorrow is time enough.

I bought some bland Chinese food and another bottle of scotch and sat outside my cabin, bundled in my coat and a blanket, an owl hooting in the distance and the stars overhead beginning to brighten. Mr. P. was the most popular teacher at my school. He said I had talent as a writer. He wasn't just saying, "You have talent, considering you're a schmuck growing up in an unimportant town with a janitor father." He'd been on Broadway. He compared me to Hemingway and Fitzgerald, promised I could one day enter that class, if only I listened to him, learned from him, did everything he instructed me to do. He promised I could become the person I'd always craved to be. If only I did what he commanded.

He delivered, too. He got me special privileges my last year in high school, promised he'd get me into Carver College and ensure they gave me scholarships. When those things happened, I couldn't deny his influence. I continued to believe he would deliver on all his promises, if only I could do the things he asked me to do, be the person he wanted me to be. The failure was mine alone, never his.

Now I wondered: was it all a lie? Did he find amusement seducing this boy who was tops in his class, who Aaron described as seeming to always have it together? Did he revel in stripping away that false confidence, peeling layers until all that was left was a frightened, clueless child? In the end, was I no more to him than a fresh dick?

A dick that couldn't even stand up, as it were, to its meagre responsibilities.

I didn't know whether to be angry or sad. I felt both, and they didn't mix well. I thought of how Sarah had once described anger and sadness as opposite ways to deal with the same emotion. I'd been hurt, and I didn't know whether to throw things at the wall or curl up in fetal position in my bed. Both seemed attractive; neither seemed enough. And so I drank.

Eventually I stumbled inside and flopped on the bed. When the silence seemed too loud, I turned on the television for distraction. It was still on when I woke to find myself bathed in tomorrow's sun.

...

The phone book in the motel office provided what I was looking for: Jonathan Piretti, #2 Old Becket Road.

I tried to imagine meeting him. I had no memory of his house, other than what had been in my writing. I imagined standing on his lawn, waiting like some Old West gunfighter for his enemy to come out. But when he did appear – a wide shadow only – I slunk up to him like the child he always turned me into, head down, arms at my sides, timid and obedient.

"You're not a teenager anymore."

My voice firm but not confident, I tried to imagine a conversation. "Didn't you see?" I asked him. "Couldn't you tell?"

"I was only trying to help you. To teach you. Look who you've become. Your father was a janitor, your mother lived her life in fear. Look how far you've come. You can't say I didn't help you."

"It almost destroyed me."

"But it didn't."

What doesn't destroy you makes you stronger. He doesn't say that, and I don't reply. Sometimes, what doesn't destroy you leaves you living your life in fear.

I imagined him turning defensive. "What we did was consensual. You were legally an adult. It's not like I took advantage of a child."

"I felt like a child. Emotionally."

"That's why you needed me."

I fought to speak the truth. "You hurt me."

"I never coerced you. You could always have said no."

"I only wanted to be like everyone else."

"But you didn't. You wanted to be special. I made it so you were."

Finally, I found the question I was terrified to ask: "Did you mean any of it? What you said about me? Was any of it true?"

...

It was a modest white house, Cape Cod style, on a modest parcel of land at the corner of Old Becket and Long Pond Roads. Beyond the house lay pastureland, a half dozen or so cows standing still as rocks under a bludgeoning, steel-gray November sky. A row of trees blocked off the farmhouse next door.

I drove past the house several times. One car was parked in the driveway, a Subaru, in front of the closed garage door. His wife's car, probably. I doubted he still owned that red Alfa Romeo, but whatever sportscar he'd replaced it with likely occupied the garage.

I drove all the way to West Becket, a small town with a combined town hall and post office, a convenience store/gas station, and an elementary school, but nothing more. I drove back in the opposite direction, toward Mansfield, retracing the route I'd apparently walked that wintry night, naively thinking – hoping – that Mr. P and his wife would adopt me. I even drove several miles down Long Pond Road, but not far enough to find a pond.

On my next pass, I shouted, "Fuck it!" and jerked the steering wheel just in time to make the driveway. Pulling in behind the Subaru, I focused on drawing even, steady breaths.

Mounds of steel-covered clouds moved in from the west, covering the front yard in shadow. Should I sit there until he noticed me and came out, the way, I now recalled, he'd parked in front of my parents' house waiting for me to come bounding out so we could go off to one of our "lessons"?

I saw no signs of life. Curtains were drawn across the front windows, and the upstairs windows were dark. Despite the car, might no one be home?

A jolt ran through me as I glanced in the rear view mirror and imagined him pulling in behind me, blocking in my car. I scrambled out and peered up and down the road, but no cars were in sight. It felt like a fist clenched around my lungs, and only by consciously relaxing would that fist loosen enough to let me breathe.

I mounted the five steps. Pressing the doorbell, I leaned close to make sure I heard it ring. Other than the ring, I heard nothing.

I rang it a second time. Instantly it opened, as if the person on the other side had been waiting for that second ring. That person was a woman, shoulder-length brown hair streaked with gray, slightly stooped and fragile looking, her hand remaining protectively on the door as her slight frame tried to fill the open space.

Stepping back, I offered a gentle smile. It was colder on the steps, with a cutting wind, and I worried about the woman, who wore only a cardigan sweater over her dress, her free hand holding it closed at the neck.

"I'm looking for – Mr. Piretti," I managed. "Would he be home?"

The woman looked like it was a hard question to answer. Noticing the wrinkles at the corners of her mouth, the skin tight around her neck, I thought that when younger, she would have been beautiful.

And then I remembered: she was. I remembered the time I'd walked to their house, the concern on her face. The time she'd accompanied her husband to my high school graduation party, and charmed even my mother. The time, backstage after *West Side Story*, when she complimented my performance and made me believe my small role had been essential to the play's success.

At seventeen I had a crush on her. Never could I understand how Mr. P could prefer doing what he did with me over being with his wife.

"You are?" she asked, her unwavering voice and clear eyes showing an underlying strength.

I hesitated giving my name. When I finally told her, she gave a slight nod but showed no recognition. It was hard to believe she didn't remember me, not because of the impression I'd made on her, but because of the one her husband made on me.

"I was a student of Mr. P," I said, unable even now to call him by his first name.

"Jonathan had so many who loved him," she replied.

"Is he home now? I'm only back for a short time, and I was hoping I might say hello." I glimpsed the stairway beyond her shoulder, imagining him tromping down.

"I'm sorry," she said. Her eyes meeting mine were strong and apologetic. "Jonathan passed away."

Her words didn't hit like a thunderbolt, but more like a light rain, seeping into me. Another image flashed through my mind, a young doctor with curly black hair and a bushy moustache, telling me that my mother had stage four cancer and would live three months, six at most. My mother and Mr. P, two people I never believed could die.

"Oh, no," leaked out of me.

And yet, another voice from some dark recess of my uncooperative memory whispered, You knew this.

The woman – Mrs. Piretti, I refused to think of her as Mrs. P – opened the door wider. "Please come in," she said, and my legs obeyed, although my whole body felt numb, as I trailed her into a living room in disarray, boxes in corners stacked four and five high, bookshelves stripped of all but a smattering of forlorn-looking remnants. A huge empty space in one corner, that a piano used to occupy.

"You'll have to excuse the mess," she said. "I'm moving back to Maine." She removed a blanket and pillow from the couch so I could sit down, then settled in a well-worm armchair with a knitted Afghan draped across one arm. On a small table beside her, a glass of water, a pair of eyeglasses, a small bottle of pills.

"It was near the end of Spring," she said, her voice soft but controlled. "He had diabetes, you know. We were always after him to take better care of himself." She shook her head gently. "He so loved his indulgences.

"We retired together," she continued. "Three years ago," and I remembered that she'd been an English teacher too, in a different school district. "We planned to travel, but he was in and out of the hospital so much. It was his heart mostly. They say people with diabetes don't feel things that might be wrong with them. The diabetes masks the symptoms. It was that way with Jonathan. He always insisted he felt fine."

Her voice drifted into silence, her gaze sliding off to a corner of the room, a corner of her mind.

Gazing at the boxes, I thought, *Is she doing this all alone?* I recalled Mr. P saying that he and his wife had no children because they enjoyed being alone together too much. A crazy idea popped into my head: I could help her pack and move. Drive her to Maine in some rented truck. But she dismissed my offer with a wave of her hand. "I'm fine," she said. "My brother will come get me when it's time."

It was time to go. "Thank you for letting me take up your time," I told her. "I'm very sorry for your loss."

I took her hand when she offered. It was dry and soft and reminded me of a bird. "I can let myself out."

"Tell me your name again," she asked, and I did. She shook her head slowly. "No, I'm sorry. I don't remember. Jonathan had so many boys who loved him."

The trip to my car felt like moving across treacherous terrain, with little solid ground to trust. I backed out of the driveway without looking at the house. The steely November clouds had merged, and a light snow began to fall. For a moment the flakes looked like ashes from a giant fire. It was cold enough that when those flakes hit the windshield, they didn't melt, even with the heat turned up high.

Chapter Seventeen

Aaron changed his mind about making pizza. Instead, his table was covered with two big bowls and lots of interesting ingredients: a jar of peanut butter, two bags of frozen spinach, pasta, soy sauce, sugar, and a red spicy sauce called *Sambal Ulek.* Two big pots of water heated on the stove.

"Yeah," he told me as he worked, "I kind of came up with this myself one day. I was messing around with combining foods. The peanut butter and spinach are great together, and the *sambal ulek* adds just the right bite. I tried it with whole wheat pasta once but it was too much. It's pretty heavy as it is. It'll give you energy."

He prepared the food the way he seemed to do everything, with energy and commitment. He wore jeans and a green sweatshirt, both loose fitting. Understandably, he was more relaxed than at work the other night.

Darkness had settled when I arrived at his house. Aaron greeted me with a strong hug, clapping me on the back. "You remember this place?" he asked, and studying it, I did. It was small and long, one story, and was located right next door to the house he'd lived in with Caroline. He'd built it himself, back when I came back to the Berkshires after leaving the private school where I'd been teaching. At the time, since he was living with Caroline in the big farmhouse next door, he'd intended this to be his dojo, but then he and Caroline divorced, and he'd been living here ever since.

"We're still friends," he told me when I said I was sorry about the divorce. "She's got this new guy, he seems all right. She still asks for my help when there's a problem with the house." He laughed. "Neither one of them can hammer a nail straight to save their lives."

Inside, there was a small kitchen on one side and a hallway that likely led to his bedroom on the other, and one giant room in between. He'd sectioned off a dining area, and a space with a TV and a couple easy chairs, but most of the room was empty, with a sleek and shiny bare wood floor and a couple of wall-to-ceiling mirrors.

The shape and layout reminded me of my train station in Virginia. Had that influenced me, when I moved out of the house I'd been sharing with Jessie?

"The timing's a little tricky on this," he told me, checking the water in one of the big pots. When it started boiling, he dumped in the spinach. Then he went to the fridge and took out two bottles. "This one's mine" – he held up one with a green label. "It's non-alcoholic. It's not bad, actually. But I got some of the real stuff for you" – he handed me a bottle of Coors. "It doesn't bother me when someone else is drinking. You just have to promise to take any you don't finish with you when you go."

I laughed. "Sounds like a good deal for me."

He started combining the other ingredients in a large bowl, beginning by scooping out the entire jar of peanut butter. "I've been taking some classes," he said. "By mail. Skidmore College."

"Oh yeah?"

"It's not a big deal. I just do one a semester. I'm not out for a degree or anything. I like doing the reading, and the professors have to read and comment on what I wrote." He laughed. "I feel sorry for the one I have now. I'm sure everyone else in class writes a paragraph or two, and I'm turning in ten pages. I've always found that shit interesting."

"What course is it?"

"Introduction to Psychology. I took a history course last spring on World War II. I liked that a lot. My father got caught by the Nazis in Africa, spent a year in a POW camp."

"I didn't know that."

"He didn't talk about it much. Anyway, I thought I'd try Psychology. It's kind of bullshit, but it's interesting bullshit."

"I took Intro Psych freshman year in college," popped out of me, and suddenly I could see myself sitting far back in a lecture hall with seventy-five other students, the professor posed behind a podium on a stage.

He looked up. "So you're remembering some shit?"

"A little. The other night at the inn, a lot of stuff came back to me."

He chuckled. "Yeah, that place has a way of imprinting itself on your memory."

Another image snuck into my mind: me sitting in an office facing a counselor who sat behind a messy desk. Telling him I was depressed, unsure of my sexuality. All the while, I was thinking about Mr. P.

I pushed the memory away and sipped my beer. Aaron was stirring the peanut butter in the big bowl, mixing it with the soy sauce, *sambol ulek*, and some water from the now-cooked spinach, and alternately spinning around to stir the pasta boiling on the stove. He even managed to pause long enough to feed Ziggy, who had trotted up to me when I arrived and pressed his body against my legs to make sure I knew he wanted to be petted, then flopped into his bed in the corner and gone to sleep.

Now, he dug into the food Aaron piled in a huge metal bowl, making grunting, slopping noises. In what seemed no more than ten seconds, the bowl was empty.

"He's happy," I mused.

"He's always happy. You have to give him that."

When he'd stirred the peanut butter concoction into a smooth sauce, Aaron drained the pasta, then began the delicate operation of combining everything, spooning a little pasta into one of the empty pots, followed by some spinach and some of the sauce, all stirred together. He repeated the process until everything mixed together in the one big pot. He grabbed a couple plates, snatched a container of parmesan cheese from the fridge, and set the pot on the "dining room" table. "I think you'll like this," he said, and spooned an enormous portion onto my plate. "I like it with parmesan but you have it however you want."

He held up his non-alcoholic beer for a toast. "It's great to see you, man."

I couldn't help but smile. It seemed that I wasn't the hermit I'd feared. My best friend just happened to live three hundred miles away.

The food was incredible, the peanut butter and spinach combining beautifully, energized by the little jolt from the *sambal ulek*. We both ate as if we hadn't had a meal in days, not indelicately but with gusto and great enjoyment. Aaron cleaned his plate first and spooned out a little more. When he offered more to me, I told him I'd love to but was too full.

He'd refused my help when preparing the meal but allowed me to pitch in on the cleanup. "I can give you the recipe," Aaron said while making coffee. When it was ready, he poured two cups and we moved to the living room section, sitting side by side in the two easy chairs facing the blank screen of the television.

A memory popped, and I laughed as I recounted it for Aaron: the two of us, on the night I'd bought my first VCR, having a double feature movie night: *Das Boot* and *Sophie's Choice*. A typical date in Aaron's world?

I steeled myself and sat forward. "Can I ask you a question?"

He shrugged and nodded like there was no need to ask.

"Do you remember Piretti? The English teacher?"

He nodded, remembering. "He did that play you and Daniel were in. I don't know how he ever convinced Daniel to get involved in that. He was a piece of work, that guy."

"Piretti?"

"Yeah."

"Why do you say that?"

"He came on to Daniel once."

Something sunk in my stomach. "Daniel?"

"Yeah. Not during the play, it was afterwards. He got Daniel all these special privileges, he'd get him out of class, take him for a ride into town to get coffee. He'd bring him into the auditorium, give him private acting lessons. He kept telling Daniel he could be a real success as an actor, if only he applied himself."

"So what happened?"

"He's standing behind Daniel, showing him how he wants him to arrange his body. Suddenly this hand comes around and a finger strokes his cheek. Daniel figures it's accidental, until the hand takes his chin and turns his head, and Pirette leans over him and tries to give him a kiss."

"What happened?"

Aaron laughed. "Daniel clocked him. One punch laid him flat on his ass."

"No."

"That's the way Daniel told it. Although when Daniel told you something, you were never sure how much of it was true."

I thought back to something Mrs. Piretti had said: "He had so many boys who loved him." Was the truth that he had so many boys he tried to make love him? Had I been merely Daniel's replacement?

I wished we could move on to another subject. Maybe watch *Das Boot* and *Sophie's Choice* again. But I knew what I had to say.

"He came on to me, too. Piretti."

"He was a real sleaze."

I dared a quick glance at Aaron, who seemed to enjoy telling Daniel's story but had now turned serious. "I didn't clock him."

"He was a bastard."

"We had a – I don't know – relationship doesn't seem the right word. Senior year. He got me all those privileges you mentioned with Daniel. We sat in his car and had long talks. He said I could be a great writer, if only I let him teach me. In exchange..." My voice trailed off.

Aaron was silent too. Then he said, softly, "They call that grooming." I looked at him and he gave a gentle smile. "I read ahead in our textbook."

I told him about the writing I'd discovered, that I'd been doing before my accident. "It really shook me, reading all that. I still don't think I've recovered."

"PTSD," he said. "You don't have to be a soldier in battle to suffer from that shit."

I looked at him sideways, and he smiled again. "Like I told you, I've been reading ahead." Then he turned serious. "He abused you."

I wanted to argue. "He did things for me. He got me into college, got me scholarships. I could never have afforded it otherwise."

"You're the one who got into college, you got those scholarships. You were first in your class, for Christ's sake."

"I got put on the wait list for Middlebury." I didn't know if that was true but when it popped into my head, I said it.

"Their loss," he said, and leaned forward. "Look, maybe he had some influence, I don't know. I'm sure he wanted you to think he did. But nothing you've accomplished in your life was because of him. I'll bet it was in spite of him."

I fought the pressure building up behind my eyes, fought to steady my voice. Failed when I couldn't hold back words I had never spoken to anyone before. "I loved him. The stuff we did – I want to say the stuff he made me do, but he didn't make me. I hated doing it, but I only wanted to please him. To show I could be the person he said I could be."

I didn't realize Aaron had gotten up until I felt a strong hand squeeze my shoulder. I couldn't look at him, I just sat with my body coiled in on itself, staring at the floor.

I sensed Aaron returning to his chair. "He abused you," he said again, more forcefully. "That's what he was, an abuser. That doesn't mean he lied about your good qualities. They're probably what attracted you to him in the first place.

"He was a prick, but those things he saw in you – you're smart, and a terrific writer – those things are real, he was just astute enough to spot them, and he used them to get what he wanted.

"He probably did care about you, in his own way. But even if you give him the benefit of the doubt on that, he either wasn't able to recognize how much he was hurting you, or he didn't care enough to stop.

"But the things in you he found attractive, those things were real."

Once again we were both quiet. While I was regaining control of my emotions, Ziggy trotted over and laid his head on my thigh. Probably he just wanted to be petted, but it felt like he was telling me, "Don't be sad. There are always sticks to chase."

"Come here, you," Aaron said, and Ziggy obeyed.

"He's dead," I said. "Piretti."

"I think I read that. A couple months ago."

"Do you really think Daniel clocked him?"

"I don't know. If he didn't, Daniel wouldn't have admitted it, not even to me. But I hope he did."

"Me too," I said.

After a while, I told Aaron thanks. "For what?" he asked.

"For listening. For understanding. For not thinking I was a horrible person."

He laughed. "I should tell you about some of the crazy things I did back when I was drinking. Unfortunately, I'd probably have to start drinking again to build up the nerve."

• • •

Aaron made more coffee, then we took turns using the bathroom. When I came out, he asked, "You feel like taking a drive?"

I said sure and Ziggy, sensing something exciting, scurried over.

Aaron patted him on the head. "This guy needs some fresh air anyway."

I followed them to Aaron's car, an old hatchback smelling of wet dog, mostly because of Ziggy's felt-covered pillow spread across the back, and Ziggy himself. Aaron turned on the heat so we could roll down the windows.

"It's great your memory's coming back," Aaron said, as we headed back toward Old Bridge.

"There are still some gaps." One big one was my first sexual experience with a woman. Jessie said I hadn't been a virgin when she met me, and given all my fears, that first experience might have been monumental.

Another gap was that private school I'd taught at, then quit after a year and a half. I mentioned it to Aaron. "I never told you why I came back here?"

"I just figured it wasn't right for you."

I called up what I could remember: a Quaker school, with only about 150 students, K through 12. I taught English to grades 9 through 12 and was director of dramatics. I thought I liked teaching there, and was well liked in return. Yet I'd quit.

I would have liked to explore it more, but I felt bad for hogging the attention. I hadn't even asked Aaron how his mother was doing.

When I did, he laughed. "She's the same. She never changes. I mean, she changes from being someone who's drunk to someone who, on rare occasions, isn't drunk, or who goes from a mean drunk to a maudlin drunk, but in the big picture, nothing changes. Whatever else she is, first and foremost, she's a drunk, and I can say that because I was one too."

"It's great what you were able to do. You changed your life around."

A shrug, then a nod.

"Since you quit drinking, do you feel like a different person?"

"The main difference is that now, when I get the urge to drink a beer, or guzzle some Johnny Walker Black, I drink coffee instead. Or non-alcoholic beer."

"I can't imagine you ever going back."

"I can. It's a lot easier to say yes than no."

We'd reached Old Bridge and were heading down Main Street. As we passed the Inn, I wondered if Aaron would ignore it, since it was his night off, but he gave it a long look instead. "The guy I got working with me now is pretty good," he said. "He's got integrity, which is the most important thing."

I told him I was glad. He may only work four days a week, but he was responsible for the other three days too. Finding reliable people was no doubt hard. It wasn't an attractive job, with all that walking, and not great pay, and it wasn't easy, either, having to work all night, mostly having to supervise yourself. I thought again of Aaron saying that the real judge of a person's integrity was what he did when he knew no one was watching.

"Yeah," he said as we left Old Bridge behind. "I think you might remember this place."

The houses had grown farther apart, and finally, when woods surrounded us, he turned onto a dirt road, his headlights like lasers in the now-thick darkness. Tightly clustered trees closed in on either side, and pebbles pinged off metal as the car jounced over ruts. Ziggy stood on wobbly legs in the cramped back seat, his snout pushed out the window, drinking in the different scents, the promise of adventure.

Aaron swung a sudden right, hardly slowing, and the car bounced off the road, rattling and rocking, tall grass scraping the sides. When the car finally rumbled to a stop, it wasn't clear if Aaron had stopped or the car simply refused to go farther.

"Can you get out on that side?"

"I'll manage," I told him, using the car door to push back the wall of tall grass.

Ziggy was excited. "Come on, you," Aaron mock scolded, opening the back so Ziggy could leap out. He bounced and pranced, then shot off into the wide field that stretched out in front of us, long as a football field.

I spoke aloud the words popping into my mind. "I've been here before."

Aaron laughed. "We took you here for your celebration. When you wrote that class paper."

"I was here before that, too."

"There were lots of parties in this field."

Then I remembered. "We had our cast party for *West Side Story* here."

He laughed again. "You and about two hundred fifty other fuckers, most of whom had never heard of *West Side Story*, let alone acted in it."

I looked around and in my head heard music: *When the truth is found/to be lies...* I could see a field teeming with people. Suzanne Martin. Daniel. Mr. P, holding court.

Aaron moved away, closer to the middle of the field. I struggled through the tall grass to catch up to him.

"This is where he did it."

Daniel.

"He came the same route we took. He had one of those big-ass lugs of a car, so he was able to plow right through this field. Why should he give a shit about his car anyway? He wanted to get to this one spot. Only he knew why.

"He sat there and drank a whole fifth of vodka. Did he replay all the painful moments of his life? Toast happy moments, good people? Maybe he was just trying to drown the part of his brain that might be resisting what he intended to do."

I tried to imagine sitting in that car, first beside Daniel, and then instead of Daniel. I couldn't do it.

Then my mind brought to focus a deserted country road in Virginia, a sturdy tree waiting ahead. But I could only see it from the outside. I couldn't put myself in that car, either.

Aaron's voice popped the bubble. "Buddy Galvin, I don't know if you remember him, he was a year ahead of Daniel in school. He's on the police force now. He got a call that night to check out an abandoned car. He figured he'd find a couple kids making out in the woods somewhere. He never expected to find Daniel."

He grew silent then, and the two of us stood side by side, leaning back against the car. Ziggy bounded over and stood up on his hind legs, front paws balancing against Aaron's shoulders. Aaron jutted his head forward, letting Ziggy excitedly lick his chin.

"I could never do that. It would break this poor guy's heart."

He lifted Ziggy's front paws and set them on the ground. "He should have got himself a fucking dog."

"That accident I had – " I heard myself speaking, nothing I'd planned to bring up, nothing I could stop myself from saying – "The police who investigated weren't so sure it was an accident."

"What happened?"

"I rammed head first into a tree."

"What did the cops say?"

I shrugged, wishing I hadn't brought it up. "I was going pretty fast. There were no skid marks. One of them thought if I'd fallen asleep or something, the car wouldn't have followed the path it did."

"You don't remember anything?"

I shook my head. "I even went out there where it happened. It was two o'clock on a Sunday morning. I have no idea what I was doing out there, where I was going."

We were both silent a while. Then Aaron said, "I've been reading this book. It's called *Drama of the Gifted Child*. It's not part of the course, but I talked with the professor about some shit and he recommended it.

"Anyway, 'gifted' here doesn't mean Mozart or Shakespeare, just anyone who's smart and sensitive. High achievers like you, but also slackers and drunks like me and Daniel. There's something essential we never got from our mothers – who were wounded themselves as children – and we ended up not believing we were loved, or lovable, that instead we must be a worthless piece of shit."

He pushed out a sarcastic laugh. "I'm sure fathers fucked things up too, but this author, she focuses on the first few years of life, when the mother's at the center."

What he said made sense, but something in me resisted. I could understand Aaron blaming his own mother, but I didn't want to blame mine.

"People like us, we grow up remembering the bad stuff, feeling the pain. We hardly even think about the good stuff that made us happy. I remember when you told me how unhappy you thought your mother was, how badly you wanted to help her get rid of her pain."

It was my turn for the sarcastic laugh. "I didn't exactly do a bang-up job with that one."

"But did you ever think about how happy you made her? If she was still alive and you asked her, 'Did I make you happy?' I'll bet she'd say, 'Yes.' She'd probably be shocked you had to ask the question."

"I don't feel that," I said.

"Don't you think it's true?"

I wanted to say, *You don't know. You never heard those wails, that bleating that cut through the locked bathroom door. You don't know how she shied away, when a scared or sad little boy begged to climb into her lap, only wanting to be held.* The way she spat, "You're just like your father," when she wanted to punish me, put me in my place.

I'd met Aaron's mother, and I'd heard his stories that made my own mother seem like a saint. The details were different but the feelings were the same. The way we tried to cope was different – Aaron with booze, me by attending to her when I could, and turning invisible when I could not. But the damage was the same.

I tried to remember the good things. When I played sports in high school, my mother attended all the games. She made huge meals for me when I came home late from practice. Senior year, she made a scrapbook of all the articles mentioning my name in the local paper, not just for sports but academic awards too. It struck me that she might have been trying to show that she loved me.

I'd always thought she objected to Mr. P out of jealousy. But she might have sensed all along that for everything Mr. P gave, he would take back more.

"I always felt I had to be perfect," I told Aaron now. "When I couldn't be, I used to pretend I was invisible. Not really, I didn't think I could make myself disappear, but it's like I was trying to tell the world I'd turned myself off. I didn't want to be Matthew Winton anymore. I just wanted to be left alone."

"That's tough, thinking you have to be perfect, and if you can't be, you have to disappear. For me it was different." His laugh was breathy, gentle and sad. "I wish I'd figured out how to make myself invisible. Instead, I used to creep around the house like a burglar, hoping she wouldn't notice I was there."

We both gazed out into the empty field, Daniel's car visible only in our minds. I thought Aaron was thinking the same thing as me: if we'd been able to get into that car that night, we would have done everything we could to talk Daniel out of doing what he did. But what if either of us had been driving?

"It's a fucked-up life," Aaron said with a sigh. He clapped me on the back. "And you, my friend, need to get yourself a dog."

Chapter Eighteen

"Hey, it's me. Matthew. I guess you know that, with my name on your phone and all...

"I'm in Massachusetts. I got here okay. I saw my friend Aaron, we talked about a lot of stuff. My memory's coming back. Not everything, there are still some gaps, but I definitely remember more than before. I'm going to stay up here a little longer.

"I'm sorry I didn't call before. I was lost. I didn't know what I was doing. I'm sorry if I hurt you.

"I thought you might be home by now but maybe you had to work late. You don't need to call me back.

"Maybe when I get home, we could talk? It's okay if you don't want to, I understand."

I hung up, wishing a phone message was more like writing where you could make a draft and look it over before sending it off. How many times did I say I was sorry? Not that she didn't deserve multiple apologies. I'd been so tense, it was hard to even remember what I'd said.

After leaving Aaron's around three a.m., I'd slept until noon, and woke up wanting to call Sarah. I had no expectations, it just seemed a right thing to do.

I waited until evening, not wanting to take the coward's route and call while she was at work and couldn't answer. Even so, I hadn't reached her. Maybe she went to bed extra early. I tried not to think about alternatives, like maybe she was with some other guy. Or maybe when my name appeared on her phone, she chose not to answer.

If we never saw each other again, I could say the timing wasn't right, but it was hard not to believe I'd gotten what I deserved.

• • •

At first, my memory came back through a certainty of what I knew. As I was driving, Route 7 appeared in my mind as if I'd opened a map. I knew that Lenox was north of Old Bridge, then Pittsfield, Williamstown, and finally, the Vermont border. I knew – and knew in my mind how to find – the Pittsfield public library, three times the size of the one in Mansfield; the video store I used to frequent when VCRs first became popular; the paper mill where I worked three summers during college, the same place my father worked after he lost his job as school janitor. The cabin on the back edge of one of His Honor's properties where I lived during most of the time I worked with Aaron at the Inn.

I spent the day driving past those places, where in my twenties, I'd discovered the music of Leonard Cohen through the CDs the library allowed patrons to borrow; binged on Kurosawa films – recommended by Aaron – on my new VCR. Driving past the paper mill, I saw myself wandering at 3 a.m., my feet hot and sore in their heavy work boots. I saw myself standing in front of a mirror over a fireplace in the cabin I'd lived in, having just come out of the shower, moving to "Dancing in the Dark."

It felt like taking an outline and coloring in all the open spots.

I was visiting the places of my life. "My life," I said aloud. I really did have a life.

There were still important gaps. Why I left teaching in the middle of my second year, for instance. I'd told Aaron I loved teaching at that Quaker school. It was the perfect situation: small classes, smart students, an administration that gave teachers near total freedom. There was even a one-hour silent meditation the whole school attended in the middle of each week.

I also still had no memories of my current teaching, of the books we read and discussed, or how I managed to teach writing. And I struggled to recall key moments of my time in college. I considered driving to Maine, but in the end I settled for technology, finding a café with free internet and looking up Carver College. On the computer I recognized most of the buildings: the huge library sitting atop a hill like the giant topping of a wedding cake; the Quad that contained the all-male, all-freshman dorm I lived in my first year – the last of its kind, as the destruction my dormmates and I caused helped bring coed dorms for all. I remembered rooms I'd lived in those four years, roommates I'd had.

Then I began to see myself in those places. I saw Matthew Winton sitting in the first seat of the far right row in English class, where he sat in all classes he enjoyed (taking the last seat in classes he didn't). I saw myself standing in line in the cafeteria, feeling anxious if I wasn't with a friend or couldn't spot one already seated; the ignominy of having to eat alone.

Freshman year, having learned to play bridge and chess, I saw myself seated in the third-floor lounge, feet up on the low table, cards in hand. I argued literature with a guy down the hall, impossible questions like who was the better writer, Tolstoy or Dostoyevsky. There was a guy – Tony Riles – who stacked up empty beer cans floor to ceiling along every wall of his room; the other guy – with a Norwegian name; Sven? – with the full beard who had taken two years off before college to hike the world, making him old enough to legally purchase wine and beer for everyone in the dorm.

Over my four years of college, I could remember relationships with three women. Two of those were serious enough that I brought the women home to meet my mother, who didn't like either one, I sensed, although she never openly voiced an opinion. I didn't think much time passed after those visits home before I broke off the relationships.

The third woman was Marie, a sweet, waifish girl who would come to my room late at night to talk, and sometimes stay. She was shy, and once confessed that though she loved visiting me, she found it awkward when she had to announce whether she wished to stay the night or go. So she worked out a plan: "I'll bring my toothbrush with me," she said, "and if I start feeling that I'd like to stay, I'll put it in my shirt pocket. If you don't see it there, I won't be staying that night."

Her plan was fine with me. I never wanted to be with a woman who didn't want to be with me, and I didn't want to coax a woman to have sex when she didn't want to, so I was content to let her make the call. On nights when the toothbrush appeared in her pocket, it felt like a treat.

I had sex with all three of those women, and I didn't recall having any problems, other than the occasional "night off" from too much alcohol, fatigue, or anxiety. I thought I was a decent lover; I was attentive, and I wanted to please my partner as much as or more than being pleased myself. I remembered Mr. P saying once that during sex, both partners should be totally selfish, focused on taking their own pleasure and satisfying themselves. "That way," he said, "both people end up getting what they want." Although I doubt I ever pushed back on that idea, I secretly believed the opposite should be true: if each person focused on pleasing their partner, wouldn't an even greater satisfaction occur?

I'd tried to be that way in my sexual relations, to always be aware of the woman's needs and desires. And yet, none of those women – Joanne in sophomore year; Karen in senior year; Marie, across nearly three years, until she found a steady boyfriend in our last year – was the first woman I had sex with. That first sexual experience with a woman was still hiding behind the wall in my mind.

That night, words and images peppered my mind as I tried to sleep. Giving in, I got out of bed. It was nearly two, and I had yet to sleep a minute. I fixed some coffee in the small pot, then sat down in front of my computer and waited for those words to return. When they did, I became the recorder, simply typing the words I heard.

. . .

Freshman year. Four weeks after Mr. P's visit, you make an appointment with the college's psychological counselor. You know why but you don't know how to say it.

Floating in Crazyland, you imagine this counselor contacting Mr. P, asking him to leave you alone. You can't do it yourself, not even in a letter. You've tried: "I'm so grateful for all you've done for me but –" that's where you always end. But what? I've had enough now? I never wanted that part of it, I hated every minute? I couldn't even please you then?

You promised Mr. P you'll never say his name. But you have to say something. If you can tell even one person something, maybe you won't feel so horribly alone.

The counselor is younger than you imagined, under thirty, with a mop of blonde hair on a boyish face. He alternates between bubbling energy – making broad gestures as he speaks, sliding his wheeled-chair across the long space behind his long, cluttered desk – and slumping down in his chair as if about to fall asleep.

He begins by asking, "What's brings you here today?"

The question sets you back, though it's probably standard. It sounds too casual, as if you've walked into an ice cream shop and been asked what flavor you want.

"I don't know," you manage. "I guess I've been depressed."

He asks for more, but your response is vague; you sleep a lot, have little energy or appetite. They warned about depression in the orientation, encouraged everyone who felt that way to see a counselor. You don't know if you're depressed, or what that means. You can't bring yourself to say, "I feel sad all the time," or "I feel like there's this giant shadow chasing me."

"What you feel is normal," he tells you, "for someone who has only been in college a few months."

This prickles you. You don't want to believe that what you feel is normal, that "normal" might mean you'll feel this way the rest of your life.

"I think I might be gay."

You think maybe he'll ask, "Have you had sex with a guy?" and you, eyes lowered, will merely nod, and he'll look at you with compassion and understanding, and you'll tell him all of it. Instead he asks, "You find yourself attracted to your roommate?"

"No."

"To some other guy."

"No."

"When you wank, you think about guys?"

"No."

A smile, amused, that reminds you of Mr. P. "I don't think you're gay."

"I don't fit in," you say. "I don't feel like everyone else."

"Met any girls you like?"

A sarcastic laugh escapes you. "Sure, but they're all interested in guys that aren't like me."

"And what are 'guys like you' like, exactly?"

You shrug.

"Ever had sex with a woman?"

You pause. To the other freshman guys in your dorm, you've made up a story about the girl you dated over the summer, who let you go all the way.

"No."

"There you are. You'll meet a girl, eventually. Maybe you'll even fall in love. Given the way things are these days, you'll probably end up having sex. And I'm not going to say that then all your problems will be solved, but afterwards, you'll feel a lot different – a lot better – than you do right now."

You leave without getting close to the words you came to speak.

• • •

I pushed back the chair, dropping my arms. My shoulders and lower back ached, my eyes burned. I went to the bathroom, returned to my chair. I wasn't done, I couldn't escape into sleep, not yet.

• • •

Freshman year, not long after visiting the counselor. You're at a party at one of the frat houses for nerds, not athletes. You've been watching a woman who makes your heart race, tall and lithe with long straight black hair. You want to approach her but fear she'll laugh at your cluelessness: "Do you really imagine a girl like me would look twice at a guy like you?"

Another girl, plain looking, with a broad forehead and brown hair that looks greasy, is sitting by herself. She's eyed you from time to time, not invitingly but with a cautious smile. She likely sees you as you see her: as someone who might be safe.

When the girl who makes your heart race is suddenly surrounded by a cluster of good-looking males, party-crashing athletes, you walk over to the plain girl and start a conversation. Her name is Maureen Bahnsen, from Caribou, way up north, been to Canada but no state other than Maine. Wants to be a German major and hopes to spend junior year on exchange in Munich.

She lives in a dorm across campus. You walk her home. When she stops outside the building entrance, her body language makes it clear she won't be inviting you in. Still, you've enjoyed her companionship, and she's smiled a lot more once the two of you started talking. Tomorrow is Sunday, and when you ask if she'd like to meet for brunch, she says yes. All that's left is to decide how to part. You despise these moments, hate feeling awkward and uncertain. The only consolation is that she seems to feel the same.

In the end, you stumble together into a quick kiss on the lips. Walking back to your dorm, you feel an elation far out of proportion to the facts.

. . .

You cultivate the relationship slowly, warily. On a Friday night a few weeks later, she invites you to her room. Her roommate and boyfriend are packing to spend the weekend at a private chalet. Incredibly, her roommate is the woman who made your heart race at the party where you first met Maureen. Her boyfriend is the son of a TV newscaster. You feel you're meeting royalty.

Finally, you and Maureen are alone. You've kissed before but never with the kind of passion that might lead to something beyond. It's a struggle sometimes to get her to open her mouth. But you like how she feels snuggled against you, and you love being intimate enough with a girl to be able to embrace her when you want, or playfully smack her butt.

On this night you've brought a book, because that's the kind of date Maureen prefers, even on a Friday: a boy and girl stretched out in bed together, doing homework.

You like the novel you're reading for English class, but time passes with painful slowness. It's like having to eat your vegetables before being allowed dessert, stretched out over hours.

Finally you close your book, turn onto your back, stretch. "I'm studied out for one night," you say. There's something dutiful in the way Maureen tidies up her books and papers and sets them on her desk.

You stretch out your arm and she slides into the groove. You can feel her chest moving up and down with her breath. Even the light pressure of her body against yours forces you to shift to accommodate your erection. Maureen is a virgin but not a prude; with no animosity, she's told of nights she dragged her pillow and blanket to the lounge even though her roommate and boyfriend swore they could be quiet, if she wanted to stay in her own bed.

You struggle to tamp down expectations for what might happen tonight, alone with a girl in a room left to the two of you for the next two days.

You kiss her, gently at first but then more insistently, using your tongue as you've been taught. When she presses her front against yours, you slide your hand along her back, burrow beneath her shirt to caress her naked back, marred only by the bra strap across her shoulder blades. You slide your hand farther down to cup her jean-clad buttocks. It's the first time you've touched her sexually in an intimate place. She moans and presses her body harder into yours. Encouraged, you wedge your hand between her legs.

She stiffens, pulls away. "You're going too fast," she whispers, a little out of breath.

"Sorry."

The kiss resumes. Her body presses into yours so tightly there's no room for your dangerous hand. Eventually, she lets you cup her breast, over bra and shirt, and later her legs part enough to slide one of yours between them, which she clutches tight.

That's as far as she lets you go. "I really like you," she vows. "But I can't go all the way. I'm saving myself for marriage."

If you weren't so frustrated, you might have found her phrase "going all the way" arousing. But you've barely made it to first base. When she gets up and straightens her clothes, brushes her hair, and asks if you'd like to meet for breakfast, it hits you hard: your night is done.

. . .

She doesn't like it when the relationship cools. "We can do other things," she offers. She lets you unbutton her shirt, unhook her bra. She winces when you pinch her nipple, even gently, and wriggles like she wants to snake away, but she kisses more passionately, her mouth opening more readily. One night she removes all her clothes but her panties and lets you press your hand against the cotton-covered mound between her legs. An intensity shoots through her, and she lets you spend the night, her roommate gone again, both of you wearing underwear, you pained by your erection.

"Sex is the most intimate way two people can share their love for each other," you insist, but she won't give in.

The frustration's too hard to live with. You alternately think about breaking up, then asking her to marry you. You convince yourself you love Maureen, promise yourself, then her, you will feel the same afterwards. You hold back the word marriage, but make it clear you're devoted to her.

When it happens, you're gentle, considerate. "Are you sure?" you ask more than once, and as it's happening, "Are you okay? Does this hurt? Does this feel okay?" You want her to feel nothing but good. You tell yourself the pleading in her brown eyes is passion.

Afterwards, you're thrilled by your performance. You are normal after all. You're excited thinking about the semester break to come, when you'll go home and tell Mr. P.

Feeling obligated, you work hard at being Maureen's perfect boyfriend. You stay over most nights when her roommate is away. Some nights the two of you have sex, on others, you say, "That's okay, I understand," when she doesn't feel up to it. You love the increased intimacy she allows you to have with her body. You can touch her where you like, however you like, provided the two of you are alone; she flinches at being touched in public.

Over Christmas, Mr. P shows delight but doesn't seem to recognize this as the earth-shattering step you believe it to be. Your evening ends parked in his car, running for its heat, between snowbanks at the deserted lake. You don't perform any better with him than before, but it doesn't bother you as much.

Not suddenly, but over the weeks and months that follow, you realize you are tiring of Maureen. You're astounded that the sex that once felt like the most profound experience of your life has begun to seem routine. There are nights when you say, "I'm not up for it," because you don't want to put in the effort. You notice she doesn't have much to say about things that interest you, and vice versa. You've never connected with her friends, nor she with yours.

You understand what's coming. First you try the coward's approach: "Maybe we should just step back a little, give each other space."

She won't allow it. "Are you saying you don't love me anymore?"

In your head you hear Gordon Lightfoot: *I don't know where we went wrong but the feeling's gone and I just can't get it back.*

She cries. Gets angry when you try to comfort her. That surprises you; you've always thought of her as timid. Calls you a son of a bitch. Orders you to get out. In a way this is easier; like being whipped when you deserve it. Once the whipping ends, you think, *I can move on with my life,* your blistered back proof you've served your sentence. You think, she hates me. As she should. Even that makes splitting up easier.

You see her a couple more times, bursting with apologies she doesn't want to hear. She wants you to explain: "You said you loved me, then you didn't love me. Which was the lie?" You offer an answer that turns into an intellectual exercise she wants no part of. "All right," she says. "I get it. You were after one thing, and I was fool enough to give it to you."

You don't reply. The fear gnawing in your gut is that she's right.

With your dorms on opposite sides of campus, you eat in separate dining halls. A German major and an English major don't share the same classes. On the few occasions you spot each other, you quickly look away, your face hot and tight, while she changes direction to ensure the two of you won't come close.

Over time, you marvel at your ability to move on. At how easily you can forget. How easy it is to live with guilt. You wish the best for her. Hope she makes it to Germany junior year, maybe meets a nice German guy, gets married and starts a family.

· · ·

You tell yourself you've escaped unscathed. Until the end of that summer between freshman and sophomore years, you give your mother a birthday present, a framed, professionally-done photograph of yourself with your new look: a full beard and hair to your shoulders. The face in the photograph feels genuine, the first time you've looked at yourself and felt that your outer self matched the person who resided inside.

You wait until your father's gone to work to bring out the box. Your mother's smile is awkward, uncertain; accepting gifts has never been comfortable for either of you. She opens the box, slides out the frame. She has to flip it over to see the image. Instantly, you know. She doesn't like it. You have spent your life reading her moods.

She looks at you, then back at the photograph, as if she's only just now realized the two images belong to the same person. A small, forced smile curves her lips. "When did you have this done?" she asks, as if that's the real mystery.

"Before I left school." You're hoping that for once you've read her reaction wrong, that given time, she'll realize what it means to you, for her to accept you as you want to be.

"It was certainly a surprise," she says, as if describing having run into someone on the street she's been trying to avoid.

You figured at least she'd put it on her vanity until you go back to school, but in the days that follow you see no sign of it. She's tight lipped and formal, as if following instructions called, "The least you can do and still be a mother."

As you're packing to return to school, things blow up.

"I don't know you anymore!" she shouts. "What you have become. What you're doing up there in that place," that place being college.

She pulls a folded paper out of a drawer and waves it in the air. "Explain this," she cries, and can barely find the breath to read a few lines: "I will never forgive your son for what he did to my daughter. He is a vile and selfish human being. He ought to be locked up. And you should be ashamed to call yourself his mother."

You reach for the paper but she yanks it back. "I don't know what you're doing up there," she says, "but you'd better take a long hard look at yourself. That woman is right: I'm ashamed to call myself your mother."

You don't respond. It's clear who the letter is from. What words could you possibly say?

You and your mother never speak about this again. Years later, after she's died of cancer and you help clean out her room, you search for the letter but instead find the photograph of yourself with beard and long hair buried in the bottom of a box in her closet, the glass cracked in several places.

Chapter Nineteen

The sun had just begun to clear the horizon when I pushed back my chair and stumbled off to bed. I didn't bother undressing, just flopped on top of the blankets, kicked off my shoes. I thought I would sleep easily, but my mind refused to still. Maureen's mother was right, I was a vile creature. Certainly what I'd done to her daughter had been vile; I'd used lies to steal something precious from her, something she could never get back. It didn't matter that I'd convinced myself I really did love her, that I wasn't just after sex; that only proved I'd lied to myself as much as I'd lied to her. Nor could I honestly blame Mr. P or my mother or the counselor, although I wanted to. Finding someone else to blame eased the pain when you yanked the knife blade out of your own heart. But in the end, no one else is responsible for what a person does in his life.

What other excuses could I fabricate? I was eighteen years old. Didn't all eighteen-year-old males obsess about sex? Wouldn't most of them do anything to get it?

I doubt Maureen could ever forgive me. I hoped I hadn't ruined her life. It felt like something broke between my mother and me, that day I gave her the photograph of myself and she waved that letter in front of me. I had thought that through my gift of the photograph, I was sharing with my mother for the very first time who I really was inside. And maybe that's who she saw.

As I lay there, another Matthew Winton strolled into my mind. Another time and place. Another memory that had fled, now ready to return.

I dragged myself out of bed, back to my computer.

•••

She's tall, almost your height, and slender, lithe and sinewy. Brownish-blonde hair to her shoulders, eyes that are gray-blue, except, you learn later, in certain light, when you can detect flecks of violet. Intense; spoiled, and emotional, she doesn't wear her heart on her sleeve but in every pore of her being, her facial expression, the gestures and sounds she makes, the way she holds her body. Even her beauty is defined by her emotions.

You watch her walk across the stage wearing a sleeveless white top and tan slacks with no pockets in the back. Her arms long and loose, her whole body not dancer-loose but free-loose, as if she's used to sprawling, as if she's certain she has the right.

You on the other hand keep close to the chest, closed in, tightly clasped. Like the character Thomas Mann said lived like a clenched fist.

She's well developed for a young woman of seventeen. You notice this watching her move about the stage during rehearsals for the play your students will put on later in the fall. You've cast her in the one female role, as one of those glasses-wearing, hair-in-a-bun ugly duckling types who finally lets down her hair to become a beautiful swan. Only you've seen the swan from the start.

You're twenty-two, beginning your first year at Warrentown Friends School. You're still focused on the newness of everything, and on the discovery that in order to teach four classes every day, you have to keep coming up with things for students to do. She's in your class but at first you hardly notice her. You couldn't guess that she'll become one of those flowers that blossom suddenly, that go home one day a girl and return a woman. Or enough of a woman to let you fool yourself into thinking she's no longer a girl.

And you cast her in this play about rebels and iconoclasts, celebrating individual conscience over bureaucratic conformity.

On stage isn't where you notice her first. That happens in your class. Watching her on stage simply adds a new dimension.

In class she volunteers a lot, says intelligent, sophisticated things. Discussing *Macbeth*, she mentions Kurosawa's *Throne of Blood*. No one else in class has heard of *Throne of Blood*, or for that matter, Kurosawa. She doesn't hide her frustration when others don't join the conversation at the level she wants them to; glares at you indignantly when you bypass her insistent waving arm to give others a chance to respond.

She often stops by your desk after class. "What do you dream of?" she asks one day.

You beg her pardon.

"What's your dream? What would you be, if you could be anything?"

You think about joking, "king of the world." Instead you say, "I don't know. I've always wanted to be a writer, I guess. You know, write the Great American Novel?"

She makes a "humpf" sound. "I thought that's already been done. *The Great Gatsby?*"

You're feeling impish. "I don't know. That's a great book, but I don't think it's even Fitzgerald's best."

She stares at you, lips parted, like you've dared something obscene.

"Tender Is the Night," you say, and she turns to go as your next class of students barges in.

A few days later when she plops her books down on her desk you notice the one on top: *Tender Is the Night.*

A week later she's back at your desk. "Promise me something," she says, and you make a gesture like you'll consider it. "Promise me you won't end up living out your life in some small town in upstate New York."

You smile. Perhaps if you were older, with more experience, you'd be amused at this precocious teenager. But you're not older, you're barely five years her senior, and you've never been on this side of the teacher's desk before. You're lonely, too, and although you like what you call the "controlled intimacy" of being a teacher of teenage students – where you can decide how much of yourself to reveal – you also like engaging in intellectual gymnastics and being challenged. It's hard not to see her as a peer.

"Well, you know," she says, preparing to deliver a line she's clearly practiced, and feels satisfaction at having come up with, "a great writer once said, 'There are only the pursued, the pursuing, the busy, and the tired.'"

Fitzgerald – though you can't recall where the quote came from. You prepare for her to ask, "Which are you?" but she leaves that question for you to ponder, turning on her heels and walking away.

• • •

On stage she flirts with you, at times haughty, dismissive, embarrassed, charming. You alternate teasing her, teaching her, and treating her as one of the team. Eventually you are able to corral your eyes from her curvy figure, the fleshy buttocks, swelling breasts. The play's a big hit, and afterwards, she introduces you to her parents. Her father is dean of a music school, her mother a moderately well-known pianist. You think how your father was a janitor, your mother worked in a factory. "She's a very special young woman," you tell them, and they beam as if to assure you, they know.

. . .

"Merry Christmas," she says on the last day before break, and pulls from her bag what is clearly a book, festively wrapped. She shoves it into your hand and races out of the room.

It's Fitzgerald again, *The Crack-Up and Other Essays*. It's a new copy but flipping through, you notice passages highlighted in yellow and starred. One of them is the quote about pursued or pursuing. Another is a famous one you recognize: "The test of a first-rate intelligence is the ability to hold two opposed ideas in the mind at the same time, and still retain the ability to function. One should, for example, be able to see that things are hopeless and yet be determined to make them otherwise."

Another is simply this: "It takes two to make an accident."

. . .

Three days back from Christmas break, she shows up at your door as you're preparing to go home for the day. She's been sullen and silent since school started up again.

She looks like a lost kitten searching for a friendly door. "Are you okay?" you ask. She looks like she's about to cry. "Come in."

You close the door behind her, and somehow the two of you end up against the wall in a corner of the room, where no one can see you through the windows. Have you coaxed her here, or followed her? When the tears burst forth, she rests her head on your shoulder and you stand stiffly, arms outstretched but careful not to touch her.

"Will you hold me?" A plea and demand both.

You flinch at a noise outside the door, look desperately around. "Here." You take her hand and lead her to the supply closet, opening the door, flipping on the light, closing the two of you inside. You push away the notion that to be discovered in here might cost your job.

When she presses back into you, you open your arms, palms settling on her back, high up, then fleeing when you feel the clasp of her bra through her shirt. "Talk to me," you whisper. "What is it?"

She tries, succeeds only in starts. "I thought about it all the time – I tried – I don't know how –"

She presses into you again, buries her face, her tears dampening your chest. You try not to think about how well she fits in your arms, how long it's been since you held another person.

Finally she draws back her head, serious tear-glistening eyes peer into yours. She takes a breath, forces out the words: "I love you."

The rebuttals in your head never get close to being spoken: *You can't. I'm your teacher. You don't really know me. It's a crush, that's all.* Later, you'll wonder if you kept them from her out of fear they might convince.

When her hands touch your face and she rises, you lower your head so your lips meet, mouths hungry, her whole body now pressed tight against your own, the sweet smell of her hair mixing with a muskier scent, and you squeeze each other as if to merge two bodies into one, the desire sexual, yes, but also literal, opening up your skin so she can climb inside. You know that you have never felt so alone as you will feel when her body no longer touches yours.

Today, underneath the hanging bare lightbulb in the unheated closet, you'll only kiss and touch and press, to prove yourselves to each other; this closet's too small for more, and you've never been gymnastic anyway, and besides, you're still the adult in the room. Still, you will drink all you can of this intoxicating moment, assuring yourself you have all the rest of your life to regret it, and atone.

• • •

The hardest part is getting time alone with her. It's hard, too, having her in class. She doesn't talk anymore, acts like she's never met you before, while you fear every time you look at her everyone else in class knows exactly what you're imagining.

A handful of her closest friends know. They are her partners in crime. Sometimes after school they walk downtown to have coffee and a bagel at Morey's Deli. One day one of those friends, Alexandra, slips you a folded note as everyone is leaving class. "Come to Morey's," it says. "Don't go in, she'll come out to meet you. 3 p.m."

It's hard to get through the afternoon, for the thrill you feel, the tightness in your chest.

You enjoy feeling like a spy. Think it would be fun to show up wearing a fedora and dark glasses, maybe a fake mustache. Recently she gave you another book – or rather, you found it sitting on your desk one day, no note – but she'd talked about the book before: *Harriet the Spy*, written for children, but you can see her playing Harriet, embracing that role.

After your last class of the day, you have to wait for the buses to leave before you can get to your car. You sit at your desk looking busy so none of the other teachers will come in to chat. You don't want to be late because every minute after three will be agony for both of you.

At 2:58 p.m. you drive past the small shopping center housing Morey's, circle back through the parking lot and pull into a space far enough away your car won't be noticed by anyone not looking for it. You try to picture the next few minutes. "Don't go inside," the note said. There's a record shop next door, you might pretend to be window shopping. Your apartment is closer into the city, and when you've shopped around here, you've run across students from time to time.

Then you spot her, standing in front of a dumpster at the far end of the mall, one fist clenching her long coat closed around the neck.

You drive up, she gets in. You begin to lean toward her, perhaps to kiss her, but she barks, "Go!" and you drive, out the nearest exit and onto Main Street.

"Where to?" you ask.

"I have to be back by four-thirty." She seems angry, like this was a bad idea and you are somehow responsible.

"Should I park somewhere and we can walk? Or do you want to just sit and talk?"

"Turn right," she says, and then directs you through the neighborhoods she's grown up in, then back into traffic. "Turn here," she orders, and you swing into the parking lot of a much larger mall, that looks like a fortress. "Drive around behind."

It's isolated in back, with the windowless back wall of the mall rising in front and a tree-covered hill behind. There are a few dozen parking spaces, about half of them full with cars you suspect belong to employees. You wonder for a moment if she once worked at this mall, though you find it hard to imagine her serving customers in a department store, or crazier, an ice cream shop. "Corner pocket," she says, pointing to the last spot. "Back in."

You obey. It's February, a little warmer than it's been, but still only 50 degrees, and you leave the car running for its heat. She rolls down her window halfway. You could ask, "Are you hot?" but the gesture seems more like an act of defiance, as if she expects one of her parents to show up and demand she roll the window up. She's hunched in the seat, staring somewhere between her feet and the glove compartment.

You remain silent, looking from her to your surroundings and then back again. You've learned to wait out her dramatic moods. She finally pushes herself up in the seat, still guarded, and mutters, "What, we're finally alone and now you won't kiss me?"

For an hour, that's all you do.

At four-twenty you ask if she needs to go.

"We've got time. My ride will wait."

"Who's picking you up?" You have to ask it a second time before she answers.

"My mother."

You pull away from her, start the car. "Alexandra will cover for me," she argues, but you put the car in gear and drive.

"So what if she sees us?" she mutters, scrunched down in her seat again, but as you near the mall with Morey's in it, she tells you to pull over so she can get out and walk the last way.

There's no parking lane on this street, so you have to stop traffic to let her hop out. She looks offended until you lean over and give her a goodbye kiss. Then she's out the door, with no words or a glance back.

• • •

You're sitting in the back row at the Spring concert, waiting for the start, when a folded piece of paper comes fluttering over your shoulder. You snare it, look up to see Elizabeth walking past, betraying no sign that she knows you. She's walking a little behind her parents – her younger sister is in the choir. Although you met her parents after the play, you have a chance to study them now. The woman is tall, large-boned, wearing a sleeveless green dress, dark hair cut short. There's a toughness about her, a sense she'd readily trade that dress for jeans and a sweatshirt, but there's an elegance to her movements, too, and the smell of wealth.

The man is shorter, a bit paunchy, balding, though his dark hair is long on the sides, and he has a white-flecked dark beard. He looks every bit the university professor, with his tweed jacket, patches on the elbows, and loose khaki slacks.

Taller than her father, lankier than her mother, Elizabeth trails with shoulders slumped. You've watched her walk down halls and thought, she's a woman, but she looks like a child now, wilted and obedient.

Except for that folded piece of paper. You get up, slink into shadows at the back of the room. Unfurl it. "Cafeteria kitchen," it says. "Watch when I get up."

Your heartbeat quickens. You've come to this concert hoping for an opportunity like this. A few stolen moments, spitting in the eye of the forbidden. Her touch makes you feel that the two of you are above the world, freed from its norms.

Midway through the concert, a figure rises in the dark. You stare at the floor as she passes. After you hear the metal click of the door being quietly closed, you count to ten, rise and follow. The hallway is bright and empty, and you think of the times you went with your father after dinner to play basketball in the gym while he cleaned the high school. You have always felt at home in an empty school.

The cafeteria is down the hall, the door unlocked; in this school, no one locks doors. The only light comes from the red glowing "Exit" signs above the other doors. Your arm is grabbed, tugged, and you tumble into her in the dark, recognizing her by feel and scent. She giggles, then says, "Sssh," as if you are the one making noise. In the dark your lips have no trouble finding each other.

Your bodies press hard together. You've been erect since before you entered the cafeteria. You want her badly, but you're not crazy; if she's gone too long, her mother will come looking. Besides, for all your adult passion, your touching has been adolescent: kissing her breasts through her bra and shirt; squeezing her buttocks as you press your fronts together. Despite the sexual frustration you know will torment you until you get home later and relieve it yourself, you have never pushed for more.

"We have to go back," you whisper.

"I won't see you," she answers, meaning the week ahead, Spring break, when her whole family's going to New York for a concert.

"I'll be here when you get back."

"The week after," she says, and names the date: a Saturday. "I'm coming to your apartment. I'm going to spend the night."

She has always been the aggressor. You accepted it because she was the one who had to devise ways to get away from those around her; you had no one to escape from. Still, you recognize that it's important for you to play the pursued, not the pursuer.

"Can you do it?" you say.

"Alexandra will help. I'll tell them I'm sleeping at her house."

Parting kisses hard enough to make your lips hurt.

You sit in one of the cafeteria chairs to catch your breath after she's gone. Intermission will be soon, so you go to your classroom, turn on the light and sit at your desk, presenting a picture of a dedicated teacher catching up to any parents wandering the halls. When the concert resumes, you go home. In bed, you masturbate, hard.

• • •

The train station rises high above the street, the platform shielded by a chain link fence, the roof backdropped by sky. She stands against that sky, her silhouette in shadows, then steps into the sun, hands in her coat pockets, her blonde hair glistening, cheeks rosy from the cold. You realize that a part of you has never believed she would come, while another part wishes she had not.

On this Saturday morning, no stream of businessmen get off the train. College students, mothers with small children, elderly couples moving carefully, clutching to railings, and you think how the world grows more dangerous, the older you get.

The world is not dangerous for her. She is the last one to descend the stairs, making an entrance, not looking at you, perhaps imagining she's being admired by all the world. A grin betrays her when she reaches the bottom, and she can't help but giggle in delight. When she slides into your arms, you surreptitiously glance side to side, from habit, before meeting her kiss.

"This way," you say, lifting the small bag she's set at her feet. An *overnight* bag, you think, tasting the thrill of the word and what it forebodes. You had sex in college, but this feels like something you've never experienced before.

"Here," you say, guiding her up the stone steps to the door of the old Victorian house divided into six apartments, yours on top on the left. You have spent the week cleaning and decorating, though there's not much you can do with a three-room apartment that came with all the furnishings. You believe she'll like the front room, have already pictured her sitting on the window seat gazing down at the firehouse across the street.

It's the first place she goes to, not sitting but leaning forward to peer out the glass. She hasn't even taken off her coat. When she straightens and glances back, you know that she approves.

You set her bag on the chair in the bedroom. That room is small, your bed along one wall, a chest of drawers along the other, barely room to walk in between. You have to keep the shade down on the one window because of the proximity of the house next door.

Her silence doesn't concern you. She despises small talk, will always choose silence over the trivial. Other than the kiss when she first came down from the train station, she hasn't touched you either. You sense that she is settling, like a cat getting used to new surroundings, but also secretly reveling that for the first time ever, your time together won't have to be stolen. You have the rest of the morning, the afternoon and evening, all night and the next morning too. It feels close to forever.

Finally she slides off her coat. She's wearing a purple sweater and the same tan slacks you used to admire her in on stage. You'd love to ask her just to walk around, let you drink her in; if you had a camera you'd take pictures, but instead you etch those images into your mind: her here.

You take her coat to the closet and hang it up. Not realizing she's following, you turn and almost bump into her. You both laugh. "So," you say.

"So," she says. "Here we are."

Like two teenagers, you think, left home alone. Except when you were a teenager, nothing like this ever happened.

You kiss, then are disappointed when she pulls back, until she says, in a breathy whisper, her cheeks rosy again not from the cold, "Let's go into your bedroom."

She watches you watch her as she slips her sweater over her head, unbuttons the shirt underneath. Unbuckles her slacks and slides them down, steps out of them and folds them neatly on the chair. She is wearing flesh-colored underwear for an instant you mistake as nothing.

You tug off your shirt and jeans, don't fold them as neatly as she has her clothes. She draws you to her, but instead of embracing she sits on the bed, coaxes you beside her.

"I can't wait to sleep with you," she says, and giggles. Then turns serious. "But there's something I have to tell you. We can't have sex." She looks at you, her expression serious, anxious too. "I made a promise to my mother."

At first you think, has she told her mother? Does her mother know she is here? Letting loose your hands, she stares at the opposite wall. "When I started high school, my mother and I had 'the talk,' you know? She asked me to promise two things: as long as I lived at home, I wouldn't do drugs, and I wouldn't have sex. 'Once you leave for college,' she said, 'your life is yours. But while you're here, please promise me those two things.'

"She's afraid I'll get pregnant, fuck up my life. Or go nuts and run off and get married. The same with drugs—" a forced laugh. "You might have noticed, I can be kind of intense sometimes."

She shrugs. "In a way, the reason doesn't matter. She asked me to promise and I did. I gave my word."

You realize in the silence that she's waiting for a reply. It's hard for you to process. A part of you feels let down, frustrated, another part is relieved. No part of you wants to try and talk her out of this decision.

"What can we do?" you finally ask.

A laugh escapes her, there's joy inside it, and she stands. When you make a move to stand too, she holds you back, then gets you arranged on your back stretched out along the bed. Her hands struggle with something behind her back, then she whips off her bra and twirls it in the air like a lasso. "Geronimo!" she cries, and leaps into bed.

. . .

You ride into the city, visit the art museum, catch a matinee of the film *Cousin, Cousine*, which instantly becomes "your film," and on the ride home, speak French to each other. You cook her a meal taught to you by a previous girlfriend, mussels and asparagus in a lemon sauce, and feel a little guilty when she asks where you learned to cook like that and you reply, "I picked a few things up here and there." You laugh to discover she's brought some schoolbooks with her, including the novel, *Anna Karenina*; she needs to write a paper for her other English class, though she swears not to worry, she's got all Sunday night for that, and anyway, first she has to finish reading the damn thing.

"It's a great book," you say, and she grunts.

"I know, but she could have given us more than a week to read it."

You've got your Theater of the Absurd books piled up beside you, the Ionesco, Beckett and Sartre, and with the two of you at opposite ends of the couch, your bare feet toy with each other beneath the blanket you share. You wonder if she's having as much trouble concentrating as you are, thinking only of getting back into bed with her and pressing your strategically almost-naked bodies together.

. . .

"This is going to be hard," she says. You're lying together in bed, her head in the crook of your arm. What's preceded is a circus of passion and frustration, with a bit of comedy added in, although neither one of you is ready to appreciate the humor yet. Kissing and squeezing and fondling, your teeth gently nibbling her breasts, her teeth not so gently biting your shoulder, your hand sneaking down to the waistband of her underwear, to be drawn away by her hand, then her hand sneaking toward yours, drawn away by you. Your hand sneaking back, only this time her hand does not race to the rescue, and you have to stop yourself.

"It's all right," you assure her. "I love just to touch you. To feel our bodies close."

That's true, if not perhaps the whole story.

"The thing is," she says, "if we did it, my mother would know. I can't lie to her. Even if I try, she'll know."

"It's okay," you vow. "I understand."

At least, you want to understand. You admire that she can have such a close relationship with her mother. That she has integrity. That she's such an incompetent liar. The needle skitters all over on your moral compass, and sometimes you lie so well you even fool yourself.

"We'll manage," you tell her. "Even without that, I love being with you ten times more than I've ever loved being with anyone in my life."

She's silent a moment, then in the darkness, you glimpse a smile. "Only ten times? I'd have thought it would be a hundred."

"There's still time. But that means you have work to do," you say, then jackknife away from the semi-playful punch that seeks your stomach.

•••

"This is going to be hard," she says. You're standing with her at the train station, and this time she's talking about going back to the public world where you're a teacher and she's your student.

"We'll do whatever we have to," you say.

"You better not look at me too much in class.

"And don't go staring at my ass when I walk back to my desk."

You're shocked; you wonder if you've been doing it without realizing. Who else has seen you? Yet you stay playful, admitting, "I love your ass," and grab her there.

"Yeah, well stop loving it in front of eighteen horny teenagers." And wriggles free.

Then the lights flash and you hear the train approaching, and everyone else on the platform except the two of you turns to look for it. Neither of you wants to let the other go. The moment feels too final, and even though you are able to think, *If this is the only day we ever have, it will live in your mind forever*, it feels like something at the core of you is being ripped away.

•••

She's sitting in the window seat with legs drawn up, knees in the air, reading *Crime and Punishment* while the sunlight pours in around her, golden off her hair, whitening her tan slacks. You look up from the table where you're grading papers. You don't want to grade papers, you want only to look at her, admire her, drink in the fact that once again she is here. She's been coming most Sundays of late, having told her parents she needs to visit the main library in the city for a research project.

Late in the afternoon she puts away her book and walks to you, holds out her hand and you take it. Like children navigating a path through the woods, you find your way to the bedroom. She giggles, and it's a race to see who can strip off their clothes the fastest and leap under the blankets, the winner sniggling at the loser, although no one loses when both your bodies come together. Her feet are cold and she burrows into you. You feel the slick material of her underwear, as your own cages your erection, and you caution yourself to tamp down your lust for her, and wonder, will there ever come a time, and then it does.

Face flushed, eyes deep and open, like gates finally unlocked. She draws you close, whispers. "Make love to me."

Chapter Twenty

No sun was visible in the oatmeal sky. I didn't know if it was morning or late afternoon. I rose, wincing at the stiffness in my lower back, the soreness in my neck and shoulders. At some point, I'd given up drinking coffee in favor of Scotch. The empty bottle rolled around at my feet.

I didn't bother trying to sleep. Sleep was peace, which I didn't deserve. I had sought to reclaim my past, believing nothing could be worse than emptiness. I was wrong.

I took a shower. I had nothing more to drink, and I couldn't remember the last thing I'd eaten. The cabin felt small and stuffy and I needed air. Despite my aching body, I needed to move. I went out to my car.

A light rain fell outside. It felt cold enough to freeze, but when I slid my foot across the blacktopped patch of the driveway, it gripped the rough surface.

There was little traffic on this late afternoon in early November. When I lived around here – before I stumbled into the constant, choking traffic in the suburbs of D.C. – I used to enjoy driving; I'd go for a drive to help me relax and clear my head. It would be nice if I could recapture that feeling now. But I couldn't deny the agitation roiling inside, or how my hands trembled when loosened from the steering wheel.

Elizabeth and I did not have sex that night in my apartment. At no point in our relationship did resisting prove harder. Throughout that night, she and I alternated being responsible, she wanting to give in and me resisting, then she resisting as I begged for her to give in. For a long time, I held that up as a badge of honor, and proof that my love for her was genuine and selfless. I did love her, even now I believe that. But I cannot deny that had I been her age, a fellow student, she would have had no interest in me.

Our relationship ended gradually. Her father got her a summer job at the college where he taught, and then her focus turned to Oberlin, Ohio, where she was headed for college. At first, there were letters, several each week, and I answered each one promptly. But the frequency dropped off as her new life blossomed, one or two a week at first, then one or two a month. I mimicked her schedule, taking days to answer each letter, adding to it whatever seemed worth sharing. I didn't want her to think she was occupying my thoughts more than I might be occupying hers.

By the time she came home for Thanksgiving, we both knew the relationship was over. I wrote her a long letter when I decided to quit my job, and she answered, wishing me the best as one might to a distant relative moving to a new country halfway around the world.

I came up to the stop sign in Old Bridge, the inn to my right. I didn't know if Aaron was working tonight but if so, it was too early for him to have started. A right turn would send me in the direction of his house, as well as the steady and safe Route 7 that continued all the way up through Vermont. I turned left.

Soon, the old mansions of Old Bridge turned into modest homes, then farmland. I passed the dirt road that would have taken me to Danvers Field. There was also a back way I vaguely recalled could get me to Old Becket Road, but there was nothing for me there anymore. Flashing through my mind was that night I walked to Mr. P's house, dreaming that he might adopt me.

Even now, I wondered: what if he had done that?

I loved him. I hated him. I missed him. I was glad that he was dead. Amid all this confusion, I never once wished I'd never met him.

I had no excuse for what I did to Maureen. Lots of teenage guys are overrun with hormones, and I had extra problems. When I first got to college, I'd been able to block out both Mr. P and my mother, pretending to live in a new world. But Mr. P coming to campus changed that, proving he could reach me anywhere.

Why Maureen? I'd known what I was doing. I was confident I could convince her to have sex and she wouldn't hurt me. I didn't think about how much I would end up hurting her.

I had taken something precious from Maureen. Although I could argue I was just a confused kid with a terrible history and no one decent and strong and kind enough to set me right, I knew I was lying when I promised Maureen my devotion.

Maureen's mother was right: I was a vile creature. Not worthy of being my mother's son.

• • •

Dusk was settling, the sky now a dark blanket. The drizzle quickly blurred the world again as soon as the windshield wipers passed. I seemed to be heading toward New York State. There were fewer houses out here, only an occasional hamlet in between miles of fields and forests. When an approaching car flashed its headlights at me, I realized I hadn't turned mine on. It was cold inside the car. Leaving the cabin, I'd grabbed my coat but hadn't bothered to put it on, and now it lay in the seat beside me. I thought vaguely that this must be the reason I felt cold.

It wasn't hard to justify my relationship with Elizabeth. A five-year difference in age isn't that significant. In many ways, she was more mature than me. And the feelings she raised in me were more powerful than anything I had felt before, or since.

But I was the teacher, in the position of power and responsibility. Was I really any different from Mr. P?

And what of the years after that? Had there been other Elizabeth's? What exactly had happened between me and Lisette Sorenson, daughter of my college's dean of Arts and Sciences?

Because thoughts of Elizabeth brought a second memory I couldn't elude.

Maria Alvarez was nineteen when she returned to Warrentown Friends for her senior year, having been away the previous two years on an exchange program in Brazil. She seemed older than that, more mature, experienced sexually too, from the way she flirted, the sidelong glances. She was small but fiery, with dark eyes and jet black hair; I'd never realized that a woman could be sexy without being beautiful. And she'd heard, apparently, that I had a reputation.

In the early months with Elizabeth, we both seemed to be fighting whatever attraction we felt for each other. It was like a wave that grew so powerful we couldn't stay on our feet when it finally rolled over us. At least, that's what I told myself. It was nothing like that with Maria. From the start, she was looking for a conquest, something to add spice to her otherwise boring senior year back in the states after frolicking in Rio. I went along with her flirting, thinking it a harmless diversion I could easily control. Also, I was a little bored without Elizabeth.

On the day before Christmas break, Maria invited me to her house, a thank-you dinner for all I'd done for her – I'd written several college recommendations and carved out extra chunks of time when she came to me for advice, although it seemed to me she could have easily solved her problems on her own. Her house was enormous, in one of the richest Philadelphia neighborhoods. I expected to meet her parents (who hadn't appeared on Parent/ Teacher night), perhaps a sibling or two. I wasn't surprised by the servant who greeted me at the front door; a house that large ought to have servants. But when Maria appeared in a sleeveless dress that was almost too elegant to be sexy, I looked from side to side, before asking, "Your parents?"

"Oh, they're away," she said, as if speaking of a car taken to the shop. "In Spain right now. They come and go."

And so Maria and I had dinner alone together, with her cook serving the food and the man who'd greeted me at the door pouring wine. She told me her father owned several companies in Spain, and her stepmother enjoyed taking vacations. "They won't be back until New Year's," she said, the invitation clear in her voice.

She was sitting at the head of the long table with me to her left. A couple times I distinctly felt her stockinged foot slide up and down my leg.

Afterwards, she suggested we go upstairs so she could show me the house. I can't deny suspecting what might happen if I accompanied her up those stairs. The servants had disappeared. It wasn't just the look in her eyes or the assuredness with which she'd run her foot up the inside of my leg beneath the table; it was all the frustration and desire built up over the previous year with Elizabeth, the disappointment when our relationship ended, an underlying disgust with myself for what I'd allowed to happen, all mixed to stoke the voice in my head that told me, "What the fuck. Who cares anyway. She's already an adult."

I want to deny what I did. I want to tear that page out of the story of my life. I want to justify my actions. She was legally an adult. She was mature for her age. She was not a virgin. What we did was consensual; she took the lead. Neither of us pretended we had any deep feelings for each other. It was, as Mr. P had described it, sex as play.

And it was wrong.

In the morning I called up the principal. She was a petite woman with gray hair, though no older than forty. She had a way of listening that suggested she knew most everything you'd done in the past, but she wouldn't bring any of it up unless you spoke of it first, or unless you crossed a line that forced her hand – although if I hadn't crossed that line with Elizabeth, I didn't know where that line could be.

"I've been struggling all semester," I began, calling on words I'd created and practiced all morning. "This is a wonderful place, the people are incredible, it's the absolute best situation for a teacher I could imagine. But I've thought about it a lot, and I'm convinced I need to resign."

I was vague about reasons: I needed to commit to my writing, see if I could do it; as wonderful as it was at this school, it simply wasn't right for me at this time. I admitted that down the road, I might regret this decision, but for now it was something I had to do.

She didn't seem overly surprised, though I believed her when she said she was saddened. When she asked when I might want to leave, my answer of "Right away if possible" did seem to take her aback, but she promised to immediately begin looking for a replacement.

I spent the holidays alone, locked up in my apartment, watching a lot of mindless TV and drinking a lot of Scotch. Crazy thoughts swirled through my head: I could visit Maria Alvarez, guilt-free since I wasn't her teacher anymore; if I called Elizabeth, probably home from college, might she say she wasn't so enamored of her new life, and even missed me a little? But I didn't answer the phone when it rang, and I called no one other than the principal, who told me, two days before New Year's, that she'd found a long-term replacement. I went to school for a day before the students returned, to fill in the woman replacing me and say goodbye to some of the teachers, but I never saw any of the students again, saying goodbye in a note the principal read to the whole school at the next Wednesday meeting. By then, I was already back in my parents' house in Massachusetts.

No one ever asked me, "What's the real reason you left?" It wasn't Maria or Elizabeth or Maureen or anyone, other than me. I left because I could not trust myself.

...

The rain now contained bits of ice that gathered in the corners of the windshield. Around me were several shades of dark, the slick shiny black of the pavement, the deeper black of the forest on either side, the gray-black of the sky dense with clouds.

The rare car approaching or popping up behind startled me, and I slowed until I was once again alone. It was hard to believe there were other people in the world going about their own lives, oblivious to me.

So much of my life had been built upon lies. I loved my mother, yet I pretended to be invisible when her need became inconvenient. I made her ashamed to call me her son. The lie I'd told myself was that I'd tried my whole life to make her happy. I'd tried, from time to time, when it suited, but hadn't I always cared more about pleasing myself? Wasn't that the thing his wife had said about Mr. P? "He so loved his indulgences." Was I any different?

Another lie: that I had loved Maureen Bahnsen, had not simply seen her as a safe person I could manipulate to get what I wanted. Another: that I was not following in Mr. P's footsteps with Elizabeth. Agreeing to her wish not to have intercourse was a pretty flimsy badge of honor. If she'd never made that request, we'd have gone at it like rabbits every chance we got. As I had done with Maria Alvarez, at least for one night.

And now? Nineteen years later, had I suddenly reverted back to the ways of Mr. P with Lisette Sorenson? What had happened that Sunday night, driving through what little wilderness was left in Northern Virginia? Had I seen the future and determined to prevent it?

I'd been writing about my relationship with Mr. P at the time. Had I continued, I would have gotten around to also writing about Maureen and Elizabeth and Maria eventually. My father had recently died, leaving me the last surviving member of my family. Perhaps it was all too much for me. In my writing – far more than in the rest of my life – I tried to cut through the lies and excuses designed to cushion the impact of all the wrong I'd done. To plow through all the bullshit.

Memories not only proved you were alive. They made you re-live your life. Every time I wrote about or remembered Mr. P, I lived all over again those nights in his car or outside beneath the summer stars. I felt all over again the fear and frustration and indisputable weight of my own failure. Remembering Maureen showed all over again how vile I had been.

I peered into the darkness, leaning forward, and suddenly I was there, in Virginia, in my car speeding along the deserted roads. I had a destination which was not a destination but a goal. At some level I knew what I would do, though I kept the actual words at bay. It's the guilt that wears you down, that breaks you, the knowledge that there is only one way to escape it, to bring you the kind of honest sleep that ends in peace.

The fork in the road looked familiar, the giant oak at its point. Was I remembering this tree, having set it aside in a recess of my mind where I could find it again when the right time came? Or perhaps it might be something mystical, déjà vu, or simple coincidence.

I knew this was the place, this was the moment. And felt a part of me bail, fly off searching for some safe space high above. The part of me left behind pressed down hard on the gas, clutching the steering wheel tight. It's funny, how in my imagination I thought I could let go of the wheel and stretch out my arms, as if I were merely a passenger. Instead I had to hold on tight. There must be intention from the first note to the last. I could not flinch, could not waiver. No part of me could be left to wonder if this was, at last, the right thing to do.

Sixty, sixty-five. The steering wheel trembling now. Creaks and pings in the metal, like an old body getting out of bed in the morning. I watched myself from high above, perched on one of those poles, admiring the old junk of a car speeding down the empty road.

Seventy-five, eighty. The car quivered and shook. The force of it pulled me back inside myself, my hands turning white gripping the steering wheel so hard. Eighty-five. A whistling sound, was it coming from outside or within? My whole body holding tight to this bucking bronc.

And then I saw only the goal. I pushed harder, the car starting to rock, as if this really was a bronc I was riding and needed it to go faster.

There was only the moment. I was ready to embrace it. To make love to it. To die in its arms.

And then something happened. Something touched me, light as a fingertip, a butterfly. I flinched, just a bit. I knew only this: today, at this moment, I wanted to live.

My foot lifted off the gas.

When I hit the brake, the car rumbled and jerked, fishtailing on the slick road. It felt as if the back half of the car broke away, held only by a single chain allowing it to swing freely side to side. I tapped the brake, and the car seemed less out of control, though still not under control, and when it finally stopped, I found myself spun around and facing the way I'd come.

Not in Virginia, smashed into a tree – but sitting in the middle of an intersection in upstate New York, smothered in darkness, icy pellets making a clicking sound as they bounced off the roof of my car.

My body trembled, a shivering that passed through me. The different shades of darkness had all merged into a solid inky black. In the stillness I heard Aaron's voice: "I could never do that, it would break this guy's heart," with a nod toward Ziggy. There were hearts I'd already broken. What about my own?

That night, I had set out intending to die. In the last moment, I'd pulled back. Out of fear? Regret? Had it been God's hand? Coincidence? Simple physics?

Did somebody want me to still be here? If not God, per-haps myself.

I was in my car still sitting in the middle of the intersection. The car had stalled. I tried the key and breathed a sigh of relief when the engine turned over. Carefully, I pulled to the side of the road.

When I was at Aaron's house, he'd shown me a quote from Kierkegaard that made us both laugh, even as it cut like a samurai's sword: "If you hang yourself, you will regret it. If you do not hang yourself, you will regret it."

Either way, there's going to be regret.

It wasn't a new concept, that life equaled suffering. But it seemed to me there were two kinds: the suffering inflicted upon you, and the suffering you inflicted on others. Too often, trying to escape that first kind of suffering had led me to inflict the second.

How do you break the cycle? Was it as simple as Aaron's solution, to get myself a dog?

For Aaron, life was a perpetual battle. He'd toughened himself up enough to stand tall and demand, "Come on, motherfucker, give me your best shot." Whereas I seemed to say, "You don't have to beat me. Just give me the whip and I'll do it myself." Was there a way for both of us to find peace?

There's a certain peace right now, said the voice in my head, in what you chose not to do.

I turned the car around and headed slowly, carefully, home.

Chapter Twenty-One

Flopping into bed and closing my eyes brought a deep and dreamless sleep. I awoke to sunlight pouring in through the windows. I lay on my back, stretching and thinking perhaps I would stay in bed all morning, then bundle up and move out to the Adirondack chair, perhaps carry it over to the edge of the pond, the water black and still these days, in preparation for winter. I would have liked to stay in bed not just all morning, but for the rest of my life.

Then a door opened in my mind and the words began to flow out. I'd thought that rush of words was over, but soon their volume and insistence got me out of bed again. I fixed some coffee – no scotch today – and began moving those words from my mind to the screen.

. . .

Seven a.m. on a Monday in December, you're just home from your all-night shift at the Inn, when your mother calls to tell you she feels like someone is pile-driving a railroad spike into the back of her skull. You drive her to the small hospital in Mansfield, which sends her to the larger hospital in Pittsfield, twenty miles away. For three days they do tests, and your mother relays the results. Your father is working the day shift at the paper mill, and you're working nights at the Inn, so when you visit, you miss the doctors. That doesn't worry you, as your mother has always been the one to take charge of important information.

They're not sure what's wrong, she says, but they've ruled out cancer. You call her friends to relay the good news. Then on the fourth day, instead of sleeping after work you go to the hospital, where one of her doctors asks if you will walk with him. "I have bad news," he says. "I'm afraid we found the source. It's in her lung, and it's very serious."

The doctor is young, perhaps not yet thirty, with a cultured British accent that doesn't match his deep tan and bushy dark hair. "The source of what?" you ask.

"The cancer, of course."

Seeing your surprise, the doctor ushers you into an examination room and closes the door. They've known it was cancer since the second day, he explains, when the CT scan showed a half dozen tumors on her brain. All subsequent tests have been to find the source, so they can determine treatment.

"I'm afraid it's too widespread for surgery," the doctor says. "I haven't spoken with your mother yet, not in these terms, but I have to tell you that the level of cancer your mother has is incurable. The best we can do is make her more comfortable, minimize her pain."

"You said you told her?"

"No. I wanted to speak with you first. I thought perhaps we could tell her together."

"I don't think I–"

He lays a hand on your arm. "I'll do the talking. It would help if you were there."

You interrupt when the doctor reaches for the door. "You said – how long does she have?"

"We try not to get into the business of predicting. Every disease develops differently. A lot will depend on how she takes to the treatment."

"Can you give me some idea?"

His dark eyes soften. He began the conversation by saying how fond he'd grown of your mother, and at that moment you believe him. "Patients with a condition as serious and advanced as your mother's usually survive an average of three to five months."

Months. You were expecting years. You recall an old television show about a guy with a terminal illness who sells all his possessions to travel around the world. The doctors gave him a year to live, but the series lasted three or four seasons.

"We don't tell the patient that sort of information unless they specifically ask," the doctor says.

Your mother doesn't ask. She looks childlike lying there with the half-her-age doctor patting her hand. "I've got some news to tell you, and I'm afraid it's not as good as we've been hoping," he begins.

You back away. Your mother takes the news calmly, apologizing for putting everyone to so much trouble. Later she apologizes to the nurses for having a vein that's hard to find. When you are alone with her and ask how she feels, she says, "Relieved." For years, you will wish you asked her what she meant.

You take care of your mother as best you are able. You drive her to the hospital for radiation treatments and take her shopping afterwards, or to lunch. When she starts losing her hair, you help her buy a wig. When her legs get so thin she has trouble walking, you rent a wheelchair and hire a carpenter to build a ramp beside the front steps.

You borrow on your own life insurance policy because you want to have enough cash that whenever she asks for something, you can always say yes. Finally, when it's clear she will have to stay in bed all the time, you rent a hospital bed you set up in the living room, making her the center of the house.

Your father helps as best he can. You know he could never care for her the way you do. Regardless, he can't afford to take time off from work.

During your mother's final weeks, you give her sponge baths as she lies in bed, carry her to the toilet and clean her when she's done. She's lost all her hair except for little tufts scattered around her scalp like shrubs across a desert, and she never wears her glasses anymore, so the world must have grown blurry to her. When she becomes incontinent, the doctors allow the hospital to admit her. She goes into a coma on the second Friday in May, and on Mother's Day, she dies.

That night, after you finish seeing to all the business matters, after taking your father home and sitting with him until you sense you can leave him alone, you cry with an intensity you have never felt before. It's as if your insides are being scraped raw, leaving a hole that will never be filled. In a flash, the world becomes a different place, and in your mind you become an orphan.

• • •

Across from a bowling alley, and in between an Italian restaurant and a house converted into a store that sells carpets, a narrow asphalt road descends a gentle slope, crosses over a brook, and continues through a patch of giant pine trees, their orange and brown needles carpeting the rich black soil. Beyond the pines is an enormous garden, a garden of gravestones. First come the oldest, weathered slabs from the 1700's, a few even the 1600's, though the names and dates would be visible only on an etching. Then the wealthy and the renowned, statues of angels and soldiers on horseback, a mausoleum or two. And finally, rows and rows of ordinary folk, separated into sections by the road that now shoots off arms in all directions. And then, beyond the final row, a patch of undisturbed land, investment in the future.

I'd been here before, most recently this past summer, when they buried my father. I remembered little of that day, though not because of amnesia. I assumed I spoke at the service, rode to the cemetery in one of those long black cars, but it was all a blur to me now. I recalled many people I didn't know coming up to me at the wake to say what a gentle and generous man my father was, but I don't remember if there was anyone to sit with me, all my family now gone.

I had a general sense of where my parents' graves might be. I began by searching several rows closer to the front, where I found my grandparents: Maggie Mae Heller and Charles A. Heller, their deaths seven days apart, sharing one gravestone. As with so many things in my past, I wished I could have gone back to a time when they were alive, and told them how much they meant to me.

My parents were buried closer to the back, at an angle of one o'clock. Two modest stones, thirteen years apart, side by side: Irene Heller Winton, devoted wife and mother; Edwin Joseph Winton, loving husband and father. Someone had left a flowerpot in front of my father's stone, but the plant inside had withered and died, the dirt in the pot hard and dry.

It was another beautiful day for November, a cloudless blue sky, the sun comforting. I stood there for a long time, letting my thoughts settle.

"I'm okay," I said at last to my mother's grave. I wondered if I should look up at the sky, as most people seemed to do, but I felt more connected through the earth.

I only wish you were married.

That's what my mother confessed, a few weeks before she died. The words came like a blade out of the darkness, the voice surprisingly strong. I stood in her bedroom doorway having just turned out her light and said goodnight. She had never directly acknowledged that she was going to die, not in my presence anyway; I never talked about the future except with lies to encourage her to rest and grow stronger, feel better.

Her words weren't a criticism, just a simple statement of something she wished, the kind of thing she'd have never said aloud before she got sick. And I didn't hear it as I might have heard it before, one more example of how I'd failed her. "I'll be all right," I told her, my voice surprising me by its strength, too. "You don't have to worry."

I halted, afraid my voice would crack if I tried to say more. As I waited, her breathing grew soft and regular, a sign she'd gone to sleep.

"I'm okay," I said again to her name etched in the stone. I wished I had known her differently. So much of my memory had returned, but I still saw her only from one perspective, as the child who needed something from her she could never quite give, the adolescent and older teen who volleyed between wanting to please her and trying desperately to break free, the young adult who lived as if she didn't exist except for mandatory Sunday phone calls and whenever I needed to be rescued. To the twenty-eight-year-old man who, at least for the four and a half months she lived, finally devoted himself to her.

But my imagination never reached inside her; I never saw the world through her eyes, felt what it might have been like to be her. She could never confide in me. She tried, but I heard every secret longing as proof that she really should have left us, all those years ago, gone off and lived her own fulfilling life, no matter what being abandoned might have done to her too-needy son. Back then, I vowed to convince her through my love and attention that she had made the right decision to stay with us, that I could make her life fulfilling and joyful. The task was Herculean, and I was not up to it.

I could remember all the stories: her irrational fear of snakes and her father's cruel "cure"; how he stole baseball from her, deeming it inappropriate for girls. How she met a British officer during the war, but he died, or left her. How she wanted to be an artist but gave up that dream to become a wife and mother instead.

I had never known her as a friend. Or even as a mother, in many ways. When I was a young child, a portrait of Jesus hung over my bed. In Sunday school they said Jesus always watched over us all, knew everything we did and thought and felt. Somewhere along the line, I got confused and transferred all those Jesus-powers to my mother.

"I'm sorry," I said. I didn't list specifics; there were too many to name. "I love you." What struck me wasn't the words but the verb tense: I loved her, yes, and I love her still.

"I hope you've found peace." This time, as I spoke, my eyes slide to the right, connecting the two stones, the two names, the two people, husband and wife.

. . .

On my way back to the cabin I stopped in a strip mall and wandered into a bookstore. I felt as I had the first time I tried to type or drive my rental car, as if some force inside me was taking charge, a force that knew more than I did, almost like a child tugging on my sleeve, wanting to show me something that would make me smile. I called it muscle memory but somebody else might have used a different term.

I was led to a bookcase filled with fiction. As I scanned the shelves, one book seemed to stand out brighter than the others, almost as if it glowed. I slid it free. *The Great Gatsby*, by F. Scott Fitzgerald.

I read the epigraph, then the next page: "Once again, to Zelda."

I turned the page and read: "In my younger and more vulnerable years my father gave me some advice that I've been turning over in my mind ever since."

I knew the next sentence, before my eyes found the words on the page: "Whenever you feel like criticizing someone..." And suddenly, everything came back. The speaker was Nick Carraway, friends with Jay Gatsby, who loves Daisy, who is married to Tom Buchanan, who has a mistress whose name I couldn't recall – but that was okay. There was a woman named Jordan, and everyone drove past an ash heap overlooked by the eyes of T. J. Eckleberg. The light on a dock at the end.

I had taught that book. I could remember teaching that book. One of the lessons had been on "felt reality" – the truth of how something feels, regardless of its factual nature.

I exhaled, my whole body relaxing. Not only had I taught this book before, I knew I could teach it again. An image popped into my head: Professor Matthew Winton, sitting at a teacher's desk facing a semi-circle of students, each of us holding that book in our hands.

I was a teacher. Teaching was something I knew how to do.

I quickly scanned the shelves for other "glowing" books. There were none, but the book next to *Gatsby* caught my attention. Fatter than the novel, it was also by Fitzgerald: *The Crack-Up and Other Essays.*

The photograph of the typewriter on the cover felt familiar, but I did not open it, instead sliding it back onto the shelf.

The strip mall with the bookstore wasn't far from Friendly's. Still enjoying the warm sun, I walked toward the bright red and white brick building. Approaching the empty space in the far corner of the parking lot, it felt as if I'd walked through a doorway into a room drenched in sadness. This was a spot where the ghost of Mr. P would always live. There were other such spots scattered throughout the town, graves in their own right, Mr. P and Matthew Winton etched upon the stones.

It was time to go home.

• • •

Back in my cabin, I found my phone sitting on the desk. I still wasn't used to it enough to remember to take it with me wherever I went. Opening it, I saw there was a voicemail message. I thought it might be Aaron, calling to see if I was still around, or Jessie with some news from the college, or maybe even the motel proprietor wanting to know how much longer I would stay. But it wasn't any them. It surprised me, looking at the number that showed up on my screen, how quickly I'd memorized it. I sat down, pushed a few buttons until I found the one that brought forth her voice, and held the phone to my ear.

At first there was silence, and I wondered, *Did she really leave a message?* I tried to picture her on the other end of the line; had she been surprised that I didn't answer, perhaps changed her mind about what she wanted to say? Was she wondering what I'd wondered a few nights ago, if I'd seen her name and decided not to answer?

She didn't identify herself. She didn't have to, since her name showed up on the voicemail, the first and only voicemail I'd received on this phone.

"I'm glad you made it there safely," she began. "It's great that your memory's come back. I always had faith that it would, given time, and I'm sure being back where you grew up helped a lot."

A pause. Her voice sounded pleasant, and genuine, although reserved, even wary. Like she was afraid something she didn't want to say might slip out if she wasn't cautious.

Or maybe I was imagining that.

"Before, it was such a crazy time. Sometimes I wonder if I dreamt it all." A chuckle. "Trust me, I'm not usually so – I don't know what the word is – aggressive? – with guys, even ones I like." Another chuckle. "Especially ones I like."

Another pause. "Things around here have been a little boring. That's okay, I guess. Maybe it's good. I don't know. When you get

back, if you want, give me a call. I don't know what will come of
it. I guess we'll have to wait and see."

Chapter Twenty-Two

I lost count of how many times I drove past her house. Sarah lived in one of those long, narrow, two-story houses connected to several other houses on each side. The houses looked new, each front door painted a different color. Sarah's was purple. The houses had their own parking lot, accessed on a feeder road allowing people to escape the fast-moving cars on Route 29.

Once again I drove past her house, continued on to the next light, turned into a shopping mall, circled back, and did it all again.

On the night before I planned to leave Massachusetts, I'd sat out by the pond, bundled in blankets, and considered not going back to Virginia at all. Aaron could likely get me a job, if not at the Inn than at one of His Honor's other properties, and I could teach a course or two at the local community college. I had enough money in my savings that if I wanted, I could live a few years without working at all. It would be a quiet life, a solitary life, but that seemed to suit me. I could go for long walks and bike rides, maybe take up yoga and meditation. Live a life in which I didn't hurt other people, or hurt myself.

I wasn't excited about a job where I would have to stay up all night and walk what amounted to several miles, especially as I got older. And at the end of such a life, what would I have? I did enjoy teaching, and my students generally seemed to think I was pretty good at it. As a writer I'd had only minor success, but I'd heard from people who'd been moved by what I'd written. Despite my propensity toward seclusion, it mattered that I do something positive with my life, not just refrain from doing something negative, and when I tried to define what "positive" might entail, I always came back to helping other people.

And then there was Sarah. I had little hope that we could have a relationship, even as friends. But I wanted to try.

. . .

It was six o'clock and already dark. Lights were on in most of the houses, including, suddenly, the one with the purple door.

I pulled off the main road.

I'd called her my first night home. She'd been polite, generous in her enthusiasm for my memory returning, but distant, too. When I asked if I could see her, she said, "Not tonight. It's too close to my bedtime," but eventually she suggested I come by her house after work the next day.

Now, stomach roiling, knees weak, I struggled up the front steps. Curtains across the windows kept me from seeing inside.

As I reached for the doorbell, the door opened.

Startled, I stepped back as Sarah appeared on the other side of the glass storm door. Her hair was pulled back tight and she still wore her uniform. Although she wore a smile, she looked tired. When she opened the storm door, I backed down a step to make room.

"You're back," she said, as if she only now believed it. But there was something welcoming in her voice.

I nodded.

"And you know who you are now."

"I think I always knew," I told her. "But it was like knowing the earth is round. You know it because the books tell you it is, but this is more like knowing because you've just returned from a flight to the moon."

She was standing in the doorway with the door held open, me a step below. I thought about the first time she showed up at my hospital room. At the time, she knew more about me than I knew about myself.

Another image snuck into my mind, her getting out of my bed, naked, and walking to the bathroom. I remembered the feel of her pressed up close against me. Now the space between us seemed immense.

"Come in," she said, stepping back. "I need to change." She gestured toward the living room, which seemed neat and unlived in, almost like a showroom. "It'll only take a minute."

"Wait," I blurted, louder than I'd intended, as she started up the stairs.

Halting, she noticed for the first time the box I was carrying. "Did you get me a box of chocolates?"

"No, I –" I tried to collect myself, recall the words I'd practiced through most of the night. After we'd spoken on the phone, I'd been thrilled that she'd agreed to let me take her to dinner. But during a mostly sleepless night, I realized that for us to have any chance together, I would have to share what I'd learned about myself, share who I'd been, who I was. I did not feel capable of speaking the words to explain or describe what I'd discovered about myself and my life, not as honestly as I'd written them down. I wanted her to know everything; I did not want to spend every day worrying she'd reject me the moment she learned of some secret in my past I'd kept from her. I could not change my past, couldn't erase what I'd done, and if any part of that was going to drive her away, I wanted it to happen now.

I slid the cover off the box. That morning I'd gone out and bought a printer, hooked it up to my laptop, and printed everything I'd written, about my mother, about Elizabeth and Maureen, about Mr. P. The result was a hefty pile.

"I want to tell you about my trip. About my life. Everything – who I am, what I've done. Even the things I'm not proud of. I don't want to keep secrets anymore."

Still two steps above me, she came down and we stood on the same level.

"You want me to read this?"

"You read a little of it already," I said, but this writing was different. It felt like I was writing my life, I said. I forced myself to look into her eyes. "Unless you've given up on me. I understand if you have. Then I guess it wouldn't matter."

Slowly, she took the box from my hands, looked from it to me. "You want me to read it now? Before dinner?"

"Maybe we should postpone dinner for another time. If you still want to go."

"You mean after I read your book?" Holding the box in the palm of one hand, she raised and lowered it, pretending it weighed a lot more than it did. Her smile made me laugh.

"It's not exactly *War and Peace*," I said.

"It better not be. In college I used that book as a door stop."

"You don't have to read it all. But who I've been – who I am – it's in those pages. I want you to know. If you care to know."

"And while I'm reading, are you going to sit here watching me?"

"Oh, God no," I answered, horrified.

"So you're going to leave me here with homework to do and nothing to eat."

Even though the teasing in her voice was unmistakable, I apologized.

"You realize what this means? One dinner might not be enough to make up for all you're going to owe me."

I smiled, but it felt like I'd just slit open my chest, revealing the darkest portions of what lurked inside me, and handed Sarah a flashlight.

. . .

I spent the next day determined to keep moving. I dealt with the mail and all the dust that had accumulated in my absence, searched through the papers in my office, collecting syllabi and class notes for the courses I taught last spring, that I'd agreed to teach again. Thankfully, studying the list of books, I could recall the characters and the storylines, I would be able to teach these books. It helped that I'd kept voluminous notes.

When I picked up a stack of papers, an envelope dropped to the floor. It had been opened previously, and I recognized the handwriting: letters tiny and cramped, the pen pressed down hard, as if words were wild horses requiring all one's strength to tame. In the upper left-hand corner, a sticker: Edwin J. Winton, 11 Hollenbeck Avenue, Mansfield, MA 01230.

Inside the folded letter was a newspaper clipping. I opened it and Mr. P stared back at me. The heading read, "Jonathan Piretti, Broadway actor and teacher." An obituary.

There was more cramped writing in the letter, a block of it squeezed into the top of the sheet: "Mr. Piretti died last Thursday. He was your friend. They had a big memorial service. I couldn't go. Love, your dad."

The obituary was lengthy: the play Mr. P had been in on Broadway, other plays he'd done in regional theater, celebrities he'd acted with – Angela Lansbury, Robert Preston. His teaching, first at Mansfield High School, then at Bear Mountain Regional. Plays he put on at high school, benefit galas he'd organized for local charities. "He was always giving back to the community," said a member of the town council. Survived by his wife, Laura Waters Piretti.

I didn't remember receiving the letter, which was postmarked in early June. But clearly I'd received it, opened it, read it. That was why I wasn't shocked when Mrs. Piretti told me her husband was dead. Had I started writing about him after receiving that news?

I reread my father's letter. The brevity and directness were typical, as he struggled with both writing and reading. I think he read only one of my published stories, the tale of a newlywed couple whose marriage was already showing signs of trouble. I'd borrowed many of the details from what I'd observed with my parents, and when my father surprised me by asking to read it, I handed it over with trepidation over how he'd react. It wasn't a long story but it took him over an hour to get through. "It's a good story," he told me, and in the uncomfortable silence that followed, I thought perhaps that was all he'd say. Then he laughed, his gentle, nervous laugh that used to anger my mother so. "Some things seemed familiar," he said, "but I know the husband wasn't me, because my name is Ed and his name was Al."

The depth of my relief made me giddy. "That's right, Dad," I told him, and took the story away.

I stared at his handwriting again. He was already having serious health issues by this time. He needed regular blood transfusions, although the mystified doctors couldn't figure out where his blood kept disappearing to.

It shocked me that he'd outlived my mother by so many years. She used to talk about all the exciting things she would do when she was finally on her own. Her death hit my father hard; at times he had that fearful, lost look of a teenager about to lose his mother. But he adapted; my father always adapted. He enjoyed being a widower in a town full of widows. We talked on the phone most Sundays, and he told me once how he'd had five dates with five different women the previous week. Even though he later confessed that two of these "dates" involved him driving the women to their doctor's appointments, I still found his social life impressive.

About marrying my mother, he told me several times, "I was the luckiest guy in the world."

I'd driven back to Mansfield to see him a couple times during the last year of his life. To my surprise and delight, he had a live-in girlfriend, a widow nearly eighty. They looked after each other, and the neighbors helped, too, mowing his lawn, shoveling snow. As always, everyone liked my father.

During those trips, I finally came to view my father for the man he was. It came after forty years of seeing him for the man he was not. He didn't resemble my friends' fathers; he didn't play ball with me in the backyard, or show up at all my games, taking me for ice cream afterwards. He didn't give me advice about life or sex or what it meant to be a man. He didn't seem to be capable of making his wife happy. He was not a man I wanted to emulate.

After my mother died, I met with a counselor, a woman about my mother's age, and although our focus was on dealing with my grief, I also talked about my mother's unhappiness and her frustrations with my father, how she often threatened to leave, how I'd tried so hard to be the son she wouldn't abandon, even while my father kept screwing things up.

"Perhaps she didn't want to leave," the counselor said. "Perhaps she needed someone to blame. It sounds to me as if your father standing gently by while she verbally abused him was an act of great love on his part. He was helping her by accepting her resentment. Taking on the blame. And taking it away from you. It's quite possible he protected you."

I couldn't accept her view at the time, but now, holding that slim paper in my hands, I missed my father, and I wished I could see him again.

• • •

At lunchtime, "Sarah" lit up on my cell phone a split second before it rang. "I finished my homework," she said. "Do I get my dinner now?"

The lightness in her voice brought relief, but I remained wary. "You still want one? With me?"

"I told you before. I never turn down a free meal."

We arranged to meet at her house that evening. "A little later this time," she said. "So I can change out of my uniform."

When I asked where we might go to eat, she mentioned a Vietnamese restaurant nearby. "Have you ever had Vietnamese food?" she asked, tentatively, as if I might not remember.

"I have," I told her. "I like it."

Part of me wanted to keep her on the line, to ask about her day at work, about her mother, if she really read what I'd written, if she'd agreed to this dinner figuring it would be our last. Instead, I said, "I'll see you tonight," and hung up.

All afternoon I couldn't focus on anything. I knew at some point I'd have to speak with Lisette Sorenson, but now didn't seem the time. I did not believe anything had happened between her and I. As I went back over the times we'd spent together, chatting in the coffee shop, having a conference about her writing in my office – the door left open, as always when I was with a student – I could admit that I enjoyed her energy and emotion, the ease with which I could tease her. I could acknowledge that she cast a striking figure. And there were things about her that reminded me of Elizabeth. But I wasn't twenty-two anymore, and I was not interested in her in that way. I didn't know if I'd unknowingly given off signals that she and I might become more than conscientious teacher and exceptional student, but if so, I would apologize and make clear there was a line that could not be crossed.

I started off on a long walk, thinking it might help work off some nervous energy, but soon after heading out, I turned around and returned home, fearing the walk might tire me out too much. I sat out back, bundled in a blanket, staring at the slit in the earth the train tracks made, as far as I could see. I went over everything I could remember was in the writing I'd given her, wondering if I should have left some parts out. Two people in a relationship didn't have to tell each other everything, did they? They ought to be allowed some privacy.

And yet, those things that shamed me, if kept secret, would lead me right back into telling lies, to others and to myself.

I also thought, this writing isn't half bad. Could I do something with it, build it into something someone might publish? It felt easier to tell it to the world than to admit it to Sarah, or even more, to myself. Maybe I could call it fiction, say I'd made it up. Not that anyone would want to read something like that. Stories about people with amnesia pop up all the time on cheesy soap operas.

I didn't write it to publish it. I wrote it to recapture myself. It helped me do that, and I shouldn't expect more. And now I would get to see what Sarah thought of the person I'd discovered.

. . .

No longer in her uniform, Sarah looked elegant in gray slacks and a blue top, her hair loose and settled on her shoulders. Make-up and jewelry, too, and a familiar scent that whisked me back to the night we lay together in bed.

The box with my writing sat on a table by the door. Slipping on her coat, she caught me looking at it. "Do we need to take this?" she asked, and shrugging, I replied, "I don't need it."

"I didn't take notes." She laughed gently. "I hope that doesn't lower my grade."

I gathered up the box. "I'll throw it in my car."

A few times, walking down the sidewalk and stopping at the corner to wait for the "Walk" light, our shoulders brushed, and once our hands gently collided.

"It's nice having all these shops and restaurants I can walk to," she said, "even if they are inside a strip mall. I know people who would be shocked we didn't drive. Nobody walks around here, except from their car to the store and back again. Of course, the roads around here aren't exactly pedestrian friendly. One more reason I prefer to hike in the woods."

"Have you been hiking out west lately?" I asked, loud, to be heard over the rush of cars and the clicking noise the traffic light made.

"I've been too busy. My mom's been a little under the weather lately, so I've been helping her out."

"I hope it's nothing serious?"

"Just the flu. But she likes being babied when she doesn't feel well." She laughed. "I guess she's earned that right."

I wondered if I'd ever get to meet Sarah's mother. Even now I continued to remember more about my own mother, and yet I still felt something vital was missing.

The restaurant was crowded but Sarah had made a reservation. "Always on top of things," I told her, and she answered, "I have to be." It struck me that I'd never really asked her what it was like to be a police officer, about the danger she might face, and even more, the trauma from some of the horrible things she'd likely seen. She joked about getting stuck in the office or her butt growing numb from sitting in the cruiser so long, but watching a body being extracted from a crushed car smashed into a tree might be mild in comparison to dealing with murderers and pedophiles. I hoped I got the chance to hear her talk about some of that, to be someone she could open up to.

I remembered how my father used to tell only funny stories from the war, glossing over what it was really like to be stationed in lands occupied by the Japanese. His favorite story involved the time he was sitting on his cot in a tent somewhere in India and a buddy, who had always seemed a little unstable, suddenly pointed his pistol at my father and fired. "I thought he was going to kill me," my father exclaimed. But it turned out that a cobra had climbed onto the cot and was about to strike my father. "He saved my life," my father said.

That was the worst moment my father ever mentioned about the war.

Maybe people just didn't want to talk about the most painful things. Or read about them either. Maybe my life would have been easier if I really could have forgotten everything.

My mother used to hang laundry on a post in the back yard, putting the intimate things, underwear and the like, on the inside, then surrounding that with shirts and pants, then hiding everything with sheets and towels on the outer rim. I remembered how in college I'd bought some white slacks and my mother chided me because she could see my underwear through my clothes. The implication was obvious: you didn't show other people private things.

I couldn't live that way. When I was young, I used to sneak into my mother's bedroom, not to snoop around but just stand there, hoping something in the air might show me the secrets of her heart. Why was she so unhappy? What could I do to change? These were the questions that tormented me, long before I got around to considering the more traditional ones, such as Who am I? and What do I want my life to be like?

Now, seated across from me in the restaurant, Sarah said, "I have a dilemma. I love their spring rolls, but I also love their summer rolls. I can never decide which to get."

"Why not get both?"

She laughed. "Then I won't have room for dinner."

"It's a tough call," I said, enjoying the playfulness in her tone.

She pretended to be thinking hard. "I could get one and you could get the other, and then we could share."

"Mix up the seasons?"

"I don't think that would be a problem. Each order comes with two rolls."

"Sounds like the perfect number. Two people, two rolls."

"Or four," she said.

"I'm a little nervous about taking such a bold step, but if you're game to try, I'll go along."

She laughed again. "You're a real trooper."

I was about to say, no, you're the trooper, but it felt like our little routine had gone on long enough. She seemed in a good mood, comfortable around me, not openly angry, horrified, or disgusted. That was encouraging, even though she was careful to maintain a physical distance.

It felt like we were starting over – or like one of those first times she visited my hospital room, when I assumed that after she left, I'd never see her again.

"So what's good here?" I asked, studying the menu.

"That's the dilemma. Everything's good."

"Do you have a favorite?"

She made a face like I hadn't been paying attention. "No," she said. "I don't have a favorite. I have twelve of them."

"I see," I said, as she named a half dozen favorites. The whole fish sounded interesting but might be too involved. There'd been a heaviness lodged in my stomach ever since I handed over my writing the night before. Even walking here with Sarah, I wasn't sure I'd be able to force myself to eat. But Sarah's mood, along with the enticing smells and sights of food being brought to other people's tables, made me realize how hungry I was. I'd had only coffee and an English muffin all day.

"I was thinking we might get a bottle of wine," I said, once we'd both decided what to order. "Chardonnay?"

"It's okay with me. But I'm not the one who has to drive home."

That stung a little, which made me wonder what I'd secretly been expecting. Was I thinking she'd either say she didn't want to see me again, or suggest we pick up right where we left off?

"I'll go easy," I promised.

When the waiter appeared, after Sarah said, "spring rolls," I said, "summer rolls," and she gave an approving nod. She ordered grilled shrimp and I got lemongrass chicken. I noticed an unoaked Chardonnay on the wine list I remembered once buying for myself, in the days before the accident. After I ordered it, and the waiter left, Sarah laughed. "I think the last time I saw you, you didn't know a thing about wine, and now you're ordering 'unoaked Chardonnay.'"

"My memory's back," I said, and she grinned.

"It really is. I'm very happy for you."

The way she said it sent me back to her first few visits to my hospital room. She was a generous person with a good heart. Her offers to help me then had less to do with who I was than who she was, and had nothing to do with her wanting something down the road.

And this felt like a gentle, friendly goodbye.

I looked around. The dining room was crowded, our table near the middle, closer to those around us than I'd have wished. It was noisy, too, the clacking of plates and silverware, so many voices blending into one wall of sound. Not the best place for a serious conversation, but I feared I wouldn't get a second chance.

"So you did your homework." I leaned close so I wouldn't have to talk too loud.

"Did you really write all of that in the last couple weeks?"

"Most of it. One part I wrote over the summer. Before the accident."

I couldn't bring myself to identify that section in a more precise way. It would be different, to actually speak the name "Mr. P" out loud, than to let it sit in ink on a piece of paper. Somehow, Sarah knew. "It was horrible," she said. "What he did to you."

She'd leaned forward too, but still I had to strain to catch what she said. She glanced into my eyes and then looked down at her hands smoothing out the cloth napkin in her lap.

"I don't want any of that to seem like an excuse for the things I did afterwards. A lot of what I discovered I'm not proud of."

"There's no telling how deeply that affected you. You loved him, and he took that and used it to abuse you."

Aaron had used that word too. Abuse. But I didn't want to paint Mr. P as a monster. Sarah was right: I'd loved him.

"Did you really feel that? That I loved him?"

"Absolutely. He was describing a world you dreamed of, promising you could have that world, if only you did what he said."

I wanted to ask, *Do you think he loved me?* But there was no way she could know that. Even if it felt that way on the page, that was only my take on things, not Mr. P's.

She leaned forward again. "Why did you write all that?" Before I could respond, she clarified. "What I mean is, why did you want me to read it?"

I'd thought about that a lot the last two days. "So much of my life was a blank," I began. "And then finally when it began to come back, it was like, 'Yes, this is who you were, this is who you are.' And I wanted you to know that. I mean, you had to put up with this person who wasn't much more than a stick figure. I wanted you to know who I was, but I knew I couldn't just sit here and tell it." I forced a laugh. "I guess that's why I became a writer in the first place: so I could put into words the things I couldn't speak out loud."

There was only one thing left to be said. I took a breath, steeled myself, and dove in. "I'm hoping there's a chance we could have some kind of relationship – whatever that might be – and if that happened, I didn't want to be keeping secrets from you."

She gave me a soft smile. "So this is everything then?"

"Maybe not everything, but it's the worst of me. Not the greatest hits but the opposite."

A part of me hoped she'd object, say it wasn't so bad. Before she got the chance, the waiter arrived with our food.

• • •

"I think your writing is beautiful," she said, as we sipped coffee after enjoying the meal. While we ate, our conversation contained little of consequence. The dining room was half empty now, and considerably more quiet. It was as if the room were a giant beast that, sated with food, slowly drifted toward sleep.

"I was never an English major or anything, but I can appreciate good writing. You don't just tell a story, you put the reader in the story, make them feel what you felt while it was happening."

"I feel it again myself," I said. "When I'm writing it."

"That must be hard."

I shrugged. "Hard" was one of those words that seemed irrelevant in this context, but I didn't know how to explain that.

The room had grown not only quieter but darker, and the shadows softened the edges when I looked at Sarah, or felt her looking at me. The wine contributed; I tried to go easy but hadn't accounted for an empty stomach. I remembered the last time I saw Sarah before I left for Massachusetts, how I was afraid to look into her eyes, fearing she'd see all the demons lurking inside. I wanted to believe there were no more demons to conceal. But that didn't mean we could see into each other's hearts whenever we liked. I didn't know what she was feeling right then, what she was thinking about us going forward. I hoped she could tell that I knew my life would be less without her in it.

"I have a confession of my own to make." She leaned forward. "My partner and I, we were never fully convinced your accident was an accident. My partner had a feeling, and he's seldom wrong. There was nothing we could do, you really could have fallen asleep –"

"It wasn't an accident."

She looked surprised, maybe not over what I'd said as much as that I'd spoken it aloud. The writing I gave her didn't include anything about the night I'd driven around upstate New York.

"I was in a bad place, it felt like I just kept sinking lower and I didn't know how else to get out." I tried to force a laugh. "It wasn't a lot of fun being me."

Or being with me, she had every right to say.

Instead she said, "I was afraid of something like that, when I came to see you in the hospital. I thought there might be things troubling you that hadn't been resolved. I was afraid –"

"That I'd do it again?"

She didn't respond, but maybe she didn't need to.

"You were worried about me," I said. "I figured that's why you kept coming back."

She stiffened. "That was true at first. It was also true that I liked you. You were funny, and I was impressed how composed you were, considering what you were going through. I probably would have been tearing my hair out in your situation. I'd never really thought about what it might be like to be so alone." She smiled. "Other than my time at the academy, I don't think I've ever been anywhere without friends or family close by. You seemed to have no one. I wanted to help.

"And then I fell for you."

"Why?"

She laughed. "Believe me, it was nothing I was expecting to happen. Maybe I'm a sucker for good writing. I mean, I liked that story you published, but what really knocked my socks off was that piece you wrote about your mother locking herself in the bathroom and crying, while you sat on the floor outside in the hall. It broke my heart.

"And then this –" she made a gesture as if the box with my writing sat between us on the table. "It's not just the writing – like I said, I never was an English major. It's how hard you work, what it means to you to tell your own story, to get it all right."

She grinned. "Besides, you were cute, all befuddled like that. There was so much you didn't know, but you never got angry or morose, you were like, "Okay, I don't know this so how can I find it out?" You weren't somebody looking for a way to give up.

"I admit, I was a little ticked when you went off to Massachusetts without me. No, not ticked, deep down I understood this was something you needed to do on your own. I was disappointed, because I thought we would have had a good time together. But I was ticked off when you didn't call."

"I did call." I forced a laugh. "You wouldn't believe how long it took me to build up the nerve. And then you didn't answer."

"I was in the shower. And your message said not to call back, so I didn't.

"But that's okay. You needed to focus on yourself, in the place where you grew up. I admit I came up with a few choice curse words for you, from time to time. That's not a bad thing, I guess, increasing your vocabulary."

"You can share them with me any time you want," I said.

And then we both understood we'd finally reached the place we'd been headed to all along.

"The truth?" she asked.

Steeling myself, I nodded.

"I really like you. I guess we don't really know each other, not all that well, but I'd like to keep trying. I don't know what that means, where that will lead, but I'd like to give it a try.

"But it hurts when you shut me out. I understand that you grew up believing you'd only be accepted, or loved, if you acted a certain way. When you didn't feel up to acting that way, you shut yourself off. But I'm not like that. When I care about someone, I care about all of them, all the time."

"Do you think you can forgive me, for all the stupid or cruel or just wrong things I've done?"

"I think the real question is, can you forgive yourself?"

I knew that she was right, and the elation I felt was tempered by the fact that I didn't know how to forgive myself, didn't know if I could.

"I'll try," I said, and her hand settled halfway across the table, palm open. I reached out and touched it, tentatively at first, and then more tightly.

"You shouldn't be driving," she said when we returned to her house.

I told her I'd be fine sleeping on the couch.

"My bed's more comfortable." She laughed. "It's bigger than your bed, by a lot."

It stung a little that she didn't like my bed. I wasn't sure the bedroom had space for a bigger bed, but I figured I should investigate.

"Maybe we can try it," I said, "and if it doesn't feel right, I'll move to the couch."

She laughed. "That's another thing I love about you. You're just so darn romantic."

We came together then, just holding each other, and it felt right, our bodies connected like this, each body giving to the other. I was in no rush, I wasn't thinking about sex, I just wanted our bodies to reacquaint, and rediscover all the ways we fit together.

. . .

I felt a little guilty, getting home at six a.m., because neither I nor Sarah got much sleep, and she had work, while I could tumble into my too-small-for-two bed. I woke a few hours later, took a long shower and fixed coffee. Last night, when we finally broke through the time and distance that had built up between us, I had no difficulty sliding inside her, and wanting to stay that way forever.

Now I went into my office, because there was one more thing I remembered, and after a long search I found it, a card still in its envelope.

When my mother got sick, the minister of my parents' church came to see her often. Reverend Lucy was short and heavy-set, smart, funny, gentle, and strong. I was enormously grateful to her. I could never have found the courage to speak with my mother as honestly and directly as Reverend Lucy did.

After my mother was admitted to the hospital, I was alone in my parents' house when Reverend Lucy came to the door. I was puzzled, because Reverend Lucy knew they'd taken my mother away; she'd ridden in the ambulance with her. That day she was somber, but steady as always, exuding what I might have called hope, although it wasn't hope as usually defined, not some hope that my mother would miraculously recover. It was a larger sense of hope, for all humanity. It was faith, I realized now; she genuinely believed that my mother, and everyone, would eventually be cradled in the arms of God. I had never felt that kind of faith, not without doubt, but I found her belief powerful, and something I might wish to seek.

"I won't stay," she said, not bothering to unbutton her coat. "I'm on my way to visit your mother."

"She's in a coma," I said, having returned from the hospital that morning.

She shared a gentle smile. "I'll sit with her. Is your father with her now?"

I nodded.

"Perhaps you'll join us later."

I had to work that night. Aaron would have taken my place if I asked, but I preferred being active to waiting. The doctors had been cautious with their words, but I sensed they didn't believe my mother would awaken.

Reverend Lucy withdrew a white envelope from her inside coat pocket. The edges were a little bent, and she took a moment to flatten them.

"Your mother asked me to give you this. She asked me to wait until – But I think it's okay for you to have it now."

The envelope was warm, having been inside the reverend's coat. It felt soft, too, not crisp like when it first comes out of the box. Nothing was written on the outside.

"Well," the reverend said, "I'll be on my way."

I met her gaze. I hadn't cried, although I'd come close several times, usually in quiet moments when alone, away from my mother. I didn't know why I tried so hard to hold back my emotions in her presence; it wasn't as if she didn't understand she was dying. She accepted that certainty more fully than I did.

When the reverend was gone, I walked into the living room and sat on the couch. Growing up, I hardly ever sat on the couch, but because of the hospital bed set up in the living room, I'd had to remove the other chairs. I felt exhausted, not from lack of sleep so much as overall wear and tear, as if I'd run a marathon.

A few times over the last few weeks, I'd come by the house to find my mother and the reverend talking in quiet tones that halted when I appeared, the sense of interruption so pronounced that I apologized and made up an excuse about having to go back out. Sitting on the couch now, beside the empty bed, blankets pulled back, mattress and pillow still showing the indentation of my mother's body, I wished I'd asked the reverend to come sit with me, talk to me in the gentle, reassuring voice she'd shared with my mother. But she had many people who needed her more. Her congregation, though small, was filled with people my mother's age or older. I was twenty-eight years old and believed I did not need religion. Or perhaps I thought religion did not need me.

The envelope wasn't sealed, the flap just tucked in. I drew out a standard Hallmark-type card, "To my son" embossed on the front in fancy, colorful letters, but with no generic verse inside. Instead, in the middle of the blank white space were three hand-written lines, like a weary caravan trudging across a desert, each fragile letter struggling to keep from toppling over.

How can I say how much you've done for me?
How can I say how much you've meant to me?
You have always been my light and my life.

It wasn't signed. She must have run out of strength.

. . .

When I lost the memory of my life, I felt robbed of the proof of my existence. Who was a person but the memories they'd accumulated? You remembered this person, or that, to prove you'd loved and been loved. Places proved you'd traveled. Accomplishments validated your work. Friends showed you'd shared yourself. It wasn't just proof that you'd lived, it was a record of what that life was like: a person was the totality of what they'd done. Losing my past life cut me loose from everything mooring me to the world, to my life, to my self. I'd had no idea who the president was, what wars were going on around the world, who had won the World Series — actually, the last twenty-seven of them. I could not picture my college or the first school I'd taught at, or any of the places I'd lived after the age of thirteen. I could not fathom all that I'd lost. The people I had loved, or who had loved me. The music I listened to, the books I'd read. What I liked to eat for breakfast. I did not know what made me happy or sad.

When I lost my memory, a part of me feared it might never return, but a larger part believed that when it did return, all the pieces would fall into place, my past would be settled, even resolved, and I'd be able to move on. What I learned is that the past is never settled, its effects linger in the fabric of your being. I remembered something Mr. P had said when I'd half-jokingly announced I would run away from home to escape my mother's influence. "You can't get away from her because wherever you go, you take her with you. She's inside you now." And yet you have to move on.

Along with my memory, also taken from me were the illusions built up over the years, created to protect myself, to convince myself I was a good and decent person, that the worst things I'd done weren't really my fault. And when my memory returned, those illusions were gone forever.

I had recaptured much of that past, not just the details or memories, but the emotions too. I could feel what it was like to be the boy Mr. P kissed, fondled, tried to make respond. I could live inside the heart of that boy sitting outside the locked bathroom door, certain that when his mother emerged, it would be to leave him forever.

There were happier memories: the time I spent with Elizabeth, despite the questions that relationship raised; that paper I wrote for American History back in high school, and the party Aaron and the other students threw me to celebrate. My first published story, the first time I taught a class. Lots of small moments, too, that I coaxed myself to remember; times I felt happy or safe or peaceful around my mother, my father, my friends, my students, by myself. And with Sarah.

In rare moments, I could see these memories as simply things that happened. I could feel their sorrow or joy but not be ruled by those emotions. Instead, I could look with an understanding and empathy at that boy sitting outside the bathroom, but also at the woman weeping inside, even the man rushing back to the store desperate to correct his mistake. To see them all, understand them all, love and forgive them all. That was the place I hoped to one day reach.

Gratitudes

I am deeply grateful to those wise and generous writers who read this manuscript and helped me make it better: David Giannini, Jessica Sticklor, Ben Obler, and my editor, Jodie Toohey, who saw something in my book that might matter to people who read it. I also want to thank Pam Bachrach, Greg Juskalian, Karen Houppert, and Don Gallehr for their understanding and support over so many years. To Michelle Brafman and Kelly Ann Jacobson: thank you for helping me navigate what happens after an editor tells you your book will be published. To Christina: thank you for being who you are, for believing in my work, and for loving me so generously. I also want to thank my fellow students in Jessica's novel workshop at Gotham Writers, and to all those in the Johns Hopkins MA in Writing Program – students, alums, faculty, and administrators – thank you for constantly helping to remind me that striving to write with honesty and courage is a worthy endeavor, and when the only choices are to keep writing or to give up, we might as well keep writing.

Acknowledgements

"The Radio" was previously published, under the title "2.25.64" in *Craft Literary*

"My Father's Court" was previously published in *Confessions: Fact or Fiction?* Edited by Herta B. Feely and Marian O'Shea Wernicke

Fitzgerald, F. Scott. *The Great Gatsby*

Fitzgerald, F. Scott. *The Crack-Up and Other Essays*

"Ruby Tuesday," written by Mick Jagger and Keith Richard; performed by the Rolling Stones

"Chuck E's in Love" and "Last Chance Texaco," written and performed by Rickie Lee Jones

"If You Could Read My Mind," written and performed by Gordon Lightfoot

"Dancing in the Dark," written and performed by Bruce Springsteen

About the Author

Mark Farrington recently retired after nearly forty years of teaching writing, the last twenty-five of them in the MA in Writing and Teaching Writing Programs at Johns Hopkins University. He has published short stories in *Carve*, *Craft Literary*, *The Valparaiso Fiction Review*, *The Louisville Review*, and other journals, and has published creative nonfiction and articles on writing and the teaching of writing in several National Writing Project publications. Farrington's short fiction has won the Editor's Choice Award in the Raymond Carver Fiction Contest, the Dan Rudy Fiction Prize, second prize in the Dame Alice Throckmorton Fiction Prize, two honorable mentions for the Momaya Prize, and an Individual Artists Grant from the Virginia Commission on the Arts. He is a four-time winner of the Outstanding Faculty Award in the Johns Hopkins MA in Writing Program; other teaching awards include an Outstanding Service Award from the Northern Virginia Writing Project and an Outstanding Alumni Award from the George Mason University English Department. He grew up in Great Barrington, Massachusetts, earned his B.A. in English and American Literature from Colby College, where he graduated cum laude, Phi Beta Kappa, and completed his M.F.A. in Fiction Writing from George Mason University. Farrington has recently moved to Maine with his wife Christina and their Springer Spaniel Maddie, after living for more than thirty years just outside Washington, D.C. *Loss of Life* is his first novel.